The Taking of Hill 1052

For Karl Dauberg—
one of those 1st MarDiv
Marines, about whom &
for whom this book
was written!

[illegible]
2011

Other books by J. Birney Dibble, M.D.

Fiction

Pan

Brain Child

Non-Fiction

Outlaw for God

The Plains Brood Alone

In This Land of Eve

The Taking of Hill 1052

Birney Dibble

NPI

Northwest Publishing Inc.
Salt Lake City, Utah

The Taking of Hill 1052

This is a work of fiction.
All characters and events portrayed in this book are fictional,
and any resemblance to real people or incidents is purely coincidental.

For information address: Northwest Publishing, Inc.
5949 South 350 West, Salt Lake City, Utah 84107
SP 2 16 94

PRINTING HISTORY
First Printing 1995

ISBN: 1-56901-164-8

NPI books are published by Northwest Publishing, Incorporated,
5949 South 350 West, Salt Lake City, Utah 84107.
The name "NPI" and the "NPI" logo are trademarks belonging to
Northwest Publishing, Incorporated.

PRINTED IN THE UNITED STATES OF AMERICA.
10 9 8 7 6 5 4 3 2 1

Dedication

This book is respectfully dedicated to the corpsmen of the Third Battalion of the Fifth Marine Regiment in Korea.

And to Barb and Dan, who kept me writing fiction.

Illustrations

The illustrations on pages 2, 118, 250 were drawn by Eric Dibble, the author's son.

Table of Contents

Maps

The Characters

(Unless otherwise indicated, all members of the Third Battalion, Fifth Regiment, First Marine Division, Fleet Marine Force Korea)

Butch—battalion surgeons' Korean houseboy
Everly, Dr. Ronald—Battalion Surgeon
Fogarty, Captain Sean—Commanding Officer, George Company
Haldicup, Captain John—Forward Observer, Marine Air Corps, attached to 3/5
Hoffman, Chief Hospital Mate Otto—Senior corpsman
Jensen, Private Ira (The Great Dane)—George Company
Jepson, Hospital Mate Jim (JJ)—Corpsman, Headquarters and Service Company
Kaminski, Private Ted—Rifleman, Item Company
Kowicki, Second Lieutenant Stan—Commanding officer, second platoon, George Company
Lavierri, Dr. Mike—Surgeon, Charley Medical Company
Lee, Yung-kak—Korean interpreter attached to 3/5
Marne, Major Bob—S-3
McCallister, Lieutenant Colonel Emory—S-6
Micleson, Lieutenant Ansel—leader of helicopter-borne platoon
Newman, Private Orville (Buckshot)—George Company
Ormsdorf, Commander Walter—Commanding Officer, First Medical Battalion
Overman, Dr. Fred—Battalion surgeon
Rainey, Sergeant Harold—George Company and head non-commissioned officer of "Rainey's Raiders"
Rohn, Corporal Ned—Ambulance driver
Runninger, Lieutenant (j.g.) Bob—Chaplain
Sanders, First Lieutenant Rory—Commanding Officer, Weapons Company

Selkirk, Major Ralph—S-5
Smith, Hospital Mate 3rd Jason—Second platoon, George company
Stanfield, Captain Alec—Forward Observer, Marine Air Corps, attached to 3/5
Svenger, Private Aage—George Company and "Rainey's Raiders"
Thorpe, Corporal Jerry—George Company and "Rainey's Raiders"
Tollander, Corporal Joe—Ambulance driver
Washington, Gunnery Sgt. Moses—McCallister's "gunny"
Wright, Captain Bill—S-2
Yung, Dr. Il-song—Korean doctor assigned to Charley Medical Company

Author's Note

A special note to the Marines who were with 3/5 of the First Marine Division in Korea: Please remember that this is not a historical account of your battalion in Korea. Rather, it is a novel. In order to make it work, some liberties had to be taken with dates, troop movements, and the position of various outfits at certain times.

Furthermore, except for references to historical people like Dean Rusk, Douglas MacArthur, "Iron Mike" O'Daniel and a few others, any resemblance of the characters in this novel to actual persons is purely coincidental.

Sincerely,

The Author

Prologue

It was over in a second.

I sat back on my heels with the bloody knife hanging from my hand. I started to shake, a gross trembling that racked my entire body. I knelt down again and pulled the blanket up over the man's face.

With the care my corpsmen would have used to clean a scalpel, I wiped the knife on the snow and then dried it on my pants. As I stood up I slipped it back into the scabbard, put the scabbard back in my parka pocket and zombie-like started back up the hill.

The wet stuff running down my cheeks started to freeze and I wiped it away with the back of my mitten.

I'd never killed a man before.

Book One
The Men of George, How and Item

One

A stiff wind whistled through the fur lining on the hood of my parka. I shivered a little and snugged up the ties running around the waist and hem. It was the 7th of November, 1951. I'd been in Korea exactly five days and had not yet acclimated mentally or physiologically to living out of doors in the Korean winter.

I stood with Marine Major Bob Marne on a fifty-foot embankment above a frozen mud road leading through Camp Tripoli to the motor pool area. Below us the riflemen of George Company moved past.

All we could hear was the occasional muffled thump of a canvas-covered canteen, the sussurration of packboards on parkas, the shuffle of 200 pairs of combat boots slogging quietly and resolutely in a double column along the frozen mud road.

The outfit I'd just joined in their reserve bivouac, 3/5, the Third Battalion of the Fifth Marine Regiment, was going back into the front lines to replace the Second Battalion of the Seventh Marine Regiment which had been in one hell of a tough sector for almost three months.

It was an eerie, stirring, depressing, magnificent sight. Brilliant moonlight glancing off the snow lit up the scene below us. I could easily discern individual trees on the mountainside a thousand yards away. Heavy, sharp shadows rippled on the ground as the men moved easily up the mountain jeep-track despite their full packs.

Elements of Weapons Company attached to this line company followed after the infantrymen. Mortar crews carried foot-plates on their helmeted heads or tubes on their shoulders in addition to M-1s. Flame-throwers carried their steel double tanks on one shoulder and their packs and rifles on the other. Machine gunners shouldered barrels and tripods.

In the half-dark, maintaining an interval of fifteen paces, they hugged the edge of the road, ready to hit the dirt at the first sound of incoming mortars or artillery.

"George Company, Jack," Bob Marne said. "Item'll move up tomorrow night and How the next."

"Yeah," I said with a soft chuckle. "I know. Your old outfit till they kicked you upstairs by making you a major."

"George was the best damn company in the battalion. I had its command all during the fall offensive. Now look at me." Even in the dark I could see that infectious grin I'd already come to love.

"A rear-echelon pogue like me."

He laughed and I thought to myself, well, not really.

The long double line of Marines moved on until the last of them disappeared into the darkness.

Quietness descended on the tent camp from which George Company had come, but that stillness was broken by the booming and flashing of American big guns to the south and incoming Chinese mortar and artillery landing on the American lines to the north.

As we scuffed back to our own tent through six inches of powdery snow I said softly, "What's it like up there, Bob, where those guys are going?"

He stopped and without looking at me stood silently for a long moment, staring out over the valley of the Nam River below us.

Then in a deep bass voice that occasionally vibrated with fully controlled emotion, he told me what it was like in the front lines of a Marine battalion in the mountains of Korea in the winter. He didn't tell it like I've recorded it, of course, but this is what I remember—and will never forget—from that monologue of his.

Trenches dug into the sides of the mountains.

Sand-bagged bunkers and exposed foxholes.

Blizzards sweeping across the frozen rice paddies, swirling through the trenches and into the bunkers.

A world of men only, where speech is coarse, where unbridled obscenities and profanities scar every conversation, where young men deprived of sex grow beards and mustaches to prove their manliness—like middle-aged men suddenly growing beards when their sex lives are in disarray.

A biting cold that is an ever-present enemy.

A twenty-four-hour-a-day job, with no time off, no weekends, no holidays.

The wounded and the dead.

The almost constant rumble of artillery behind the Marine lines throwing shells onto the enemy.

Fire-fights along the front lines that sound like several strings of fire-crackers exploding simultaneously.

Chattering machine guns.

A world so saturated with fear that it goes almost unnoticed, because if you do think about it you go crazy.

Patton tanks with their 850 horsepower V-12 Continental engines growling up the mountain tracks.

B-rations out of #10 cans when the lines are quiet—hot when it's dumped into steel mess pans and cold by the time it's eaten. C-rations when the lines are active, little cans of beans or stew or spaghetti heated on a can of Sterno. K-rations on patrol or on the move, canned ham and eggs, beef or pork loaf, desiccated graham crackers, tasteless cheese.

Stretchers and jeep ambulances and chopping helicopters.

The walking wounded. The crawling wounded. And the dead.

But worst of all, overshadowing all thoughts and actions, the long black nights and the loneliness.

He stopped talking and I felt a chill in my bones colder than the Arctic winds sweeping down from North Korea.

We felt our way carefully back to our tent, chuckled softly at the snores of our three tent-mates, and slipped into our mummy-bags. I could hear Bob yawn explosively and then subside almost instantly into the regular slow breathing of deep sleep. He knew what it was like in the front lines and he knew he was going back up there. He was a professional Marine. And he fell asleep like a baby with its stomach full of warm milk.

I lay with my hands behind my head, relaxed, yet awake. George Company gone, Item tomorrow, and How the next night.

And with How would go our Headquarters and Service Company. Back into the mountains from which 3/5 had come three weeks before for a rest from the tyranny of war.

Now in my mummy bag I could feel the slow onset of drowsiness overcoming me. I was not a professional Marine, but a civilian doctor dressed up like one, and I didn't really know what it was like up there. But the hypnotic rumbling of our big guns soothed my tense muscles and I drifted off into an untroubled sleep.

Two

The next morning, November 8th, the cold sun shone down the line of tents that George Company had occupied for three weeks, and which they'd left standing for the next company coming off line into Camp Tripoli. George Company wouldn't need tents where it had gone.

As I walked briskly down the deserted company street toward Sick Bay, my thoughts turned slightly maudlin, wondering which of those boys who'd camped here would not come back.

Now I continued on down the road through the How Company area, watching with interest the various activities in which the company was engaged. During the three weeks off the line, every day was structured to keep the men busy so they wouldn't have too much free time for brooding about recent experiences in the line, or for worrying about going back.

The time in reserve had not gone slowly for those

men. Too fast, if anything. They'd gotten what they'd come for: food, rest, and security. Most of them had been up on line for many months, living in cold unheated bunkers and eating Charley or K rations.

Now, back in Camp Tripoli, their officers had made sure that there was plenty to do: gun drills, marching drills, inspections, boxing matches, volley-ball, baseball, camp improvement projects, lectures on everything from gonorrheal prophylaxis to machine gun emplacement. In the evening, after hot chow, the men saw movies like *David and Bathsheba*, or Claudette Colbert in *Let's Make It Legal*.

Morale was high. The men were happy, young, vigorous. And they were alive.

And immortal.

Not one of them felt that he was marked for death in those cold mountains to the north. Maybe the guy in the next bunker. Maybe his buddy next to him. But not himself. Besides, today is today, and tomorrow never comes. Even though George Company moved out last night, and Item Company goes tonight, and How tomorrow…

But they were not immortal. That fact had been driven home for me just two days before. I had stood on a sidehill above the Nam River watching my battalion coming out of their company areas. With the infinite precision of combat-hardened and Corps-disciplined Marines, the helmeted, battle-dressed battalion marched down the company streets onto the open flats beside the frozen Nam-gang. They moved with almost casual ease, loose-limbed, arms swinging in absolute synchrony. Their platoon non-coms marched five paces to the right, setting the pace quietly: no need for cadence-calling in this battalion.

Along the sides of the road to the river, men of the Korean Service Corps crawled out of their make-shift canvas tents and stood watching somberly. A gentle breeze ruffled their baggy quilted jackets and pants. The ear-flaps on their alpaca bunny hats bobbed as the men spoke softly to one another. They loved these Marines.

High above the river towered the rounded hills and jagged mountain peaks, green where there were pines, white where there was snow, and brown where there was neither. Serpentine, narrow, three-foot-deep trenches ran everywhere on the hills and across the flats, safe-holes to dive into if a mortar or artillery barrage started.

The marching men came to a halt in phalanxes of squads, platoons and companies. Scattered here and there were boys in almost new fatigues, replacements newly arrived in the 14th Replacement Draft, filling out the battalion's complement of 1,000 men.

From squad leaders to platoon lieutenants to company commanders to Battalion Commanding Officer Lieutenant Colonel Emory McCallister, rolled the report: "All present or accounted for, SIR!"

McCallister saluted sharply, stepped back a full pace and barked, "Gunnery Sergeant Washington!"

Moses Washington saluted McCallister, right-faced to salute the flag, about-faced to stand before his comrades. He made no speech, did not need to. All knew why they were here. Washington began to read from a list, his voice carrying easily through the crisp mountain air.

"Corporal William Bennet. Private First Class Joseph Bradford. First Lieutenant Charles Ceton. Hospital Mate Third Class Ralph Dawson. Private Samuel Dresser..."

On and on the voice of the sergeant boomed out the names of the men who were not present but were accounted for, who had gone up with 3/5 three months before but who had come back prematurely—in body bags.

The men in the ranks stood rigidly at attention. For the first time in three months their helmets sat squarely on their heads, their boots were free of mud and snow. Brass and oil-polished steel reflected the noonday sun. Leather gleamed. Canvas canteen covers and bayonet sheaths, faded and scrubbed almost white, attested to the pride these men took in their appearance on this occasion.

Sergeant Washington read out the last name on the list. There was a long silence. The Stars and Stripes cracked sharply at the top of a forty-foot white pole behind the battalion's senior officers. The men in the ranks stared straight ahead.

Then a battle-dressed, helmeted bugler put his horn to his lips with black-leather-gloved fingers. Sweetly, mournfully, clear as a bell in the cold blue air, Taps sounded and resounded against the hills.

There were more than a few moist eyes in those ranks of tough young Marines staring straight off into space.

Three

Despite the snow and sub-freezing cold, a baseball game was in progress just outside my Sick Bay. I stopped to watch. The infield was flat, but the outfield was out in the terraced rice paddies. Right field was three tiers higher than left field so the right fielder looked as if he were standing in the bleachers. Chasing Texas leaguers required the skills of a mountain goat.

I knew all the corpsmen by now and some of the Marines. One of the Marines from Item Company, a big tough kid by the name of Thaddeus (call me Ted) Kaminski, stopped the game and shouted across to me, "Hey, Doctor, we need a good third baseman."

I was flattered, not by being called a good third baseman, but by the fact that they had already accepted me—an officer—in their games. I'd read Norman Mailer's *The Naked and the Dead* and remembered clearly how General Cummings had humiliated Lieutenant Hearn and then told him, "The Army functions best when you're frightened of the man above you and contemptuous of your subordinates." I'd never worked that way and didn't intend to start now.

Maybe it's different in the Medical Corps. I don't know. But I wasn't about to obey the "non-fraternization" rules. As far as I was concerned, those rules were written by and for officers who weren't accepted by the enlisted men and needed to formalize their estrangement with a statute. Al Chamberlin writes in *Circle of Courage* that it was the officers who got no natural respect from their men that hid behind the non-fraternization policy. Amen to that.

So now I laughed and shouted back to Ted, "Can't right now. Maybe later."

As I went on to Sick Bay, the game continued and I heard a roar of outrage and then Kaminski bellowing, "Kill the ump."

Fred Overman and Otto Hoffman were sitting on water cans in the sun outside the Sick Bay quonset hut, playing cribbage. Fred raised a hand in greeting and said, "Funny damn war."

Dr. Fred Overman, the other battalion surgeon, had been with 3/5 for two months. He was a little guy, short and stocky, but his movements were quick and graceful. I'd liked him right away. We'd had some long talks about the duties of a battalion surgeon, and about the corpsmen who worked with us.

Chief Hospital Mate Otto Hoffman was our senior corpsman. He was a lean, wiry man of about thirty—an old man in this world of twenty-year-olds. Like 20% of the troops in Korea, he was a "retread" from the Second World War. He knew his job and he knew how to handle his men. A strict disciplinarian when he had to be, he was fair, and the men knew it. He never bawled out a man in front of an officer and he never held a grudge. They also knew that he'd made Chief the hard way, one rank at a time. I'd already found myself listening to him and watching him, learning something every time he made a move.

"Yeah?" I said now to Fred. "Why's this a funny war?"

He told me.

The last time he'd seen Ted Kaminski was about four weeks before, up on the front slope of Hill 722. Overman had gone through the Item Company lines on the MLR (Main Line of Resistance) in the dead of night with his jeep ambulance to pick up a wounded man out between the MLR and the OPLR (Outpost Line of Resistance). In addition to a veteran rifleman as driver, and a corpsman, he'd had two riflemen from Item Company with him.

Kaminski had been one of those riflemen. That night he'd been all Marine: on his head a helmet with torn, brown-and-yellow camouflaging, a bandolier of ammunition slung slant-wise across his chest, two hand grenades clipped to his web belt, a twenty-pound Browning automatic rifle (BAR) held naturally and easily in his right hand as he gripped the roof of the bouncing jeep with his left.

Later, while Overman and his corpsmen were working on the wounded, oblivious to everything but the job at hand, they heard the light patter of tennis-shoed feet swishing through the snow only a few yards away. The medics froze. Chinese soldiers were on the run toward their own lines and were at first unaware of the Americans crouching over the stretchers.

But one of the wounded, semi-conscious and in great pain, groaned loudly.

One of the Chinese stopped, located the Americans, and charged.

That was what Kaminski was there for. He shouted to the working men, "Hit the deck," which they did as Kaminski barked at his buddy, "Kill the son of a bitch." And they did.

"Now," Fred said to me with a wry grin, "I hear this same guy shout, 'Kill the ump.' Same vehemence. Same inflection in his voice."

I didn't have as much trouble reconciling those two Kaminskis as I did the two Overmans. Only a few weeks before he'd been kneeling in the snow on a windswept mountain side, saving some Marine's life, while two other Marines shattered the stillness with their BARs. Now he sat there in the sun, radiating nonchalant confidence and good humor, telling a tale of danger and heroism as if he were relating the outcome of a football game—or a bingo party—or a chess game, for God's sake.

As I stood there listening to him, I seriously wondered if I could be that gung ho and handle such a situation. Because, I thought, these guys are really something else and maybe they're built differently than I am. And I remembered what Eric Sevareid had said, matching my mood at that moment: "The GI's performance in Korea outmatches the behavior of those who fought our wars of certainty and victory. This is something new in American society. This is something to be recorded with respect and humility."

I wanted to ask Fred just what had gone through his mind.

Was he numb? Scared? Did his hands shake as he splinted shrapnel fractures and suture-ligated life-threatening artery punctures?

But I didn't ask. That wasn't the kind of question you put to guys like Fred Overman. It would have been too embarrassing for both of us.

Four

Item Company moved out that night under cover of darkness, just as George had done the night before. Next morning their company streets were empty but George Company's bivouac had been taken over by Dog Company of the Second Battalion of the Seventh Marines. The streets and tents boomed with the shouts and laughter and singing of men long deprived of any such outlet for their coltish energy.

There were, too, whoops of joy as men bear hugged others they hadn't seen for weeks or months even though they'd been in the same trench line.

"You still alive, you ugly old Polack?"

Or, "Hey, whatcha been doing for excitement lately?"

Or, "Holy shit, man, they let dumb Swedes like you carry a loaded rifle?"

Big grins.

Or maybe a little more serious, "Why, you big black

son of a bitch, you did make it back from 616. Di'n't see ya again, thought mebbe..." And the answer with a poke in the belly, "Aw, man, no Chink gonna shut off this old nigger's water."

Or more serious still, "Ya hear that Tex bought the farm?"

"Yeah. Fogarty put him up for a Silver Star."

"Numbah hockin' sixty-nine! St. Peter gonna pin it on him?"

H&S Company and How Company were due to leave Camp Tripoli that night at 2200. I was ready to go an hour earlier and stood by my jeep ambulance with my gear.

Backpack strapped to my packboard and propped against the front wheel of the jeep ambulance. Brown camouflage-covered helmet perched on the pack. Parka draped over the hood of the jeep. M-2 carbine cleaned and lying with two 15-round and one 30-round clips on the stretcher on the jeep's lower rack.

I was dressed for cold weather: skivvys (boxer shorts and T-shirt), brown wool longjohns top and bottom, wool shirt, brown wool pullover sweater, green wool pants, inner fatigue jacket, alpaca-lined vest, outer field jacket, green wool scarf. Topping all this was an alpaca-lined hat that we called a "bunny hat" because it had long ear flaps that tied under the chin or on top of the head.

Strapped around my waist over my field jacket was my web belt, a K-bar knife with its seven-inch blade and a .45 automatic on the right, canvas-covered steel canteen on the left, canvas cartridge case just to the left of the buckle in front. My pockets were jammed with candy bars and two Unit-l First Aid kits. I carried a pen light and a fountain pen in the left front pocket of my fatigue jacket.

Fred Overman was still in Sick Bay stealing what we'd need on line and knew he'd never get through regular channels. I sat on the rear deck of the ambulance talking to Ned Rohn, a new driver assigned to our jeep ambulance. Ned was a former How Company machine gunner who'd been wounded three times and thus became eligible for duty out of the lines. After his third wound, when he was ready to leave the field hospital—Able Medical Company—they'd cut orders for him to some really rear-echelon outfit back in Inje or Uijonbu or somewhere. He'd fought it. He hadn't wanted to leave his buddies in 3/5. They compromised by giving him my ambulance.

It was hard for me to comprehend a man being wounded three times and not wanting to get out of the combat zone. At least three times, probably many more, Ned Rohn had been in some kind of hell of whining bullets, fluttering mortars and screaming artillery shells.

But here he was, not obviously the hero type, a tall, wiry man, 21 years old, with a flat-top haircut, long sideburns and a slightly crooked nose. His smile was a bit crooked, too, but it gave him an air of nonchalance rather than menace. The bill of his faded, frayed fatigue cap was bent into a half circle and worn low on his forehead so he looked at the world through a tunnel. His dark brown eyes flashed with intelligence and good humor. Both knees of his pants were torn open.

His field jacket was unbuttoned and on his green skivvy shirt I could see a small gold cross hanging from a thin gold chain. To offset this, he wore a .45 automatic on his right hip and carried a 30.03 Enfield rifle in the cab of the jeep.

He said he liked the aught-three better than either the M-l Garand which the line Marines carried or the M-2 carbine that was issued to us medics.

"Sort of goes with this old jeep, don't it, Doctor?" He

patted the jeep ambulance on the hood like it was a faithful old cow pony. I laughed. The jeep had been new a long time ago, saw action somewhere like on Guam or Okinawa, was mothballed for five years, now was Rohn's pride. He was forever washing it down and tinkering with the four-cylinder engine.

All but one of my mental pictures—and all of my snapshots—catch Rohn with a big grin on his face. He was that kind of a guy. Always telling jokes. He loved a good pun and a slapstick spoonerism. He was one of the cleverest guys with reparteé I've ever known.

Rohn had his serious side, too, which he effectively hid from the rest of the Aid Station. But I recognized it and he was soon aware that I saw through the facade. Now as we stood talking by the jeep, I said, "You finished high school, Ned?"

"Just barely, Doctor. Wasn't cut out for that sort of life, I guess. But I can fix anything. Long as it's got moving parts. Once I took my Mom's grandfather clock apart just to see if I could get it back together. Mom come in and seen the few thousand parts scattered all over the living room floor. 'Theodore,' she said—I knew I was in trouble when she called me Theodore. 'What in tarnation you doing?' Took me three days but it worked better'n it ever did before."

He grinned that sardonic little grin.

"See you're married." I pointed to his wedding band.

"Yeah, over a year now." He looked down at the ground and I was going to let it go, but he said, "We were too young to know that we were too young." He glanced up at me. "She hasn't written in more'n a month."

"Lots of guys haven't got much mail lately. Big storm over by Yong Dong Po."

"Yeah, that's prob'ly it."

We heard the roar of a jeep coming up the Sick Bay road. It slid to a stop and Moses Washington, Colonel McCallister's gunny sergeant, jumped out of the CO's open jeep. The sergeant was a tough old black guy of about 35, a retread, one of those "grizzled veterans" of the Second World War.

His gravelly voice was even hoarser than usual from a cold I'd been treating since I came up to 3/5. "Evenin', Doctor. Hah-yah, Ned. Change a' orders, Doctor. Second serial shoves off at 0400 tomorrow 'stead a tonight. Don't know why. O'ny God and the colonel know."

I laughed. "And neither's talking to the grunts?"

"Ya got that right, Doctor!"

He jumped back into the jeep and spun off in the direction of the How Company encampment.

So we got another night's sleep in the tent.

I accepted the change of orders as just another of those incomprehensible vagaries of military life. I'd plugged into my slot in the battalion with a minimum of fuss. I'd been brought up in a Depression-era home where you gratefully accepted the good things and shrugged off the not-so-good. My Dad was a cabinet-maker and there weren't many people buying cabinets in the 30s. In the summer he hauled garbage at a church campground two days a week with an old broken-down gray horse and a farmer's almost-broken-down hay wagon. In the winter he shoveled corn cobs out of trucks into the coal-chutes of people who couldn't afford coal, which included us. I had a paper route and cut lawns and shoveled snow and turned my earnings into the common pot. And we survived.

So now I unstrapped my mummy bag from my packboard and went down to the pyramidal tent I shared with Bob Marne, Fred Overman, and the two Marine Air

Corps officers who were our Forward Observers, responsible for calling in Marine and Navy air strikes and directing their bombing runs.

Bob Marne was still down with the brass working out the details of our move. Overman was already in his mummy bag, one visible eye balefully staring at the scene on the cot ten feet across the tent from him. Alec Stanfield, one of the fly-boys, sat on his cot with a bottle of Vodka in one hand, a Korean hymn book in the other.

Holding the book also was Butch, our twelve-year-old Korean "houseboy." They were singing "The Old Rugged Cross," Alec in English, Butch in Korean. Alec was well on his way to stupefaction but his high tenor voice harmonized beautifully with Butch's soprano.

John Haldicup, the other FO, sat on his cot, directing the choir with a waving hand clutching a bottle of The Glenlivet. When he saw me come in he put his finger to his lips with an exaggerated "Shhhhh!" which was louder than any noise I would've made.

I declined a "snort" and decided to write a short note to my wife Ingrid. I started it, "After waiting for the mortar and artillery barrage to lift, we stormed out of our foxholes...oops, wrong story. That's one for Lorrie when she grows up and I tell her how I won the war." Ingrid didn't think that was at all funny, as I heard very clearly in her return letter a couple weeks later.

I wrote "Free—Air Mail" on the envelope and addressed it. I scrawled my return address in the left upper corner:

J. Q. Lord, Lt. (MC) USNR 503770
H & S, 3/5, 1st MarDiv FMF
c/o FPO, San Francisco, CA.

I stripped down to skivvies and crawled into my mummy bag. Oh-four-hundred would soon come.

Haldicup ended the song with a dip of his bottle. Butch rolled out his sleeping bag in front of the pot-belly stove and lay down on it. He would crawl in only after all "his" officers were in their sacks, and only after he'd gone outside to change the oil can hooked up to the stove so it wouldn't run out during the night. He raised a hand to me and said with a big grin, "Goo-night, Ilene." I laughed and answered, "Goodnight, Irene." I'd taught him the song just a few days before.

John and Alec corked their bottles, went outside to use the mortar tube stuck in the frozen ground, came back in and soon were snoring hoarsely.

Five

I didn't go to sleep quite so easily. Going into combat for the first time gives a guy a thing or two to think about. Even though I thought President Roosevelt was pretty clever when he said at the start of World War II that all we had to fear was fear itself, I was troubled by the fear of being afraid when I found myself under fire.

Could I continue to work like Overman had done when his position was overrun by Chinese troops?

Would I panic?

Run?

I was a well-trained physician. I'd had basic Marine combat training for three months at Camp Pendleton.

But I didn't delude myself that training as a doctor and training for combat was the same as working as a doctor in actual combat.

I tried to switch gears by thinking back over the past week. Our landing at Sokchori just a week before, on

November 2nd, was still fresh, so I let my mind drift over it, hoping to quiet the beating of my heart and dry the sweat on my palms.

That day had dawned cold and misty. I stood on an upper deck of the 12,000-ton troop transport *William Weigel.* There were 5,000 Marines with me on that ship, all but a couple hundred headed for front line regiments. The gray ship smelled of cold metal. Everything I touched felt clammy.

Because of the dense fog hanging low on the gray water, all I could see at first was a whiteness everywhere. The ship was at anchor, its engines stilled. We rolled slightly in the groundswells headed for the beach, a novel sensation after eighteen days at sea.

As the unseen sun slowly brightened the day, I began to make out the silhouettes of mountains in the distance. Cold-looking mountains, rising 5,000 feet out of the sea. I remembered reading that the name "Korea"—meaning "high and beautiful"—derived from the Koryo dynasty that flourished from 918 to 1392. From where I stood, the mountains did look beautiful. The time would soon come when they would look like Hell.

The U. S. Navy hospital ship *Consolation* lay at anchor two hundred yards off our starboard quarter, the three red crosses on its white side standing out clearly now in the mist. Tied up alongside the *Weigel* was a Landing Ship Tank (LST), waiting to take us ashore.

The PA blared, "Now hear this! All hands lay below and prepare to disembark. Repeat! All hands lay below and prepare to disembark."

I went below. My seabags were packed, their grommets secured with combination locks. Ready also was my 55-pound backpack, personal gear inside, shelter half, rolled-up mummy bag, blanket roll, and entrenching tool strapped on the outside. My web belt lay on my cot. Attached to it with metal hooks that fitted into steel eyelets were my canteen, K-bar knife, and ammo holders. I clamped it around my waist, struggled into my pack, picked up my M-2 carbine, and climbed the ladder.

The tenseness in the air was palpable. No one was boisterous that morning. No one whistled or sang. There was no griping either. We were mentally prepared to disembark. This was what we'd ridden this ship for and we were all glad to get off. Two and a half weeks on borrowed time was long enough.

The enlisted Marines had lived a troglodyte existence in the caverns below decks, emerging daily, a company at a time, for brief exercise periods on deck. When the sea was rough, their vomitus ran first up and then down the aisles between the quadruple-decker bunks as the ship pitched and yawed. Some played poker and cribbage in never-ending games, some read paperbacks by the dim yellow overheads, some read pocket New Testaments (I envied them their faith), some talked of the girls they'd left behind and wondered, like every soldier in every war, who those girls would be sleeping with tonight.

Now they stuffed letters and pictures into their pockets in case their seabags got separated from them. I'd already put the picture of Ingrid holding Lorrie into my shirt pocket. We didn't carry wallets. There was nothing to put in them that we'd need in the First Marine Division.

There was no harbor and no dock at Sokchori, just a narrow shingle of rock and gravel. We trudged down two gangplanks from ports on the messdecks of the *Weigel* onto the LST. Standing quietly in full combat gear, most of us tipped slightly forward at the waist to balance our packs, our rifles at trail arms.

As the gangplanks swung back aboard the transport,

only a few attempts at rough banter broke the silence. A tall Texan standing in front of me turned his head and shouted to a friend, "That bitch ya shook off in Oceanside'll never getcha now." And another man behind me grunted and said, "At least he's got a girl, Tex. More'n you kin say!"

But most of the men stood quietly, like I did, wondering what the hell was going to happen next. The feeling of anxiety deepened when the metal doors of the transport clanged shut. The ship's company cast off the mooring lines which had held the LST close to the Weigel. With just a bit of melodrama I thought, "Hey, those doors just shut out my real life..."

The LST slowly pushed its flat prow up onto the beach. When I trudged ashore through the tank exits under the weight of my seabags, pack, and carbine, the beach was nearly deserted except for the shore party battalion supervising the landing. A gruff staff sergeant directed us doctors and a dozen Marines to a "Six-by." The truck had a gray plywood door with the names Mike and Steve painted in white on it. Steve was the driver. Mike was a brown and white terrier sticking his head out a square hole in the door. I detoured to pat the dog on the head, got a sloppy kiss from Mike and a big grin from Steve.

We climbed into the back of the open truck and sat on our sea bags. The shore party sergeant barked, "Shove off, Mac," and our truck pulled into line with the rest of the convoy and set off into the mountains.

The MSR (Main Service Road), cut by a bulldozer into the side of mountains that often sloped upwards at sixty degrees, was spotted with teeth-jarring potholes and so narrow that the entire convoy stopped several times at the bottom of an ascent to wait for trucks coming down the mountain. Tank tread marks in the frozen road hummed under our wheels like warning strips on highways.

During each halt we piled out of the trucks to stamp our feet and swing our arms. The temperature was below zero and the cramped confines of the crowded trucks caused a progressively numbing cold. My nose and sinuses ached and my eyes blurred with tears from the fine spray of snow swirling around us as the wind picked up powder from the hillsides. The snow wasn't deep—only an inch or two in most places, and the roads were completely clear, frozen hard.

We'd left the mist at the seashore. The sky was a pale blue, the sun a hazy white, the hillsides dark green except where the snow showed through. It would have been perfect weather for skiing.

Three hours later we rounded a bend and saw below us a tent city stretched out along the Nam River valley. Fifteen minutes later we were in the city, which was identified by a red and yellow sign as the headquarters of the First Marine Division. Beneath this sign was another, "Clear your weapons," obviously meant for those men coming back from the front lines. Already impregnated with the desire to do everything right, but knowing it was a dumb thing to do, I self-consciously slid back the bolt of my carbine and checked the chamber.

The other doctors and I were dumped unceremoniously near a pyramidal tent strong-backed with four-inch-thick pine logs. A wooden door hung in a shaky frame of two-by-fours. Sandbags surrounded the tent to a height of about four feet, piled around the strong-backing. A sign said, "Division Surgeon."

One by one we filed in and received our assignments from a cheerful Navy corpsman in Marine fatigues and a soft cap. Stenciled on his left sleeve was a caduceus between the two inverted V's of a Hospital Mate Second Class and the "crow"—actually an eagle with outstretched wings. He had every right to be cheerful. He'd been up where we were going and he'd been there long enough to rate a rear-echelon job. He grinned and said, "Three-five for you, Doctor. They're in reserve up in Camp Tripoli."

I looked at the mimeographed order sheet listing all six doctors in my draft. My name was followed by "Bn. Surg. 3/5." Battalion Surgeon, Third Battalion, Fifth Regiment.

I spent that night in Division Headquarters with the other doctors in an unheated tent lighted only by a flickering kerosene lantern. The kerosene gave out, no one knew where to get more, so we went on candle-light-savings time for the first of many dozens of such times. We tried to play cards and were defeated by the numbing cold. Laughing, griping, mumbling black witchcraft against the Chinese Communists and the First Marine Division, we crawled into our mummy bags and went to sleep.

Now, a week later, on the eve of my entry into the ranks of combat veterans, I rolled over in my sleeping bag and listened once more to the soothing rumble of our big guns.

And fell asleep.

Six

It was pitch dark at 0400 the next morning. Butch had gotten up a half hour earlier and had turned the stove up to warm the tent for us. I don't know how he did it without an alarm clock. Perhaps he just set his internal clock like I used to when I was going duck hunting.

He shook me gently and said, "We go now, Doctor Rord."

The road from Camp Tripoli to Regimental Headquarters wound around through the heavily forested mountains, taking the path of least resistance. Here it followed a streambed, there the slope of a mountain, looking for a place to go over, finally being forced up onto a ridge. It clung precariously to the ridge line, then jumped down, descending between blown-up trees and bushes. Now and then it serpentined up the side of the mountain with such sharp switchbacks that one could easily have jumped from the road onto a truck on the road below. In one of my first letters home to Ingrid I wrote, "...these awful hills—where everything is either perched on top of a hill or hanging on to the side of one."

These mountains weren't the Rockies or the Alps. They were more like the Ozarks or the Smokies or the Black Hills—two to five thousand feet high, none topping out above the tree line. But I would find that sometimes in the early morning, when the clouds were low and mist swirled around the peaks, boys from Colorado and Montana would look up and say, "Hey, that reminds me of home!"

Our convoy had road priority—troops returning to combat, not to be held up without cause, and no vehicles to be separated from the rest without reason. There were no civilian vehicles. We moved slowly, no more than ten miles an hour and usually less, in the dark, headlights off, taillights and brake lights disconnected, no glowing cigarettes or flaring matches. Until you've driven an icy mountain MSR in pitch darkness, you haven't really lived.

We traveled in two "serials"—two strung out lines of vehicles starting two hours apart. Overman had left at 0200, fourth in the first serial in the crackerbox, a squarish, enclosed ambulance that could carry two stretcher cases or half a dozen non-stretcher cases.

Since Korean civilians weren't supposed to be up where we were going, Fred had stowed Butch away in his ambulance. Colonel McCallister, our battalion Commanding Officer, knew Butch and didn't care, but there were those rear-echelon security Marines who would have dragged him off by his ears.

I followed in the jeep ambulance near the end of the second serial, thirty-fifth in line, our red-and-yellow Sick Bay sign wired to the front bumper. Ned Rohn was my driver. I sat in back on the jump seat across from the stretcher racks. It was about five degrees above zero and I was glad I'd put on all the warm clothes I owned.

I had a lot of time to think, sitting there in the dark, in that jeep ambulance grinding slowly up towards the battle lines. One of the things that bugged me was how I'd respond if all of a sudden I was under fire and had to keep working.

I'd read the World War Two stories from the Pacific and from Europe.

Army guys ignoring bullets and mortars to drag wounded men into shelter.

Marines wading through shoulder-high surf onto an island beach, while the Japs (we still called them Japs then—hatred dies hard) picked off the officers and the corpsmen and the noncoms if they could identify them.

Suicide charges against entrenched machine gun positions.

Sailors battening down hatches over the screams of men below, saving a ship while sacrificing their buddies. The roar of a sergeant in France, "Come on, you sons a bitches, ya wanna live forever?"

Pilots clinging to the controls of dying aircraft long enough to allow their crews to escape but not long enough for themselves.

The stories were endless. And carried a common theme. Heroism. Personal heroism. In Marine parlance, they were gung ho. I will sacrifice myself so that my buddies will live. I will fall on that hand grenade. I will control this airplane till my crew have all jumped.

Or did they really think?

What goes through a man's mind under that kind of stress?

What would go through my mind if I were ever to be in a position of danger when a job had to be done? At that moment, as I sat in the jeep, hanging on to the stretcher rack in front of me, I seriously doubted if I could make myself into a hero.

It took our serial over two hours to reach regimental headquarters. Our track led us through mostly empty country, abandoned by the Koreans and not usable by the troops. But just as it got light we crawled through a valley filled with the big guns of the Eleventh Marine Artillery Regiment, stretched out for almost a mile. Huge searchlights six feet across scanned the skies.

"What the hell are those for?" I shouted.

Rohn turned his head and shouted back, "Artillery spots." He had the jeep in double-reduction gears to slow it down while he maneuvered it through the tortuous S-curves. As he answered, we came alongside a gun emplacement just as it fired. The jeep jumped a good six inches sideways and I felt my hair stand on end and my ears ache. I swallowed hard.

"God damn 'em," Rohn said with a crooked grin. "Second time in a week. They must see me coming."

"What size gun was that?" I asked.

"One-fifty-five. Millimeters. About six inches."

We drove in silence for a few moments. Then I asked, "How far back of the front lines are we, Ned?"

"About two miles, Doctor. This place is called 'Artillery Valley,' headquarters of the Eleventh Artillery Regiment. They're stretched out for about a mile, have about half the division's big guns, maybe more. The rest are deployed along the front lines behind the infantry battalions."

Then we were out of the valley again, climbing steadily through the dense pine forests. It was getting light and I was getting hungry. There was a box of K-rations at my feet under the stretcher rack. I debated cracking it and then thought better of it. I'd have to be a hell of a lot hungrier to make the effort worthwhile. I mean, after all, who'd expend any time or energy for what I knew was in those boxes? Not me. Not then, anyway. There'd come a time. Several times, in fact.

The convoy stopped at the Seventh Marines regimental headquarters while our CO, Lt. Col. McCallister, conferred with the Seventh's commanding officer. Rohn veered out of the convoy and pulled up to the regiment's aid station where Fred Overman was waiting for me.

Chief Hoffman stood by the crackerbox rear view mirror, shaving dry.

"Above and beyond the call of duty," I called to him.

And Rohn said, "Bet he's going falking in the worest."

The Chief just smiled.

"Come on, Jack," Overman said. "I'll show you the aid station. A little fancier than ours up on the line, but similar."

The aid station was in a 16x32 squad tent, a dark green monster. Half the floor was covered with planks recovered from shell cases, one of the advantages of their location close to the artillery.

So we settled on the Sick Bay stretchers for a rest while the regimental surgeon, a friend of Fred's, started to bring us up to date on what was happening up front. But then Ned Rohn stuck his head through the tent flap. "Movin' out, Doctors."

Seven

In November of 1951, a year and a half had gone by since Harry Truman sent the Americans across the Sea of Japan to the "Land of the Morning Calm."

Seoul had fallen to the North Koreans in the summer of 1950. It was retaken by United Nations forces in the fall of 1950. It fell again when the Chinese intervened in the winter of 1950-51. Then it was retaken by the U.S. in late winter of 1951.

So in November of 1951 that once proud city, which I would never see, lay sprawled in its own rubble south of the front lines near the west coast. The lines themselves jumped from hill to hill across the breadbasket of Korea around Munsan and Inchon in the west, then followed ridges and mountain tops to Wonju and Inje in the east.

The *Blitzkrieg* was over.

The *Sitzkrieg* had just begun.

The truce teams of the two warring factions were

already meeting almost daily in the quiet little village of Panmunjom, immortalized by its geographic position in the neutral zone between Pyongyang, capital of North Korea, and Seoul, capital of South Korea. Little progress had been made except to stabilize the front at what later became the DMZ (demilitarized zone) along the "Kansas" line.

The war was only half over but no one knew it then. There would be another 12,300 Americans killed in action in that last half, almost as many as during the first half.

The sector of the United Nations lines controlled by the First Marine Division was in the mountains which ran north and south along the east coast for hundreds of miles—almost the entire peninsula. On both flanks of the U.S. and Korean Marine Divisions were American Army divisions.

The front line was well north of the 38th parallel in this area. It slanted southwest from Kosong—a small town on the east coast, sixty miles north of the 38th parallel—to the mouth of the Han River, about thirty miles northwest of Seoul and ten miles south of the 38th parallel.

The biggest town in our area was Inje, which lay about thirty miles inland from the seacoast and about eight miles north of the 38th parallel.

Running north from Inje to the MLR was the Namgang River—and it was along this river that most of the major Marine encampments were located: Camp Tripoli, Division Headquarters, Able Medical Company, the 11th Artillery, and so forth. The valley formed by the river was the only area flat enough for large encampments and formed a natural pass through the mountains for the development of roads. Before the war moved through, only narrow walking paths and bullock tracks crossed those mountains and the people living there were among the most isolated in the world.

Just to our west, in what was now a U.S. Army sector, lay the famed "Punchbowl," an almost flat plain seventy square miles in area nestled in the midst of high mountains, won during the spring offensive of 1951 by the Marines of 3/5. There Ned Rohn had been wounded twice, the first a minor wound just two days after arriving in Korea, the second, also minor, two weeks later.

His third wound had been much more serious. He'd been crouched behind his machine gun when a mortar round landed twenty-five feet behind him and sprayed his back with half a dozen fragments. The surgeons at Easy Med had dug most of them out, had evacuated him to Able Med where five days later the wounds were all sutured. Within two weeks he was ready for action again and was sent up to 3/5's H & S Company as our ambulance driver.

A little farther to the west was "Heartbreak Ridge," taken and lost and taken again. The American boys who died there were just as dead as those who had died six and seven years before on Iwo Jima and Peleliu and Okinawa. The islands had become mountain ridges, the Japanese had become Chinese, the palm trees had become pine trees, and the blood ran just as red on the white snow as it did on the white sand.

But the boys in Korea wrote home with a plea that was never heard during World War Two: "You want to know what you Americans can do about the Korean War? All any of us ask over here is that you *remember us*."

The road from regiment to the MLR was narrower, bumpier, more rutted, and in general more primitive. On the map it showed up as a series of dashes: -- --. In other words, a track. But it was a track only months old and had not yet had a chance to compact like jeep and 4 WD tracks have done in the mountains of the U.S. It wasn't used much because those in the rear didn't go up to the front unless they had to, and those at the front couldn't go back unless they were replaced, wounded, or killed.

At one point we bobbed across a river on a pontoon bridge built by the combat engineers. In another place, on a side hill, we slithered by a gaping hole where half the road had been nudged off into the river by an artillery round. We watched first with alarm and then amusement as a truck ahead of us slid sideways, then backwards, thirty feet down into the river and later had to be pulled back up by a Sherman tank.

The sound of our own artillery became more and more muffled. When we stood by the ambulance during rest breaks, we could often hear the shells whirring overhead. (Not until they start their downward plunge near the end of their parabolic arc do they start to scream.) Occasionally a shell exploded above us with a dull thud and a puff of smoke. "Airbursts," Rohn explained.

I asked, "Don't they ever hit anyone?"

"Don't seem to," he answered, then corrected himself. "Yeah, I did hear once of a corpsman who had a small fragment come through his sleeping bag, but that's all I ever heard of."

It was a bright sunny day, almost windless, warm for November, around forty degrees, and the rock-hard track was softening in the sun. Where rice paddies lay in terraces which was almost everywhere in these mountains, the snow had melted from the curving, grassy brown edges but remained deep and white in the flat fields.

A few Korean civilians were on the road, nonchalantly ignoring the Xth Corps orders that stated flatly that no civilians were to live north of a line connecting the regimental headquarters of the various outfits along the MLR.

Kids with massive loads of brush stacked high on their A-frames struggled up the steep slopes and stepped off into the dirty roadside slush to let us pass. They grinned and waved.

For half an hour our jeep was caught behind a man leading a bullock pulling a "honey cart" loaded with six large wooden barrels full of fresh human excrement on their way from villages to rice fields. The stench was not at all like honey, but we couldn't pass and so crawled at two to three miles an hour until we came to a wider place in the track.

Two old papa-sans in long flowing white robes and black bird-cage hats stood reflectively as they watched us creep by.

Three nicely dressed young men stood along the verge and waved to us. They all wore starched white blouses, baggy white trousers, and thin black or white overcoats that looked like the laboratory coats I wore in medical school. Two wore stiff brown hats that looked like folded and partially opened grocery bags. The other wore a felt Alpine-like hat with a wide ribbon and narrow brim.

One gave us the O.K. sign with thumb and index finger and shouted in English, "USMC number one! USA number hocking sixty-nine!" Interpretation: "Marines the best. Army the worst."

I laughed and shouted back, "KMC shay-eel," which Butch had taught me meant "Korean Marine Corps Number One." That elicited broad smiles and a delighted clapping of hands.

In one little blasted village a small gaggle of school-age children played in a snow-filled ditch. All wore thin white socks and rubber slippers. I wondered that their feet didn't freeze. Maybe they did.

The children crowded close to the slowly moving jeep with their hands outstretched, calling with big grins, "*Kuadtsa scoshi*-bit?"

"What're they saying?" I asked Rohn.

He laughed. "*Kuadtsa*, Korean for candy. *Scoshi*, Japanese for little. Bit, you understand."

(A *scoshi*-bit of history here: the Japanese had annexed Korea in 1910 after five years of "protectorate" status and controlled it until 1944, enforcing their culture, including language, on the Koreans. The Japanese military government had deprived the Koreans of freedom of assembly, association, press, and speech. Now, in 1951, many uneducated Koreans still used Japanese words and phrases, often unaware that they did so.)

Then, before long, I realized there were no more civilians on the road. Nor were there any other vehicles. The big guns of the 11th were muffled. Not so the thud of incoming stuff on the lines not far ahead of us. The sounds of battle were as clear as a Fourth of July fireworks display in the city park.

Rohn pointed to the ridge ahead of us and I saw a flight of four Corsairs swoop one at a time below the ridge and heard the sharp crackle of .50 caliber machine guns and then the booming of 500 pound bombs as they exploded on the Chinese lines. I wondered how many human lives were snuffed out in those few seconds. But they were the enemy, right? They'd attacked us, hadn't they? It was all right to kill them, wasn't it?

Uh huh.

None of us in that long convoy voiced it, but it was a day when it was good just to be alive. We all knew that we were headed back into combat and life seemed even more precious.

But there was no incoming fire on us now and no threat to life from flying steel. The jeep ambulance crept up and around and down again, keeping pace with the rest of the convoy. I gazed upward at the towering white mountains and then downward at the steep wooded slopes into the white valleys.

I closed my eyes for a moment, thinking how good it'd be when I'd be going the other way. I thought of Ingrid back in the States and fantasized a bit about our reunion in 'Frisco or LA or wherever I'd land in a year or so. I remembered reading somewhere that any ordinary housewife could become a charming lover by greeting her husband each evening dressed only in a radiant smile and a gingham apron. I planned to write Ingrid with the suggestion that when she met me on my return she could forget the apron.

But that kind of thinking had to have some control so I made myself slide back into the present. As I did so I realized that Rohn was doing an unusual amount of shifting from regular gears into double-reduction gears, and then back again, especially on the downward grades, never putting his foot on the brake.

When my curiosity could no longer be checked, I asked, "Saving Old 99's brakes, Ned?"

He patted the dashboard. "Old 99899 ain't got brakes any more, Doctor. They finally went out on that last hill before Regiment."

We were on a particularly steep, hairpin curve. Rohn put in the clutch, shifted into neutral, and said, "Watch."

He slammed the brake pedal down to the floorboard. Nothing happened. By now we were careening around the curves like a motorcycle in a motordrome, rapidly catching up to the truck in front of us. Unnerved, I white-knuckled the seat, thinking that now there was no possibility of shifting into low, much less tractor gears. But Rohn did wrestle the stick into second and pumped the brake. We slowed down.

"See what I mean, Doctor?"

I nodded my head. I saw.

Slewing in the mud around the nose of a hill we came suddenly upon a row of half a dozen pyramidal and squad tents clinging precariously to the back slope of an east-west ridgeline. Below this shelf was the rest of the command post of the Second Battalion of the Seventh Marines. This encampment would now become the site of our Fifth Marines' Third Battalion Headquarters and Service Company.

Rohn maneuvered the ambulance out of the convoy and slid to a stop by the Aid Station. I climbed out and gazed around me. I was suddenly overwhelmed by the enormity of what I was undertaking, what I'd been brought here to do. This bivouac, I thought, this isolated mountain outpost, this camp under the guns of the Chinese Communists, will be my home away from home until our outfit is relieved by some other outfit in three or four months. Then we'll go into reserve for a few weeks and then go back up on the line in a different sector for three or four months. By that time I'll be due for rotation back to a field hospital where I'll stay for four to six months. Then I'll go home.

I had it all figured out.

Someone had dubbed that row of tents on the ridge "Mercy Row" because in addition to the Aid Station there were the tents of the corpsmen, doctors, and chaplain. Between Mercy Row and the motor pool stood a huge green cross, twenty-five feet high, the cross-bar at least six feet across, constructed of hundreds of pine branches lashed together, their color locked in by the cold.

Sandbags were piled around all the tents, especially high around the 16 x 16 pyramidal tent labeled in yellow and red, "Sick Bay." Another blue and white sign stuck between two sandbags said, "Aid Station." The ground around the station was littered with fuel cans, stretchers, huge steel-handled wooden trunks, and other odds and ends of medical and non-medical gear. They needed another tent. I made a mental note to nick Chief Hoffman's ear with a gentle request that he cumshaw one from the Army.

The troop-trucks of the convoy pulled off fifty yards away into the motor pool area. The Marines of How Company piled out of the trucks, stretching arms and legs, running in place to push blood back into cold feet. I knew how they felt. One open truck with our 3/5 corpsmen stopped beside our jeep and the corpsmen jumped down and looked around.

Fred Overman, who'd arrived two hours earlier in the First Serial, was standing by the crackerbox, talking to Dr. Roger Hendricks, the battalion surgeon of 2/7, who'd come out to greet us.

The corpsmen, too, had all come outside and were standing in a grinning row, watching their reliefs rolling in. I had a pretty good idea how they felt, too. In just a few more hours, as soon as darkness fell, the last company of 3/5, How, would go into the line to replace the last company of 2/7, Fox. Fox would leave with its H & S Company—including these aid station corpsmen—for Camp Tripoli, the reserve area which we'd just left.

Eight

How Company went up into the lines that night to reconstitute 3/5 and complete the relief of 2/7. Fred Overman and I stood on the shelf of Mercy Row and watched them go. It was a replay of the night Bob Marne and I had stood watching George Company moving out of Camp Tripoli. But tonight it was pitch dark, the moon and stars now blocked by a thick layer of clouds that had moved in during the afternoon. All we could see were indistinct shadows moving along the track below us.

I didn't envy those guys at all. It was cold, bitter cold, probably around zero. The wind was coming up and it felt like snow. I was reminded of the night Ingrid and I had stood on the rickety porch of her father's cabin in the wilderness of northern Manitoba. We'd come in on snowshoes from the plowed road almost a mile away with food for several days. With our arms around each other we listened to the wind howling across the frozen lake and through the tall spruce forest.

"Maybe," Ingrid said, "we'll get snowed in!"

"Yeah," I said, "wouldn't that be great? Just you and me and the timber wolves."

We went back in and sat by the roaring fire with glasses of brandy and talked far into the night. Well, we didn't just talk. I think it may have been that night that Lorrie was conceived.

Now Fred and I went back into our little two-man Arctic tent and lay down on the ground on our sleeping bags. I reached over and turned up the dial on the tiny oil-burning potbelly. Gradually the chill left but it never really got warm.

If Fred had been nonchalant when we were in reserve, he was all business now. He was leaving for the trench line in the morning to man our forward aid station. Now he pulled a metal ammo box over to him and extracted a list of all the corpsmen in the battalion.

Twenty were scattered along the line, one or two in each of the nine infantry platoons, two or three in the Forward Aid bunker, and two in Weapons Company. We had a dozen corpsmen assigned to the rear aid station, three or four on each shift of eight hours, though shifts meant little when there was work to be done. Everyone pitched in whether he was "on call" or not.

"Up on the line," Fred said, "each of these guys is pretty much on his own. Before we went into reserve at Tripoli, I didn't really know them too well. When a WIA came back to me with a sloppy field dressing or a poorly-placed splint, I didn't usually know if it was because the corpsman was incompetent, or because he'd been under fire with the rest of the platoon and just couldn't do any better under the circumstances."

He took a long drag on his cigarette and continued.

"Now, after those three weeks in reserve, I know them all much better." Patiently he ticked off each man by name, detailing their strong points, their weaknesses, who could be depended on, who needed a little encouragement and help, and who needed careful watching so that he didn't make any serious mistakes.

The next day Overman went up to the forward aid station bunker in the lines. He wanted me to get acquainted with life in the battalion before going up. He said the lines were quiet now and he didn't mind going up.

I was left in charge of the rear aid station, a 16x16 pyramidal tent, half the size of the one at the Seventh Marines' Headquarters. Overman was right; this wasn't as fancy. No shell box flooring here. The floor—or "deck" as we old salts called it—was Korean dirt, pounded hard by the combat boots of the doctors and corpsmen. The stretchers were laid on frames made of small pine trees, the wash basin a helmet liner set in an eight-inch artillery shell casing, soap dish a C-ration can, "medicine cabinet" built of wood from shell boxes. Heat was furnished by a small pot-bellied oil burner in the middle of the tent.

Fred had seen me taking all this in when we first arrived and had said with a grin, "Nothing's too good for the boys at the front—and that's what we get!"

Fred was right about it being quiet. About 90% of the time it was deadly dull. Most days were an unending repetition of nothingness.

No place to go.

Very little to read. There were some Armed Service Edition books around and I read Herman Wouk's new book, *The Caine Mutiny*, and then Stuart Cloete's *The Turning Wheels*. I wrote home to Ingrid to send me Daphne Du Maurier's new book, *My Cousin Rachel*, and A. J. Cronin's latest, *Adventures in Two Worlds*.

We had breakfast at 0900, the best of which was rubberized pancakes and over-fried bacon (just like Ingrid liked it). Sick call for H & S Company personnel—almost always minor aches and pains—took about thirty minutes. Then there were a few aid station duties to attend to, like signing the Emergency Medical Tags of wounded men who'd been evacuated the day before, and checking out Chief Hoffman's duty list, and stuff like that.

Lunch was what someone had gotten in a "care package" from home, usually crackers and brownies and cookies. The big meal of the day was at 1600 and was ladled out of a big pot onto our mess tins. It was all canned stuff, of course. No fresh meat, fruits, or vegetables. I was already missing those things and wrote Ingrid, "If you thought I was a fresh fruit eater before, watch me when I get home!"

I soon found that Chief Hoffman was a Navy reserve doctor's answer to prayer. He ran the show, but he always deferred to me and made it appear that I was the boss. All I needed to do was suggest something and it was done. After we'd been up there about a week, I said, "You know, Chief, it'd be a good idea to have a bunker between the aid station and the 'copter strip in case a landing 'copter draws incoming fire."

That afternoon I went over to the aid station and the bunker was almost finished. The Chief had merely had to say, "The doc said…" and it was done.

This was a novel experience for me. I'd never had that sort of power. I could understand, for the very first time, that to have power over other people is fine wine in a long-stemmed glass. I wrote to Ingrid that night, "I'll sure hate to leave my little kingdom up here on the hill…" She didn't think much of that as I found out quickly in her return letter.

I saw very few WIAs in rear aid because, first of all there weren't many. I think for the month of December we averaged only two or three a day. Secondly, Fred Overman saw most of them in his forward aid station and sent them out directly from the lines, over our heads to the rear in helicopters. Sometimes it was hard to believe that we were "in combat."

I guess I was a little disappointed. Then I thought, my God, what am I thinking? Do I want it to be busier? Do I want more guys to get their legs and hands and heads blown off? I was glad I hadn't voiced my disappointment. It wasn't long before I looked back on those first weeks with nostalgia, for we were in a lull before the storm.

And if it was dull most of the time, it sometimes *too* exciting. It was, like some airman said in World War II, hours of pure boredom interspersed with minutes of sheer terror. Even with Fred Overman up on the line, I was subject to call from areas which were easier for me to reach from rear aid than for him. I got calls in the middle of the night from the lines. "Yeah, Doctor," a corpsman reported, "we got a man hit here, like you to see him." Or a platoon commander phoned back, "Six men just exploded a land mine, Doc. Two are bad but the other four look okay."

And then there would be a fast, jolting ride with Ned Rohn along roads that were not much more than wide trails, not daring to use lights or even a flashlight to see the road, knowing that if the jeep went off the road it would very likely hit a land mine. So I just sat back with one hand hanging onto the stretcher rack across from the jump seat where I always sat, the other hand holding either my M-2 or my .45 in case I'd spot infiltrators, trusting to Ned's night vision and steady hand.

The carbine was clearly the more accurate weapon of

the two at anything more than ten to fifteen yards. But to be accurate, you had to hold it steady with both hands and aim it. How are you going to do that in the dark, on a rutted, pot-holed road, while hanging onto the jeep for dear life with one hand?

So I usually rode with my mittened hand on the leather strap that held my .45 in its holster. My index finger protruded through the leather mitten shell into the trigger finger extension of the wool mitten liner, ready to unsnap the strap and pull the weapon, which I carried with the magazine full but the chamber empty.

Besides, I'd never really have to use it, would I?

Sometimes it would be a daylight run down a road zeroed in by the gooks' mortar crews, who waited for a vehicle or group of men to expose themselves.

Like the time in mid-November when I got a call from How Company that two Commonwealth Division Turks from a prisoner-taking patrol had come back through our lines badly shot up.

Rohn and I took off.

We were crawling up Hill 812—the backside of How Company—where a track branched off to the Second Battalion of the First Marines. A mortar round landed in front of our jeep. I could hear the fragments whizzing over our heads, not like the pinging whine of a ricochet-ing bullet, but more like the whuuuuush of mallards' wings as they put down their landing flaps right over your head.

The hole in the road made by the mortar shell was three feet deep and six across.

Rohn looked at me with those penetrating black eyes. "Somebody up on 1052 goofed, Doctor. We shoulda been dead."

"What do you mean, Ned?"

"They could a used a proximity fuse that explodes above the ground like a Bouncing Betty except lots more power. Bigger shrapnel, too. But that round must've been like some of our 81 mm. mortars that got a detonator fuse that delays for a tenth of a second and gives the round time to penetrate a bunker or whatever before it explodes. Saved our lives, them using a round like that. If it'd exploded on contact, it'd've sprayed an area 100 yards in diameter."

Another time, in late November on a different track, in a swirling snowstorm, we came down the hill back of the George Company lines, rocking and swaying and bouncing on the frozen road. Wind and snow sucked in the open back of the jeep ambulance, covering both the patient and me with powdery snow.

The lines were quiet. The Marine we had on the stretcher had a fractured femur which he'd gotten while reinforcing his bunker. A log had gotten away from him and pinned him against the sharp verge of the trench. He was in a lot of pain from the movement of the bouncing jeep and asked us to stop for just a few moments and allow him to catch his breath.

We stopped at the little stream at the bottom of the valley. I shot another quarter of morphine into the guy, deep in his deltoid.

"Let's give it about fifteen minutes to work," I said. "We're not in any hurry. They can't see us from 1052 in this snowstorm."

"Okay Doctor—"

But the snow squall thinned out rather suddenly and within minutes a 120 millimeter mortar landed in the track about a hundred yards behind us. Rohn and I looked at each other.

"Stray round?" I asked, and knew it wasn't.

"They can see us now from 1052," Rohn said.

The next round was fifty yards away. We hit the deck, bounced right up, and scrambled into the jeep. Rohn took the ford in the stream at full speed. I hung on to the injured Marine with one hand and the stretcher rack with the other.

The Marine's teeth ground together, his eyes squeezed shut with drops of moisture at the corners, and there wasn't a damn thing I could do about it.

The next rounds landed in a saturation pattern, three or four of them, centered on the middle of the river, thirty yards behind us now but a few feet from where we'd been parked. Rohn put the pedal to the floor and we got out of there into the relative safety of the H&S Company ridge.

Too close.

A week later, after the lines had been real quiet for several days, I got careless. There'd been almost no incoming at all, no patrols, no attacks by the Chinese.

Overman had come back to rear aid and we played gin rummy in the daytime and poker with rifle bullets at night. The weather was cold, clear, and sunny. McCallister sent a truck back to Inje for a couple dozen cases of beer. The corpsmen played volleyball in the snow and I joined them a few times.

One bright sunny morning I got a call on the EE-8 field phone from a corpsman up on the line in George Company. A couple of the Marines had been wrestling in their bunker and tipped over a helmet liner full of burning kerosene that they were using to heat the bunker. One guy had a small burn on his thigh, and the other guy had burns of his hands that would need some attention.

"What should I do, Doctor?" the corpsman asked. "Send him back to you, or directly to…"

"I'll come up and see him," I said, glad for the excuse

to do something besides sit and contemplate my navel.

"You don't need..."

"Sit tight, Mac, I'll be up in half an hour."

Rohn drove me up to the backside of George Company and I told him he might as well just sit and wait. If anything started up, he could either join us in the bunker or shove off back down the hill to H & S and pick me up later.

There was absolutely nothing coming in. I couldn't even hear anything anywhere in our sector. In defiance of all common sense I walked over the crest of the ridge and stood leaning against a tree above the trench system, contemplating the scene before me.

The heavily wooded ridge dropped sharply below me into the valley, then rose again onto another ridge where the Red Chinese were dug into their trenches and bunkers. It was a beautiful sight.

So quiet.

So peaceful.

The bark of the tree I was leaning against exploded three inches from my hip. I froze, then took a step forward to jump into the trench. Another bullet plowed into the snow at my feet, splattering frozen mud and dried oak leaves and snow over my boots. I jumped into the trench and fell to my knees just as a third bullet thunked into the tree just above my head.

I don't remember hearing shots. They would have been coming from Hill 1052, which was close enough for the sound of a rifle to be heard. But it was obvious that a sniper had me spotted.

That volley of rifle bullets whistling around me was a very personal thing. A man, another human being, who didn't know me from Adam but knew I was the enemy, was trying to kill me.

ME!

Can it get any more personal than that?

Even as I lay there flat on my belly in the cold sunlight, I could see the trunk of the tree on the edge of the trench with the freshly splintered yellow wood where the brown-black bark had been torn away. I didn't think much about it right then. Only later that night when I was eating from a can of C-ration beef stew, did the thought overpower me that I might have been killed. My fingers hadn't trembled up on the line but they did as I ate that stew.

For a couple of weeks we again endured a stretch of boring routine. Then, in the first week of December, on one of the coldest days we'd had yet, I got a preview of the battle for Hill 1052, which was germinating in the generals' minds back in Division. Fortunately for my peace of mind I didn't have a premonition, which was just as well because even if I had been able to see into the future, there wouldn't have been anything I could do about it.

I was actually back behind the lines of How Company watching a mortar crew in action. Somewhere up in How Company an FO was shooting an azimuth with his helmet off to avoid deflecting the magnetic needle. He radioed the coordinates back to Lt. Rory Sanders, who listened carefully and then barked orders to his crew. They fired a round.

Waited.

Heard the round hit.

Sander's radio squawked and he relayed the message, "Up 300, right 50."

Fired another round.

Waited.

Heard the message from the FO and relayed it, "Zeroed in. Fire four."

Four mortars dropped one at a time into the tube and exploded out in about six seconds.

The radio squawked, “Got him.”

“Clear out,” Sanders shouted.

The crew quickly began dismantling the mortar barrel from the footplate.

Too late.

An enemy mortar fluttered in. We all dropped in unison and all escaped the flying steel except Sergeant Todd Fehling, the crew chief. He took a chunk in his belly.

We leaped to our feet and four of us dragged Todd into a thick clump of trees. With a wry grimace I pulled off the tape holding a bottle of serum albumin to my hairy calf and started it in Todd’s forearm vein. While I was working, I heard Sanders order a Marine back to H & S to get a stretcher. We hunkered down and waited. I thought Todd was going to be all right if we could get him out to Easy Med in a hurry.

Suddenly we heard the gooks running down a draw to the left of us, shouting orders and blowing whistles. All we could do was stay quietly right where we were.

The mortar crew lay on their bellies in the snow, rifles pointed in the direction of the whistles and running feet. Rory Sanders sat with his back against a tree, his trigger finger on the trigger housing of the .45 resting in his lap.

If the gooks had cut back to the east behind us we’d’ve been completely cut off from our own lines and would’ve been sitting ducks for capture or killing. The mortar guys would’ve gotten some of them, but they couldn’t have held out very long against the number of Chinks we heard running down that draw.

We lay there for over two hours, listening to the battle, wondering just when the gooks were going to find us. Gradually the sounds of battle shifted to our west, then finally north of us again. Slowly it became clear that the probe had been driven back by the left flank of Able Company of the First Battalion. We got Todd Fehling out of there and 'coptered him to Easy. I never heard what happened to him but I'd guess he did all right.

As the weeks passed, I began to realize that I'd been baptized by enemy fire and hadn't panicked, hadn't stood benumbed, hadn't thrown away my rifle in a desperate frenzy of fear. Even with Chinamen close enough to hear them running in the snow, I'd kept my head, had continued working on Todd almost as if I were in the relative safety of the rear aid tent.

I knew now what it was like to be in combat.

Oh, I knew it wasn't like wading ashore on a Pacific island through a hail of machine gun bullets, or like storming a hillside with a thousand other men and fighting hand-to-hand in the trenches with bayonet and K-bar. But it was enough of the real thing to give me confidence that I wouldn't make an ass of myself if things got worse.

So there were times when I was very happy just to be bored. I liked to stand outside my tent as the sun set. It was that period of the day when everything was in limbo and everybody was suspended between what they'd been doing and what they were going to do. The sick bay watch changed. The anti-guerrilla patrols came back. The officers, just come from staff meeting, stood in groups of two or three, passing the time of day or taking care of odd scraps of business.

Except for the occasional rumble of artillery to our rear or a firefight up on the front, it was quiet.

Peace in the midst of war.

Happiness in the midst of unhappiness.

The wind of God brushed lightly against the hearts of men committed to the task of preventing other men from preaching dialectical materialism and atheistic ideologies, from over-running a people who had renounced that way of life.

And then jets roared overhead, night fighters with errands of death and destruction. Or a jeep ambulance roared in from the lines or a helicopter chopped overhead with men wounded and dying. And one night a B-29 bomber in flames circled our position, growling like a big truck climbing a hill, coming down fast, and crashed in No-man's Land with an explosion that lit up the sky. Only five parachutes flared so I knew five others had gone down with the plane. And I was brought up sharply from reverie to the cold hard fact that "out there," even then, men were fighting and dying.

Everything wasn't so peaceful, after all.

I wrote a long letter to Ingrid in mid-December, "It's a strange sort of life, one which I'll probably never encounter again—at least I hope not. But I'm happy. You can't be otherwise. You can't sit and brood all day because you're not home with wife and other loved ones and friends. You have to be philosophical about it and take every opportunity that comes up to improve your morale and that of your men. I'm sure that when I finally do get back to you I'll have many pleasant memories of Korea. Gradually the unpleasant memories will fade out and I'll feel a sense of pride in having served 'Corps and Country' in a useful capacity. And then maybe all the days of separation will not seem to have been in vain. Let's hope so. I believe I can truthfully say that it isn't the U.S. I miss, but you and the home we had together. In a few more months I may change my mind about not missing the U.S., but I feel now that if only you were here, everything else would be all right. Just being away from the U.S. hasn't affected me like I thought it would. Life doesn't just stop for the period of time you're away from your country. You're the same person you were before. You react the same and talk the same and in essence live the same. Before I left the States I had the vague idea that everything would sort of be in a state of suspended animation until I came home. And then I'd just take up where I left off. Not so."

I'd learned that when those doors clanged shut on the *Weigel* a month before they hadn't closed on "my real life." This was my life. What could be more real?

On the 15th of December, exactly two months since we'd sailed from San Diego, I stood outside the aid station watching the sun dropping behind the ridgeline to the west, throwing the camp into shade, but still lighting the mountains in the east and south. The sky was blue, the cumulus clouds white, and I had to admit that it was a beautiful sight.

But then a patrol came in from a day of anti-guerrilla action.

Their leader, Randy Carpentier, a second lieutenant, was covered with mud and snow from head to foot. It was clear that he'd spent part of the day crawling on his belly, either into trouble or away from it. His helmet sat awry on his head as if he'd begun to get a headache from the tight pressure of the helmet liner on his temples. He lifted his boots heavily as if they weighed a ton and there was a sucking noise with each step as the mud gripped his boots.

His carbine was slung over his shoulder as if it were part of him and it was also covered with mud beginning to cake on the stock and barrel. The muzzle, bolt, and trigger housing had been kept carefully cleaned and oiled.

His radio man followed him closely, carrying a "300"

radio with which the lieutenant had kept in contact with the battalion Command Post throughout the day. Following him were the three fire teams of four men each, slogging along in the mud and snow, tired, dirty, hungry, sick of it all.

Bringing up the rear was the platoon corpsman, guardian of their physical welfare, often the unsung hero, sometimes the lauded hero, his men swearing by him, once in a while at him.

I knew the corpsman. His name was Jeff Madison. He was black. He'd been with Item Company for three months, now was attached to this platoon doing special operations. He'd handled cases of amputation from land mines, belly wounds from small arms fire, multiple body wounds from mortar and shrapnel. He'd seen American boys die in his arms, helpless to aid them.

Two months later during a chow break Jeff would sit on a land mine about five feet off the path and blow off his right buttocks along with the sciatic nerve and femoral artery. He would survive, but with his leg amputated at the hip.

It takes all kinds of men to fight a war. There must be those in mortar-shelled front line bunkers, like those in George, How, and Item Companies of the Third Battalion. Their faces were dirty, unshaven, and haggard. Their eyes stared blankly. When a buddy in the next bunker was killed by incoming, they said, "He didn't know what hit him."

And there must be men like Sergeant Andy McPherson—his lower leg gone, blown off by a Russian foot mine. His only comment to me was, "I guess this finishes my career in the Marine Corps."

And there must be men like Second Lieutenant Stan Kowicki, who led a reinforced platoon against the enemy one moonless night. In that action he won the Bronze Star for his courage, for his stamina, for his stealth. The medal was pinned on him in front of Colonel McCallister's tent. He stood in the snow two paces in front of the platoon which had stayed with him and supported him in the maneuver for which he was being decorated.

There was also our Chaplain, Bob Runninger, one of the inhabitants of Mercy Row. He was an unassessable asset to the battalion. By that I mean you couldn't measure in concrete terms what he did for the men and officers of 3/5. Every morning he went up to the front lines and crawled from bunker to bunker. Talking to the men. Cheering them up. Praying with them. Sometimes I'd be up there, too, and I could see their eyes taking on an individuality, losing that blankness which marked them as "front line, infantry." The tenseness in the muscles of their faces relaxed. It was the power of God working through "Chappie."

And there were men like Alec Stanfield. It was he who'd sung "The Old Rugged Cross" with Butch. He was 28 years old, veteran of four years piloting Marine Corps fighter planes in the Pacific in WW II, six months piloting Corsairs in Korea. Now he was finishing five months of front line duty as a Forward Observer, directing air strikes against the Communists.

Alec sat on my cot that evening of the 15th, clutching a bottle of Canadian Club in one hand, resting his chin in the other. The silk black and white ascot at his throat seemed to parody his mood. The Coleman lantern was out of fluid and we sat in the light of a candle stuck in a whiskey bottle. He was the picture of abject dejection. A handsome man, his face was marred only by a scar on his lower lip where flying glass from his Corsair's windshield had hit him, his eyes beginning to get just a little glassy from fatigue and alcohol.

Alec had been married eight years, had two children. He had everything but a future. By the time he could get out of the Marine Corps he'd be thirty years old. The only jobs he'd had were temporary ones between wars. He was one of many—the lost generation—forced to fight two wars to preserve the unity of a country, the first an applauded war to save the U. S., and now Korea, the Forgotten War.

Nine

And then there was Major Bob Marne. We spent a lot of time together in those early weeks back on the line when there weren't many battalion operations going on. That would soon change but for now it was quiet.

Bob was the S-3, the operations and training officer, so he worked closely with the C. O. and the Exec in planning sorties against the enemy.

I liked him from the start. He had an easy way about him, quiet and unobtrusive, the opposite picture one usually has of a hero-type combat Marine. He was only 5' 10", almost six inches shorter than I am, solidly built like an NFL quarterback. He wore his black hair very short in a brush cut.

In several ways Marne was not a typical Marine officer. He was 35, older than most at his rank, a mustang, a former enlisted man who'd worked his way up through the non-commissioned ranks to staff sergeant in the

South Pacific. He'd been with the Third Marine Division then and made the landing on Guam on July 15th, 1944, wading chest-deep in the warm salt water sweeping in to the long, almost straight beach named Nimitz Beach after the War to honor Admiral Chester Nimitz, but then unnamed—stretching south from Orote Point.

He'd distinguished himself there, quite obviously, because he'd been awarded a Silver Star, a Purple Heart, and then a battlefield commission as a Second Lieutenant. He would never have said it, perhaps wouldn't even have thought it, but he likely would have agreed with Al Chamberlin who wrote, "Promotions and responsibilities come fast in combat to those with the brains and guts to bear them."

At first he wouldn't tell me what he'd done except to say that it was only what anybody would've done. I pretended to accept that, knowing it wasn't true, knowing he knew that I knew it wasn't true.

He was one of those men who didn't have to brag about his accomplishments. I'd already noted in my short life that it's the guys who do the most talking about their conquests—war, sports, women, whatever—who in reality have the least to talk about.

Clearly this was not an original observation on my part. As one example among many, Will Comfort in his masterpiece, *Apache,* the story of Mangus Colorado (Red Sleeves), says, "...the one who talks most and is most eager to be understood is ever the disciple, the master being him (sic) who has nothing to explain. All can see this, save the disciple himself, or one meshed in his own deeds."

Getting his commission had helped Marne with the decision to make the Corps his career. He'd worked up to captain in the six years between wars and had just been promoted to major before I joined 3/5.

We sat in his tent or mine, reflecting on many subjects. He had a philosopher's interest in the subjects considered "cultural" (in a derogatory sense) by most Marines: ethics, mores, and religion. We had some dandy discussions. Bob Runninger, "Chappie," was often there, but one night when he wasn't there Marne and I got off on the relative merits of Oriental and Western theosophy. I took the side of Western religion (primarily Christianity), just for the purpose of debate, I claimed, but mostly because I didn't know anything about Oriental religions.

Marne asked me, "Why don't you believe in reincarnation?"

A very pertinent topic for Marines in combat.

I laughed. "Because it's so patently ridiculous."

He said, "Did you know that there're many millions more who believe in reincarnation than don't?"

I was in a cul-de-sac. How do you argue with that? I tried. "Well, Bob, the majority isn't always right, you know." Enter Henrik Ibsen's Dr. Stockmann spouting off in *Enemy of the People*. But I didn't have Ibsen's genius, so Bob just grinned superciliously and won the point.

I didn't let it go that easily, however. "So," I said, "what're you going to come back as?"

He thought it over for a few moments. "Hell, I don't know. Maybe a bird. Yeah, an eagle. A bald eagle. Did y'ever see one catch an updraft and climb right up into the sky without moving a muscle? White head and tailfeathers catching the sun?"

I nodded. I could see it. Yeah, if Marne came back as a bird he would be an eagle.

But it was his own personal philosophy that intrigued me. He seemed so gentle and kind that I found it hard to accept that he was a battle-hardened Marine who'd had to kill many men.

One day in mid-December when we were enjoying a boring, peaceful lull, I asked him how he reconciled his kind of life with his beliefs.

"Jack," he answered, "did y'ever hear of Sergeant York?"

"Sure, everybody has."

"Once he was asked the same question you just asked me. He said, 'I knew those men up there was tryin' to kill my buddies. I figgered if I could get rid of them, my buddies'd be safe, and there'd be less killin'. So I kilt 'em.'"

In his novel, *The Last of Days*, Moris Farhi deals with the essence of Marne's and York's philosophy. He says that a soldier attains innocence, purity, and sanctity by fighting and killing the killers. I wonder if Marne felt innocent, pure, and sanctified when he tried to dodge that Chinese bayonet on the north slope of Hill 1052 in March of 1952.

One night, a few days before Christmas, when the lines were eerily quiet, Bob and I played a round of bridge against Chappie and Jim Jepson, one of my H & S corpsmen, an HM 2. Marne's cards were incredible and his skill adequate so he made one bid after another.

We were all drinking Scotch—even Chappie—from a bottle Alec Stanfield had smuggled over from Japan on his last R & R. Marne was normally a very light drinker so he began to show the effects in his eyes. It didn't affect his luck or his play.

When he made bids of Six No-trump and Seven Spades only two hands apart, Chappie said, "I give up," and slumped back on the cot.

Jepson got up and started to leave. He didn't mind fraternizing with us officers when it came to bridge or volleyball or in Sick Bay. But to sit around just talking and drinking with commissioned officers bothered him.

"Stick around, JJ," I said. "No need to run off."

He stopped and looked down at Marne with a half smile. "I will if the Major will tell us what he was doing when he got his Silver Star and Purple Heart."

I half-expected Bob to clam up and thereby send Jepson out of the tent in a bit of disarray. But flowing in his veins was enough adrenaline from his two slams and enough alcohol from the Scotch to relax his inhibitions and unlock his memories.

"Sure, JJ." He settled back against his rolled-up sleeping bag, ran his hand over his brush, looked straight off into space, then glanced at me with a sudden mischievous smile. "There I was, covered with slime and leeches, crawling through the steaming jungles of Guam in my green skivvy shorts."

We all burst out laughing and Jepson sat down with a thump on the end of Marne's cot.

Marne sat forward a little, his smile slowly draining off his face. "Sounds funny now, sitting here in the middle of a Korean winter. But in fact, that's exactly how it was."

Then he told us what it was like in the Pacific and what he'd done to earn a Silver Star and a Purple Heart. He told it without bravado and in such a matter of fact tone that I had the feeling that he'd rehearsed it in his mind for years, not ever having told the entire story to anyone.

"I thought that our corpsman was dead. I'd seen him go down like a sack of grain tossed into the back of a pickup truck. That was two hours earlier, just before it got dark.

"Our line was ragged. Of my thirteen-man squad there were only seven left. Not even two complete fire-teams. The second lieutenant in command of the platoon came crawling along the line, trying to re-organize what was left of his three squads.

"'Sergeant,' he said to me, 'we're going to have to pull back a little before morning. We're too thin.'

"'Yes, sir.'

"'Chuck's still out there?'

"'Yes, sir.'

"'You heard him?'

"'No sir, but he's still there.'

"The lieutenant rolled on his side against the bole of a coconut palm. He scratched a mosquito bite on his chin and I could hear his fingernails grating on his three-day-old beard. In the dim light of the stars his face was completely invisible.

"'We'll go get him,' the lieutenant said, 'before we move back.'

"'Yes, sir.'

"There was never any question about leaving him behind. I'd seen men killed recovering a dead body. But that's one reason for the high esprit de corps in the Marines. You know that someone will always come after you, whether you're dead or alive.

"The silence in our sector was complete, the rifles and BAR's stilled. The soft slurp of entrenching tools digging foxholes had ceased. In the near distance, over behind Baker Company, the 120s thumped occasionally just to keep the Japs in their own holes.

"I took off my helmet and ran my hand over my crewcut to sweep the sweat off my head. Rivulets ran down my grimy neck. Mosquitoes whined and bit. I knew I'd have to pull leeches off Chuck's arms and neck when we brought him back. Or maybe I wouldn't. Leeches liked live blood.

"'Who d'ya want, Bob?' the lieutenant asked.

"Unhesitatingly I answered, 'Amery, Jock, and Big Grunt.'

"The lieutenant's helmet strap slapped against the tree as he nodded. 'Check your gear,' he said and slithered off.

"I checked my gear and reached for the K-bar at my belt. I'd never used it. I hoped I never would. Shooting a man—even a Jap—was one thing. Fighting him with a knife was another.

"We moved out at midnight. I took the point. My canteen slapped at my side and I wished I could've left it somewhere, but I might never have found it again. And in that jungle, good water was harder to come by than food. I felt my feet sloshing in my boots—they hadn't been dry for a week, eight days to be exact. I'd stopped wondering how long it took to get jungle rot. It didn't seem to be very important any more.

"I moved slowly, a step at a time, feeling the jungle floor for roots and vines, pushing slowly through the knee-high undergrowth, brushing lianas and succulents aside quietly with elbows and shoulders and my M-l held at port arms, my eyes staring into the darkness. I could feel Big Grunt's knuckles in my back gripping my web belt. ('You're the God-damndest biggest grunt I ever seen,' the DI had said the first day we'd mustered in boot camp, and the name had stuck.)

"I knew exactly where Chuck had gone down. A dozen times before it got dark, I'd plotted the course I'd have to take, knowing I'd have to go out there if Chuck didn't come back on his own. There was a narrow trail for the first forty yards, well worn, probably a supply route for the Japs before we'd moved in. Then there was a palm tree sheared off shoulder high. I felt it now and knew it was the right one.

"Around the stump. Bear left, off the trail, about ten

degrees. Feel for a rotting tree trunk lying half buried in the dank muck. Line up directly perpendicular to it and move straight ahead about twenty yards to a thick growth of bamboo. Circle the bamboo—too dense to go through—about five paces.

"Strike out boldly, though quietly, into standing water up to my knees.

"Chuck was just on the other side of the water, about thirty more yards, at the base of a giant breadfruit tree. The water felt cool on my legs. The putrid stench of the black swamp rose around me. Clouds of mosquitoes whined and bit. I stumbled slightly and felt Big Grunt's hand tightening on my web belt to steady me.

"The ground rose slowly until I was out of the water.

"I put my hand out in front of me to feel for the breadfruit tree, felt nothing, and moved slowly along the edge of the standing water a dozen yards. Felt nothing. Felt panic. It's got to be here. Took one more soggy step and felt the rough bark.

"I edged my boot forward and moved it in an arc. Touched something soft. Something human. Put my hand down into a sticky mess of blood and clothes and flesh.

"I straightened up, put my left hand back, grasped Grunt's wrist, and pulled him around to my side. I could hear the soft slurps as Amery and Jock moved alongside Grunt.

"'Got him,' I whispered.

"By pre-arranged plan, Amery and I moved off a step to either side, M-1s at port arms, index fingers on safeties. Grunt and Jock moved between us, rifles slung on their backs, lifted Chuck, started back.

"The machine gun spit fire and lead from thirty yards away. Ambush. Mud and leaves and water splattered over us and Grunt stumbled and fell, then struggled to his feet, unhurt. He and Jock disappeared with Chuck. I never saw any of them again.

"Amery was dead, but I didn't know it then. I lay semi-conscious, two bullets in my belly and one in my flank. The Japs bayoneted both of us to make sure we were dead. So to my perforated bowel was added a collapsed lung.

"The platoon found me in the morning, when instead of retreating, they were reinforced and able to advance. I didn't remember it at all when Big Grunt carried me back to H & S Company. Later I wanted to thank him but Big Grunt was one of the Marines who died on Guam, that beautiful green gem in the Marianas Archipelago."

We all sat quietly for a while, ruminating on the story. Finally Jepson sort of half smiled and said, "So you did all that just for a corpsman?"

Marne laughed softly. "Dumb stunt for an otherwise rational human being."

"I thought you were a Marine," I said. That brought a few chuckles.

Jepson got up to go. "Thanks, Major. Hope you're around if I ever catch it."

Ten

Christmas Day was quiet. There were no firefights along the line. It seemed as if even the Chinese were reluctant to mar the day. Chappie held a short service down in the motor pool clearing where the six-bys and the crackerbox were parked in a ragged line.

Somewhere Chappie had gotten a four-octave bellow-type organ powered with foot pedals. Jim Jepson played it with a touch that seemed almost professional. He sat on a wooden artillery shell box, head bared, his eyes staring over the heads of the hundred men and officers of the H & S Company who'd gathered in a semicircle around Chappie and the organ. JJ's .45 automatic slapped lightly against his thigh as he pedaled the bellows. He played half a dozen carols to which everyone knew the words. His voice was as pleasing as his playing.

That evening Marne and I invited JJ over to Marne's pyramidal tent to sing for us. He stood in the middle of the tent while about twenty of us medics sat on the pounded earth floor. In his cold weather combat uniform and with his bunny hat held in his raw, red hands, he sang, "O Holy Night," "The Holy City," "The Lord's Prayer," and several others.

Then he sat down on Marne's cot as we wiped our eyes.

"Got anything else in your repertoire?" I asked.

With a winsome smile he broke into the "Toreador Song" in Spanish or Italian or whatever it was originally written in. Then he sang "Old Man River," and finally, "Because."

Let me tell you, that was a moving experience, sitting there in the half-light of a kerosene lantern half a mile from the front lines. But all was as quiet as the Western Front and on the Don.

New Year's Day of 1952 came and went almost unnoticed.

Action along the lines seemed to be picking up little by little. King George VI of England died on February 6th and the flags all stood at half mast for ten days. Lincoln's birthday passed completely unnoticed. Then Washington's birthday. Fred Overman's time on the line was drawing to a close. He was due for rotation back to the rear, possibly even when the 18th Replacement Draft arrived around the 1st of March. I spelled him up in forward aid for a week or two at a time.

But then came the day when Bob Marne was asked to pull a Sergeant York. Only on a bigger scale.

Marne's problem, and therefore by definition ours, was a classic one in warfare: control of the High Ground. In the heat of battle it is absolutely essential to get up on that next hill, that next ridge. In the aftermath you must keep that position. Castles, forts, strongholds of all kinds have been built on the High Ground from the time of the Israelites under Joshua up to the time of this war.

Opposite all the United Nations lines on the ridgelines of Korea was another ridgeline. And opposite our Third Battalion of the Fifth Marines was the tallest mountain in our sector, Hill 1052. Every man in the battalion knew about it. It was a factor we dealt with daily. It was from 1052 that the three shots had come that almost got me.

We called it Luke the Gook's Castle. From up there the Chinese could see everything that went on along a big chunk of our lines, the entire sector of the UN lines held by 3/5 and at least one company of 2/1. Their snipers could zero in and their forward observers could direct mortar and artillery fire.

"My assignment," Bob told me, "is to figure out a way to take that pile of rock." He looked askance at me, a twinkle in his dark brown eyes. "Want to go take a closer look?"

We were sitting on empty shell boxes in Sick Bay. It was the 26th of February. I'd just finished examining a young Marine who'd been hit by a Bouncing Betty the night before while on patrol deep into No Man's Land out in front of our MLR. He had dozens of small fragments of steel in his back, but none had penetrated his chest or belly.

Before answering Marne I said to Chief Hoffman, "Evac to Easy in the jeep ambulance. No need for a 'copter."

I filled out the EMT and said to the Marine, "You'll probably be back up here in a couple of weeks." He was pleased, I could tell by his expression. Then I turned to Marne and answered his question. "I'd like that."

We left the next morning in the CO's jeep and went up

the tank road that serpentined its way to the right flank of George Company, still in defilade, almost to the top of the ridge. We left the jeep about fifty yards from the skyline and picked our way up a narrow ravine to the top. Dropping to hands and knees we scrambled over the top of the ridge and rolled into the trench. With Marne leading the way, we crawled another hundred yards along the trench to a bunker situated just at the point—or nose—in a bend of the ridge.

Marne ordered me to stay put while he eased himself onto his belly and slid down into the six-foot-deep foxhole in front of the trench. After a few moments he motioned to me and whispered, "Okay, come on down."

I rolled into the foxhole and stood on the fire step and raised my eyes to the level of the top of the trench. My heart beat a little faster and sweat broke out on my back despite the frosty air. I didn't really like the idea of having my helmet in the crosshairs of some Chinese sniperscope. I already knew what that was like.

The Rock, Hill 1052, the mountain called "Luke the Gook's Castle," seemed to stand naked against the sky. It was an impressive sight, the barrenness of The Rock accentuated by the green of trees and brush around its base. Worn smooth by the winds of centuries sweeping down from the tundra and the mountains of Manchuria, it stood proud and defiant, unconcerned by the wars of us puny men, seemingly oblivious to the whine of bullets and the scream of shells, the burning and blackening of napalm that had scarred its surface. In normal times, foxes and raccoons crouched in its caves and crevices, and under its hanging ledges perched crows and magpies, sparrows and finches.

There was a small Buddhist monastery on the very summit, partly obscured by leafless and blasted trees. I could see the reddish-brown tiles of the roof and the pagoda-style architecture. Marne told me that we were making very effort to avoid hitting it with our bombardments. Then he added, "They tell me there's a path up to it from the north side."

Interesting, I thought, and wished I could just climb up that path and wander around in the monastery. At that time I had no premonition that I would do just that, although not as a camera-toting tourist.

Because the lines here bent south for about 3000 meters, almost two miles, The Rock was almost due west of our position. Its summit at 1052 meters (3450 feet) was almost 200 meters higher than the one we stood on.

This very height was the clue to the problem.

A valley stretched out between the two ridgelines, a small stream winding through it. On all sides as far as we could see were heavily-forested mountains, set so close together that they formed almost continuous ridgelines. Indeed, the hill on which Marne and I stood was actually only the highest point on a ridgeline that stretched in a crooked line to the north and south.

The Castle had to be taken, yet it seemed well-nigh impossible. In a rapidly advancing war it might even have been by-passed by capturing the surrounding terrain, leaving it to be either insularized or abandoned. For very good reasons this could not be done now.

Marne swept his glasses over the surface of The Rock and pointed out to me the tiny openings, no more than pockmarks from this distance, which were the mouths of tunnels leading back into a virtual beehive blasted out of the solid rock.

"Bill Wright tells me," Marne said, "there's an entire company of men—about two hundred—living in that Rock."

Captain Wright was our S-2, the guy in charge of our battalion intelligence. I told him once that the term "military intelligence" was an oxymoron. His face was blank until I told him what an oxymoron was, then he laughed politely but with an aggrieved look. He didn't like anyone to make fun of his specialty.

"Reminds me of Peleliu," Marne said. He sat down on the frozen mud fire-step and I crouched beside him. We were jammed together like sardines in that narrow hole. "That was a bad battle, as William Manchester said, fought at a bad place and a bad time."

He grunted, a mirthless laugh. "If I'da stayed a sergeant I wouldn't even have been there. They'd've sent me home to recuperate. But when they commissioned me on Guam two months earlier—I was still in the hospital—they transferred me from the Third to the First Division. They needed second looies real bad. So I got to make two landings two months apart."

"Lucky you!"

"Yeah. At least I didn't get shot up on Peleliu. We made the landing without too much trouble. Then we tried to move north through the Umurbrogol Mountains. The Japs had shipped in professional miners to connect up the natural limestone caves with tunnels. There were as many as a thousand infantry in there at a time. They'd made entrances that looked out randomly around the compass so they could set up a crossfire almost everywhere. We had over 1200 KIAs and over 5000 WIAs."

He stood up and adjusted his binoculars. "We called that ridgeline Bloody Nose Ridge."

A blare of sound suddenly filled the air.

Instinctively Marne ducked down. Then he laughed. "There they go again."

It was eerie, all right. Coming from the crest of 1052

was a high-pitched voice screaming, "You American Marines. You have been sent here by those fat, rich business men who make many dollars selling guns to the United States Army. And where do they spend their nights? In bed with your wives and sweethearts."

This sort of talk went on for at least five minutes and was followed by a tirade against the American imperialists who had started the war against the peace-loving people of North Korea and were even now trying to sabotage the peace talks at Panmunjom where right-thinking Communists were trying to end the killing. Finally, they stopped talking and began playing some of the most dirge-like music you've ever heard.

Eventually they quit. Marne shook his head and stood up. He swung his glasses off to the east, his practiced eye assessing the terrain from a military standpoint. As he made his observations he thought out loud. An assault from the northeast would force the attacking unit to climb a small ridgeline, drop into another shallow valley, then climb the base of The Rock. The element of surprise would be gone as soon as they crested the first ridge. This would be nearly as suicidal as a direct frontal assault.

He surveyed the approaches from the southwest. They were almost as improbable as from the northeast because the stream at the bottom of the valley made a wide U-shaped bend at that point and was too wide and deep there to wade. Even a night crossing in rafts or boats would be impractical, unthinkable actually, because the opposite bank was known to be patrolled at night by the Chinese. Any sizable force would be detected long before an attack could be launched.

Logically there was only one approach that could be made. That was a straight frontal assault, with a horrible loss of men. Marne could not bring himself to accept this. He ducked down and looked at me with a twisted, almost agonized expression on his face.

He sat on the fire step again, deep in the foxhole, musing, again more to himself than to me, "Where is that Rock vulnerable? What did I learn on Peleliu that I can use here? There must be some element of surprise. How? A decoy raid somewhere else to divert the Gooks' attention? A pincers movement around the mountain, maybe then followed by a frontal assault? Parachute troops onto the backside?"

He'd pinpointed the problem but had come up short on the solution.

Eleven

The lines stayed quiet in our sector but off on our right flank we could hear the First Marine Regiment taking a terrific beating. Scuttlebutt had it that it was either a prelim to a major Chinese offensive aimed at the First or a feint at that sector as a prelim to a major offensive against our Fifth Regiment.

On the 29th of February I was on my way down to Sick Bay for H & S Company sick call when Chief Hoffman came puffing up the road from Bob Marne's pyramidal tent office. He waved a paper.

"You got TAD to Charley Med for a coupla weeks, Doctor!"

"The hell you say."

"Take a look."

He was right. He handed me a poorly mimeoed copy of orders. There it was in purple and white: Lt. (s.g.) John Lord, etc., etc., Temporary Additional Duty, etc., etc.,

Charley Medical Company etc., etc.

So I packed up, said good-bye to the corpsmen and cheerio to Fred Overman, who'd come back to rear aid when he got word of my transfer. Butch's eyes brimmed with tears as he stood ramrod straight two feet in front of me. Then he bowed slightly from the waist, his hands at his sides. As he straightened up, a faint and trembly smile tugged at the corners of his mouth. "You come back taksan quick, Number One Battarun Surgeon. We sing goo-night Ilene many more time."

I shook his hand. "You betcha."

I stopped by Marne's tent but he was as surprised by my orders as I was. He grinned and said, "Don't stay long enough to miss all the fun up here."

He meant Hill 1052, I was sure. Even as I thought that it might be a good idea to miss out on the upcoming battle for Luke's Castle, I said, "Wouldn't miss it for the world!"

My orders were to report directly to Commander Walter Ormsdorf at Able Med on my way to Charley. I was getting curiouser and curiouser by the moment.

Rohn took me back in the jeep ambulance. As usual I sat in back on the jump seat opposite the stretcher rack. I hadn't really been up on line all that long—less than four months—and I really hadn't felt a sense of pressure or strain or anxiety. But as soon as we cleared security at the H & S perimeter and started down that road to the rear area encampments along the Nam-gang, I realized I was beginning to relax from a state I didn't know I was in.

There are no words to describe the feeling of relief that intensified as I moved farther and farther back from the front lines.

First we passed that point that I knew was out of range of rifle and other small arms fire, the personal stuff: where a Chinese soldier sits in a bunker or up in a tree and takes careful aim at you with a sniper-scope. Or maybe a gunner crouching behind a machine gun with a thirty degree traverse just raises the muzzle a bit to spray you and your buddies on the hillside across from him.

Then next, as we pulled back farther, we got out of range of the mortars: that's when a mounting sense of light-heartedness really set in.

The mortars are sort of personal but not like rifle bullets. The guys working the tubes usually don't see you at all. They're just robots dropping rounds into the open mortar barrel. But there's a sharp-eyed observer up on his OPLR spotting for them and reporting your position by radio. He sees your jeep or your truck, or maybe he sees some activity along the trench line, or maybe he penetrates the camouflage of a Sherman tank or a recoilless rifle. And he calls in the coordinates to the second lieutenant in Weapons Company—or whatever the Chinese equivalent is—and the lieutenant barks out the orders and pretty soon the stuff starts fluttering in on you.

Then as Rohn and I continued rear-ward through the snow and mud, we moved back out of range of even the longest artillery.

That's the really impersonal stuff.

Some anonymous joker once said that artillery lends dignity to what otherwise would be a vulgar brawl.

Well, maybe.

Anyway, those gooks two or three miles back of their lines never even know what they're shooting at, much less who. Their officers often don't know. Oh, there'll be FO's somewhere up on line, but they don't usually direct artillery fire at an individual bunker or truck, much less one person. They just saturate an entire hill or village or segment of trench line.

Finally, as we came in sight of Able Med, I realized

with a bit of a shock that now we were out of range of everything but airplanes and the Chinese hadn't had much in the air since our fly-boys shut down MiG Alley between Pyongyang and the Yalu River.

Now a deep feeling of relief flooded my mind and my body. Now laughter came more easily and I joked with Ned about these poor rear-echelon pogues who didn't know what it was like to be in a real war.

Thoughts tumbled through my brain that I'd blocked out before because it was unlucky even to think them. My thoughts could now range freely into the near future (hot chow, real coffee, warm tents, and most of all, freedom from fear), and then into the more distant future (eventual transfer from the lines to rear-echelon poguedom, and probably R & R to Japan).

And then I really free-wheeled it and let my mind roam all the way home, to Lorrie and Ingrid and Mom and Dad and my new practice in some small city in the USA.

Able Med straggled along the banks of the Nam-gang just like all the other encampments of any size. We felt out of place in our mud-splattered jeep with weapons on our hips, helmets on our heads, mud on our boots, and ammo holders on our web belts. We were in a different world back there, one which after only four months I'd almost forgotten existed.

I made an observation which came to me as a bit of a shock: the further we got back of the front lines, the more people were "shook up" at the thought of being in a war. I never changed my mind on that.

I noted something else which shouldn't have surprised me but did. An American flag whipping in the breeze on a twenty foot pole brought a surge of emotion that started tears in my eyes. I saw Ned's eyes lingering on the flag and knew he felt it, too. Breathes there a man with soul so dead…?

Ned knew his way around and soon found the aluminum sided-and-roofed building with two nine-foot barn doors labeled "A MED." Beside it was a quonset hut with a red and yellow sign, "CO 1st Med Bn." Commander Ormsdorf was in charge of all five medical companies—field hospitals—in the Marine Division. His immediate superior was the Division Surgeon back in Division Headquarters but he ran the show.

"Go get some coffee, Ned," I said. "This shouldn't take long."

With a lop-sided grin on his face, he came to rigid attention, the heels of his scuffed and muddy combat boots thunking dully together, saluted sharply and said, "Aye, aye, sir."

I returned the salute with a smile and said, "Oh, yeah, we can't forget that back here, can we?" I couldn't remember him ever saluting me before. We'd gotten kind of relaxed about the courtesies of military life up front.

The quonset was snugly warm, too warm for me, actually, after having lived up on the line for four months.

Ormsdorf was a jolly little fat man. He had the face of Charles Laughton, the body of Nikita Kruschev, the smile of the Mona Lisa, and, I found quickly enough, the tough mind of Douglas MacArthur.

Over a cup of very bad coffee he said, "Dr. Lord, two things have happened at the same time at Charley Med. One, as you're no doubt well aware, is that the First Marines up in front of Charley are under a bombardment that our G-2 thinks will be followed by an all-out offensive. Charley's already getting a steady flow of casualties. If the Gooks come down in force, Charley'll be busier'n hell."

He settled back in his canvas camp chair, bit the end off a White Owl, spit the flakes into his hand and flicked them into an empty C-ration can on his desk. His eyes crinkled at the corners as he sucked the flame from a lighter into the end of the cigar. "Not exactly a Havana but better'n nothing." He set the Zippo on the table. On one side was the shoulder patch of the First Marine Division: a big number 1 with the seven stars of the Southern Cross on a blue background.

He blew a ragged smoke ring and continued. "Second thing. In a couple days the CO of Charley, Lieutenant Commander Roland Ramsey, leaves for home on regular rotation. His relief's on the way but he's not here yet. So we need a temporary replacement for God only knows how long, maybe as long as two weeks."

"Yeah," I said, "the 18th replacement draft ought to be here pretty soon."

"Yes, with Fred Overman's relief. But Ramsey's relief is flying over and we don't know where the hell he is."

"Can't you hold Ramsey till he gets here?"

"Doctor Lord, he's a *lieutenant commander*!" He set down his cup and eyed me with a twinkle in his eye. He *was* Charles Laughton and this was a movie set I'd wandered onto. "Besides, I really want to get Ramsey out of here. He's been here too long already."

"Yes, sir," I said, for want of anything better. In the Navy and presumably all the other services you were always on safe footing with that response, or the even better, "Sir!"

"We've sweat this for a while, wondering what to do. No one's happy with any of the doctors at Charley as a replacement—even short term—for Ramsey. All good doctors, some of them terrific surgeons, y'understand.

But not the command type. So we've been looking over our list of battalion surgeons. You had a two year internship and two years of surgery at Cook County Hospital. Right?"

"Yes, sir."

"Your fitness reports are excellent." ("Fitness" had nothing to do with physical fitness. The reports were filed by people above you in the chain of command—in my case, Fred Overman, the regimental surgeon, and possibly the Division Surgeon. People who saw you at work and could evaluate your "fitness" for your job.)

"I wouldn't know about that."

"Okay. So, no more beating around the bush, Dr. Lord. You're our choice."

This time I came right out with it. "Sir!"

In the next hour we talked about the problems I'd face. First of all, I was only 27 years old. Secondly, the billet called for a lieutenant commander but there were none available. Thirdly, in my command I'd have a dozen doctors and eighty corpsmen for the medical work, plus 120 Marines for security, supply, radio, food services, ambulances, trucks and a few other things.

As I look back I wonder I didn't panic and refuse the command, but at the time I was supremely confident that I could handle the job.

Rohn took me back north over the frozen, rutted road to Charley Medical Company, which was located in what was left of the little village of Hwanggi. His lopsided grin was a little more skewed. "We're gonna miss you up in 3/5, Doctor."

"I'll be back."

He shook my hand and took off. I watched him go. We'd been through quite a bit together. As he disappeared from sight down the frozen MSR, headed back to the front lines, I wondered if I'd ever see him again. It struck me then that one aspect of our lives is the kaleidoscopic redistribution of people. Old friends are left behind as we move or they move on. New friends are made and then they too disappear. Sometimes old friends pop up again in new situations only to disappear from sight again later. In service the kaleidoscope turns faster, especially in a theater of war. Sometimes I envy those people who live out their lives in the same town—even the same house—where they were born.

Rohn had left me off in front of the administration tent. A green-painted frame eight feet high supported a black ship's bell with "C" MED and something in Korean painted in white on it. An Hn checked me in and showed me the way to the doctors' tent.

I carried my pack and M-2 carbine, and the Hn carried my sea bag up there. I stayed there for just one day and two nights, getting to know the other doctors.

When Roland Ramsey left, Mike Lavierri would be the senior surgeon. He was only thirty-one years old but had four years training at New York Memorial. Mike had three other surgeons to rotate with him on the big cases. There were nine other doctors, all with experience in trauma on rotating internships but with no formal surgery training.

Sam Sortie was our only trained anesthesiologist but several of the others had had some experience in spinal and regional anesthesia.

In addition we had a Korean doctor attached to our hospital. Yung Il-song was from Seoul and had studied at the University of Korea in Seoul. He'd had little formal surgery experience but a great deal of practical work during the past year and a half at Charley.

I spent long hours talking with the C.O., Roland

Ramsey. Then when he sailed out of there I moved from the doctors' tent into Ramsey's command post, the only house still standing in Hwanggi. I had one big room all to myself, a wooden floor under my feet, a jeep, and the men called me "skipper." It was a heady experience.

The Marines, being a unit of the Navy have no doctors, corpsmen, nurses or medical facilities of their own. So when they go into combat they draw on Navy personnel for those functions. Assigned to the First Marine Division in Korea was a battalion of five medical companies: Able, Baker, Charley, Dog, and Easy. All five were actually forward-area hospitals under Commander Ormsdorf, who reported to the Division Surgeon in Division Headquarters.

Charley Medical Company when I joined it lay about four miles behind the right flank of the First Marine Division. Behind the left flank was Easy Med, behind the Korean Marines was Dog Med. Baker Med was on paper only. Ten miles to the rear was Able Med, the nerve center for the others, handling some surgical cases but primarily concerned with administration, emergency dental work, and non-surgical emergencies. We called Able Med the Wastebasket Company. If you didn't know what to do with a non-surgical patient, you said, "Oh, hell, send him back to Able!"

Charley Med and the other Medical Companies corresponded in many ways to a Mobile Army Surgical Hospital (MASH) behind the U. S. Army lines. There were a couple of major differences. MASHs were 10-20 miles behind the front lines. And they had female nurses.

I visited a MASH once and came away with the distinct impression that the nurses were an unnecessary and unwanted distraction. You couldn't help seeing them as women. If you were single and not averse to premarital sex, or married and not averse to extra-marital sex, you'd be in competition with a hundred other guys for a dozen nurses. If, single or married, you were opposed to casual sex, you'd still be tempted daily by the mere presence of women in such a tight little society. I thought that it was a mistake to station nurses in such an environment.

Twelve

There didn't seem to be any resentment from the doctors about my appointment over their heads. I got the feeling that none of them had really wanted the job, which may have been at least part of the reason Ormsdorf had bypassed them.

Commander Ormsdorf's timing was perfect.

On the 2nd of March, a Friday evening, my first night in my little Korean house at Charley, darkness an hour old, I heard the roaring flap of a helicopter settling onto the landing strip about thirty yards from my sliding paper door.

Only minutes later a new roar filled the sky as a second 'copter sailed overhead, banked and circled, waiting for the corpsmen to race up the little hill back of the security Marines' tents to mark the second strip with flashlights. Then it too settled in with the distinctive and all too familiar flapping sound.

I was sitting with my feet up on the desk the corpsmen had made for Ramsey out of some packing cases from an artillery shell shipment. A *Time* magazine on my lap lay open to an account of the war in Korea. Although I was right in the middle of that war I knew very little about what was really going on. I had to read John Osborne's editorial about the "waiting, fighting 8th Army" in order to comprehend the total picture.

I resisted the urge to run out and help unload the casualties. I was the *Commanding Officer*! There were many eager young Hns who would look askance at a skipper doing their work. But then, over the purring of the two parked whirlybirds I could hear a third 'copter circling the hospital. Running feet pounded the frozen paths as doctors and corpsmen headed for the triage tent. I grabbed my fatigue cap—no helmets back here—and ran after them. Trotting down the path from the doctor's tent were Yung Il-song and Mike Lavierri. I joined them and said, "Looks like no sleep tonight."

"Won't be the first time," Mike said, "but it's been a little dull around here lately."

It was an unfortunate remark and I cringed. I remembered that I'd caught myself thinking the same thing when I first arrived up with 3/5. So I bit back the sharp retort that formed in my mind. Because of his skills in surgery, Lavierri hadn't had the customary tour of duty in a front line outfit, which may have caused him to identify a little less with the wounded men.

But for me and the majority of doctors and corpsmen at Charley, each wounded Marine was a man who might have been a buddy in the trenches. And who knew about cold bunkers and dirty foxholes and fluttering mortars. And about singing bullets and flying steel and white phosphorus. About long convoys and clanking tanks and rumbling trucks. About loneliness and boredom and the infinite patience of the trenches.

We shared the knowledge that Death comes to the wary and the unwary alike. That he rides on the long steel bayonet with a cold gray hand pointing the way. That he rides the artillery shell with his shrouds streaming. That he guides the flying missile with a death's-head grin.

The frontline doctors and corpsmen know these things and do not have to voice them. They know how thin the line is that separates life from death, and how fast the mask of stillness shrouds the form. They know how quickly a startled angry heart can be calmed by the softly beating wings of silent peace.

They *know*—and look into each other's eyes with mutual respect and admiration. And to hide this emotion from themselves and from each other they laugh and tell sick jokes and cuss and go back to their jobs with wry grins on their faces.

I pulled Mike back as the others went on and said softly, "Knock off that kind of talk, Mike, it doesn't sound too good. I know what you mean, but most of the guys who just came off the lines won't."

"Sorry, skipper, I didn't mean it the way it sounded."

"I know, Mike. Forget it."

Both patients from the first 'copter were in the triage ward, a 16x32 squad tent, when we got there. Their stretchers lay on the double row of foot-high wooden rails that ran the length of the tent on either side. Within a few moments, two more were brought in from the second 'copter.

Dr. Don Simonstad, a general practitioner from California, got up off his knees where he'd been working on one of the wounded men and turned to Mike. "Belly wound, Mike. Chunk of omentum poking through. Not much loss of blood, I'd guess, 'cause his pressure and pulse are real good. One for you?"

Mike nodded. "Yeah, let's go, unless the other one needs it more."

"I don't think so. Looks good. Multiple small shrapnel wounds, but nothing important that I can see."

Two corpsmen picked up the stretcher and gently lifted it till its short bent-steel legs cleared the rails, then slid it forward, the back man stepping carefully over the rails. They carried him down the long ward and then turned left into the connecting operating tent.

I walked over to the other man.

"Hi, Mac," I said with a grin, "how're things going?"

"Great, Doctor. Got a powerful bellyache though." He was black, a real giant of a man.

I knelt down beside him and pulled his dungaree jacket up and his pants down. "Tell me if it hurts." My fingers prodded the outer edges of his abdomen without response, but when I touched the central area around the navel, he tensed his muscles involuntarily and grunted, "Right there, Doc, real sore right there."

"Looks like one of these fragments might've gone into your belly." I looked at his EMT. "Jesse Carter, eh? Where you from, Jesse?"

"Chicago, Doctor."

"Hey, I know that town real well. Interned at Cook County Hospital."

His eyes lit up. "You gotta be a good doctor then!"

"Jesse, we may have to take a look inside there later. Right now it doesn't look too bad. We'll keep a close eye on you."

I looked up, found HM3 Ross Tompter standing beside me. "Take Jesse on down to the holding tent. We may have to operate on him later."

A truck rumbled up outside the tent. A few moments later in came eleven walking wounded with bandaged arms, heads and legs. "O.K., guys," I said, "you can sit down over along the wall. Kelly, go rout out the day crew and then make sure all the doctors are on their way. Dr. Yung, you start at one end and I'll start at the other and we'll get these men triaged."

Even as I spoke, another 'copter settled onto the strip near my command post, a jeep ambulance squeaked to a halt outside the tent, and in a few moments four more stretchers were brought in and laid on the rails.

"Don," I barked, "take a look at those fellows, will you? Let me know if you need any help. I'll try to move these walkers on out as fast as I can."

While I sorted them out, I was able to piece together what had happened up on the line. All the wounded were from the First Marine Regiment, which held an S-shaped, two-mile-long front stretching east from Hill 812 to Hill 575. My battalion, 3/5, was on their left flank and a Republic of Korea Army division on their right.

No one knew why the gooks were coming down the road like they wanted those hills. Of course, if they took 575 it would lay 812 and the 3/5 sector wide open for encirclement. As it turned out, they didn't take it on this offensive, but they would later when I was there. That was when we tried to take 1052, Luke the Gook's Castle, and...but that's getting ahead of my story.

I got to work triaging the wounded. I sorted them into categories: those who could be operated upon under local anesthesia, those who needed general anesthesia, and those who could safely wait for hours or even longer while the more urgent cases were taken care of.

There was a fourth group. Another group who would wait, who would wait only for death. There weren't very many, but in every big fight there were badly wounded men who didn't die right away. If the numbers of casualties were few, and there was a surgeon free, and anesthesia was available, these men were given the benefit of heroic measures. And once in a great while one of these "hopeless" cases could be pulled through.

But when casualties flooded the hospital and every doctor and anesthetist were needed for urgent cases that had a good chance for survival, it was an accepted maxim that occasionally you literally had to put some unfortunate men aside and let them die.

Nobody talked about those boys. They were usually unconscious or at least deep in shock. They couldn't even say, "Save me." There were no relatives present to plead their cases. The doctor would complete his exam, bow his head in thought—or in prayer—and then make his decision.

I was looking at just such a case now. A corpsman.

He'd been down on his knees working on a wounded man when a Chinaman with a burp gun came up behind him and pumped four .45 slugs into his back in one burst. "Buuurrrppp" had gone the gun, and the four bullets stitched themselves across the corpsman's back, traveling upward through kidneys, stomach, diaphragm and into the lungs. The man was unconscious, his pulse uncountable, his blood pressure unmeasurable.

If he'd been the only casualty there, he would have gotten the works. As it was, I said to Tompter, "Put him in D ward. No surgery contemplated."

I moved down the line of stretchers. Tompter stayed with me while another corpsman worked just ahead of us cutting off or unwrapping the bandages from the wounds so I could inspect them.

Rarely did we do anything to the wounds during this

first exam. Another corpsman following behind the doctor rewrapped them to await definitive surgery. But we gave blood to those who needed it, started IVs with normal saline if the patient was headed for major surgery, put down naso-gastric tubes for belly wounds, gave tetanus toxoid to everyone, and did other necessary procedures to treat shock and ready the men for definitive treatment in the operating tents.

We saw every conceivable type of war wound in the triage ward at Charley Med. Shrapnel and bullets hit without foresight and at random, sometimes injuring vital structures and sometimes missing them by fractions of an inch. Here was a man with a broken arm from a rifle bullet; he was sent to the holding ward with his arm splinted to await surgery. The next two cases had multiple shrapnel wounds all over the body, but without major wounds that required general anesthesia; they were sent immediately to the minor operating tent to await debridement. The next man had the major part of his left thigh torn away by a fragment of an artillery shell. He went to the holding unit to await surgery. The next man had a buttocks wound, the frayed handle of a Chinese "potato masher" grenade still sticking out of the jagged hole; he was sent back to minor surgery for its removal.

The hours ticked by rapidly. By 0200 (2 A.M.), nearly a hundred wounded men had been admitted, and more were on the way. Most of the walking wounded were now waiting outside the admitting and triage tent, having been examined and found not to need urgent surgery.

I went into the holding ward to check the patients there. Two of the patients who had been in good shape when sent there were deteriorating and had to be given immediate priority. The corpsman had died moments after I sent him back. The others were doing well and could await their turn.

On another ward check about 0400 I stopped again to see Jesse, the black Marine who'd had the "powerful bellyache."

He was dead.

I was shocked, heartsick. I called over the corpsman in charge of the ward.

"When did you see this guy last, Frank?"

"Fifteen, twenty minutes ago, Doctor."

He looked down at Jesse, looked up at me with real pain showing in his weary eyes. "He's dead?" He stooped over and flicked an eyelid. Still unbelieving he put a hand over Jesse's mouth. "He is, isn't he?"

He put a foot up on the rail and leaned forward on his elbows. "I was just talking to him. He asked when we were gonna get to him. I said real soon now." He wiped the back of his blood-smeared hand across his forehead. He needed to talk this out and I let him go. "I asked him if he felt worse. He said no. I didn't take his blood pressure. He wasn't sweating or cold or anything. God Almighty!"

He looked up at me and the agony I read there made me look away. "What happened, Dr. Lord?"

"Look at his conjunctivae, Frank."

Frank pulled down Jesse's lower eyelid and exposed the stark white membrane. "He bled to death, didn't he, Doctor, right under my eyes? Right here in front of me. God, I'm sorry, Doctor!"

"Not your fault, Frank. Mine, if anybody's. Must have a small hole in his aorta. Only thing I can think of."

Even though I was only four years older than he was he needed the comfort of a fatherly hand on his shoulder. I did just that. "Come on now, let's get back to work."

He gripped my arm just above the elbow, smiled weakly with trembling lips and tear-blurred eyes, then moved off slowly, shaking his head. I watched as he started preparing another Marine for surgery. He worked slowly at first, then more and more rapidly, and soon was working at top speed again. But I knew he hadn't forgotten what had happened.

I never would.

I can still picture the entire scene.

The body of Jesse Carter lies on his stretcher, about halfway down the ward on the west side of the tent. On his left is the stretcher of a Marine with his left hand mangled by shrapnel. On his right is a Marine clutching a bandage over his right eye. Frank the corpsman, stares at Jesse, unbelieving.

Jesse's face hangs before my mind's eye, his eyes half open, sightless.

Dead.

By 0600 the steady flow of wounded men had begun to slow down a little, but there was a backlog of almost fifty unoperated cases. Some of the more serious cases, like belly wounds and compound fractures, were waiting too long for surgery. It had long been Medical Battalion policy not to evacuate men parallel to the lines, that is, from one front line medical company to another, and there were no trained surgeons back at Able Med. But it seemed to me that now there was adequate reason to change the policy.

I got on the EE-8 field phone to Commander Ormsdorf to convince him we needed help. I could see in my mind's eye the usually jolly, round, Charles Laughton face now blinking the sleep out of his eyes and thinking hard.

"Yeah, all right," he said, finally. I knew he was shouting at the top of his lungs but I had to strain to hear him. The little black phone line strung by the communications people didn't have relays and it was ten miles back to Able Med.

It was good news to me as Ormsdorf shouted, "Okay, Dr. Lord, we'll clean you out. But not to Dog or Easy. I'll send up some Sikorskis and ship 'em to the *Consolation*."

The *Consolation* apparently still lay off Sokchori where I'd seen her a few months earlier. She rotated with two other U. S. Navy ships, the *Repose* and the *Haven*, and with the *Jutlandia*, a converted Danish cruise ship.

"Thanks, skipper," I yelled.

Hurriedly I re-examined all the serious patients in the holding ward, working down the line of stretchers perched a foot off the floor on their wooden rails. I marked twelve men for "'copter evac," the rest for holding to be operated on at Charley.

It was obvious that Wally Ormsdorf believed in the maxim that if something is worth doing, it's worth doing now. I had just barely finished when a big Sikorski landed on the strip down by my command post and the corpsmen began loading stretchers into it. It could take six at a time.

Shortly afterwards another came in and took the rest of the men I'd tagged.

Thirteen

About 10 A.M. I decided I'd had enough of the triage ward. I'd been in there for almost sixteen hours straight with only short break for gulps of coffee. I hadn't slept. No one had. I knew from my experience at Cook County Hospital that I'd be okay until about four or five in the afternoon. Then it would hit me. Hard. At County that was fine. I was never on call two nights in a row and could usually get away from the wards by late afternoon. I would have supper, have a beer or a glass of wine, watch some dumb TV show till seven or eight, and collapse.

Now, with no one coming on duty to relieve me, I didn't know what I was going to do if I couldn't get some sleep some time during the day.

I found out.

I'd sent Yung and Simonstad back to the Minor Surgery Tent hours ago and now went back there myself. I asked them if they'd like to work Triage for a while and both agreed. Then I changed my mind and asked Yung if he'd like to stay in Minor Surgery for a while. He readily agreed to that, too.

As their C.O. I could've ordered them but there was little of that kind of baloney in the medical corps. Not at our level, anyway, and not with most reserve officers.

There was an occasional Regular Navy captain-type jerk who was so insecure or gung ho that he had to order people around, but usually those guys could also make sure that they didn't end up in Korea. And back in the States you knew you had to put up with a certain amount of military garbage.

While Simonstad finished the case he was working on, I walked into the small tent which contained the scrub basin and brushes. I soaped my hands and arms, then scrubbed off the dirt and blood and vomitus that had accumulated in my knuckles and under my fingernails. I'd washed frequently during the past sixteen hours but hadn't had a chance to really scrub.

I stood with my eyes closed, half asleep, hands mechanically working with brush and soap, mind jumping from thought to thought.

Wonder when this will let up. Getting pretty tired. No end in sight.

Poor Jesse. That was my fault. He said I must be a good doctor if I trained at Cook County. Sure.

Drop of sweat running down my eyebrow. I rubbed my forehead across the sleeve of my white T-shirt.

Hope my mail finds me down here. Should hear from Ingrid soon, see how she likes her new job. She and Lorrie had moved back to St. Paul where her parents lived. They were glad to have her, and her Mom was more than pleased to take care of Lorrie so Ingrid could work. Ingrid was making over $200 a month, most of which she could save. The Navy was sending most of my pay (about $400) to Ingrid so we figured we'd build up quite a nest egg during my year in Korea.

Huh! Lorrie'll be almost three by the time I get home. Won't know me.

Should've had Yung go into triage. He works hard in minor surgery but can't turn out the cases as fast as Simonstad.

That Yung! They tell me he's the hardest working guy they ever saw. Almost always the first man down when the 'copters come in. Always the last one to leave. Funny how little anyone knows about Yung Il-song. The inscrutable Oriental. Good man. Has a wife somewhere, Seoul I think, but never asks for special leave. Apparently doesn't go see any of these little sheba-sheba girls, either, that keep working their way up to the lines.

Simonstad woke me from my reverie. "O.K., skipper, take over. They'll have the next guy up for you in a second. What's the matter, you sick or something?"

I opened my eyes and grinned. "No, just resting. Just like the old internship, *nicht wahr*?"

"*Jawohl*. But at least back there we could usually count on sleeping the next night."

"Yeah." We both knew that even if the wounded stopped coming right then we had another long night ahead of us.

I wiped my hands on the green towel hanging from the wooden rack next to the basin and walked back into the Minor Tent. Two corpsmen were lifting a Marine up onto the sawhorses. He lay on his belly with a large dressing over his left buttocks. I put on my gloves and started drawing up procaine from a bottle held by the corpsman. The corpsman pulled off the dressing. I glanced at the wound and was surprised to see a large piece of wood sticking out of it.

"My God, man, you still here?" I exclaimed, recognizing the potato-masher handle. "Thought you'd've been done hours ago."

"Guess they thought I could wait, Doctor."

The corpsman scrubbed around the wound with liquid green soap. I placed my sterile towels and anesthetized the skin and muscles as well as I could. Several times I hit the wood with the needle as I probed deeper and deeper. That's great for sterile technique, I thought. Finally I felt I'd numbed it as much as I could.

I made an elliptical skin incision around the protruding wood and controlled the bleeding. Then I grasped the grenade handle with a heavy Kocher hemostat and pulled. I pulled harder. It started to move slowly, then faster and faster like a champagne cork, and finally slurped out with a gush of blood. The fragment was nearly four inches long, one inch in diameter, and fragmented on the distal end. The flow of blood was profuse and I placed a gauze sponge deep into the wound and held it there firmly with my fingers.

The grenade handle had severed the gluteal artery but with a figure-of-eight stitch I controlled it. Then I debrided the wound of splinters and other debris and packed it open with Vaseline gauze and fluffed gauze.

"All done, Mac," I said.

"Got it sewed up already?"

"Oh, no. We never do that here. We leave it wide open to drain for five to ten days. Then any dirt or other junk we might've missed will work its way out. Prevents infection. Somebody back at Able or maybe the hospital ship will close this up when it's ready. Sorry if I hurt you. That thing was really deep. You want it as a souvenir?"

"Hell, no." He grinned. Then he grinned wider. "That hole'll be kind of hard to explain to the boys in the locker room, won't it, Doc?"

"You can always tell 'em an old witch stuck her broom up your ass."

With a mischievous smile, incongruous under the circumstances, he said, "Wish there was a coupla young witches around here about now."

I chuckled and went into the scrub tent to wash up. I was dripping with perspiration and when I stripped off my rubber gloves water splattered from them. I poured myself a drink from the five gallon water can on the ground and gulped it thirstily. I remembered then that I hadn't eaten yet and realized I was voraciously hungry. None of the others had eaten either. I walked back into the Minor OR.

"Dr. Yung, why don't you and Harry Golden go get some chow. When you get back, Don and I'll go over."

I watched Yung for a moment, the small brown hands in the 6 1/2 gloves working carefully in the debridement of a nasty shrapnel wound of the face. The Marine he was working on lay with his eyes closed, but opened them as I came up to the stretcher. He asked, "He doin' a good job, Doc?"

"The best, Mac, the best," I said. The Marine closed his eyes again. Yung shot me a grateful glance. His hands had a very faint tremor now as they laid the Vaseline gauze into the wound. I'd touched a sensitiveness in Yung I hadn't been aware of. We walked off together and I queried, "Things going O. K., Dr. Yung?"

"Very fine, Captain. Taksan number one." He paused for a split second. Then without looking at me he said, "You did a very good thing to me now."

"Well, I meant it." And I was glad I'd sent Simonstad into triage instead of Yung.

I turned to my next case. The corpsman was scrubbing a Marine's leg which had a dozen or more jagged puncture wounds.

"These don't look too bad, Mac. Probably keep you out of action a month is all." I talked almost continuously with the Marine as I injected each wound with an ellipse of procaine.

Most of the boys liked to talk. There was a release in talking. Whether they'd been on line a few days or a year, they'd been under constant discipline. Furthermore, the mere fact that they were wounded indicated that they'd just recently been under tension in a life and death situation over which they had practically no control.

They'd sat in their bunkers waiting for the rounds to fall, or they'd crouched in their foxholes hoping they were concealed from sniper fire, or they were climbing a hill or running a valley, all the time listening for the flutter of a mortar round coming in.

And then they felt the blast as it blew them to the ground. They took stock of themselves and tried to determine the extent of their injuries. If they could, they crawled or walked back to the forward aid station. If they couldn't, they called for a corpsman and were carried out on a stretcher.

I cut ellipses of skin from around the shrapnel wounds, then cut similar ellipses of fat and muscle from around the tracts which led to the metal fragments embedded deeper in the leg. Most of the shrapnel I removed easily, along with bits of cloth, dirt, leaves and other debris blown in by the blast or carried into the wound with the metal.

There were smaller fragments of metal that I couldn't remove easily and I left them in place. I knew that a few of these would have to be removed at a later date, but most would cause no trouble and it was never worth the time and effort to try to get them all. Debride the wound, stop the bleeding, pack it open, cover it up, and ship the patient out. Next man.

Morning eased into afternoon…night came and we'd been up for 36 hours without sleep…night passed…morning came and we'd been up for 48 hours without sleep. The wounded kept coming. In trucks and jeep ambulances and helicopters. There was no sign of a letup. Periodically I called Commander Ormsdorf and soon a flight of Sikorskis would come in and take off with the backlog of serious unoperated cases and stable post-op belly and chest cases.

Ormsdorf sent up a crew of Marines from Able Med to put up five 16x32 squad tents to use as post-op recovery wards. I could hear them laughing and talking and had the urge to run out there and ask them what was so damn funny and didn't they know there was a war on and would they kindly knock off the brouhaha. Fortunately I recognized that I was getting irrational in my fatigue and that those gyrenes had every right to be happy. I closed my eyes and clenched my jaws and kept on cutting. A couple of hours later one of those Marines came to the door of the Minor O.R. tent and said, "Sir, we got the tents up and the pot-bellies goin' and is there anything else we kin do while we're up here?"

When we got the tents fairly well heated with pot-belly stoves, we emptied out our old wards to take the newly operated cases. And Ormsdorf, God bless him, sent two six-by trucks up from Able and took twenty-five walking wounded back to have their debridements done there. I wished I could've seen the looks of horror on the faces of the internists and pediatricians when they were called out of their snug bunks to do surgery!

Fourteen

We were all beginning to show heavy, dark circles under our bloodshot eyes. Small drops of tears trickled from the inner corners. The supply of surgical caps ran out so we tied masks onto our foreheads to keep loose hairs and sweat from dripping into the open wounds. Some of the corpsmen wore their green fatigue hats backwards like a baseball catcher's.

A visitor would have thought it a ludicrous sight to see doctors and corpsmen running around the tents in big combat boots, white skivvy shirts, green fatigue pants, and two masks tied to the front of their heads.

Nobody was laughing.

Those laughing the least were the doctors and corpsmen in the main operating tent. Theirs was the toughest job of all. It was here that life or death operations were performed. It was here that legs were saved or sawed off, bellies were opened in order to stem the flow of blood and liquid feces. Shattered kidneys were removed. Livers were sutured. And through it all the principles of good surgery had to be observed.

Even when the sweat pours down your face and stings your eyes.

Even when your hands tremble from fatigue.

Even when your brain is numb from sleeplessness.

About 10 A.M. on the second day, thirty-six hours since the first copters arrived and fifty-two hours since anyone had slept, I took my turn as first assistant in the main operating tent. I worked with Mike Lavierri. We made a good team.

Mike was a good surgeon and I'd done enough surgery to be a good assistant. Doctors who don't do surgery make very poor assistants. They don't know what the surgeon is going to do next, whereas a good assistant anticipates the surgeon's next move. Not needing the surgeon's directions, he speeds up the surgery by holding the right tissues in the right way, uses the right retractors in the right place.

A good assistant keeps the surgeon out of trouble when his intense concentration may cause him to overlook the proximity of another organ, or to forget a minor but potentially important step.

A good assistant anticipates the use of special sutures or instruments and asks the nurse or corpsman to get them onto the back table before the surgeon asks for them.

The assistant must be patient with the slow or meticulous surgeon, agile with the speedy operator, a buffer for the scrub techs or nurses with a prima donna, a foil for the wit of the self-styled clown. The assistant must be all things to all surgeons and, most importantly, must keep his hands out of the way yet always have them in the right place!

Dr. Sam Sortie was seated in the center of the O.R. tent between the head ends of two operating tables. With his left hand he was giving a general anesthetic to a patient on one table. With his right hand he arranged the medicines and instruments for the induction of the next patient on the other table. Sam was preoccupied, concentrating intensely, his mind working on two entirely separate problems at the same time.

Two corpsmen brought in the next patient and lifted him gently off the stretcher onto the other operating table. His battle fatigues had been replaced by dark blue pajama-like pants. His torso was pale white, contrasting with the deep tan of his face and hands—a farmer's tan, my Dad would've called it. He was about 19, strong of face and body.

He had two small defects: a hole in his abdomen just below the ribs on the right where a bullet had gone in, a slightly larger hole in his left flank where the bullet had come out. His eyes were slightly glazed from the pain, his cheek muscles bulging from jaws set hard. His respirations were quick and shallow as the rapidly-developing peritonitis splinted his belly and diaphragmatic muscles. I hated to think what it looked like between those bullet holes. He groaned a little as he was eased onto the operating table.

"Easy, buddy," a corpsman cautioned, "we just about got 'er."

"The IV's run sub-q, Joe," Dr. Sortie remarked. "Better start another one."

The corpsman straightened out the patient's right arm and tied a rubber tubing tightly around the upper forearm to fill out the veins below it.

"He had any atropine yet, Joe?" asked Dr. Sortie.

"No, sir, just MS about an hour ago."

"Better give him 1/120th when you get the IV going."

"Aye, aye, sir."

Deftly the corpsman pulled the vein taut with the fingers of his left hand, inserted a long needle into it, then threaded the needle up to the hub. He reached up and pulled out the loop on the rubber tourniquet. The blood flow in the needle adapter reversed and the saline ran in a steady stream. Another corpsman punctured the rubber adapter and injected the carefully measured dose of atropine.

During this maneuver, Dr. Sortie had kept his left hand mechanically squeezing the bag on the anesthesia machine supplying his other anesthetized patient with oxygen and gases. He now nodded to me, and as I took over the bag, he turned his full attention to the Marine waiting to have his belly opened. He picked up a large syringe filled with yellow sodium pentothal and anectine (succinyl choline chloride) and injected about half of it into the IV tubing where the atropine had just been given.

Watching the boy's face carefully, he saw the muscles go slack, then begin to twitch faintly. Soon most of the heavy muscles of the body were twitching also. When they too relaxed, he positioned himself at the patient's head, inserted the laryngoscope deep into the throat, lifted up the epiglottis with the curved tip of the scope, reached blindly for his instrument table with his right hand, found the endotracheal tube and slipped it through the vocal chords into the trachea.

Working quickly now, the patient's entire muscular system paralyzed from the anectine, Dr. Sortie attached the double, black rubber, accordion-pleated tubes to the endotracheal tube and pumped pure oxygen into the lungs with a series of forceful squeezes on the black bag. He took the pulse and blood pressure, found them to be

O.K., and filled the balloon at the end of the endotracheal tube with five cubic centimeters of air from a small syringe to make an airtight system.

"All set, Mike, you can scrub," he said to Lavierri as he sat back on his stool. He took both anesthesia bags again, adjusting the valves regulating the rates of flow of the different anesthetic gases. Sweat poured unheeded down his face and neck and arms.

Mike grunted and he and I went out to the scrub tent.

"Man, that's a cool customer we got in there," Mike exclaimed. "He's been sitting right there doing that since ten the night before last. Mechanical man."

"Yeah, a robot. Did you ever try doing two generals at once, Mike? One's enough for me."

"No, never tried it. Wouldn't have believed it if I hadn't seen it with my own eyes."

The patient was scrubbed from nipples to mid-thighs, then painted a bright red with merthiolate. A gowned corpsman draped heavy sheets over the patient as Mike and I gowned and gloved ourselves. Mike moved to the patient's right and I to his left.

The corpsman slapped a scalpel into Mike's hand. The scalpel grooved a long red line from rib margin to groin, a few inches to the right of the midline.

Sponges daubed, clamps clicked, catgut flashed into square knots.

Scalpel again and the shining white fascia split to show the heavy rectus muscles beneath.

The handle of the knife and a finger split the muscles from end to end without apology to the now-denervated central strands.

Tissue forceps on the peritoneum, scalpel to nick it open, Mayo scissors to widen it. An ugly-looking and foul-smelling mixture of old dark blood, fresh red blood, and brown liquid feces poured onto the drapes as the intestines bulged through the incision onto the field.

"Upper abdomen first, Jack," Mike said.

With my right hand wielding a cupped Mayo retractor I lifted the patient's left rib cage upward. I slipped my left hand into the abdomen and pulled down gently on the colon, exposing the anterior wall of the stomach and the rest of the contents of the upper abdomen. Gently, slowly, Mike explored the entire abdomen while I stayed just ahead of his searching eyes and exploring fingers with my retractors.

Like most surgeons, he talked his way through the exploration. "Missed the liver somehow. Stomach's all right. Colon looks O.K., the bullet went behind it. Here's the hole where it went through the gastrocolic ligament. Here's two holes in the jejunum. Two more in the ileum."

He ran the entire small bowel carefully through his fingers. "Two more holes. Two more. Eight so far. Ten…twelve…saw a guy once with 23 holes in his small bowel…never did find the bullet or the other hole, bullet must have been inside the bowel…twelve…guess that's it, Jack. Let's have some plain catgut, Vern, on an intestinal needle, three-oh."

Vern Toy, the corpsman on the Mayo table, was already poised with the suture. He always was. Most of our OR scrubs were every bit as good as their counterparts in civilian hospitals in the States.

One by one Mike placed "purse-string" sutures around each hole, asked me to tie them down snugly, then inverted them with several sutures of fine black silk. Running the bowel again, he checked for any missed perforations. Then the circulating corpsman poured several liters of warm normal saline into the abdomen and we sucked it all back out.

"Pretty lucky guy at that," Mike mused. "Nothing vital hit. Not too much spillage. The peritonitis will clear in a few days. Shouldn't have much trouble. Let's close."

The operation had taken just under an hour to complete.

Fifteen

Another man was brought in from the holding ward. He too had only one wound, but a mean one. A large flying fragment from a mortar had ripped through his left leg, tearing off all the muscles on the inner and anterior aspect of the leg from mid-thigh to knee. The bone was intact but laid bare for a distance of almost six inches. The main artery, nerve, and vein had been blown away. The leg below the knee lay useless on the stretcher, bluish-white in death.

Mike Lavierri studied the wound, his head moving slowly from side to side. I knew what he was thinking. Even if the defect in the artery could be bridged with a vein graft, the leg would be flailing without nerve supply to the muscles. And, of course, the skin was gone, so nothing was available to cover any blood vessel replacement.

Mike placed his hand on the shoulder of the anxious Marine. "It's got to come off, Mac. No way to save it. Sorry."

His voice was compassionate and his eyes held fast to the Marine's. The Marine nodded his head almost imperceptibly, sucked in his breath involuntarily, and said quietly, "Figured that myself, Doctor. And the doctor up front said the same thing. It even feels dead. Hardly any pain at all."

It was a short procedure and Mike had me do it so he could close his eyes for a minute. I think he was as close to sleep as you can get and still stand up. I tied off the retracted and clotted femoral artery and vein. Sharply incised the sciatic nerve. Incised the few remaining muscle bellies. Sawed through the bone. Debrided away some of the muscle and skin which had been devitalized by the tearing action of the shrapnel. Packed the end of the stump with Vaseline gauze and a handful of fluffed gauze. And wrapped the stump with elastic bandages.

It may have been a short operation, but it was a mutilating one, distasteful to us both. Patching up holes in the gut was one thing; chopping off a leg was another. One was constructive, the other destructive. Both had the primary aim of saving life. Both patients would have died without surgery, but the psychological effect on us surgeons was different, to say nothing about the physical and psychological effects on the patients.

There were counterparts in the civilian practice of medicine. A major factor in my original decision not to specialize in surgery had been the steady procession of mutilating operations through the surgical theater during my internship. Leg amputations, breast amputations, radical neck operations with removal of mandibles and tongues, cancer operations of many kinds. One after another they came, each patient different but each losing a part of his body in the fight against disease. It was often incredible how much of a person you could cut away and still be left with a living, breathing, human being.

But many other phases of surgery were exciting, of course, and ultimately they'd won me over and I'd gone into surgery as a specialty. Surgeons were already reconstructing blood vessels, bone, even the heart and lungs. Heart-lung machines were being experimented with and someday soon the human heart would be brought to a voluntary standstill to allow the surgeon to cut open the heart and repair defects deep inside. New techniques were already in use which allowed surgeons to bypass the carotid arteries in the neck while the carotids were opened and cleaned of cholesterol deposits and clots and calcium plaques. These procedures and many more were awaiting only the development of skilled young men to learn and perfect them.

Meanwhile, hundreds of those potential surgeons like me were being siphoned off from their internships and residency programs to do routine medical work in Army and Navy hospitals and dispensaries. What a tragic waste of time and men.

The third day was ending and the third night began. Fatigue was a grasping specter, a hollow-eyed and blood-smeared devil standing by every man. I could feel its heavy hands pressing my eyelids down, dragging at my shoulders until they ached with dull pain, knotting my stomach so I couldn't even eat, squeezing my temples with steel-banded fingers, buckling my knees when I relaxed for a fraction of a second.

While the doctors worked, the corpsmen stood asleep on their feet, rousing more and more painfully each time. While the corpsmen switched patients, the doctors leaned against the tent posts or sat on a cot and closed their eyes for precious moments. Several of the corpsmen began to hallucinate, reliving experiences they themselves had

had on line, and had to be carried unconscious to their tents.

The third night was the worst. The constant flow of men from the lines was lessening, but the aching fatigue in each man resulted in slowing down of reflexes. Minor techniques such as starting an IV became major undertakings. The surgeons' eyes blurred over, making them stop to close their eyes till the blurring cleared. Even Sam Sortie, the mechanical anesthetist, was starting to have difficulty getting his patients asleep and then awake.

It was a nightmare.

Book Two
Getting Set

Sixteen

Unnoticed by all, the nightmare was about to end as a Sikorski helicopter settled onto the 'copter pad near my CP while another circled slowly, waiting for the other to clear its cargo. We heard the 'copters, of course, but we'd been hearing them for days.

The sun rose fiery red on the horizon as the first 'copter settled in. Two corpsmen trotted in a drunk-like stupor to bring in more seriously wounded men. To their surprise, then, out climbed a half dozen men in shiny new green fatigues, clean new combat boots, cameras slung around their necks, eyes glancing warily around them as if a Chinaman with a burp gun might be hiding in the bushes.

These men were American Navy doctors and corpsmen sent over from Japan to relieve the men of Charley Med.

So it was all over for us for awhile. Mike Lavierri,

Sam Sortie, Yung Il-song, all the other doctors, Ross Tompter, Vern Toy, and all the other corpsmen who had worked so long and so hard, were able to sleep again, knowing that the wounded men were being taken care of. We would be up again in a few hours if the casualties kept coming and the new men needed help.

But now our waking nightmare ended with sleep. Sleep to erase the memories of the mutilation we had just tried to correct, sleep to forget the carnage that man had perpetrated against man in the name of a Godless Communism.

A sleep which was not anesthesia, and a sleep which, unlike Jesse Carter's, was not death.

We nearly slept the clock around. When we finally awoke early on Tuesday morning, the 6th of March, everything was quiet except for the usual sounds of a military base. An occasional truck rumbled by. The off-duty corpsmen played volleyball in the snow up on the hillside 'copter strip. The thin purr of an L-19 observation plane hummed in the near distance. Every five minutes the guns of the 11th Artillery thundered in volleys of four.

The devil in my nightmare still played his hateful tune in my head. Never had I seen such carnage even on the worst nights at Cook County Hospital. I learned later that we'd triaged 1,004 wounded men in those three nights and two days.

We did 142 major operations under general anesthesia—belly, chest, and amputations—an average of over two every hour.

We evacuated 153 walking wounded to Able Med for minor debridement.

We shipped 288 severely wounded men to the *Consolation*—forty-eight Sikorskis with six stretchers in each.

We lost twenty-one men during or after surgery. The time spent on several of those might have been better spent on others, but sometimes that's not obvious at first. And, to come up with the understatement of the year, it's awfully hard to say, "Take him to D Ward. No surgery contemplated."

Three men came in DOA.

If my arithmetic is correct, that means we operated on 397 WIAs in the Minor Surgery Tent under local anesthesia. A high percent of those minors were multiple shrapnel wounds. Five, ten, twenty, even thirty wounds in a single body, but none of them breaking bone or penetrating the belly or thorax. Many would have been called majors in a stateside hospital.

When the smoke cleared and my brain started functioning again, I was so proud of all those guys that I wanted to recommend every one for a Bronze Star with a Combat V. The irony was that I, as commanding officer, was to be decorated with a Bronze Star on the recommendation of Wally Ormsdorf. The commander came up to Charley before I left for 3/5 and told me he'd already sent in the papers. I protested that if I got one, everybody should get one. Ormsdorf retorted, "Look, Jack, you're the guy who held Charley Med together…"

"I did no such thing, Commander Orms—"

He grinned that Quasimodo smile. "I say you did. Someone's got to be decorated for that action up here at Charley and I'm selecting the C. O. That's you!"

I shook my head. "Commander, this isn't a joking matter. That's not fair to the other doctors and corpsmen."

He sobered suddenly. "You're right, Jack. Sorry. But listen, will you? I've talked to the people up here. They say you were everywhere, organizing, encouraging, directing 'copter traffic, triaging, operating, assisting at surgery, even carrying stretchers and mopping up vomitus."

He smiled. "I may even recommend that you be kept here instead of being sent back up to your line outfit."

"Oh no, you don't! That's where I draw the line."

And so it was that I got the first of two Bronze Stars. And, false modesty aside, I really earned the second one.

The crew from Japan stayed with us for three days. They didn't have much to do, were disappointed, and said so. I heard them talking in the mess hall. Daryl Sims, a tall, good-looking young guy just a couple years older than I, was saying, "Yeah, y'know, I hate this just sitting around. I came over here to work and there's nothing to do."

I looked down the long table at him and asked quietly, "What kind of work you looking for, Dr. Sims?"

"Why, trauma, of course."

"Where's that trauma supposed to come from?"

I kept my voice low and the messhall went suddenly still as the others stopped to listen.

He looked hard at me, quizzical at first, then grasped my meaning but not my thoughts. "Why, from the front lines, of course," he said.

I could feel the tension in the tent and wondered why Sims couldn't. Mike Lavierri in particular was mesmerized. He froze with his fork halfway to his mouth, then rested his elbow on the table, the fork hanging in mid-air. I'm sure he was wondering if I was going to be as gentle with Sims as I had been with him a week earlier. I wasn't.

I said, "Perhaps you'd like to cut off Bob Marne's leg? He's the S-3 up in Three-Five, my battalion. Or how about digging a slug out of Jim Jepson's belly? He's one of my corpsmen in rear aid up there. Or how about

Colonel McCallister or Chaplain Runninger or maybe some of the grunts up in the trenches like Buckshot Newman or Ted Kaminski or Ira Jensen...oh, I could give you the names of a lot of my friends up there that you could get a crack at if only they'd get wounded in action. Maybe you'd like to amputate *my* leg when I step on a land mine for your convenience?"

I was getting worked up and I knew it. I stood up, looked around, and left.

They got the picture real quick and stayed out of my way after that. But I could see them eyeing me across the ward or across the compound. It was a look of mixed wariness and respect.

The corpsmen heard about my little speech and picked up the ball. From then on until the packaged surgical team left, they snapped to attention whenever I came on the ward. They barked out "Aye, aye, sir!" at my slightest command. Without a fuss they wore their fatigue caps square, their fatigue jackets tucked into their pants, their pants folded neatly into their boots.

I wished Wally Ormsdorf or Lieutenant General Seldon with his red ascot or even "Iron Mike" O'Daniel would just drop in for a visit.

The team went back to Japan with their anesthetists and corpsmen and lab techs. They were really a good bunch of guys, pulled out of comfortable billets at Yokosuka or Sasebo or somewhere. They'd enjoyed their brief tour of what they called the front lines, but they were glad to leave.

That long-lost new CO of Charley Med finally turned up. He hadn't been lost at all, of course. He was regular Navy and had used his rank and his savvy to catch a few days in the flesh-pots of Tokyo. He hadn't wanted to come to Korea but had bowed to the conventional wisdom of the Armed Services which held that combat duty enhanced an officer's chances of getting the star of an admiral or general.

So he took out his hostility on the rest of us, bitching about almost everything and everybody. I was so mad at him by the time I left that I gave him an exaggerated Australian salute, you know, with the palm turned outward and the arm so stiff it vibrates.

Well, after only eight days at Charley Med I returned on the 9th of March to my own outfit in the real front lines, the Third Battalion of the Fifth Marine Regiment of the First Marine Division. They welcomed me back with sincere warmth—I was one of them—part of 3/5. It was almost like a reception line up on that shelf of Korean mountainside called Mercy Row.

Jumping the line entirely was Butch. He came charging out of my tent and literally slid to a stop in the snow about five feet in front of me. He held his arms stiffly at his sides, then bowed deeply from the waist. "Butch taksan happy see Number One Battarun Surgeon." That formality over, he straightened up and actually leaped into my arms.

Ned Rohn was so glad to see me that he almost forgot he was an enlisted man and I was a commissioned officer. He had to restrain himself from hugging me and settled for a two-handed handshake. Bob Marne did hug me—in a manly way, of course—and clapped me on the back with his big leather and canvas gloves. Chappie shook my hand warmly. "Good to have you back, Jack. We've missed those all night bull sessions."

The corpsmen popped out of the aid station and their tents, waved and shouted, "Welcome back, Dr. Lord."

And, you know, I was glad to get back up there. When I'd taken off for Charley Med ten days before I hadn't been at all unhappy. But now that I was back on line I felt like I'd come home. In just eight days I'd had my fill of rear-echelon-poguedom.

Oh, I knew I'd be going back to Charley or maybe Easy someday. And maybe I'd be ready for it in another six months or so. But for now this was where I belonged.

Or so I thought.

Seventeen

Fred Overman came back to the rear aid station as soon as he heard I was back. It was real quiet along the lines now, had been for a couple of days, but he'd been pretty busy while I was at Charley Med. A fair number of casualties from the First Marines had fed back through 3/5's forward aid station and then back to Easy Med.

Fred had stayed up in forward aid during the entire offensive, leaving Chief Hoffman to handle rear aid.

I wasn't surprised.

Fred was one of those guys who likes the places where the action is. Away from administrative duties. The kind of a guy who likes roughing it or at least doesn't mind it as much as some of us. I really think he preferred the forward aid station in the trench system where he didn't have anyone to report to, except once in a while to me and even less often to the C. O.

"Any word on my replacement?" Fred asked me.

"Yeah, matter of fact. Came in the 18th replacement draft. He's in regiment now."

He didn't look as happy as I thought he'd be. Then he brightened. "It'll be good to get out of here."

I grinned. "Somehow I don't think of you as a rear-echelon pogue."

He laughed outright. "You got that right."

Then he sobered. "When's the DivSurg sending up what's his name?"

"Everly. Didn't catch his first name. Probably in a couple of days."

"Guess I'll run back up to George Company then and say good-bye to the troops."

"You don't need to do that."

Again that laugh that was sort of a bark. "Yes, I do."

I knew what he meant.

He said as he turned away, "I'll have Joe Tollander drive me up part way in Rohn's jeep ambulance, if that's okay with you."

"O.K. with me? You're still the boss."

He was gone within the hour, back up to where his friends were, to say good-bye.

The Division Surgeon, in his infinite alcoholic wisdom, sent Dr. Ronald Everly up to us that same day. He arrived about 1600 just after we'd finished our second and last meal of the day.

Everly climbed out of the passenger's side of the jeep, snapped to attention when he saw me, looked around for a flag to salute and of course didn't find one. So he turned back to me, saluted, and machine-gunned me with, "Lieutenant-junior-grade-Ronald-Everly-reporting-for-duty—SIR!"

At first I thought he was clowning, but he wasn't. He was dead serious. And of course he was only exercising proper military etiquette. When you report aboard any

Navy ship or station, you salute the ensign (usually the flag) and then the officer of the deck, even if he's below you in rank, even if he's a non-commissioned officer.

But this was ridiculous.

Everly was a tall man, lean and straight, and affected a pencil-thin black mustache. He was dressed impeccably in clean combat gear, pants creased and tucked into boots. On his almost new, unfaded green field jacket his name was sharply stenciled on the left pocket just above USMC and the Marine Corps emblem of globe, anchor and eagle. He wore a single silver bar on his right lapel and a gold leaf with acorn on the left.

He even wore a camouflaged helmet that contrasted with the long-billed cloth fatigue caps or bunny hats the rest of us wore around the rear aid station unless we were in a training operation, under inspection, or actually under fire.

I glanced down to see if he still wore the canvas leggings we'd worn in combat training at Pendleton. He didn't, but somehow he'd already obtained a service .45, slung on his right hip from a web belt, a canteen on his left. And—I couldn't believe this—he wore a blue ascot around his neck, tucked down inside his fatigue jacket. I wondered if his hair was slicked down with Brilliantine.

I shouldn't have been so catty. He really did look sharp. Just incongruous.

Not that the rest of us looked sloppy. Fred Overman wouldn't have tolerated that in the aid station nor McCallister in the H & S Company. But we just weren't so—so ritzy.

With a big grin I saluted him with a wave of my hand to the bill of my cap. "Welcome aboard, Dr. Everly. I'm Jack Lord."

"I assumed you must be."

He didn't offer to shake hands. I didn't know if he was afraid to get his hand dirty or if the salute had taken care of that formality.

He looked around him with a puzzled look on his face. "Is this it?"

I couldn't resist. "Is this what?"

"Where the Battalion Surgeon works."

I looked over his shoulder at the Aid Station, a sharply set pyramidal tent that Chief Hoffman had strong-backed with lumber cumshawed from an Army MASH.

I glanced over at the half dozen of my now-relaxed but battle-hardened corpsmen who'd come out of the tent to see their new battalion surgeon.

I looked down at the long line of H & S Company pyramidal and squad tents stretched out along the Soyang-gang.

"This is it," I said. "Pretty fancy, eh?"

With a twist of his lips that hovered between disgust and sneer, Everly said, "Very."

I wondered what he'd say when he got his first look at the inside of our forward aid station—a dark, cold, smoky, slightly larger than average bunker in the trenches.

I wondered what he'd look like after a week up there where your hands and knees were always dirty from crawling around on all fours, where your face and neck were always dirty from the lampblack, where your entire body was always dirty and stank to high heaven because there usually wasn't enough water to bathe in and ice cold even if there was enough.

"Let's take a look at the aid station," I suggested. "Your driver can take your gear up to our tent."

My corpsmen stepped politely aside as we approached. As I went in I heard Everly say sternly, "Don't you men salute commissioned officers?"

I was shocked. This was a wartime Marine bivouac a half mile from the front lines, not a Navy ship or a stateside hospital. There were times when I saluted: when the commanding general or the division surgeon approached me directly. But I never required my corpsmen to salute me and I didn't know any battalion surgeons who did. The flurry of saluting and clicking of heels back at Charley Med had been solely for the benefit of the OR crew from Japan and had been voluntary on the part of the corpsmen.

With a shake of my head, I turned to go back out but Chief Hoffman had already solved the problem. I heard him say curtly, "Ten-shun!" and heard the scuffling sound of the men coming to attention. And then, "Hand salute!" and there was a rustling of fatigues as the hands came up. Everly's voice said sharply, "Carry on, men, I'll be in the area all day."

My God. This guy was going to be trouble.

When he came in I said in as offhand way as I could, "Military etiquette isn't as important here as it is in noncombatant areas."

He sniffed. "It is to me. My father was an Army colonel under Patton and one of the last things he said to me before I left for Korea was to maintain discipline at all costs."

"Well, I won't argue with that, Ron—"

"Ronald, please—"

"O.K., Ronald. But somehow I don't equate saluting under these circumstances with discipline."

"I do."

As I showed Ronald around the Sick Bay, I kept telling myself, slow down, boy, you've got to live with this guy for at least three months, probably four or five.

Surprisingly, he liked the setup and said so. "Looks

like you've got things pretty well under control, Jack. I think I can work here."

God be praised, I thought, bit my tongue, and changed the subject. I told him how we handle what little paperwork there was, what the password was in case he had to make a run up to the front lines that night, and a few other things. He seemed more than slightly bored as if he knew all this already.

Maybe he did.

I hadn't, when I came up to 3/5. It wasn't part of our orientation at Pendleton or anywhere else.

But he said, "Thanks, Jack," and asked, "What's the tactical situation now?"

I almost said I hadn't read my *Time* magazine yet that week but said instead, "What do you mean, Ronald?"

"You know, what outfits are on our flanks, what operations are planned...?"

"Oh, yeah. Well, Bob Marne, our S-3, is working on something but I've been down at Charley Med for a week and just got back today." I wasn't about to tell him about the upcoming assault on 1052. He'd be down in the 5-6 tent telling them how MacArthur would have done it. Or how he himself would do it.

So I just said, "We've got army divisions on both our flanks."

"American Army or gooks?"

I sat down on an artillery shell packing case. "We got any coffee, Chief?"

Chief Hoffman had followed us in and was standing off to one side with a bemused look on his face. I was sure that he'd dealt with officers like this before and would know how to handle Everly. He came to stiff attention and said smartly, "Aye, aye, sir, coming right up." Then to a Third Class corpsman, "Rick?"

Rick Simpson, one of my better men, scurried out. I didn't like using corpsmen as go-fers but that was one custom ingrained in the Navy medical services that I hadn't fought.

"Ronald," I said. "'Gook' is a derogatory term that we reserve for the enemy. It's like calling a Negro a 'nigger.'"

He nodded. "O.K., point taken. But I've heard some pretty sad commentaries on the South Korean troops."

"They've done as well as they could with the training and the support they've gotten."

He nodded again and then without thanking him accepted a cup of coffee from Simpson.

He sat down on another packing case, swung one long leg over the other and seemed to relax.

"Where'd you go to med school, Jack?" he asked me.

"Illinois."

"I went to Harvard."

I didn't doubt that for a moment. It stuck out all over him. I'd known another Harvard med school graduate back at Great Lakes before I got orders to the Fleet Marine Force. He'd griped about everything. Zion, the little town where a lot of us married men lived, was too puritanical. Lake Michigan was too cold and not "for Gawd's sake" at all salty. Chicago was too hot and had no character like New York and Boston. Illinois was flat and grew corn and pigs. Wisconsin, just across the border, was still populated mostly by wild Indians, wasn't it? *Et cetera, ad infinitum et nauseum.*

I felt like saying to Everly, "Well, good for you," but again I bit my tongue. Instead, I said, with a grin, "I won't hold that against you."

He didn't think that was at all funny. My corpsmen were hiding big grins behind their hands. That wasn't good, of course, because they'd have to work with this s.o.b. But you can't legislate respect any more than you can legislate morality.

Lieutenant junior grade Ronald Everly was going to have to prove himself to these guys just like I'd had to. Let's just hope, I thought, that he's as good as he thinks he is.

"Well, I should think—" Everly began, but just then a blast shook the tent. We all swallowed quickly to equalize the pressure in our ears. We knew what it was and were unconcerned. Not so Everly. His eyes went wide, his body tensed with his arms straight down at his sides. "Was that a bomb? Sounded like it was right outside."

Chief Hoffman laughed and said, "Just an eight incher firing over our heads, about 300 yards back. We get the shock wave every time."

Everly's face was a shade paler than usual. He glanced over at me. I almost felt sorry for the guy. Harvard Yard was never like this.

Eighteen

We talked a little while longer and then I said, "You might as well get settled in, Ronald. Let's go up to our home away from home."

We filed out, the corpsmen following us, relaxing a little, two of them laughing and talking about their own imminent departure from the battalion to rear area outfits.

The smiling face of one of the corpsmen turned suddenly sour. I followed his pointing finger to the ridgeline to our north as he said, "Look, Doctor, here comes Joe Tollander in the ambulance you sent up with Dr. Overman a couple hours ago. Looks like trouble to me."

We stood suddenly silent as we watched the jeep crawling down the ridge on the tank road from the lines. It picked up speed when it reached the CP area and then slid to a halt in front of the aid station. Corporal Joe Tollander's eyes sought me out and then he shouted, "Guy shot in the chest, Doctor, accidental. Didn't look so good when we started out."

Fred Overman leaped out of the back and watched quietly as two corpsmen gently but swiftly pulled the stretcher off the racks and carried it at a run into sick bay. I jogged over and arrived just in time to see an ashen face with lifeless eyes disappear into the tent. A corpsman at my elbow said, "Christ, that's Al Samuels. He's dead!"

I ducked into the tent and watched in a sort of horror as Overman knelt beside Samuels. He pulled back the heavy OD blankets and attempted to feel a pulse. Then he pulled down the zipper on the Marine's parka, pulled the fatigue jacket out of his heavy wool pants, and applied a stethoscope to the motionless chest. I could see, just above the left nipple, a neat round hole surrounded by dark blood mixed with the gray of powder burns.

Powder burns? Strange. Was something going on up front that we didn't know about?

It was clear to me that Overman was following an ingrained routine, a stereotyped formality implanted by dozens of experiences just like this one. Samuels was so obviously dead. Blood and saliva had run from his mouth in his last agonies and were now drying. Overman could see all this. But there was a formula to follow, a priestly function to observe.

"Let's roll him over," he said finally.

"Sir."

"Okay, far enough."

We gazed blankly at the exit wound, a fist-sized hole in the man's left chest just below the tip of the scapula. An emergency battle dressing had been taped on by the corpsman on line, but it had been soaked off by a great quantity of blood and lay soggily on the stretcher.

They gently let the body roll back and covered it with a blanket.

"How the hell did this happen?" I asked as Fred stood up. Fred gestured toward Tollander. "Tell him, Joe."

The ambulance driver stepped forward. "Al was gonna climb down into one of those deep foxholes, y'know, the ones with fire steps we use on watch? Relieving his buddy to go heat up some chow in their bunker. He handed his M-1 down to the guy, butt first. His buddy, his *buddy* mind ya', reached up and grabbed the rifle by the trigger housing and the damn thing went off. J'ever hear of such a crazy stunt."

He looked around the circle of men. Nobody answered.

Fred said, "All right, Joe, get him back to regiment. Take the cracker box. I'll notify his C.O. The rest of you get back to work."

He looked over at me. "Was that my relief out there?"

"Yeah. That's Ron—sorry, Ronald—Everly."

His nostrils flared and there was the bare hint of a smile in his eyes. I knew he'd gotten the picture. Under other circumstances he would've come up with some witticism, but with the dead Marine lying on the ground at his feet he just turned to Joe Tollander and said, "I might as well go with you. Seems as if I'm not needed in this battalion any more."

"Sure, Doctor, I'll wait for you."

"Won't take me long," Fred said.

Two men lifted the stretcher and took it outside. The corpsmen dispersed slowly, mumbling to each other about the incident. Several had known Samuels when they'd been attached to his line company.

Fred and I went back outside. To Everly's questioning glance, I said, "He's dead."

"You give him mouth to mouth?"

Overman shot little black darts from his eyes. "No."

"No resuscitative measures at all?"

To try to bust up what I saw could be a nasty confrontation, I put my hand on Everly's sleeve and said quickly, "He was dead, Ronald."

"But I've seen..."

Overman had already had enough. "Stow it, buster," he said and started down toward his tent.

"You can't talk to me..."

Overman turned and stood facing Everly, weight on his right leg, left knee slightly bent, his thumbs caught in his web belt. Hanging low on his right thigh from a thin leather waist-strap was a .45 automatic in a worn, chocolate-brown leather holster. Several leather strips hung in a braided tail from the lower end.

His once dark-green fatigue jacket was now faded and frayed, encrusted with old dried mud, the right sleeve stained with fresh, dark red, liquid blood.

His green wool pants were muddy and baggy at the knees but were neatly tucked into his rough-worn combat boots so that they folded over the tops like a paratrooper's.

His soft fatigue cap was squared away on his head, pulled low over his eyes, the vertical silver bar of a Navy lieutenant j. g. catching the slanting rays of the sun.

He was a veteran of eight months up here and he looked it. In Navy parlance he was an old salt. A Marine might have honored him with the term "grunt" or "crunchie." His mouth was set in a straight line and his eyes blazed.

Behind him his corpsmen and Joe Tollander stood in a ragged phalanx, caught in stop action as they loaded the dead Marine into the box-like ambulance with the Red Cross painted on its sides and the steel chains on all four wheels. Their eyes glared their challenge to anyone who would take issue with their battalion surgeon.

If I hadn't already seen Overman in action, hadn't seen the way his corpsmen idolized him, I would have known in that instant that this guy Overman was my kind of a guy. I wondered what he was going to say.

He didn't say anything.

He just stood there for a full ten seconds.

Spun on his heel.

Walked away.

Perfect, I thought.

I said to Everly, "Wait for me here," and caught up with Overman. As we walked toward our tent up the rough path gouged out of the hillside, I'd already forgotten Everly. The senseless death of the young Marine filled my thoughts and there was no room for idiots like Ronald Everly.

I knew that an accidental death could happen anywhere: at home, in training, in Korea. I'd already found that accidental combat deaths were much more frequent than I'd supposed they'd be.

Sometimes they were caused by the so-called "friendly fire." These were almost always in a confused situation.

An American Corsair comes out of the clouds over what he thinks is a Chinese encampment, lets go his eggs, pulls up into the clouds, never seeing that his bombs fell on H & S Company of 2/7 of the First Marine Division.

An NCO of the British Royal Marines at the battle of the Chosin Reservoir is gunned down by American Marines as he tries to make his way back to his own outfit.

A propeller-driven Navy plane swoops in over the wrong side of Eerie where Al Chamberlin is fighting for his life with Love Company of the 179th Army Regiment and drops a 500 pound bomb.

Almost everyone who's been in combat can tell you a horror story about friendly-fire KIAs. That kind of incident was bad enough.

But what really got to me were the truly accidental deaths: mortar tubes exploding, jeep and truck accidents, accidental weapon discharges like Al Samuels'. At Charley Med I'd operated on a Marine who'd been hit by shrapnel from a hand grenade accidentally tossed into a warming bonfire. He said that three men had been killed.

And back at Camp Tripoli, before we moved back on line, I'd been called to see a big Negro Marine who'd been playfully practicing "fast draws" with a corpsman whose .45 was supposedly empty.

It wasn't.

And then there was Lt. Rory Sanders, one of my tent-mates at Camp Tripoli and leader of the mortar platoon with which I'd been trapped behind How Company. He bought the farm a month after I left 3/5, when I was already convalescing in my hospital bed on the *Consolation*, then in Inchon Harbor. The handsome, blond, young, second lieutenant in Weapons Company was cleaning his .45 in his tent back of the lines on a beautiful sunny Easter Sunday morning in April. The azaleas were purpled out all over the hills high above Seoul where the rice didn't grow, forsythia lined the little streams with yellow gold, the war was almost over. The .45 was not empty after all, and Rory Sanders lay dead on the pounded mud floor of his tent.

Now as Fred gathered his gear together in our tent, he asked me, "Can you finish up the inventory, Jack? I'd like to get the hell out of here before someone changes their puny little minds!"

I grinned. "Sure, Fred. How many bottles of paregoric did you use in that dysentery epidemic last week?"

"Five quarts. Leaves three. Now may I leave—sir?"

"Run along, you rear-echelon pogue."

We shook hands. There was no attempt to hide my envy or his sheer joy. In fact, he said with a leering smile, "I want you to know I'm leaving the battalion with mixed emotions."

"Yeah, how's that?"

"With happiness and joy!"

I drew back my fist as if to sock him one. He put his palm up against my fist with a laugh. "You'll be going back one of these days," he said.

"Some day. Sure as death and taxes. Oops, bad simile. So long, Fred."

The change of doctors in the aid station was effected in a matter of minutes. Overman threw his packboard, seabag and M-2 into the crackerbox. Everly threw his packboard, seabag and M-2 onto Overman's canvas cot in our Arctic tent. Overman left with Tollander and roared off with a parody of a salute to me and a baleful stare at Everly. Everly stayed with me and our corpsmen.

Transfer accomplished.

I wondered how long it'd be before I took off in a jeep for a permanent assignment in the rear. I wondered how I'd feel. There would be "happiness and joy," of course—an elation of the spirit. But I was sure that there would be an inexpressible sadness in leaving 3/5 and its officers and men. So it would be a real mixture of happy and sad emotions—further mixed with anticipated nostalgia. You're already planning the reunion. But in your heart you know you'll never see these guys again and you're saddened further. The kaleidoscope turns. The moving finger writes, and having writ, moves on…

I kept Everly in rear aid for a couple of days, trying to orient him a bit. He maintained that know-it-already attitude and finally in disgust I told him he was ready to go on up to the forward aid bunker in the George Company lines.

That woke him up and I could see the wheels turning. He didn't say anything but I could almost hear the, "Why don't you go up?" I ignored the look in his eyes and called an unnecessary "staff" meeting while Everly got his gear together.

Nineteen

There was considerably more action in 3/5 than there had been when I'd left just a week before for Charley Med. H & S Company practically writhed with activity. Jeeps from Regiment buzzed in and out. Occasionally a 'copter chopped in, left off a man or a manila envelope, and chopped off again. Colonel McCallister strode about the CP as if he were planning the second Inchon landing or another drive to the Yalu.

Visiting VIPs strutted about in their camouflaged helmets and freshly pressed "battle fatigues," taking pictures, acting tough. One of the visiting majors even carried a swagger stick. As long as they didn't have to prove how brave they were, they could pretend they were.

If they really were tough, why were they trying to *act* tough? Some of the officers peacocking around were from supply, PR, medical, intelligence. Important, necessary positions. We couldn't have gotten along without them. But, by God, they didn't need to act as if they were combat types.

I got so I could spot a real combat type who for some reason was now out of combat. He came up from the rear in a jeep or a truck, not a 'copter. He was squared away but not pressed or ascotted or swagger-sticked.

He didn't wear a helmet unless he was headed for the trenches or had just come back. Even if he outranked me, his eyes met mine with a friendly, steady, neutral look, not a glance that said, "Hey, guy, don't ask me any questions that might blow my cover." He did what he'd come to do and left, didn't prolong his visit with some dumb show of busy-ness.

When I watched some of those preening pretend-heroes, I couldn't help remembering when I was a boy making little lead soldiers out of discarded plumbing pipes and lining them up in strategic battle lines. Give me strength, I muttered.

I didn't see Bob Marne much because he was holed up a lot with the S-4 and the S-2, the battalion Supply and Intelligence officers. And he was up on line for several days at a time. I knew something was up and it had to be Luke the Gook's Castle.

I was a lot busier myself. The warming weather and decreasing snow cover had stimulated activity all along the line. There were no major offensives going on anywhere in our sector, but squad and double-squad raiding patrols were starting to be more active. Firefights frequently broke out both day and night. Prisoner-taking and reconnaissance patrols were sneaking through No-man's Land and getting into trouble.

Artillery and mortar bombardments had tripled or quadrupled on both sides. Three-Five in particular was taking a pounding from artillery and mortars, due, Colonel

McCallister insisted, to our vulnerability lying under the guns of Luke the Gook up in his castle. He was undoubtedly right. All I knew was that I was getting a steadily increasing flow of wounded and dead.

On March 13th we had to move the entire H & S Company, including our rear aid station. We were in defilade, of course, but the gooks tried to wipe out Item Company with their very mobile 76 millimeter artillery. Their accuracy was so poor that many of their shells were sailing over the top of the hills and landing in the battalion command post.

With tongue in cheek, I wrote to Ingrid, told her we'd moved because "the stray rounds disrupt our peaceful pursuits in the battalion CP, make chow late because the mess men are hiding in their bunkers, break up the aid station volleyball games, and get the colonel's clothes dirty when he has to hit the deck."

A new weapon for mass destruction was being used in our sector. Rockets. Six mobile units, each with 24 rockets in three rows of eight tubes, fired in sequence at five second intervals. So for twenty-five seconds there was an almost constant booming noise. For a few seconds all was quiet and then there was a muffled but louder roar of exactly the same duration, that is, for twenty-five seconds, as they hit targets on the enemy MLR. When they fired at night, twenty-four brilliant fingers of light followed the unguided rockets, foreshadowing for the world what was to come in missile warfare.

Apparently the rockets bothered the enemy more than anything else so the rocket crews hitched up their units immediately after firing their riffles because they knew they'd be bombarded by the enemy within minutes.

Ned Rohn in the jeep ambulance and Joe Tollander in the cracker-box were kept busy running back and forth from the lines to rear aid. Ron Everly, still up in forward aid, was even busier than I was, of course, because he was seeing all the casualties and bypassing us in rear aid by evacuating many by helicopter. They whirled over us toward the lines more often than they had for a long time, whizzing down the valley, skimming the ground until they reached the backside of the MLR, then chopping back over us headed for the Medical Companies or maybe the hospital ship *Consolation* lying off Sokchori.

Why all the activity? What was the purpose of all this? Why didn't we just sit and look at each other across the valleys and rivers and the coils of barbed wire? Why, for God's sake, did we keep on killing each other?

Well, one official reason is that the DMZ had to be fixed somewhere and each side had to try to get as much territory as it could before the final settlement of the Kansas Line. The brass liked to call these activities an "active defense."

Dean Rusk, Assistant Secretary of State for Far Eastern Affairs summarized the second official reasoning: "We must make it in the interest of the Chinese Communists to accept some stabilization (of the lines) by making it so costly for them that they cannot afford not to accept (a truce)."

That may have soothed ruffled feathers and perhaps helped dry the tears of parents and wives back home, but I think a major reason for the persistent activity was a lot more basic, a lot simpler than that.

I'll tell you what I think.

I'm pretty well convinced that the senior career officers running this war, sitting back in Division Headquarters or maybe even in Corps Headquarters, were having fun. By fun I don't mean they thought they were at a party. But they were doing what they'd been trained to do and that's always fun. Or perhaps a better word would be "enjoyable."

They'd spent their professional lives studying Carl Philipp Gottlieb von Clausewitz, Napoleon Bonaparte, Chester Nimitz, James Van Fleet, and Douglas MacArthur. Most of them had had experience in the Second World War as junior officers. Then for five or six years they found themselves at a barren stateside training camp or perhaps a cold-war encampment in Europe.

The frustration of professional soldiers without a war to fight would have to be similar to that of trained surgeons treating head colds and diarrhea. Now the frustration was over. Now they did have a war to fight. Not a very big one. And not much going on with the lines stabilized.

But it was a war. Now they were in charge. So they sat around their charts and their up-to-the-minute contour maps marked "Korea 1:25000 Transverse Mercator Projection, prepared by A. P. I. G-2 Section, 1st MarDiv, FMF." (The one I saw in the 5-6 tent in late February of 1952 was dated November, 1951. You can't get much more current than that.) And they say, "Hey, let's send out a patrol from George Company of 3/5 and have them take a crack at Hill 1052."

I like the way Al Chamberlin puts it in his book, *Circle of Courage*. "While the peace emissaries shuffled and dealt their diplomatic cards at the conference table for political pots, the fighting forces shuffled their men and weapons and dealt death for tiny geographical pots along the 38th parallel."

F. Scott Fitzgerald wrote in *The Beautiful and Damned*, "In their childish hearts two out of every three professional officers considered that wars were made for armies and not armies for wars."

Even Bob Marne was caught up in the charade. I asked him, "Bob, why are we planning this big offensive against Luke the Gook's Castle?"

There was a blizzard raging outside and nobody was doing anything on either side of the barbed wire. Butch sat on my cot. We were all eating freshly popped popcorn.

Yeah, popcorn. Ingrid, instead of sending popped corn to cushion the brownies and tollhouse cookies like she usually did, had sent a bag of unpopped corn. I sent Butch next door to Sick Bay for the big enameled wash basin. I cut out a piece of cardboard from a beer case the size of the top of the basin, scrubbed out the basin, cumshawed some oleo and salt from the galley, and popped the corn on the pot-belly stove.

Marne stopped munching and answered, "I thought that was obvious."

"To control the High Ground?"

"Right."

"My question goes back another step then. Why don't we just stop shooting at each other and then it wouldn't matter if they held the High Ground."

He shook his head in bewilderment. "There's a war going on, Jack."

I nodded my head as if I understood. I didn't understand at all. I mean, wouldn't it be simpler to just draw the Kansas Line right down the middle of 1052 and 812 and all those other hills strung out across the breadth of Korea and stop killing each other? But no, there was a war going on and military minds were going to see to it that something was done about it.

And over on the other side, they were following the principles laid down in 1938 by Mao Tse-Tung in his book, *On Protracted War*, written at the height of the Sino-Japanese War but not known to the U.S. military until 1954:

"Enemy advances, we retreat.
Enemy halts, we harass.
Enemy tires, we attack.
Enemy retreats, we pursue."

So we were fighting a war and men on both sides were getting killed and wounded. My job was not to question why but to do my professional best to minimize the carnage brought on by those other professionals. Maybe I'm being unfair, but I saw enough to believe that I'm not being the least bit unfair.

During the next few days I asked Rohn a couple of times how Everly was doing up on the line. He knew what I meant, of course. He knew that I talked to Everly by field phone daily about patients, but he knew that that wasn't what I wanted to know.

Rohn put me off once with, "Oh, he's doin' okay," and later with, "No problems, Dr. Lord."

The third time I pinned him down. He'd just completed a run back to Easy Med and we stood by his jeep outside the aid station. "I get the feeling," I said, "that Dr. Everly isn't exactly captivating your hearts up there."

He grinned that lopsided grin and shuffled his feet like a kid caught with his hand in the cookie jar. He slipped the gold cross up out of his jacket and twirled it in a circle. "You got the picture, I think, Doctor."

"What's wrong?"

He hesitated. He didn't want to get in the middle of anything having to do with commissioned officers, especially two who were so close to his own case.

"Ned," I said," "this is strictly between us two. I ask as a friend. It goes no farther."

He hesitated just another second or two then decided to take me at face value. "His attitude, Doctor." He eyed me with a look half quizzical and half accepting, then made the final plunge. "He's a horse's ass, Doctor. Gripes about everything. The chow's no good. His bunker ain't built right—not strong enough or something. He should a stayed in H & S and you shoulda gone up there again. He ain't puttin' his brilliant mind and exceptional trainin' to their full value."

He held up for a moment as I nodded my head and looked down across the frozen rice paddies terraced below us. I could only think, so what else is new? I wasn't exactly preparing myself for a practice in the States either.

Then Ned said, "You were up there, Doctor. You know we all gripe about that same stuff…"

I laughed. "Yeah, there's something wrong with morale unless the troops are griping, that sort of thing?"

"Yeah, Doctor. It ain't a lot a fun. But this guy is something else. He really means it."

"Thanks, Ned. I appreciate your candidness. And I meant what I said about this staying right here." I knew that candidness came hard for an enlisted Marine talking to a commissioned officer about a commissioned officer.

I turned the matter over and over in my mind. The last thing I wanted to do was leave him up there if it would put our wounded men in jeopardy. That's always one of the main concerns of anyone in a command position. For the non-coms and officers on the line it was a constant worry. Now I had the problem.

I decided that so far I hadn't seen Everly mess up on anything. And he wasn't up there to be liked. If he did his job, and didn't make any more goofs than the average battalion surgeon on line for the first time, there was really nothing I could do.

Twenty

Two mornings later, on March 14th, I was sitting in my tent writing Ingrid. Ned Rohn scratched on the side of the tent and called out at the same time, "Trouble up in George Company, Doctor." He ducked his head and came in.

"I could hear it," I said as I stood up. For a couple of hours there'd been a more or less continuous rumble along the lines, not much small arms but lots of mortar and an occasional artillery round. From where our H & S Company tents were located I couldn't tell if it was George or How that was getting it.

"Dr. Everly wants you up there," he said.

I buckled on my .45. "He hasn't called me."

"No, sir. The call came from Captain Fogarty to the 5-6 tent."

Now that was strange. Not unheard of, but strange. Captain Sean Fogarty was the commanding officer of

George Company. The 5-6 tent was the tent where Lieutenant Colonel Emory McCallister (6—battalion commanding officer) and Major Ralph Selkirk (5—battalion executive officer) lived and worked.

McCallister, like most battalion COs, usually let us doctors run the aid stations. Among the many decisions, important and trivial, that we had to make continuously, were how the wounded should be evacuated (jeep ambulance, cracker-box, truck, 'copter), which corpsmen should be sent up from the rear aid station to relieve wounded or tired corpsmen on line, and not least, when the doctor on line should call for help.

"McCallister want to see me before I go?"

"No, sir."

We piled into the jeep ambulance and crawled up the tank track that Marne and I had taken when he showed me 1052. And, as before, we left the jeep when it would have been risky to go any higher, about fifty yards from the top of the ridge.

Above the sound of the engine we could hear stuff coming in all along the line, but very little was coming in on George Company as Rohn circled the jeep to point it back down hill in case we needed to get out of there in a hurry. Suddenly the incoming picked up considerably and some of it wasn't too accurate and was landing on the back side of the ridge, that is, all around us.

"Run for it," I hollered as Rohn slammed down the clutch, put the stick in reverse, shut off the engine with the toggle switch, and dived out the door.

There was no need to duck or dodge. The shells were falling randomly. Nobody was shooting at us. We weren't in the middle of a saturation pattern as if they'd seen us. We scrambled almost to the top of the ridge, still on the back side, still in defilade as if that made any difference.

I dove into a deep crater just as a round landed very close by. I waited a few seconds for Rohn to pile in on top of me. When he didn't, I knelt in the thigh-deep hole and there he was, sitting on the ground about ten feet away, holding his helmet in his hands.

"Ned," I shouted.

He just sat there, slumped forward, legs straight out in front of him, eyes open so I knew he was just stunned. He started to tip over so I crawled out and dragged him by the shoulders into the shell hole.

We scrunched down as far as we could, which was pretty good for anything except a direct hit. I no longer wondered if two rounds could land in the exact same spot. I'd seen many craters that were obviously made by two or more separate shells.

For several moments we lay like two spoons in a drawer, Ned in front of me. He rolled over and with the faintest of smiles handed me his helmet. There was a hole in the left side that I could put three fingers into. I looked up at him and he turned his head to one side. I felt his temple and found a slight scratch and a small lump.

I handed him his helmet and he put it on without another word about the incident.

"How you doing, Doctor?" he asked, "You get hit?"

"I guess not. Don't feel anything. But I don't see how I could've missed getting hit."

"Doctor, once I was carrying one end of a stretcher—over in the Punchbowl—when a round landed. The guy on the other end damn near disappeared. The patient we was carrying got killed. I stood there with the two handles of the stretcher. Didn't have a scratch. Just stood there wondering where the hell all the steel had went."

His face was covered with mud. Blood ran in a steady stream down his cheek from a ragged gash in his face.

There was another tiny fleck of blood on his neck. I pulled out my Unit-1 but put it back because I knew I couldn't do much in that crater except stop the bleeding with pressure and put on a bandage. I reached down into the pocket of my field jacket and got out a small combat dressing. With it I applied steady pressure to the wound for a few moments, then taped it in place.

"Number four, Doctor."

"Yeah. Some guys have all the luck."

"But don't put me up for another Heart."

"You earned it, Ned."

"They'd transfer me to some goddamned rear-echelon job quicker'n you could say 'Luke the Gook.'"

Then he looked at me, looked away with a strange smile that approached a leer, looked back at me and broke into an uncontrolled guffaw.

"What the hell's so damn funny?" I asked.

"You're face, Doctor, it's covered with mud. You look like Jeff Madison over in Weapons Company. Or maybe like you're gettin' one a them mud facials."

"Very funny. Maybe it'll improve my already too handsome face."

"Yeah, maybe. Sheba-shebas, watch out. But they'd never let you into an operating room that way!"

I chuckled. His grin grew wider. I laughed outright. Our grins sort of froze as a whistling flutter coming in close forced us to duck down with our faces in the mud. This was getting to be no fun. The round landed at least ten yards away but the ground shook and dirt and snow and chunks of shrapnel flew high in the air and settled to earth all around us and over us. Rohn grinned. He didn't have to say that that was a close one.

"We gotta get out a here, Doctor," he said.

"I know. I've got to get my bearings. Should've done

that before we got this far. Which way is the aid station from this hole?"

"To the right. About three bunkers down."

"All right. Go on, I'm right behind you."

Now we did duck and dodge as we crossed the ridgeline, dropped over it for twenty or thirty yards, and hit the trench line running. On hands and knees we scrambled down the line toward the aid station bunker.

The trench system of the United Nations lines extended along the entire length of the Main Line of Resistance from east to west coast. It was frequently elaborate, improved on by each successive outfit as they found time and opportunity.

James Brady, writing about Korea in *The Coldest War*, says, "The fighting was as primitive as Flanders Fields in 1917 or Grant's siege lines before Petersburg during the Civil War."

But, judging from pictures I'd seen, our trenches and bunkers were nothing like the trench systems of Europe during the First World War. Our trench was very narrow, no more than two feet wide in most places. It was only about three to four feet deep, snaking through the pine trees and along barren ridges so that a round landing in it would be limited in the area it could spray with flying steel. "Chappie," our rotund chaplain, frequently complained laughingly that there were some boys up on the line he never saw because there were places in the trenches that he couldn't squeeze through.

Along the trench, cave-like bunkers had been dug out of the side of the hills 20 to 30 feet apart. With the exception of special-use bunkers such as for ammo or supply, they were all in enfilade, that is, on the side of the hill or ridge exposed to the enemy lines.

Most of the riflemen's bunkers were about four by

eight feet and only three to four feet high. The front half was reinforced with logs and sandbags. The floor was frozen hard in the winter, soft and often muddy in the spring and fall, dusty in the summer. The opening was usually covered with a heavy burlap cloth nailed to the overhead log.

In each of these tiny caves, with little heat or light, two men lived for months at a time. Their only light was from candles. Their only heat came from fuel oil burned in a helmet liner, a tiny C-ration tin, or a #10 can cumshawed from the galley back in H & S Company. Their faces became black with dirt and from the oily soot of the fuel oil, their eyes bloodshot from the smoke.

In front of each bunker was the deep, uncovered, on-watch foxhole like Marne and I had used on his reconnaissance and like the one Al Samuels was climbing into when he was killed. Back of the trenches, over the ridge in defilade, were open foxholes dug big enough to hold a mortar crew and their weapon.

The forward aid stations, occupied by two to four corpsmen and usually one of the battalion surgeons, were considerably larger since they had to accommodate stretchers and up to a dozen men at times. But even these were usually no more than ten by fifteen feet and only four to five feet high.

The company commander's bunker was about the same size, maybe a little smaller.

The bunkers were built to withstand mortar rounds of the three sizes that the Chinese used: 60, 82, and 120 millimeters, or in inches, 2.4, 3.1, and 4.7. All were supplied by the USSR. The Soviets also supplied the Chinese with 45 millimeter and 57 millimeter anti-tank guns but I never saw those used where I was.

We were not in good tank country although a tank

column did occasionally rumble up our road to the MLR where they could be positioned to fire point blank at specific enemy targets. One time a squadron—or whatever you call a bunch of tanks—set up a hundred yards from our CP, fired a dozen salvos, then skedaddled before the Reds could retaliate, leaving us to take the pounding that followed. McCallister was livid—as angry as I've ever seen him—because we lost three men and half a dozen trucks.

Even inside the bunkers you could usually hear the bigger mortars coming, unless other noises blanked out their sounds. The sound they made was a high pitched whir, a fluttering sound, caused by the tail fins rotating at high speed, spinning like a rifle bullet or a football thrown by a rifle-armed quarterback. You could hear them coming closer and closer, and if they exploded on the roof, dust and dirt rained into the bunker. Sometimes the mortars would find a weak spot and penetrate farther, even into the bunker itself.

Inside the bunkers the warning flutter of the smaller mortars couldn't be heard, so the sudden explosion and raining sand and dirt and dust was the first indication of a direct hit or near miss.

The artillery shells were different. They were 151 millimeters, or almost six inches, in diameter. By the time they got to us in the bunkers or trenches, they whined, almost screeched through the air, terrifying in intensity. A direct hit on even the strongest bunker caused its total destruction.

That screaming whine stopped the conversation of all but the most stoic. Especially when it was obvious that this one was going to be close. The tell-tale scream kept getting closer and closer until there wasn't room in the ears for any other noise, and no room in the brain for any other thought, and we merely waited, hoping we'd hear the explosion.

This was one of the hells of the front lines.

Sitting.

Listening.

Feeling.

The air full of fluttering mortars, the screech of artillery.

The thuuu-wuuump of explosions farther down the line.

The deafening blast of explosions close by.

Knowing that the artillery shell travels faster than sound. Knowing that if you can still hear it coming, you're all right because that shell is way ahead of that awful sound. (It really is true that you never hear the round that gets you.)

Feeling fear creeping in around the edges of your consciousness, not completely blotted out by the enforced ennui of the trenches.

Feigning nonchalance, trying not to show your fear because none of the other guys seem bothered.

Knowing—hoping—that they feel just like you do and are trying to hide it from you.

Twenty-one

Well, Rohn and I weren't sitting now.

We were headed for a bunker where we could sit.

Just before we reached the forward aid bunker, a Marine came crawling out of it as fast as he could move.

He screeched to a halt. We faced each other, helmet to helmet, on hands and knees. I could read the urgency in the eyes that stared at me through the layers of dirt and soot. "Doctor Lord! Am I ever glad to see you. Two guys in a bunker next to the skipper's has got hit bad. I'm goin' down to get 'em."

I thought fast, wondering where the corpsmen and Everly were but not wanting to take the time to find out. "Get in the aid station, Ned, I'll go down the line to see these men."

"But, Doctor..."

"Get moving!"

"Sir!"

The other Marine flattened out in the trench and Ned crawled over him.

"Your name, Corporal?" I asked.

"Jerry Thorpe, sir—"

"Okay, Jerry, lead the way."

I bellied out and Thorpe crawled over me. I turned around and we went back down almost a hundred yards and came to the blasted bunker. The round—probably an 82 millimeter mortar—had landed in the trench in front of the bunker door and much of its shrapnel had penetrated the burlap.

I crawled inside. One man was dead. He lay crumpled on the frozen ground, almost totally covered with blood. He'd apparently taken the brunt of the blast. His face was a mass of blood and flesh. All four extremities lay in unnatural positions like a rag doll dropped on the floor.

The other man lay in a contorted position against the back wall. His face was black with soot as usual, and through it his bloodshot eyes were glazed with pain. He said, "Take care of Jim first, Doctor, he's the worst."

I shook my head. "Too late, Mac."

"Oh, God." His eyes closed and he squeezed them shut. When he opened them there were tears at the corners.

Real men—real Marines—don't cry? Bullshit.

I looked him over. He'd taken several fragments in his left leg, about midway down the thigh. His femur was broken, that was obvious. There was blood running down his face from a small fragment that had penetrated his cheek but that didn't look too bad.

"You hurt anywhere else, Mac? You know, stomach or chest or anywhere?

"I don't think so, Doctor."

I knew what he meant. His leg hurt so much he really

hadn't had a chance to feel pain anywhere else. But it was a good sign, because if he'd gotten a wound of any significance in his torso, he'd probably be feeling that by now.

I turned to Thorpe. "Get a splint and a stretcher, will you, Jerry?"

He scurried out.

I pulled my Unit One out of my pocket and gave the Marine a quarter of a grain of morphine sulfate.

I pulled up my pantleg, started to rip off the tape that held a 100cc bottle of serum albumin tightly to my calf, then decided to hold off on starting it till we got him down to the aid station. With the rigid steel needles we had, there was too much of a chance of losing the IV in transporting the patient down the trench line. Besides, the man's pulse was strong and only a little faster than normal.

A corpsman came back with Thorpe and together we splinted the leg and put a small temporary combat dressing on the face wound. We sat for a few moments, giving the morphine a chance to work. I filled out the EMT while we waited. The man's name was Phil Gonlag.

"Where you from, Phil?"

"Remsen, Iowa."

"Corn country."

"Yeah, Doctor."

"Looks like you'll be going back there in a little while."

A faint smile creased his soot-blackened eyelids. His blue eyes were preternaturally bright against the black background. The pupils were already beginning to contract from the morphine. "A million dollar wound, eh, Doctor?"

I nodded. The kind of wound that takes you out of combat but doesn't kill. The best kind.

The incoming was still falling but it seemed to be lessening a bit. Wishful thinking, I suppose. Like sitting in your hundred-dollar-a-day resort watching the rain sweep over the lake where you'd like to be fishing, and saying, "Hey, guys, I think it's letting up a little."

So we started out. The trench was too narrow to lock the stretcher handles in place so we dragged it, trying not to agitate it too much, moving it a few feet at a time while we repositioned ourselves to make the next move.

But then the stuff started really raining in. We pulled Gonlag into the closest bunker, crowding in with the two guys already in there. Then about ten minutes later we started out again and got another twenty yards down the ditch. We were playing a game called musical bunkers. You moved when it was relatively quiet and ducked into the closest foxhole or bunker when the fluttering or screaming music started up again.

We were still a long way from the aid bunker. Not in distance really, because a fast runner could've made it in six or seven seconds if he could've stood up and taken off on a dead run. But we couldn't. As we passed by the command bunker, I made another quick decision.

"Drag him in here," I said, and we did.

Captain Sean Fogarty looked amused as he watched me crawl in. I couldn't figure out why at the moment and didn't try.

Fogarty was the company commander, the one who'd relieved Marne of the command of George Company when Marne was promoted to major. A tough Marine. I knew he too had been in the South Pacific but I didn't know much else about his combat record. Later I found out that he'd been a reserve second lieutenant (not a career officer) at the battle for Okinawa, had gone back to civilian life after the war, then rejoined the Marines when the Korean War broke out. Another retread. They were all over the place.

He sat with his back to the dirt wall, a slab of shell packing-case on his knees, a small map on the slab. Soot covered his face, and, as with Gonlag, made his deep blue eyes even more penetrating. He'd tipped his helmet back a bit so he could rest his head against the wall without removing his helmet.

"With your permission, sir," I said.

"You got it." His eyes swung to his gunny sergeant. "Keep counting, gunny."

The sergeant was trying to count the enemy rounds falling on George Company. It was a difficult job because they came so fast and it wasn't always possible to tell if the round had fallen on George or How or Item. But it was better than no count, I guess. And would provide ammunition for the persistent requests to eliminate The Gook's Castle.

Ned Rohn came crawling in, his hands and forearms smeared with drying blood.

"Not again!" I said.

He laughed. "No, sir. This ain't mine. Been helping in the aid station. Thought I better find you, case you wanted to leave."

"Not yet."

There was another man back in the corner of the large bunker. I didn't realize it for a while because I was busy with Gonlag, and the man sat with his head bowed, his helmet covering his upper face.

But then I sat back, having done all I could.

"Hello, Jack," the man said.

Twenty-two

It was Everly. Now I knew why Fogarty had smiled when I came in.

"What the hell...?"

I didn't get any further. There wasn't any need to. Everly had chickened out. Had taken refuge in the strongest bunker in this section of the trench system. He was useless.

I knew now why the call to H & S had gone to McCallister instead of me. Everly hadn't made the call. It had been Fogarty or his gunny and he'd felt more comfortable calling the 5-6 tent rather than me. I would have had too many awkward questions.

I crawled over to him on my hands and knees and sat beside him. He wasn't really panicked. Wasn't ready for an NP evac, nothing like that. He'd just made the conscious decision that he wasn't going out in the rain. A guy could get wet out there.

A tough battalion CO with a bit of the old gung ho

attitude could have made a good case for a court martial. But it was clear that Fogarty didn't intend to notify Colonel McCallister. I certainly wouldn't unless there was no alternative.

There was no need for a lecture. Who was I to do that anyway? We talked a bit about the number of casualties we'd taken so far. He seemed to have that pretty well in mind. There were three other KIAs besides the man who'd been in the bunker with Gonlag.

I decided to shake him up a little. Maybe that would help. "Ronald," I said, "all you got to remember is that these are the Golden Days."

He looked at me with a mixture of disgust and alarm. "You're over the hill."

"Just think a minute. What's past is past. Can't do anything about it. What's coming is coming and we can't do a thing about that either…"

His laugh was short, harsh and raspy. Fogarty looked over at us and turned away. Everly said, "So you're Hamlet and I'm Horatio."

It was my turn to laugh. I'd caught the reference and Everly looked surprised as I quoted, "If it be now, 'tis not to come. If it be not to come, it will be now. If it be not now, yet will it come."

His smile was tentative, but it was there, and I was hopeful. He said, "So there's more culture west of the Appalachians than we thought." His smile faded but the lost look was gone, replaced by a simple, trusting, wide-eyed stare. "We live in the present? Only the present? That what you mean?"

I had the weird feeling that I was George talking to Lenny in Steinbeck's *Of Mice and Men.* ("Tell me about the rabbits, George.")

I poked him lightly on the arm, and said softly, "Yeah,

you rum-dum, that's exactly what I mean. These days, right now, are all we've got. Which makes them by definition the Golden Days."

He didn't say anything, but he was thinking, I had to give him credit for that. I was thinking, too. Thinking that there are two days in the week that we should never worry about: yesterday and tomorrow.

Yesterday is gone, with all its faults and blunders, its mistakes and cares, its aches and pains.

Tomorrow hasn't come yet, with its possible adversaries, its burdens, its large promises and poor performances.

A man breaks down when he forgets that he can fight the battles of just one day at a time. It's not the experiences of today that drive men mad. It's the remorse for something that happened yesterday and the dread of what's coming tomorrow that does that. I wanted to say all that to Everly but it would've been too much, too preachy, and he would've known it and resented it.

So when the bombardment really let up, and Rohn and I could get out of there, Everly had gotten a brighter look in his eye. And I had to give him credit for that, too. But could I leave him up there? Was his credibility with the troops and the corpsmen destroyed to the point that they wouldn't do what he told them? You have to command respect in order to command.

Well, I left him up there. What else could I do except maybe send him back to rear aid and stay myself? Or take him with me and leave the front without a doctor in that sector.

As Rohn and I scrambled out of the trenches, Everly was directing the evacuation of Gonlag and the other WIAs. Gonlag's buddy and the three other KIAs could wait. There was no hurry. They weren't in a hurry.

I was pretty sure that Everly would be all right. As Rohn and I ambled down the backside of the ridge to the jeep ambulance, I said, "What do you think, Ned?" I knew he'd heard the entire conversation in the bunker.

"About Dr. Everly?"

"Yeah.

"He'll be okay now." We sat in the jeep waiting for the corpsmen to bring two of the evacs for us to take to Rear Aid.

Rohn turned back to me, that lop-sided grin widely askew. "Ya shoulda been a shrink, Doctor!"

I cracked his helmet with my knuckles and he yelled, "Ow!"

I sat back and laughed. "You say that so anyone else can hear and I will put you up for another Purple Heart."

He touched the olive drab bandage on his cheek. "Almost forgot about that, Doctor. Will it need stitches?"

"A few. In four or five days, if it looks okay. I'll see if I can get the shrapnel out when we get back to H & S."

"Hope this's the last one."

It wasn't.

Twenty-three

We had a battalion briefing each evening in the 5-6 tent. On that night, March 14th, I was a little late. The artillery liaison officer from the 11th Marines was concluding his report as I came in and sat down on the dirt floor.

"...and 644 rounds of mixed 82 and 120 millimeter mortar on our Third Battalion." He finished up and sat down on the ground beside me.

Everyone sat on the ground except the CO and the Exec.

They sat on canvas camp chairs behind a rough makeshift table which was buried beneath quadrangle maps, protractors, colored pencils, celluloid overlays, a battered Royal portable typewriter, and other tools of the warrior's trade. A white-gas Coleman lantern hung from a nail on one side of the tent's center-pole, a Double-E 8 field phone from a nail on the other side. A glowing pot-bellied stove stood in the center, its black pipe exiting through an asbestos-lined metal cap about twelve feet up at the peak of the 16x16 pyramidal tent. The air was already blue with smoke from a dozen cigarettes and Bob Runninger's pipe.

Two canvas cots stood against one wall of the tent, each with a neatly rolled-up mummy bag on top and a closed-up seabag underneath. Unless I was on the move, I never rolled up my sleeping bag and I never closed up my seabag, a fact I laid to the difference between a professional Marine and a civilian doctor dressed up to resemble a Marine.

"Air?" said the Exec, Major Selkirk.

Captain Alec Stanfield, the air liaison officer who had sung the duet with Butch back in Camp Tripoli, mumbled from the rear, "Nothing to report tonight, sir."

"Nothing to report?" howled McCallister, his rough smoker's voice loud with outrage, his eyes blazing. "When the hell we gonna get that air strike on those artillery positions backa the Gook's Castle?"

Stanfield pulled himself heavily to his feet. I knew he'd been drinking all day in his tent and wondered if the colonel had detected it yet. Alec's voice was calm and collected as he spoke. "But sir, I've explained to the colonel that I've requested air on those coordinates three times and…"

"Did you tell 'em we know where the guns are and that our own artillery can't hit 'em?"

"Yes, sir!"

McCallister growled and then as he asked the next question his voice rose gradually in pitch until it was half an octave higher than normal.

"And did you tell 'em we can't even build new bunkers and repair damaged ones in George Company because every time the boys climb out of their holes they get clobbered? Did you?"

"Yes, sir!"

"And what'd they say?"

"That by their calculations artillery could reach them."

The colonel's face was livid. "So now air is telling artillery what they can hit?" He slammed the flat of his hand on the table, jutted his chin out, and roared, "You put in another request for an air strike on those same coordinates!"

"But, sir…"

I groaned and thought, come on, Alex, just say "Yes, sir" one more time and be done with it. I knew that if he'd been sober he would have. It's a funny thing about these fly-boys. Almost to a man they're such nice guys that they won't turn down a drink from anybody.

In a way I couldn't blame them. After all, they were fly-boys. They hadn't joined the Marine Air Corps to rot in a hole up on the OPLR. But then, I hadn't gone to med school with the express purpose of going to a front line Marine battalion in the Fleet Marine Force in Korea.

McCallister slumped back in his chair with a dismissing wave of his hand and Selkirk continued the briefing. When it was Marne's turn he stood up. Before he could speak, Colonel McCallister used his prerogative and took over from Selkirk.

"Well, Major, how ya gonna do it?"

I smiled inwardly. This had been going on for a week, the CO asking Marne the same question every night at the battalion briefings.

The colonel wanted to send a platoon-sized raiding party—about fifty men counting corpsmen and officers—right up the front of the hill below The Rock, then split into two parts, surround The Rock, and hold there until a company-sized assault group—about 150 men—could join them and take The Rock by brute strength. It was an elementary one-two punch that might succeed but would be costly in casualties.

He could have just given the order, and might have done so if the situation were an emergency and there was no time to consider alternatives. But there was time and McCallister was giving Marne the chance to come up with another strategy.

Marne did have one partly worked out. In an earlier session he'd said, "Colonel, if I can figure out a way to get a couple squads or maybe a platoon onto the backside of the Castle, we could save one hell of a lot of casualties."

The colonel had said, "Okay, Major, we'll attack 'em from the rear then. But how we gonna do it?"

This was the question that had just been put to Marne again. He had to say simply, "I still don't know, Colonel."

I'd heard him talking to Major Selkirk just that afternoon. "Maybe we could slip men through the lines one by one and regroup behind The Rock. Maybe we could parachute in a platoon or two. Or maybe we could go down the river in small boats starting from a point well northeast of The Rock. Or maybe..." Then he shook his head and the Exec had agreed that none of these plans were feasible. They'd worried the bone a bit more but had discarded the solutions almost as fast as they thought of them.

Now in the silence that followed Marne's admission, the colonel said softly in his gruff but commanding voice, "We can't wait much longer, Major."

As Marne sat down, there was a rustling behind me and Alec Stanfield got to his feet. He spoke with the exaggerated care of an alcoholic trying to sound normal. "Excuse me, sir, may I make a suggestion?"

With a deep sigh that failed to fluster Stanfield, the colonel said, "Go ahead, Captain."

"Thank you, sir. I'm not entirely familiar with this particular tactical situation…"

In his condition he shouldn't have tried those last three words. They came out in a slurred jumble and McCallister's face froze in hard lines.

Ignoring McCallister, Stanfield continued, "…nor with the exact nature of this mission, except that it's become obvious that you want to smoke the gooks out the Castle. I was wondering. Would it be feasible to use air in any way?"

Selkirk barked, "What ya gonna do, Stanfield, parachute in from an L-19?"

The L-19 is a small, usually yellow, single-engine observation aircraft that we often saw zipping over the enemy lines just a few hundred feet off the ground.

But the air officer continued, apparently oblivious to the concern on Marne's face and the growing anger on the colonel's. "I was thinking that maybe you could take a platoon in behind that damned Rock by helicopter."

The idea dropped into the tent, hung there for what seemed like minutes, then began to glow like an overheated pot-bellied stove.

By helicopter! I looked over at Marne. The simplicity of the solution had immediately caught his imagination. I could almost hear the wheels turning in his brain and knew he was already formulating a plan in his mind. I wasn't at all surprised that he had it ready by the time the room began to hum after its initial stunned silence. He stood up and motioned Stanfield down.

"Colonel," he said, his pent-up frustration giving his words a machine-gun-like staccato, "we could take enough men—a reinforced platoon—in eight Sikorskis—and secure the rear of The Rock. G-2's got air photos of that whole area. I've seen 'em. We could easily pick out eight places large enough to land the 'copters in. The gooks are used to hearing 'copters over our lines at all times of the day and night so they wouldn't get alarmed until the 'copters were almost completely landed. I think it'd work!"

The colonel didn't seem to share Marne's enthusiasm. "It isn't quite as simple as all that, Marne," he said. "For one thing those 'copters are division vehicles. Clearance'd have to be gotten from General Seldon himself."

He stopped talking, drumming his fingers on the table. Selkirk looked back and forth between McCallister and Marne. McCallister was thinking about it, sorting it out, while we sat tensely. I think we were all caught up in the idea the way you are when something really new and exciting is propounded for the first time.

Then the colonel shook his head slowly from side to side. "No good. Just think of the risk involved. Eight Sikorskis, sixteen pilots, eight radiomen, attempting to land behind enemy lines, discharge forty-four Marines and four corpsmen, and take off again before they got shot down." He shook his head again and his eyes bored into Marne's. "D'ya think the general staff would buy that? Negative! They wouldn't risk that many pilots and 'copters."

"Look, Colonel," Marne said, "Let's look at it this way. How many boys do we lose every day because those gooks sit up on that Rock and watch everything that goes on along a four company sector of our lines?" He turned to look at Stanfield. "With all due respect to Captain Stanfield, I'd like to point out that a human life is a human life, whether it's a dirt-crunching Marine or a pilot."

There was a murmuring all around me and a nodding of heads in agreement. Almost all of those officers had had front line experience here in Korea or in the Pacific.

They knew what it was like. So I smiled to myself. It was Sergeant York talking all over again. Kill the killers to keep your buddies from getting killed.

The colonel didn't hide his smile. I liked him for that. "Marne," he said, "you're an idealist." And he didn't say it in a pejorative way like most Marine colonels would have done. "But speaking practically—and tactically—a pilot's life is worth more to the Marine Corps than that of an infantry Marine's. Now don't get all riled up. Ya been in the Corps a long time. Fourteen years, isn't it? Ya should've had that soaked in by now."

"Okay," Marne said, "if we're going to look at it that way, let's be *real* practical about it. Let's figure out how many boys we can allow to get killed before we risk a pilot's neck. How many crunchies do you figure equal a pilot, Colonel?" Marne sat down, his face suffused with dark blood.

This was hardly the tone of voice calculated to win favor with a commanding officer. The faces of the other officers in the tent mirrored their concern for Marne, but McCallister let the remarks pass as if he hadn't heard them. It was evident that the colonel understood that it was Marne's feeling of responsibility to his men that had made him rash. I was beginning to like this tough old Marine. More, I was beginning to respect him.

How many times had I heard this line of reasoning? Well, maybe they were right. Who knows? Any one part of war in itself cannot be explained in terms of right and wrong, because it's all wrong. You have to be a Sergeant York and figure out the best way to kill the most enemy troops while you have the least number of friendly troops killed.

So, well, maybe the colonel was right.

But he himself hadn't given up on the 'copter idea,

despite what he'd said to Marne. Now I heard him say, "Well, I suppose it wouldn't hurt to run this by the general. All he can say is 'no.' Who's next, Selkirk?"

"Doc?" Major Selkirk said to me.

I stood up and started giving the totals of KIAs and WIAs for the previous twenty-four hours. I glanced out of the corner of my eye and saw that Marne was lost in thought, and I believed I knew just what those thoughts were: "Eight copters, with six combat-ready Marines to a 'copter..."

Twenty-four

Late that night I walked up to Marne's tent to borrow an Air Form to write Ingrid. He poured me a cup of black coffee from the battered canteen cup on the pot-belly, then suggested I stick around a while because he expected to hear from McCallister any minute.

We were sitting side by side on his cot writing letters to our wives when the field phone rang. Marne reached across to where it hung on the center pole of the tent, pushed the butterfly, and said, "Major Marne."

I could hear the colonel's voice booming over the wire as Marne held the earpiece well away from his ear. "Marne? McCallister. The division CG not only approved of your wild scheme, he said he'd help us out in any way he could. Said this was a new dimension in warfare and he wanted to be a part of it. Anyway, I explained that we had everything except the copters and pilots. He said he'd get right to work on it. So, Marne, listen. Get together with the S-2 and the S-4 and work out a detailed plan for getting your platoon from battalion CP to the back of The Rock and bring it up to me for approval."

"Aye, aye, sir!" Marne sat there for a moment, then shoved the phone down into the stiff canvas box, hung the box on the center pole and turned to me, his eyes shining triumphantly.

Twenty-five

Inhabited villages were all around us. One, Ku-dong, actually lay in No-man's Land down in the valley between the Chinese and UN lines. Others were scattered through the mountains back of the lines. Korean Army officers went regularly to the villages to order them evacuated. Reluctantly the people would climb into the back of the trucks with battered suitcases or blanket rolls. For a few weeks the villages would stand empty. Then the villagers would inevitably straggle back. Some of the elderly peasants could not be budged without literally carrying them away; rightly or wrongly they were usually left alone.

The problem was that North Korean and Chinese sympathizers often lived in the villages, sending a steady flow of information to the enemy which resulted in pinpoint shelling, disruption of communications at crucial moments, mining of roads and paths, and many other acts of sabotage. The children, moving from camp to camp with hands outstretched for candy, became the unwitting tools of their parents, taking advantage of the Americans' natural love for kids.

Friends by day and enemies by night.

In short, the villages were a constant danger to us.

Periodically the Korean government would ask our S-2 to check out the villages and evacuate them. Our S-2 was Captain Bill Wright, a stocky, crew-cut, leathernecked veteran of the South Pacific. He would send a squad into the villages nearby to search for "guerrillas," which is really what they were, irregulars fighting against the regular forces of the United Nations.

With the assault on The Rock imminent, Colonel McCallister exercised his own prerogative as military commander of the area and ordered Wright to sweep the entire Third Battalion area clear of guerrillas, in front of the lines and behind them.

One of the first things Wright did was to clear out all the "houseboys" and men of the Korean Service Corps.

The KSCs were mostly men too old to join the army but fit enough to carry loads and perform other menial tasks around camp. Without meaning disrespect we called them "Eetiwahs," which actually is a Korean command to an inferior or a child meaning, "Come here." Our troops had heard Korean officers calling to the men, "Eetiwah," and assumed that that was their "collective" name.

Almost every tent in the CP had a Korean lad to do the laundry, keep the pot-belly's fuel oil barrel full, and help with all the other household chores. Butch was our boy. We couldn't pay him anything because we had only military script and Koreans by law were unable to accept or spend it. But he got his food and clothes and a warm place to sleep.

Wright rounded them all up with the help of the CIC and transported them back to the regimental stockade. Poor Butch. He didn't even have time to get his sleeping bag or Korean hymnal or anything. I figured I'd never see him again.

Two nights before the battalion briefing in which Stanfield came up with his helicopter assault plan, Wright had taken a reinforced squad from Item Company down onto the north slope of Hill 751, out in front of Item's MLR, to clear out a small unnamed village and then a half mile north to Ku-dong, a larger village out in front of George Company. (I was to become all too familiar with Ku-dong. With apologies for the pun, the name still rings a very loud bell in my mind.)

When they came back through George Company's lines about dawn, Wright woke me up to examine the Koreans to see if they needed treatment for anything. There were only seven, all from Ku-dong. The unnamed village had proven to be uninhabited. Not a very suspicious lot: an old papa-san and his wife, three youngsters in their teens, a baby in the arms of its mother.

They were all healthy though thin. I wondered what a stool specimen would show. Probably ascaris and maybe hookworm. But we weren't set up to diagnose tropical diseases, much less treat them.

They chattered happily in Korean to Wright. He grinned and motioned toward Lee Yung-kak, our interpreter, who listened for a while and then said to me, "They are thank you taksan for finding what sick they have and you will please give medicine now so they can go back to village."

I smiled wryly and said, "You can answer that one for me, Lee."

I watched the happy faces turn slowly sad as they

realized that they were being moved, not treated.

That night Wright had pulled an entire platoon out of George Company under cover of darkness, waited till it was light, then slogged through the melting snow back from the lines to the village of Sohuigu. This somewhat larger village lay at the junction of the Kanmu-gang—our own little stream where we got water for washing clothes—and the Soyang-gang, a tributary of the Nam-gang where all our major encampments lay.

There was no trouble at Sohuigu. With Lee Yung-kak translating, Wright carefully explained to the Koreans living there that their own government had ordered this sweep. It was a bit of a white lie, but it went over all right. They piled into trucks and were sent directly to our Regimental Headquarters for examination and transport to either a place of their choice or to one of the white-tented refugee camps scattered all over South Korea.

There was just one more village in our immediate vicinity, Puho-dong. It lay well behind our lines almost straight east of George Company, down in the valley near a little unnamed trickle of a stream. Lee Yung-kak told Wright about the situation the afternoon after the battalion briefing as we sat in the sunshine outside the Aid Station. "Are forty people down in there that village, about maybe, captain. Men, women and children. We not know if are any enemy agents. Maybe about none. Two sheba-shebas, maybe."

As Battalion Surgeon I had no responsibility for these raids except to ask Chief Hoffman to assign a corpsman to the squad. But as an excuse to get away from Mercy Row and stretch my legs a bit, I decided to go along on the patrol. Captain Wright assured me that no action was anticipated on this particular sweep.

The squad leader, acting under Wright's command,

was Sergeant Harold Rainey, pulled out of George Company for training with the troops that would go in the helicopters to the back of The Rock. He'd been a buck private in the last year of the Second World War. Like Bob Marne, he'd made the landing on Guam in July of 1944. He'd taken two machine gun bullets through his left thigh, was patched up down in New Guinea, then sent back to Guam to wait for the final push into the home islands of Japan, which fortunately never came off. He was now about 27, along with me one of the old men of the battalion. He was tall and lean, still pale-faced from a winter in the bunkers on the front lines, but starting to sunburn a little now that he was back in the H & S area.

At two in the afternoon the file of ten Marines—Wright, Rainey, and two rifle teams—strode swiftly down the road out of H & S Company, then wound up a path into the hills to the east. There was no road up to Puho-dong. I could see where jeeps and even trucks could probably make it if they had to. But the village was within walking distance.

At first we followed a trail along a little stream which could have been any trail along any mountain stream in the USA. We could have been going on a picnic. But the stream was the Soyang-gang, the mountains were in Korea, the picnickers were all men who carried M-l rifles and hand grenades instead of fishing poles, C-rations instead of lunch baskets.

The trail serpentined across terraced rice paddies, brown still and frozen hard, though the snow was getting soft in the mid-March sun. In one place we passed a completely frozen waterfall, about the size of the Lower Falls of the Yellowstone. I wanted to stop and admire it, maybe even climb over the rocks to it and get a closer look, but there was no time nor would it have been safe because of buried mines.

Wright, Rainey and interpreter Lee Yung-kak led the column. I brought up the rear and found myself walking just behind Corporal Jerry Thorpe, the young Marine I'd literally run into in the trenches when I went up to George Company with Rohn to help Everly.

The day was sunny and warmer than usual for mid-March. In the hills, magpies called raucously and cackling cock pheasants darted through the leafless azalea bushes. A rooster took off flying and Thorpe raised an imaginary shotgun and followed him. "Pow," he barked. "Nailed him."

"Nice shot," I said. "We'll have him for supper."

"Don't I wish," he said.

"You from pheasant country, Jerry?"

"Naw. City kid. Philadelphia. Oh, I guess there's pheasants out in the country some places. But I never got out there."

"Maybe when you get back."

"Yeah, Doctor, maybe. There's gonna be a lot of changes in my life when I get back. One thing, I'm goin' back to school. I didn't never graduate from high school."

"How'd that happen?" I asked, more than a little surprised. People just didn't do that anymore, did they?

He laughed, a pleasant, controlled rumble in his chest. "Improper motivation the school psychologist said. Wanted to start making some money, you know, right now, not next year. Had a girl. Had a wreck for wheels. Both needed a lot of money to keep going. More'n I could make at part-time jobs."

The column stopped for a moment as Lee and Wright discussed the choice of routes to the village. I scraped the snow off the path with my boot and sat down cross-legged. Thorpe turned around and did likewise. We didn't dare move off the trail because of land mines. The trail itself was swept often enough that it was unlikely to be dangerous. But I remembered all too well when Jeff Madison of Weapons Company had blown off his right buttocks when he was on one of these anti-guerrilla patrols. He'd sat down just five feet off the path.

I said to Thorpe, "You've been picked for the helicopter assault, I guess."

"Yeah, Doctor, or I wouldn't be back here sittin' in the sun talkin' to you. But I wasn't picked. Volunteered."

"Why'd you do that?"

"All the 'copter assault grunts are volunteers. 'Cause of Sergeant Rainey, I guess, for me. He's some Marine. Tough as nails, but human, too. When I heard he was senior non-com on this mission, I just raised my hand, too. Now I'm kinda wishin' I hadn't."

"Why d'ya say that?"

He shoved the buttplate of his M-l into the snow and leaned against the side of the barrel. "Looks like a goddamn fool stunt to me. Stupid, in fact."

I laughed. "Better not let Rainey or Major Marne hear you say that."

"They've already heard me. Rainey has, anyway, and he prob'ly told the major. Rainey and I're in the same tent. One day I was mouthin' off to some of the other guys when Rainey come in. Told me to shut up. I told him I was gettin' a bad feeling about the whole deal, you know, takin' that Rock that we both knew would've been bypassed in a real war."

"What'd he say then?"

"Told me to shut up again and what did I think this was if it wasn't a real war. Told me we had to have some confidence in the guys that run this show. Huh, I laughed in his face at that one."

But he had a smile on his face that belied his words.

I was getting to like this young fellow. For a corporal in the Marine Corps he was thinking for himself a little too much, but that wasn't all bad. Especially if he didn't stay in the Corps all his life.

He went on for a while about the difficulties in taking The Rock back from the Chinese. "You know, Doctor, I've stood in the watch hole and seen our Corsairs dropping 500 pounders and strafing with fifties on that Rock and they don't never seem to do more'n if I was to shoot at it with a BB gun."

"Yeah," I said, "I've seen it myself."

"And just this morning Major Marne was telling us that we'll be outnumbered about four to one until they move How and Item up."

"But you still volunteered for this mission."

"Yeah, Doctor. Dumb, dumb, dumb." But there was a twinkle in his eye.

Strange. One of the oddities of this conflict. Maybe of all conflicts, I don't know. They asked, why take this hill? Why take any hill? What good would it do? Who cares? Then they stepped forward a pace when their sergeant asked who'd like an extra week of R & R and all they had to do to earn it was to volunteer for a hazardous mission.

Twenty-six

The confab up front was over and we started out again along the trail. I could look back now and see the H & S Company in the valley behind us. It could have been a Boy Scout camp, it looked so peaceful down there. Then I raised my eyes a bit and there was the tip of Luke the Gook's Castle. I wondered if anyone was watching our patrol, and if they were, would they start shelling us? We were definitely in mortar range, though pretty far out for real accuracy. When I looked back at our tents in the valley they didn't look like Scout tents at all.

A hundred yards from the summit of the next hill Sergeant Rainey turned and motioned his squad in to form a semicircle around him. I followed and stood outside the ring.

He spoke softly but with intensity. "You'll see the rooftops of the village from the top of this hill. All we're supposed to do is order them out and see that they go. Right, Captain?"

"Right, Sergeant." Wright pointed his finger at Lee and swept his hand upwards. "Go take a look, Yung Kak." Lee trotted up the hill, leaping agilely from paddy to paddy. He was a little guy like most Koreans and his over-large Marine uniform flapped as he ran. He was unarmed and held his helmet in place with one hand and balanced with the other.

He slowed as he neared the summit, peered over, and after a few moments motioned for us to follow.

Below us, about fifty yards away, were five square houses, all but one framed up with wood, plastered on the outside with cracking mud, roofed with plaited straw, and arranged in a circle around the courtyard. It was odd to see intact houses this close to the front lines. Most had been destroyed by artillery, mortar and fires. These looked deserted. Lee had said they weren't.

"Tell 'em to all come out," Rainey said.

Lee cupped his mouth with both hands and called out in Korean, "All you people in there come out so we can talk to you."

No response for several moments.

Then about a dozen women and children sidled out and stood silently in the courtyard. They were a colorful but very unhappy-looking group of people.

The women were dressed in baggy trousers and quilted blouses. Several wore an apron-like skirt that billowed in the wind like a Dutch girl's. Those carrying children on their backs held them there with brightly colored wrap-around blankets tied in front above their breasts.

Two older women wore loose white cover-alls. All the women wore terry-cloth headscarves which crossed their foreheads and tied in back under their hair.

The little girls wore knee-length, colored skirts over

dark baggy trousers. Most of the little girls wore brightly colored jackets of reds, yellows, purples, and greens, very striking against their dark skin. Two of the girls carried babies on their backs. The little boys wore brown or black wool pants and jackets. All wore rubber slippers on bare feet.

There were no men at all.

Rainey said, "Ask them if there are any more inside."

Lee complied. "They say 'no more.'"

"Tell them we're going to search their houses."

When Lee translated this, one of the women spoke quickly and loudly and another dozen people came out.

Still no men.

"That all of them, you think, Lee?"

"No, Sergeant. Not if we got right news. Many more in the houses, maybe. Some are hiding. Something is maybe not O.K. here."

"You damn betcha there's something not O.K. here." Rainey hooked his thumbs in his webbed belt and pondered for a moment. He seemed to make up his mind, nodded his head sharply, but looked to Wright for confirmation. Wright said, "Do it."

Rainey said to his squad, "Murphy, take your rifle team. Rout 'em out. Search each house room by room." He looked at Wright for confirmation again. Wright nodded. Rainey said, "Shove off."

Wright said to me, "Bug out, Doctor. Get back a ways, down below the ridgeline. And don't try to be a hero. Sorry, but I didn't know we'd have any problems here."

I grudgingly obeyed and backed off a few yards where I could lie down on my stomach and watch what happened.

One rifle team scrambled down the slope with Rainey and Lee a few yards behind. Jerry Thorpe's team stayed on the hilltop with me, spread out in a line about five yards apart.

The women down below us stood stoically, unemotionally, watching the six men approaching. Several children stared up at their mothers with wide black eyes. One little girl was on the verge of tears and clung tenaciously to her mother's legs.

The Marines, one with a Browning Automatic Rifle, three with M-1s, walked abreast to the first house. It was the largest of the five, the lower three feet of its walls built with fieldstones, the upper half with wood and mud plaster.

Big, flat stepping stones lay around all four sides of the house and on the path to it from the paddies. Huge stacks of split fire wood and barrel-sized bundles of twigs were stacked around the front. Behind it was a row of three-foot-high black pots used to collect the "honey" before the war came through here. Maybe they still used them: there were no outhouses.

Lee and Rainey stayed in the courtyard as the rifle team slid the paper door aside. I could hear their combat boots clomping on the plank floors.

"No one here, Sarge," one called.

They went on to the next, a mud-floored house with only three rooms. I could sense the increasing uneasiness of the Koreans standing in the open courtyard in the circle of houses, the women restless, the children staring open-mouthed. Rainey stood tensely, body rigid, head thrust forward, right hand resting on the open holster of his .45, index finger playing with the leather strap that held the weapon in place.

That house was also empty.

As the Marines entered the next house, there was a sudden pounding of feet as two young Korean men dashed out the back and across the rice paddies. As if triggered by the running men, a dozen people poured out of the other two houses and started running wildly in all directions.

The Marines shouted, "Halt, stop, come back, we'll shoot." Lee called loudly in Korean, presumably the same instructions for I heard mixed with the stream of words the command, "*Etio sipsio*," meaning, "Come here, please."

Rainey shouted, "Fire over their heads." A volley of bullets followed the fleeing figures.

Pandemonium. The youngsters in the courtyard were terrified and ran in erratic circles, screeching, crying, sobbing, their mothers trying to catch them. An older woman—a grandmotherly type—called out sharply and the whole lot of them went screaming and yelling after the first group.

I heard no order from anyone, but one must have been given, for both rifle teams began firing into the tumbling mass of Koreans leaping from terrace to terrace down the hillside. The first two men were now nearly a hundred yards away, but one dropped and lay still. Others closer to us fell and rolled moaning on the ground. And to my horror, two women fell: the old woman who had given the order to run, and a young mother holding onto the hand of her eczema-covered four year old.

I did hear an order then.

"Cease fire."

But the firing had already stopped, the Koreans no longer running but standing terrified, or kneeling over a fallen form. There were twenty people on the ground, bloody, and in grotesque positions. Several lay very still.

The old woman was dead.

The child's mother was dead and the little one lay

beside her. As I came running up, the child recoiled from me and with terror in her eyes ran screaming down the hill to be picked up by another woman.

"God in heaven," I thought, "this is senseless." Through my thoughts I could hear Rainey ordering two Marines to run back to battalion headquarters to get transport. The rest stood uncomfortably as I did what I could, which wasn't much. We had no bandages, no morphine, no splints, no stretchers.

Eight people were dead. Another thirteen wounded lay in the snow and softening mud of the warm March day. Two of the wounded had broken legs. All I could do was arrange their limbs in a position of maximum comfort. Three others had abdominal wounds and I couldn't help them in any way.

One young woman lay doubled up on her side, both hands clutching her belly. With wide, frightened eyes, she looked at me and whispered through clenched teeth, "*Salyo chu sio*—Please help me."

"*Etio sipsio*, Lee," I called and he came running over to me with a look on his face which I found difficult to interpret. "Talk to these people, Lee. Tell them we'll help them. Tell them we've sent for stretchers, and will get them to a hospital as quickly as possible. And Lee—tell them we're sorry."

I thought I saw Lee's eyes soften for just a fraction of a second and from that moment on there was a bond between the Korean and me.

Meanwhile the first fire team had rounded up the now subdued Koreans. Jerry Thorpe's team resumed the house-to-house search. From the door of one house, Thorpe called to me, "Doctor, c'mere a sec, will ya?"

I heaved to my feet, ran back up the hill, and pushed through the narrow door into a dimly lighted room. A large wooden machine, broken into several pieces, stood in one corner. It was apparently used to spin flax into twine. Dozens of balls of twine lay scattered around the room amidst piles of light cottony flax pods looking like white cocoons.

When my eyes accommodated I clumped into the back room where Jerry was beckoning. He was kneeling beside an old woman who sat on a straw mat in the corner. His hand was on hers, his eyes looking into hers with an emotion I can only describe as compassion. Beside her was a white-haired, white-goateed man, his eyelids heavy, his baggy pantaloons and rubber slippers failing to hide the gross swelling of his feet and legs. Neither appeared afraid. The man actually looked defiant.

"Get Lee," I said softly to Thorpe. Under Lee's courteous questioning, several facts came out. The man and woman were married and had lived in that house all their married lives. He was 82, she 73. Several of the others were their children and grandchildren, but most were people whose origins were unknown to the old couple.

Were any from North Korea? "We do not know. Perhaps. It is all the same to us old folks. We do not ask that kind question of homeless and hungry people."

Where did they get their food? "The girls and children provide for all of our needs." I thought I knew how at least some of the girls—the "sheba-shebas"—made their money.

Outside I could hear the jeep ambulance and two trucks arriving and recognized the voices of Jim Jepson, Rick Simpson and Chief Hoffman. I left Lee with the old couple and went out to supervise the transfer of the wounded. The unwounded Koreans were herded into one truck which would take them to the refugee stockade at regimental headquarters for interrogation. From there they would be allowed to go to relatives in the non-militarized zones or to one of the refugee camps.

Chief Hoffman was helping Jepson lift the body of the young mother onto a stretcher. I called to him, "Chief, get two more stretchers up here, will you?"

"Aye, aye, sir," he answered, then with a puzzled look he asked, "You got more wounded up there, Doctor?"

"Just a couple people who can't walk."

Two corpsmen and two Marines came up with two stretchers and carried out the old man and woman. Mama-san upright on the stretcher, her weeping red eyes turned back over her shoulder to make sure that papa-san was coming.

Jerry Thorpe sat on his heels, watching. He looked up at me. "I guess this is part of war, too, ain't it, Doctor?"

I nodded. "Whether we like it or not."

I didn't ask him if he'd done any shooting, and, if he had, whether he'd hit anyone. I didn't want to know.

I could point my finger at no one that day, neither at those who had fired the shots nor at those who were gunned down. It seemed very likely that some of these people *were* enemy agents, else why should they have tried to get away? Or were they just panicked by the presence of armed Marines and startled into running by the screech of the old grandmother?

Who was guilty? The North Koreans? The Americans? Chinese? The South Koreans?

All of the above?

Captain Wright stood on top of a partly underground vegetable cellar watching the last of the wounded being carried down to the trucks. Had he ordered the shooting? Very likely. What were his thoughts now? I hesitated to guess.

Some day I'd ask, I thought.

Maybe when my own thoughts were clearer and the sticky red stuff was off my hands and the sounds of war were gone.

But when that all came to pass, would I still want to know?

I think that even then I was aware of the answer to that question. No, I didn't want to know. Like Marne, like York, like a few million others, I preferred to argue that a war had to be won, that all war is wrong and you can't pin the blame nor point the accusing finger at any one side or any one man.

Twenty-seven

I hitched a ride on the last truck to leave Puho-dong with a load of unwounded Koreans. The driver slowed to a crawl as we came into the H & S Company area and I hopped off.

The deepening shadows of evening climbed up the eastern slopes, turning the red-brown of last fall's oak leaves a deeper red, and the green of the new spring a darker green. Earth shone like bronze where the snow had melted or had been worn away by boots or tires. The darkening blue of the sky promised a cold and starry night.

Its raucous call jarringly out of place in the evening's idyll, a magpie glided swiftly down into the brush, its black and white feathers ruffling slightly in the breeze. Behind it and high-lighting it, an orange sun returned to its home in the Yellow Sea.

I trudged up the path from the road to the ledge where

the Mercy Row tents perched. Beyond the Row I could see Bob Marne standing in his doorway, his lean face looking tired and strained in the half-light of the falling darkness. With a wave of his hand he beckoned to me and stepped back in to his tent. I threw my helmet and .45 onto my cot and went up.

The March breeze was chilling at this time of night so as I entered he pulled the door flaps together and tied them at the top and in the middle to keep the wind out and the light in. Stooping down to the stove in the center of the tent, he turned the regulator up to nine, opened the lid to make sure the fuel was running in, waited a few seconds and then threw in a burning match. With a slight "poof" and a glow of flame the stove began to crackle as its metal expanded with the heat. Seating himself on a water can, Marne held his hands over the stove. "I'll never complain of hot weather again," he said with a rueful smile. "I feel like I could never get too warm even if I lived in the tropics the rest of my life!"

I laughed in commiseration and he looked up quizzically. "What's the matter with you?"

I told him about Puho-dong. If I'd expected outrage, I'd've been disappointed. Marne just said, "Not the first time. Likely not the last."

Bob was tired. Dead tired. He'd had a long, hard day. He didn't want to talk about Puho-dong. He told me a little about the proposed plans, now nearing finalization, for the storming of Hill 1052.

For the helicopter assault group, he'd asked for volunteers from the line companies and then picked the best men from those. They'd been formed into a platoon-sized raiding party, that is, three squads of thirteen men, each squad comprised of a squad leader and three fire teams. Each fire team consisted of a BAR-man, an Assistant-

BAR-man, and two riflemen who carried only M-l's.

(The Browning Automatic Rifle is actually a light machine gun, weighing 19.4 pounds. It has a 20-round magazine and can fire up to 650 rounds a minute on fully automatic fire. But a good BAR-man can also fire single shots with greatly improved accuracy.)

To each squad was added a flame-thrower from Weapons Company and a corpsman from H & S Company. The platoon would be under the command of Second Lieutenant Ansel Micleson (he pronounced it Mike-ul-son), with Sergeant Harold Rainey as his second in command.

In the helicopter assault group therefore there would be only forty-seven men, three of them non-combatant corpsmen.

"Pretty thin," I said. "You told me there's two hundred men in that Rock."

"It'll do," Marne said. "It'll have to do," he added and then clenched his jaws and flattened his lips against his teeth.

Marne went on. The proposed attack was to begin at dawn. During the night the artillery and mortar barrage would be unusually—but not suspiciously—heavy on The Rock. At first light, Corsairs would streak in with their bombs and napalm, followed by Marine Thunderjets.

A small party, called the decoy raiding party, would start down into the valley from the MLR at dawn, move up the south slope of The Rock, then fall back. They'd keep the Chinese occupied in front of The Rock. Micleson's and Rainey's specially trained platoon would then attack the rear slopes of The Rock, coming in by helicopter, to engage the Chinese between their MLR and their artillery, mortars, and headquarters company.

Presumably this would force them to let down their guard in front of The Rock. If and when this became obvious to McCallister, he'd order a two-company force—four to five hundred men—to move through the original decoy party to secure the rock fortress. The success of the whole operation depended on the attack from the rear.

For most of that morning Marne had worked with Lt. Micleson's platoon, the men attacking from the rear. He'd drawn sketches on paper, had traced movements in the sticky Korean clay, and had gone over and over the various points, minor and major, upon which success depended. He'd regrounded the men—all of them already battle-hardened—in the fundamentals of hand-to-hand combat, cover and concealment, movement across open terrain, and most of all, firing of any weapon from any position. Their eyes had lit up with anticipation when he told them they'd land in 'copters.

Later that day he'd spent his time with the other two elements of his plan—the decoy party, and the final assault group. They were still deployed along the front lines, of course, so he'd had to crawl along the trenches, speaking to groups of ten or twenty gathered in aid stations and command bunkers.

To the decoy party, the second platoon of George Company, he'd explained that their purpose was to make it look like they were serious about taking The Rock. They would drive forward, up onto the lower slopes, inevitably taking some fire from the Chinese, then find safe cover from which to continue engaging the enemy with the heaviest fire and the fewest casualties possible.

To the final assault group, How and Item Company, he'd explained that their mission began when Micleson's attack from the rear had the enemy confused. They would swarm off their own lines and pass through the original decoy party.

He warned them that they could expect no help from

artillery and mortars because of their proximity to The Rock and also the decoy party.

And now Marne was tired. I could see the heat from the stove begin to steal into his body. His eyelids began to fall slowly over his eyes even as he finished his little lecture. I sat watching him for a moment. A warm glow of brother-love filled my heart. I'd never had a brother but if I'd had one I'd've wanted him to be like Bob Marne. I hated to see him going into this mission. We were bound to take heavy casualties and Marne would be in the thick of the fighting. Nothing—nothing—must happen to him.

I closed my eyes, too, succumbing to the warmth and the relaxation following one of my most trying days.

Half an hour later Bob sat up with a start, waking me up for I'd fallen asleep, too. The stove was roaring and glowing red in the darkness. We'd forgotten to turn it back from nine and it was burning fiercely. Marne, sitting close by it, was flushed bright red.

I laughed. "Warm now, Bob?"

He laughed, looked at his watch, and said, "After six. Briefing's already started."

Quickly he turned the stove down to one, grabbed his cap and a flashlight off his cot, and we trotted off toward the 5-6 tent.

Twenty-eight

Operation Rock was scheduled for the morning of March 19th. On the 16th a lowboy chugged into the H & S compound with the body section of a Sikorski helicopter. The nose was badly damaged, the rotor and engine missing completely, the undercarriage badly crumpled and the wheels gone. I figured it had crashed somewhere and its usable parts salvaged.

Laughing motor pool Marines unloaded it and placed it in a cleared and relatively flat area of the battalion command post. Carpenters began building a platform to raise the carcass up to the height of a real helicopter.

Chappie and I watched from Mercy Row. "I don't like this," Bob said.

"I know what you mean and I don't either. But they're going after The Rock, Bob, one way or another. Maybe this'll be better than most."

He was silent for a couple of minutes then shrugged

his shoulders and sighed deeply. "I wish they'd settle this mess over in Panmunjom, not here."

I nodded. "Yeah. Seems so simple to us."

He glanced at me and said, "Would be simple if you'd just take all the politics out. But you can't. This a political war."

My turn to sigh. "Yeah, more than any other war we've ever fought. C'mon, Chappie, I'll buy you a cup of coffee."

His grin was infectious. "Okay, and I'd like a piece of banana cream pie to go with it."

"You got it!"

That afternoon I watched Marne, Micleson, and Rainey take men in groups of six to the hulk. They climbed aboard in full battle dress: packs, sleeping bags, entrenching tools, helmets, canteens, bayonets, K-bars, grenades, M-1s, everything. All three corpsmen's pockets bulged with Unit Ones, battle dressings, IV tubing. I knew they'd taped serum albumin bottles to both calves. I'd wanted to send a fourth corpsman with a pack of medical supplies but Marne had nixed that. "No room in the 'copters," he'd said.

I watched as over and over they practiced until they could evacuate the helicopter in a matter of two to three seconds. As each man jumped from the 'copter he ran a few yards and dropped to the ground and lay there, waiting for the order from his squad leader to move forward.

Next day, on the 16th, eight Sikorskis in two tight formations of four each roared in from the south and landed in the battalion area, two on the regular strip, two in the supply area, two in the road, and two in the cleared section where the practice 'copter body had been.

Marne wouldn't go on the 'copter mission itself but he

wanted to go on the practice runs. I wouldn't go on the mission either, but I talked Marne into letting me go along on the first of the practice flights. He didn't know it, it probably didn't make any difference, but I'd never in a 'copter before. We stood in the cold winter sunshine as Marne went from 'copter to 'copter with his clipboard, checking each detail with the precision for which he was known. He spoke to each pilot, calling them all by name as if he knew them and maybe he did.

I was assigned to the 'copter in which Marne and Harold Rainey would ride, one of the two on the regular 'copter strip. I chatted with Rainey as Marne made his rounds. We talked about the weather, the chow, the new replacement draft due in two weeks, everything but this mission. We also didn't talk about Puho-dong. That was, and would always be, an off-limits subject.

Marne came back to our 'copter, turned and shouted, "Relay this order! Saddle up!"

I heard the order go from our 'copter strip to the supply area, the road, and finally down to the cleared area where the practice 'copter had been. We went aboard, all thirty-nine riflemen plus the three corpsmen, three flame-throwers, Licutcnant Micleson, and Sergeant Rainey.

I climbed in, followed by Marne, who shouted to our pilots, "Move out."

The giant unarmed whirlybirds rose skyward one at a time and formed into two rectangles over the CP. Looking out the open side hatch, I was startled at how fast the campsite fell away below us. Then the pilot banked the bird into a turn and all I could see were the parallel mountain ridges running in a northeast-southwest direction.

I caught a glimpse of 1052 and was seized with a sudden pang of consternation. Would the Reds be tipped off by seeing the eight copters flying in formation? But, as Marne had pointed out in defense of his plan, supply copters occasionally came into camp in flights of three or four and this flight would probably not seem unusual. That we were watched carefully from The Rock, I had no doubt.

Suddenly my stomach lurched skyward and I felt suspended, weightless. The 'copter had started its descent by braking in midair and dropping straight downward. The sound of the rotors changed pitch as they were feathered and slowed.

I realized suddenly that our practice landing site was near Puho-dong. But I had no inclination, nor the time, to brood on that now. I glanced over at Rainey. His face was set in hard lines and I knew what he was thinking, too.

We'd never forget.

The forested hills flew up at us at a terrific rate. My ears felt like they were going to explode. Hastily I swallowed to open my Eustachian tubes like a SCUBA diver equalizing the pressure in his middle ears.

I caught sight of a clearing ahead of us into which the pilot was dropping the 'copter. The 'copter came within six feet of the ground with no apparent slowing, suddenly braked in mid-air with a loud flapping sound, then dropped the remaining few feet in a dead fall. I'd heard Marne warn his men about all this, but when I glanced over at him I could tell that it was even quicker than he himself had imagined.

We all sat there in stunned surprise for a few seconds, then the Marines started clambering out. Back at Pendleton I'd seen various troop maneuvers—and participated in a few. But then we were, after all, in California. Combat seemed a long way off. This practice was the penultimate exercise before the real thing.

Our 'copter was near the center of the line with three on the left and four on the right. As each 'copter landed, its people jumped out one at a time, rushed forward and fanned out until they coalesced into one continuous line.

I stood mesmerized in the open hatch and watched the action. As soon as the line was formed, Micleson shouted, "Hit the deck," and the men dropped as if shot. I could see them crawling belly-down on knees and elbows—their rifles cradled to keep them out of the snow and mud—to rocks, bushes, and trees, from where they could see and not be seen.

I jumped out and followed in behind Marne.

Marne confided to me later that they'd looked pretty good on the first run, but now he shouted loudly, "All right, grunts, on your feet. Stand steady."

He looked both ways down the line and then, "Damn it, Svenger, look at that space between you and Rafferty. A whole Goddamn regiment of gooks could infiltrate a hole like that."

He spun on his heel and shouted, "Where's Thorpe?"

"Here, sir."

Jerry Thorpe had propped his M-l against a boulder in order to spit into his olive-drab handkerchief and dab at a long gash in his left hand which had filled with dirt and clotted blood. As Marne strode over to him he stuffed his handkerchief into a pocket and quickly grabbed his rifle. "Corporal Thorpe!"

"Sir!"

"It's your responsibility as fire team leader to deploy your men. Why's Svenger way off in the boondocks? What if your A-BAR was out of it and you needed Svenger? How would he get over here without getting hit?"

Thorpe stood his ground and barked, "Sorry, sir!" I

could tell that Marne liked that. No excuses. No whining explanation. He said sharply, "Get that hand taken care of," and continued on down the line talking to the men individually. Then, turning back to his own 'copter, he called, "All right, men. Gather round. On the double!"

The men came jogging in, rifles at port arms, helmet straps tugging at chins, canteens and bayonet scabbards banging against hips. They formed in a semi-circle around him.

The men all knew Marne. Some had served under him when he'd been CO of George Company. To a man they respected him. They knew he was a mustang who'd made it into the commissioned ranks through discipline, courage, perseverance, loyalty, and a whole bunch of other things.

His lips pursed now as he watched them through eyes slitted against the setting sun. "You people were just too damn slow getting out of the copters and forming the attack line. You *got* to get out faster. Chances are you'll be long gone by the time the incoming starts. But you got to give the pilots a break, too, by getting out fast."

He pushed his helmet back on his head and wiped the sweat off his forehead and out of his eyebrows with the sleeve of his field jacket. Then he squared his helmet and said, "I can't emphasize enough the importance of regrouping quickly and dropping on command. You did pretty good, but when the steel starts flying it'll be harder. You're gonna want to drop too quickly. That'd form a ragged line. Easy to infiltrate if you have to stay there overnight. And difficult to control. Okay, let's get back aboard and try it again. We just got time to do it once more."

Twenty-nine

The lines were quiet that night and I got a good night's sleep. Before sacking in I talked on the EE-8 with Everly and he sounded okay. He never said anything about his bugout and I didn't remind him. He was the one who had to live with it.

Next day, the 17th, was about as nice a day as you could get even if you ordered it direct from God. Spring was in the air. Someone had cumshawed a volleyball from a rear-echelon outfit and the corpsmen got me into a game. There was a lot of good-natured arguing about someone—usually me—catching the ball and throwing it instead of hitting it, or whether a guy had reached over the net to spike the ball. But it was a good hour. We were stripped down to our T-shirts and were sweating heavily by the time we quit. We forgot for that hour that we were only a half mile from the front lines.

I took a bath in my helmet liner and was standing

naked as a jailbird when I heard the tent door flaps swish open. I turned my head and there was Butch grinning from ear to ear. "*Ohio gazaiamus*," he said in Japanese.

"How in the hell did you get back up here?"

He took me literally. "Walk," he said.

"No one stop you?"

"No."

It was good to have him back. For one thing, I had gotten tired of the corpsmen standing around laughing at me as I washed my dirty underwear in the Kanmu-gang.

I hadn't been up to the front line trenches for several days. I knew it couldn't last and it didn't.

This would be the night I would meet the enemy face to face. Not over a barbed wire entanglement with his burp-gun spitting bullets, but on a stretcher with his wound pouring blood.

This was only right, for I hadn't gone to Korea to get shot at, but to treat wounds, even those of the enemy.

Operation Rock was two days off. McCallister decided he needed to know if the gooks had gotten intelligence about the impending offensive. So that night two raider patrols went out from the MLR about 2200. They must have made contact almost immediately because at 2225 the first call came in from How Company to send up a doctor and the jeep ambulance.

Ron Everly was over in Item Company so I sent Tollander in our other ambulance from the motor pool to pick him up and take him over to How. I figured that the jeep could move Everly from Item to How faster than he could crawl down the trench, especially if there was much incoming that would make him hole up now and then.

At 2255 another urgent call came in from Forward Damage Control Charley with the intelligence that a patrol out of George Company had encountered the enemy and a prisoner had been shot and captured. They requested a doctor to keep him alive and a jeep ambulance to get him out.

SNAFU. Situation Normal: All Fouled Up. If I'd gone out to How myself, leaving Everly in Item, he'd've been close enough there to take care of this wounded Chinaman. It was too late to call him back.

We took the other jeep ambulance. Rohn drove and I sat in back as usual on the narrow jump seat parallel to the two stretcher racks, hanging on to the metal braces. We made our slow way along the road. I use the term "road" rather loosely. It was just a dirt track gouged and graded by the combat engineers part way up to this sector of the lines, taking advantage of natural gullies, stream beds, and relatively tree-less areas.

It was pitch dark and we couldn't use any light. Rohn drove with his head hanging out the side of the jeep, following the road by watching it go past the front wheel. We could hear the firecracker rattle of a firefight along most of the line. There also was a lot of incoming mortar along the line but none where we were.

Even so it didn't seem like a very smart idea to be driving up there, but there was nothing that any of us could about it without disobeying orders. No one even thought about doing that.

Discipline in the Marine Corps was too ingrained.

The casualness of the manner in which orders were usually given belied their authority. I never heard the Hollywoodian bellow of an officer, "THAT'S AN ORDER, SERGEANT!!" More often than not I heard, "I guess you'd better do such and so, Sergeant."

And this was in the United States Marine Corps!

Under fire, of course, the orders were crisper and the answers sharper, but I never saw a Marine hesitate long enough to need bullying into carrying out an order. I did see, once in a while, a Marine stare long and hard at an officer who'd given him orders he didn't like. But then, always, he'd respond with, "Sir!" and take off to carry out those orders.

So when I received the request to send an ambulance and doctor up to Item Company, I treated it as an order. Which it was.

The moon wasn't due up for another half hour or so. But there was starlight on the snow and I could make out the track ahead as I looked over Rohn's shoulder through the windshield. We were on the downslope of a small ridge, almost ready to grind through a small stream in the last little gully before making the final climb to the MLR.

The ford didn't look right tonight. I reached forward and gripped Rohn's shoulder. "Road block," I said.

But Rohn had already seen it and had hit the brakes. Old 99 shuddered and skidded to a stop. The engine killed before Rohn could stomp on the clutch.

At the bottom of the little hill, where the road crossed the stream, was a pile of bodies.

"KSCs," Rohn muttered. "God damn those dirty gooks."

Rohn was right. Some Chinese infiltrators had murdered half a dozen "Eetiwahs" and dumped their bodies on the bank at the edge of the ford.

There was no way around them.

Upstream the banks were too steep.

Downstream the water was too deep.

I don't think either Rohn or I considered our choices. We were on a mission, under orders. Rohn slid out from under the wheel, I scrambled out the back, and together we started dragging the bodies off to the side of the road. No shots yet. What were they waiting for?

I soon found out.

While we were working on the bodies, the Chinese guerrillas had been creeping down the draw alongside the road, attempting to reach us unseen before we could clear the road. But Rohn, battle-wary and with instincts honed in a year of almost continuous combat, saw them when they were about a hundred feet away and yelled, "Gooks! Let's get out a here, Doctor."

We jumped into the jeep and Rohn ground the starter. For aching seconds it failed to catch. Slowly Rohn pulled out the choke, knowing that if he pulled it too far and too fast, he'd flood the carburetor and we'd be two more statistics. The engine caught, back-fired and roared to life. Rohn slammed in the choke with his left hand and the clutch with his left foot, shifted with his right hand, let out the clutch with his left foot, and accelerated with his right foot, all at the same time. We shot forward as he let up on the clutch, bounced over the remaining bodies in the creek bed, and hit the road on the other side.

Shots rang out now, most of the bullets singing overhead, but one must have threaded its way through the back of the jeep between me and the stretcher racks because I heard it thump into the dash board.

I pulled my .45 and started firing out the back of the jeep. I couldn't see anything except the flash of fire from half a dozen muzzles but I hoped the ambushers would be forced to the ground and their aim distracted.

The firing stopped. They would still hear the roar of our jeep but the darkness soon covered our escape. In the daytime we'd have been visible all the way to the top of the ridge. But, of course, in the daytime the guerrillas wouldn't have even been there.

Rohn turned to speak to me. He opened his mouth but he didn't say anything. He just turned back to the road and kept driving. What was there to say? We'd walked into an ambush. The gooks knew we had to use that track and that ford. Tacticians say, "Confound your enemy by using different routes, vary your schedule."

Sure.

We would never really know why the gooks waited so long to fire. Prisoner patrol probably, Rohn suggested when we had the chance to discuss it. They wanted us alive and talking. They wouldn't have gotten much from either of us. We didn't know what the hell was going on anywhere in Korea. We got all our information from *Time* magazine.

Thirty

Now we crept slowly up the back side of the front-line ridge and crossed the trench system self in George Company on a pine log bridge. We drifted downhill about 700 yards in a southwest direction into No-Man's Land, now west of Item Company, followed the Kanmu-gang for a few hundred yards, then headed straight north, east of Ku-dong and southwest of Hill 812. Now we were due west of George Company's lines again.

I knew from my maps back in H & S that we were as close to 1052 as we could be without running into routine Chinese patrols. The Item Company line ran almost straight north and south here, so The Rock was due west of our position. I stood on the flat steel platform of the trailer hitch, my left hand gripping the canvas roof, my right hand holding my .45 in a cocked-up, ready-to-fire position.

Until half an hour ago I'd never used the .45 except in

target practice. I sure as hell didn't want to use it again now. For one thing, I was starting to shake all over, one massive malaria-like chill, teeth ramming together, neck in torticollis first to the right and then to the left and back again, back and shoulders chug-chug-chugging away, buttocks and legs pogo-sticking on the trailer hitch.

For another thing, my .45 would be no match for the Chinese burp guns, those light machine guns that went "burrrrrp" as they let go a volley of .45 slugs. (They also had U.S.-made Thompson submachine guns, as well as a good supply of aught-threes like Rohn carried, booty from the 1947 defeat of Chiang Kai-shek, who'd been supplied by the United States. It was not the first time, nor, I supposed, would it be the last, that changes in political bed-fellows turned American-made arms against Americans.)

But just holding the weapon in readiness gave me a wee bit of confidence—of optimism—of security—however badly misplaced but necessary to my mental, if not physical, health. Gradually I brought my dancing muscles under control.

Moonlight began to light the scene before us as the moon crept up over the ridge behind us to the east. To the west the outline of 1052 loomed ominously close. The summit was, in fact, only about 1000 yards away, so we were already on its lower slopes.

Suddenly Rohn slammed on the brakes. I peered through the darkness over the roof of the ambulance and saw that ahead of us was a column of men coming toward us along the track. As soon as I saw them I could see that they were American Marines. Rohn pulled off to the side as far as he dared to let them by.

The lead man was dragging something. It took a minute in the darkness for me to see that what he was dragging was a man. The Marine held the man's feet by the ankles in front of him at his waist, the man's body hanging down behind and his head bumping along on the irregular frozen track. I couldn't believe it.

I vaulted off the back of the jeep and ran around to the front. The column halted and the Marine dragging the body let him fall with a thud. He was a Chinaman. Second in line was the platoon corpsman, Jason Smith, a new man, who'd come through H & S just a week before. I'd sent him straight on up to the lines and hadn't gotten to know him at all.

He'd been holding a bottle of serum albumin connected to the prisoner. Now he handed the bottle to the third man in line and knelt beside the Chinaman.

I knelt beside Smith.

My thoughts were in a tangle. Just two days ago I'd seen the slaughter of almost a dozen non-combatants. I'd pretty well rationalized that as being necessary, or at least unavoidable. Now I found a column of healthy young American Marines, who easily could have carried this little man, allowing him to be dragged as if he were a dead deer. It would've been bad enough if the man were dead, but to treat another living human being like that was unpardonable.

So I seethed, knowing that if I said anything right then, I'd make a mess of things. Besides, my own thoughts were tumbling so fast that I wouldn't know where to start. Or stop.

"He's unconscious, Doctor," Smitty said.

We didn't dare shine a light so I examined him as best I could. In particular, I would have liked to see his pupils in order to determine the presence or absence of lateralizing intracranial hemorrhage.

His cap was gone. (None of the Chinese wore helmets.)

I knew he was an enlisted man because his hair was short and wiry; the officers let their hair grow, probably so their men could spot them quickly. His black hair was soggy wet from melting snow and matted with clotting blood. He'd been shot through the head, the point of entry and exit very close together on the right temple.

His breathing was stertorous so I quickly slipped a black, hard-rubber airway deep into his throat with the end protruding between his lips. He sounded much better. There wasn't much in the way of secretions, for which I was thankful because we had no way to suction his pharynx.

His clothes were tan in color, baggy, ill-fitting. His quilted coat was filthy and almost saturated with blood. He smelled violently of garlic. A bandolier of ammunition still angled across his chest. His tennis shoes were torn and nearly worn through; the laces had broken and had been knotted back together in half a dozen places. His wraparound leggings were loose and bloody. He had no other wounds so the blood must have come from one of his buddies.

The unit of albumin that Smitty had started earlier was running subcutaneously, so he started another one in an arm vein and taped it in place. He did it by feel, in the dark, with cold fingers. The guy was good all right. I told him so and he just grunted.

The rattle of gunfire and the thudding of mortars sounded around us in the hills but nothing was coming in on us. But we had to get out of there before some sharp-eared Chinaman heard the commotion and called in a barrage. But we also had to do what we had to do.

"How long you been with him, Smitty?" I asked.

"About an hour."

"What's his state of consciousness compared to when you first saw him?"

"Better if anything. BP's come up from 70 to about 90. Pulse's stayed steady at about 110."

"Good." I allowed myself a brief sigh of relief. As I stood up and looked around at the half dozen Marines close enough to hear and see us in the near-total darkness, I could practically hear their questioning looks. Their thoughts came clearly to me across the darkness: no one should feel good because the Chinaman was getting better.

"Who's in command here?" I asked.

A young man of about 22 stepped forward. He identified himself as Lt. Roger Mason. He was a big man and even in the dim light I could see the hardness of his face and the sharpness of his features. He wore no insignia, which was standard operating procedure for commissioned officers and corpsmen along the front lines. I always took mine off whennever I went up. We'd smartened up since Guadalcanal, when the Japanese selectively sniperscoped officers who wore insignia and corpsmen with red crosses on white armbands. The Geneva Conventions* meant nothing to the Japanese.

"I'm the platoon leader, Doctor," Mason said quietly, the softness of his voice contrasting with the sternness of his countenance.

"Any of our guys get hurt, Lieutenant?"

"No, sir. We were damn lucky. We were on a prisoner-taking patrol. Got this one, then were ambushed less'n a hundred yards from here. We drove off or killed the Chinks."

*First promulgated in Switzerland in 1864 and later modified many times to keep up with the "advances" in weaponry, e. g., gas and biological warfare and nuclear weapons.

I shook my head. "I don't get it. Isn't 812 one of our own outposts on the OPLR? Aren't there Marines up there all the time? Or at least at night?"

"Yessir. But the gooks'd apparently come across in the dark and nobody up there heard 'em. This goes on pritinear every night, y'know, Doctor."

I nodded. "Yeah, I know."

"These guys might a been on their way through our lines, for all we know. Or maybe somehow they knew about our patrol and waited for us. Who knows?"

My mind echoed "who knows?" as Rohn laboriously turned the jeep in the track, trying not to put the wheels too far off it because of land mines. Finally he got it facing back toward our lines. No one held his breath, no one ducked or turned away or said a word. But everyone knew what could happen. Knew that one minute we could all be standing there talking and the next minute be blown to Kingdom Come.

It was that kind of a war. Men from both sides creeping around in the dark. James Brady described it as "tough, murderous little brawls with men dying on barren ground...ambushes and raids and bloody dawns..."

Our jeep ambulance must've been heard for a mile or two, even in this mountainous country. This George Company platoon had been ambushed close by where we were standing. Where were those gooks now? Were they reforming their patrol? On their way back here even now? Were they the ones who'd ambushed Rohn and me?

I told Mason about our ambush. He said, "We'll send out another patrol when we get back to the line. These guys are bushed."

Thirty-one

I helped Smitty and Rohn ease the patient onto a stretcher and slide it onto the lower rack of the jeep ambulance. There were no catches on the rack, nothing to prevent the stretchers from sliding backwards except the built-in cant downward toward the front.

Smitty climbed into the back and hooked the bottle of serum albumin to the stretcher rack. He called softly to me, "Want I should stay with him, Doctor, or do you want to ride back? We'll have to take a Marine with us, too, in case he comes around."

"He's not going to come around, Smitty. But wait a sec. It'd be a good idea to send a guard along anyway." I turned to Mason and said, "You going back to the MLR now?"

"Yessir."

"Go on, Smitty, I'll walk in with the platoon. Wait for me at the MLR. I'll want to go on in with the prisoner from there."

The jeep crawled off slowly through the darkness and we waited till we couldn't hear it. As it left I got the feeling that I didn't want to be on that jeep anyway, cruising through the dark of night with a prisoner of war whose buddies might want him back, and with only one Marine and one corpsman for security.

Mason and I followed the path back up the hill. The rest of the squad fell in behind us in single file.

"You guys sure got to do some stupid things, Doctor," Mason said.

"You mean like trying to save that Chinaman's life?" I knew damn well that's what he meant.

"Yeah, you know there's not a single guy in that column back of us that would've batted an eyelash if I'd just pulled out my .45 and let that gook have it in the head."

A little irritated, I said, "Why didn't you?"

"My own stupidity, and the fact that my mission was already secured, thanks to that ambush."

"Your own stupidity?"

"I radioed the captain that I had a Chinaman with a hole in his head and that he was still alive. He ordered me to bring him in."

"You wanted a prisoner, didn't you? Wasn't that why you were out there?"

"Yeah, but not that way. It's like going duck hunting and having your Labrador find a day's bag limit of cripples somebody else shot and couldn't find. See what I mean?"

I said, "No," but he let it go.

We were still a thousand yards or more from our own lines, climbing steadily up the frozen, terraced rice paddies. The half-moon was full up now, riding high above the ridge to our east. I felt better with an entire squad—

thirteen riflemen plus Lt. Mason—behind me, presumably between me and the Chinese.

I chuckled and Mason turned to look at me. I said, "Looks like we're both acting a little stupid tonight, Lieutenant. You didn't kill him because of *your* orders, and I've got to try to save him because of *mine*."

"Your orders?" he asked. If it'd been light enough I'm sure I could have read a real question in his eyes.

"Can we rest a minute, Lieutenant? I could use a break if it's safe."

"It's safe." Now it was his turn to chuckle. I knew why he was amused. In No-man's Land, half a mile out in front of our lines, and it was safe! We squatted in the path, afraid to step off it because of mines.

I felt a lecture coming on. Half a dozen of the Marines were within hearing distance and I wanted to answer Mason's last question in some comprehensible, if disorderly, way.

"Yeah, Lieutenant, my orders." I searched for the right words, dragging them out of a world I'd almost forgotten, out of the past that was only seven months behind me, back to a time and place where the ethics of living, letting live, letting die, and killing were more exact. Where putting a gun to the head of any man was unacceptable in the extreme. I tried to project my mind into a future that was God only knew how far away. Were these really the Golden Days as I'd claimed to Everly just a couple of weeks before? Were these days a simplified version of life, or a more complicated one? The rifles cracked, the mortars crunched, occasionally an artillery shell screamed overhead, a cool breeze brushed my sweaty face.

Mason and his Marines waited, not, I knew, with bated breath for my words of wisdom, but because they had no place else to go. Besides—and I knew this at the time, too—what I had to say wasn't really for these guys, but for me. It was oath of Hippocrates time.

"I've seen lots of wounded men, Mason. And back home lots of sick men. I've worked all night long on some bum from skid row, and when he pulled through, what did I have?"

He didn't have to search for an answer. "A bum from skid row?"

"Yeah, a bum from skid row. He hadn't changed. He wasn't worth any more than before he got sick. But—and this is the important thing—he wasn't worth any less, either. I've operated on old people with brains addled by repeated strokes. And what were their lives worth when we sent them from my surgery ward back to the locked ward in the psycho hospital? Nothing. Or at least not much, by our standards. And I've worked on some rather important people, too, and sent them back to their jobs."

I waited to see if he was with me. He was. He said softly, "Yessir."

"Okay, so you got the point. But let me say this anyway. Make sure we understand each other. To me, as a doctor, I've just got to look at each human being as a human being. I can't work harder on one man than on the next. I can't withhold treatment from a derelict or a psychotic, and then give it to someone I think is more important to society. In many cases, the dividing line would be too thin. Besides, who the hell am I to judge? I just can't do it. I can't play God by trying to sort people out into save-this-one and don't-save-that-one categories."

Mason was quiet, but there was a restless shuffling of bodies in the darkness. I was glad I couldn't see their faces.

"It really boils down to this. You've got your orders, and I've got mine. You've got a job to do, but so do I. Right now that Chinaman on that stretcher is my job, because he's a human being, not white or yellow or black. And I'm going to do everything I can to save him."

I blew out a long breath and said, "End of lecture, now let's get the hell out of here."

Thirty-two

Lieutenant Mason issued a soft-toned order, "Saddle up!" and we struck off toward the MLR again. When we crossed the trench line the squad left me. I could hear them shuffling both ways down the trenchline back to their bunkers.

I no longer wondered how they found the right one. They were home again and knew exactly where they lived. Knew intimately the squiggles in the trench, where it curved around that big pine tree, where it was deep and where it was shallow, where the company and platoon commanders lived, where the communication and forward aid bunkers were. They could find their own happy little homes in the darkest of dark nights. They were home.

I jumped the trench, climbed to the top of the ridgeline and over it, down to the jeep ambulance waiting on the backside of the ridgeline. Smitty got out and I took his place on the jumpseat across from the stretcher rack.

I examined the patient. He was breathing hard, but still hadn't tried to work the airway out of his throat. He'd do that only when his level of consciousness rose to the point where his pharyngeal reflexes were intact again. So he was still pretty deep.

His pulse was steady. In the relative security of the ridgeline defilade, I shone my pen-light into his pupils. They were both equal in size and reacted readily, if sluggishly, to the light. So there was no lateralization yet, no sign of blood collecting in the subdural or epidural spaces, nothing that needed emergency surgery. That was good, I thought, and smiled wryly, because we clearly couldn't do any surgery where we were.

"O.K., Smitty, get on back to your platoon."

"Aye, aye, sir."

"Which one you with?"

"Second.

"You did a good job tonight. I'll remember that."

"Thanks, Doctor." He walked off and I felt a warm glow. It was good to have men like that working the lines.

There was an irony here.

It took good men to do what had to be done in Korea—in any war, for that matter. The goof-offs and incompetents were quickly noticed and were shipped to less sensitive jobs, usually in a rear area somewhere. The best men were selected for the most sensitive and—more often than not—the most dangerous positions. So it was they who got hurt and killed.

Quite obviously this isn't an observation original with me. 'Twas ever thus. And we did have good men in Korea, in line companies and weapons companies, in Navy Medical Companies and Army MASHs, in the Air Force and in the artillery.

And they served purely out of a sense of duty and pride in themselves and their outfits. There were no flags flying for them at home. No paper and scrap-metal drives. No outpouring of ballads and songs like, "When the lights go on again, all over the world," or, "Don't sit under the apple tree with anybody else but me," or, "Let's remember Pearl Harbor."

Victor Hicken in *The American Fighting Man* says, "They fought while politicians back home told them that the war was useless, they sacrificed while friends back home enjoyed a general prosperity brought on by the war, they fought under military and political restraint, and they gave battle under some of the most miserable climatic conditions ever faced by American warriors."

"Shove off, Ned,"I said to Rohn. We crawled back down the hill toward H & S Company, Rohn hanging out the door watching the front wheel, one hand holding on to the strut where a rear-view mirror had once been, the other hand steering the jeep. I hung onto the stretcher rack with both hands as we tilted from one rut to another and slewed in the icy track.

Lt. Mason had radioed ahead so two Korean interpreters were waiting in Sick Bay back at Battalion Headquarters. One, Kim Suk-bom, spoke Chinese. The other, my friend Lee Yung-kak, English. Between the two, our S-2, Captain Bill Wright, could interrogate the Chinaman if he ever came around.

Two pressure lanterns lit the Aid Station tent. Ron Everly was there, as was Captain Wright. Chief Hoffman, Jim Jepson, and Rick Simpson were working in the back.

Ron had come down from the lines with two badly shot-up guys from the How Company fracas. They'd already been flown out, though I hadn't heard the 'copters out where we were in the boonies.

Everly looked like hell. Three day growth of beard. Sooty face. Blood-shot eyes. Hollow cheeks. His uniform was mud- and blood-stained. His ascot was gone. He didn't salute me, but he did get up off the shell box he'd been sitting on. I almost told him to sit down and relax but his father wouldn't have liked that.

His eyes glared at me and I expected a blast of indignation for having sent him cavorting around the front lines in the dead of a winter's night. "Where the hell've you been," he asked, all traces of Harvardian English gone. "I've been worried sick. Bill Wright tells me you've been half a mile out in front of our lines!"

I wanted to say something like, "Welcome to the real world," but I held my tongue. He still needed all the help he could get and sarcasm didn't qualify as help. Instead I said, "Gotta get my daily exercise somehow."

Rohn and another Marine clumped in with the stretcher. Bill Wright stared down at the prisoner, glanced up quickly at me and said, "Whew, does he stink! Doesn't look so good does he, Jack?"

"He's semi-conscious, Bill, but I think he's coming to."

"We gonna be able to get anything out of him? We don't get many of these guys."

"If I had to guess I'd say maybe in a couple hours. No promises. Got a head wound, you know."

"Yeah, I know. Mason filled me in. We're lucky he's alive at all, I suppose. Or maybe it's not luck with you guys on the job."

I didn't tell him about how the prisoner was being handled when I first saw him. Maybe I should have, and maybe I would later, but I didn't then.

It occurred to me that I'd had to swallow an awful lot of stuff today.

It also occurred to me that I didn't really have a choice.

What do you do?

Where do you draw the line?

Once you're in uniform you don't have much say and no forum in which to say it. Where would I go with a complaint about Puho-dong? Or about dragging a prisoner by his heels? The time to voice your complaint is before you put on the uniform or after you take it off. And even then you're likely to have a Queeg-like outcome.

"Well," Wright said, "we better scram and let you guys work. Call me when and if he can talk, will you, Jack?"

"Yes, sir." I didn't have to call Wright "sir." Our rank was the same—two silver bars. But somehow it seemed appropriate at that moment.

Wright and the interpreters filed out with scarcely a glance at the quilted figure fighting for his life on the stretcher. I couldn't really blame them. Especially the Koreans, who'd seen their own families and friends gunned down by men dressed like this. Lee's father had been mowed down in the courtyard of the Seoul Presbyterian Church during the first Chinese offensive almost a year before.

Lee himself had been with the First Marine Division when it was encircled by the Chinese at Hagaru-ri at the south end of the Chosin Reservoir. So he had witnessed the full fury of the Chinese attacks: the masses of men charging into the guns of the Marines, bugles blowing, cymbals clanging, whistles screeching, the Chinese leaping over the bodies of their fallen Comrades. Now one of them lay on the floor of the aid station and Lee could not be at all blamed for his attitude.

There was an additional, most outrageous, irony. This prisoner was getting priority medical attention now, and would be treated in a Marine Medical Company. He might even be flown to a hospital ship or Japan if necessary. The interpreters on the other hand, if wounded, would be evacuated to a civilian hospital and forced to pay for their care. This was United Nations policy and frankly was often ignored by those of us in the field.

Gradually the Chinaman returned to consciousness. He began to work the airway around in his mouth and finally spit it out. I rolled him on his side and aspirated the mucus with a bulb syringe. He opened his eyes and lashed out with a fist that caught me on the side of my head. It was a reflex reaction. I don't think that he struck me on purpose. At any rate, I grabbed both his hands and gently lowered them to his side while Everly rolled him onto his back.

During the next hour he became more and more lucid and by 0300 I decided he could talk. I sent Jim Jepson for Captain Wright and the interpreters. They filed back in, sleep heavy on their eyelids, and sat down cross-legged on the hard dirt floor beside the stretcher. Major Selkirk was with them this time. He stood quietly behind the interpreters.

Wright sat looking at the prisoner, saw that he was staring back, and began asking questions in English. This was translated from English to Korean by Lee, then from Korean to Chinese by Kim. The answer was then translated from Chinese to Korean to English. It was a lengthy process.

Wright asked who he was, what outfit he belonged to, how many men were in his unit, how many troops were in this sector around 1052, how they were armed and how much ammo they had.

Wright asked if there were any NKPA (North Korean

Peoples' Army) troops in the line or in reserve. No, no *In Min Gun.*

What reserves were there? No company reserves, all in the line. One battalion in reserve about three miles back. No regimental reserve nearby.

What transport was available for the battalion in reserve?

Five or six trucks.

How many men in their Command Post?

No more than twenty.

Why were there so few reserves in the area around 1052?

Because it was impregnable.

The Chinaman answered all the questions without any apparent attempt at dissimulation. To some of the questions he said, "I don't know," and I could empathize with that answer. If I were ever to be interrogated like that, there would be a lot of questions I wouldn't know the answer to.

Then Wright got to what McCallister really wanted to know: if the prisoner had any alert from his officers about an up-coming offensive by us against Hill 1052. He answered that he himself had no knowledge of any offensives, specifically none aimed at 1052.

We all knew that he may have been telling lies carefully rehearsed for possible capture. He obviously wasn't thinking about his answers. They came out as quickly and naturally as his condition permitted. Either he was telling the truth or was lying beautifully.

Wright sat back and propped himself up with his hands behind him on the dirt floor. He looked up at me. "Wha'd'ya think, Jack?"

"I think he's telling the truth, Bill. I don't think he's physically capable of lying. What do you think, Ron?"

"I agree."

The grilling went on a little while longer, about fifteen minutes altogether.

Then the interrogators left.

Major Selkirk was the last to leave.

He stood at the door of the tent, staring down at the prisoner.

Suddenly his booted foot lashed out at the Chinaman's head. The head slammed sideways against the stretcher, then rolled slowly back, the man's eyes wide in terror, jaws clamped together, teeth bared in a tight grimace. Selkirk struck again

and then once more

and then strode out the door and was gone.

Thirty-three

The Chinaman's eyes were tightly closed now, tears of pain, fright and humiliation, squeezing out at the corners. His mouth pursed and quivered like a child trying not to cry.

It had all happened so fast that no one could do or say anything. And once Selkirk was gone, what were we going to do, run after him and chew him out? We all stood stunned for a moment. Then Ron and I rushed to the prisoner and re-examined him. There wasn't much change but what there was wasn't good.

The prisoner was weak and restless. He started to slip in and out of lucidity. Even with increased infusions of serum albumin—the only IV fluids we had available—his blood pressure slowly dropped while his pulse increased. It became obvious to all of us that if he were to be kept alive he would need further treatment in a hospital and probably would need surgery for debridement of the brain and for control of dural bleeding.

One thing he didn't have was a hematoma building up pressure on his brain. I was pretty sure of that because those cases usually have an enlarged pupil on the side of the bleeding, weakness or even paralysis on the side opposite the bleeding, and a rising blood pressure and dropping pulse. There were a lot of other signs to watch for, of course, including spinal taps which we couldn't do in the field, but the findings on physical examination were fairly reliable screening tests.

I didn't know if there was a neurosurgeon in Korea at the time. But I did know that Mike Lavierri back at Charley had been trained to do burr holes and other emergency neuro procedures. That was standard in a general surgery residency in those days. I'd done over a dozen during my three months on Ward 22 at Cook County Hospital.

"What do you think, Ron?" I asked.

This was the second time I'd called him Ron. He didn't bridle but answered as if he hadn't noticed. "Better 'copter him out. He'll never make it here."

I parted the door flaps and looked out. It was two hours till dawn. The moon was about half full and shed enough light so that I could make out the silhouettes of the H & S Company tents a hundred yards away.

I'd called in copters many times for wounded Marines when it was darker than this. Two had come in already tonight for Everly's patients.

For night evacs we stationed four corpsmen with flashlights at the corners of the little landing area. Out of the inky blackness would come the little Bell, dark itself at first, silhouetted against the sky on moonlit nights, almost impossible to see on dark nights. The pilot, looking down, could see almost nothing until he spotted our flashlights. When he saw them, he'd switch on a single but powerful spotlight on his undercarriage and settle neatly between the flashlights.

This was flying at its best, at its toughest. These pilots were real heroes. They deserved all the medals they got and didn't get all they deserved. When we drove the dark roads in a jeep ambulance without lights, the worst that could happen would be to hit a tree or slide into a ditch. If these guys lost track of the ground or the valley they were following, they'd be dead. I never heard of that happening, but I suppose it did.

Helicopters as flying ambulances had been introduced in January of 1951. So they'd been in use for almost a year when I got to Korea. 'Copters, plus Marine Medical Companies and Army MASHs, had reduced the mortality rate of men arriving at medical services to 2½%. In World War II it was 4%. In World War I, 8%.

Think about that. In WWI you had a one in twelve chance of dying even if you got to a hospital. In Korea that had dropped to one in forty. There were other factors, of course: antibiotics, whole blood and fractionated blood products, advances in the surgery of burns and compound fractures and chest wounds, better trained staff from the Hn up to the senior surgeons. But the most important factor was the helicopter.

I turned back to the EE-8, lifted it off its nail on the tent pole, cranked the handle on the battery case, and put the receiver to my ear.

"Wildbeast," answered the operator over in the S-l tent a hundred yards away.

I pushed the butterfly each time I talked, released it to listen.

"Wildbeast, give me Wild."

"Yes, sir." Then, "WILD, WILD!" he shouted as he

tried to reach regimental headquarters on the sound-powered system.

No answer.

"Line sounds dead, sir."

Cut again, I thought, by some kid I've been giving candy to. Some poor overworked Marine commo man will have to find that break tomorrow, I thought. One of the unsung heroes of Korea was the lineman, running his thin black commo cables from post to post, company to company, squad to squad, even on the front lines. He carried his quarter of a mile of line on big spools, in good weather and bad. He usually worked out of H & S Company but spent a lot of his time in much less safe areas when for some reason a line went dead.

"Try going through the Second Battalion, operator."

"Yes, sir. Wildfire, Wildfire, Wildbeast calling Wildfire.

"Wildfire," the answer came from wherever our Second Battalion was now.

"Wildfire, see if you can get me through to Wild."

From two miles to the rear I could just barely hear the operator answer, "Wild." He put me in touch with the officer in charge of dispatching helicopters. I explained my problem to him.

"Negative, Doctor, not at night. Not for a Chinaman. We'll send up for him when it's light. Keep him alive though. G-2 will want him."

The line went dead.

I hung the phone back on the wall. "That takes care of that."

Everly looked up from where he was sitting back in the corner eating peaches out of a C-ration can. "I can see his point," he said. "Why risk a pilot's life for a half-dead Chinaman? The Army pilots won't fly at night at all, even for American casualties."

I nodded agreement but wasn't sure I really agreed. I almost said, "So we're a bunch of dogfaces now?" But I was too tired to argue. The decision was out of my hands.

Chappie came in about 0400. His fleshy jowls were bright pink from the cold. God knows where he'd been all night. His bunny ears were turned up but untied so they flapped up and down as he walked.

He raised a mittened hand in greeting, pulled off his parka, and sat heavily on the other end of the cot I was sitting on. The canvas stretched tight and lifted me up an inch or so.

"Teeter totter," I said. I was getting slap-happy.

He grinned. "We can't all be skin and bones. 'Sides, look how much longer I'd last if we got captured."

I was to remember that remark.

Everly said, "Some coffee, Bob?"

He shook his head, the alpaca ears bobbing violently. "No thanks." He gestured toward the Chinaman. "Anything I can do?"

"Don't think so, Chappie."

Jepson moved a couple of steps toward us, a row of five-inch Kelly clamps hanging from a finger. "You could pray for him."

Chappie looked at him long and hard. "I could."

He eased his bulk forward off the cot onto hands and knees on the packed earth floor, crawled a couple of feet, sat back on his heels. The Chinaman's eyes remained closed.

"Lord," Chappie said, and stopped. His eyes slid sideways toward mine. He closed his eyes and started again. "Lord God, we pray for the life of this man. We ask this because he is a man, a child of yours, not the enemy. We ask, too, that you soften the hearts of the men who sit daily at the peace table so that this terrible civil war might end. That no more will men kill in order to force their ideas and dogmas on others. Amen."

"Amen." Jepson turned back to his work.

Chappie sat with us for another half hour. We mumbled non sequiturs at each other from time to time. He fell asleep, almost tumbled off the cot, then shucked on his parka and left with a whispered, "Peace," and a hand raised as if in benediction.

I looked over at Chief Hoffman who was squatted beside the prisoner. I said, "How's he doing, Chief?"

"About the same, Doctor. Pressure's come back up and is steady at about a hundred. Right pupil's starting to dilate though."

I almost shouted, "It is? When'd you notice that?"

Everly was on his feet, flashing a light into the patient's eyes. "He's right. I just looked ten or fifteen minutes ago myself, and they were normal. What do we do now?"

"Nothing. What can we do? Can't operate on him here. Might not be a subdural anyway. Could just be swelling of the brain. Not a damn thing we can do. Not even any 10% glucose."

"I never thought much of that treatment anyway," Ron said. "Too much rebound. Right now I'd give a few bucks for some urea, though." He paused, thinking, then ventured a rueful smile, "Isn't there anything we could use to open his head? Take a quick look?"

"Are you nuts? Here? I wouldn't go for that. What if we got into some real bleeding? No cautery. No silver clips. No nothing to control hemorrhage. Huh-uh. That'd be foolhardy. Sit on your hands, Ron."

Jim Jepson and Rick Simpson had a hard time accepting Selkirk's head-banging without being able to do something about it. Jim stood with a handful of bloody hemostats, staring into space. He looked over at Simpson and said, "It was like he figured that since the Chinaman had already told us what he knew, now he oughta be dead."

"Only," Rick said, "he couldn't kill him right here."

"Yeah. So he took out his...what would you call it—took out his rage...yeah, his rage...by kicking him. Should be reported."

"Yeah? To *who*?' Simpson asked.

"Hell, I don't know. Somebody."

They went back to work, cleaning and sterilizing instruments in boiling water, but I could hear them talking and mumbling about it until Hoffman sent them off with, "Go get some sleep, you guys, nothin' you can do."

They stared at him, nodded, and shuffled out. For all their rough, tough ways in this rough and tumble world of curses, profanities, and obscenities, most of these guys were corpsmen because they wanted to be corpsmen—to take care of sick and injured people. I'd seen Jim Jepson take many a wounded and dying Marine in his arms and carry him gently from jeep ambulance to Sick Bay and nurse him along as if he were going to live. Once, when a Marine died and his buddy broke down, Jepson sat down with the buddy and cradled him in his arms, holding the boy's head on his chest.

The Chief dropped off to sleep on one of the cots. The guns from the 11th Artillery Regiment behind us rumbled intermittently but all was quiet now along the front lines.

Ron and I sat at opposite ends of the camp cot, slumped in thought, tired but unable to think about sleep. So we sat and waited and watched in the flickering lamplight.

Every so often one of us would get up to check the

patient's pulse, or check his eye signs, or pump up the pressure lantern, or go outside to use the mortar tube or just to get some fresh air.

"I suppose the 19th replacement draft'll be coming out soon," I said.

"Should be. I heard there were only four doctors coming."

"Won't work down to us very fast that way."

"Looks like you'll be up here with the battalion another two or three months anyway."

"Mmm-hmm." I yawned prodigiously.

"Good," he said, and I knew what he meant. And knew what had happened. He'd finally adjusted to being a dirt-crunching Marine doctor, had given me credit for it, at least to some degree, and had become dependent on me. Without realizing it, of course.

Silence again. The two hours dragged by. Neither of us wanted to leave the other with the sole responsibility of watching our prize patient, and neither mentioned going to bed. It seemed to be tacitly understood between us that we'd both maintain the vigil. Even though there really wasn't much either of us could do now.

I fiddled with the short-wave radio Ingrid had sent me in a box of popcorn. I couldn't find the Far East Network but I picked up a Japanese station playing Western music. First was "Il Baccio" and then "Play, Gypsy" and I almost went to sleep.

Not Everly. I'd never seen him so entranced by anything. His eyes were glazed, staring off into space. His lips worked slowly, pursing and relaxing. It was a side of him I hadn't seen before. Only when they started singing "Come Back to Sorrento" in Japanese did he slowly come back to Korea. I almost asked him where he'd been and then decided I didn't really want to know. Or rather, I wanted to know, but I didn't want him to have to tell me. Let him keep that secret place. There were few enough of those secret places in this First Marine Division.

Butch came in with two big canteen cups of hot chocolate. In his broken but understandable English he said he couldn't sleep, figured we'd like something hot. He was right. It was delicious.

He stood quietly, watching us sip. I offered him some but he smiled and shook his head.

Once in a while he glanced over at the Chinaman on the floor. I wondered what he was thinking and wished I could speak Korean. It wouldn't have been right to find out through an interpreter. I knew he was an orphan. Fred Overman's predecessor in the battalion had found him on the street in Wonju trying to hook onto an American Army unit, the First Cavalry, I think. He was about twelve, maybe older. It was hard to tell because he was a little guy and yet so worldly wise from all he'd seen and been through.

"*Cum-upsum-needa*," I said as I handed him my empty cup. "*Can-tonsum-needa*," he answered and slipped out the doorway, carefully re-tying the flaps.

Dawn came. A heavy mist hung close to the ground, the air clammy, cold, penetrating. I was reminded of the morning less than five months before when we off-loaded from the *Weigel* onto the LST at Sokchori. Was it only five months? I'd lived a whole lifetime since then. A sudden, burning, overwhelming, seiche-like tide of homesickness washed over me. I gripped the door flaps to steady myself. As quickly as it came, it left.

The sun's rays penetrated coldly to the fallow rice paddies below the row of tents as Everly and I greeted the flapping roar of the 'copter with audible grunts of relief.

Jepson and Simpson stumbled groggily out of their

tent and carried the Chinaman on his stretcher down to the landing. From where I stood in the doorway I could just barely make out the vermilion flags at the four corners of the pad.

Bending almost double, the corpsmen rushed in under the whirling blades with their stretcher and were unstrapping the lids from the "coffins" on the runners before the pilot could idle the rotors and get out to help. I never heard of a corpsman being injured by 'copter rotors.

For the pilot, the name of the game was balance. If he had two casualties, he'd size them up and add sandbags to the lighter side. This morning he had just one patient so he filled the other pod with sandbags. When he was satisfied, he helped the corpsmen strap down the lids and climbed back into the idling machine.

The corpsmen ducked back off the pad and when all was clear Jepson gave the pilot the thumbs-up sign. The pilot lifted off a few feet, turned the craft precisely in the opposite direction, tipped forward and upward and was gone.

And so the Chinaman, too, was gone.

"Let's hit the sack, Ron," I said wearily.

And so we did, with another insight into this war that went nowhere, that no one was allowed to win, that sent men out to do battle in No-man's Land with nothing accomplished except to bring back a Chinaman with a hole in his head.

Thirty-four

Well, maybe one thing was accomplished after all. McCallister was happy. He'd gotten the intelligence he wanted: that there had been no apparent leak to the Chinese about our plans to hit 1052.

So we were ready to go. But I still had no idea of the part I myself was to play until noon of the 18th when my field phone rang in the aid station. I was still groggy from lack of sleep and Everly was conked out on a stretcher on the floor.

It was the S-5, Major Selkirk. "Like to have you at the 5-6 tent about 1300, Doc. Can you make it?"

"Sure thing, Major. 1300." I hung the EE-8 back on its nail. I had a brief flashback of a booted foot slamming against a Chinaman's head. Cool it, I thought.

Ron Everly squinted up from the floor. "What's up, Doc?"

Hey, I thought, this guy's really loosening up. I briefly

considered answering him in Walt Disney-ese but figured I'd better leave well enough alone.

"Selkirk asked if I could make a briefing at 1300. Actually, I was thinking of packing a picnic lunch and taking Ingrid and Lorrie to the zoo." Then I got serious. "Meeting at 1300. Odd time. Can only mean one thing. Operation Rock must be about ready to get off the ground."

I couldn't have been more right. I went over to the 5-6 tent a little while later, scratched at the flap, entered and sat down on the packed mud floor. There was a tension in the tent that was palpable. The air was blue with cigarette smoke. As the saying goes, everybody who was anybody was there. All the officers from the line companies had been pulled back for this meeting. You could tell them from the rest of us by their blackened faces and their dirty uniforms. Also by the lack of insignia.

In contrast to his crew of officers, McCallister sat relaxed in his canvas chair, a director sure of his actors, a coach with a three touchdown half-time lead. I envied him. I was the loon trying to walk on land, the deer trying to cross a freeway. McCallister was in his element.

Bob Marne sat off to one side, feet folded under him, notepad on his knee. He raised a hand to me in silent greeting. I knew he was the brains of this operation but would let McCallister and Selkirk take charge because he as the S-3 was out of the chain of command.

Selkirk stood by McCallister's side in front of a contour map pinned to the tent wall. He spoke to McCallister. "I think everybody's here, skipper."

McCallister stood up and hooked his thumbs in his web belt. He had on a new fatigue cap and had squared it low on his forehead so I could hardly see his eyes in the dim light. I wondered how he'd gotten a new hat.

"The protective fire," he said, "will be furnished by the second squad of the second platoon of George Company. That's your sector, Fogarty. They'll be set up along the nose running out from Hill 67 directly in front of George Company. The first and third squads of the second platoon will form the main body of the decoy raiding patrol. These two squads will fall back into flanking positions on both sides of the second squad almost as soon as contact has been made with the enemy. The original base of fire—the second squad—will fall back last in case of counter-attack or if heavy mortar and artillery fire is encountered. Any questions, Fogarty, or anyone else?"

There were none. These men were veterans and their orders were clear.

McCallister looked over at me. "Doc, glad you're here. I'd like you to set up a forward aid station just to the rear of the second squad. Down in this draw here, about halfway between Ku-dong and the MLR." He pointed to the map pinned to the tent wall. "As I think you know, there are still remnants of an old trench system here. One of the bunkers has been enlarged and fortified. You know where it is?"

"Yes, sir."

"Good. There's a 'copter strip about fifty yards from this track," again pointing to the map. "After we take 1052 you can illuminate it at night with flashlights if necessary, with relative safety since it'll be in defilade. We hope to be done with this job before dark, but who knows."

A ghost of a smile hovered at the corners of his eyes as he said, "And I believe your jeep ambulances can get down this same road to pick up men who don't need 'copter evac."

He knew damn well we'd just been down there the night before. But I said, "Right, sir. We've been down there a couple times and we can make it all right. The cracker-box and even six-bys can make it, too, if the track stays frozen. Only trouble we've had is getting around that tank trap. Maybe two or three men could be stationed there the whole day, if they can be spared, in case anyone gets stuck and needs help getting out."

"Yeah. Make a note of that, Selkirk. Okay...well, that takes care of that. We'll leave the actual details for you and Dr. Everly to work out."

The briefing continued. I listened attentively to the military jargon, a language which had no counterpart in any of my previous experiences before I was sent to the FMF. The details of the plan were restated for the entire officer personnel of the battalion by Bob Marne, with comments and additions by Colonel McCallister.

As I left the briefing I turned over in my mind the few things which would have to be taken care of in setting up the forward aid station out in front of the MLR. The list of medical supplies to be put aboard the ambulances was already in the hands of Chief Hoffman. A word would suffice to get them ready. There was little else to do except decide which doctor and corpsmen would go out. There were twenty corpsmen on line already but they'd have to stay with their platoons.

By the time I reached my tent, I'd already decided that I'd go. I felt a rather peculiar sensation in the pit of my stomach. I hadn't felt that way before on any of our previous missions. Call it anything you want—premonition, foreboding, hunch—but this time I was worried.

Thirty-five

I decided to leave for the MLR that night at dusk rather than wait until morning. I climbed over boxes of combat dressings and sat on the jump seat just behind Rohn. Joe Tollander, our other driver, would follow a hundred yards behind with four corpsmen. Both jeeps were jammed with gear that could be spared from rear aid. Both Ned and Joe would return to H & S after leaving the people and supplies in defilade behind George Company's lines.

Everly stood watching. I wondered if he was happy or sad to be left back in H & S to triage the wounded as they came back. A week before when he'd gone up to forward aid he'd left with a dirty look in his eye. Now he reached in the open back of the ambulance and shook my hand.

"Still time," he said, "to change your mind and let me go back up."

"Thanks, Ron, but this is my show tonight." I grinned. "Time you got some experience in rear aid."

He let go of my hand and I could see him fight the urge to come to attention and salute. His dad might have done so, but I was proud of him. Sometimes it's hard for guys like Everly not to be "proper."

It was still light enough for Rohn to see the winding, pot-holed road out to the lines, but I figured that by the time we got there it would be dark enough that we wouldn't be spotted by Red ground observers like the time we were chased down the road with mortars.

The first part of the short trip was toward the east. Sitting in the back of the ambulance I could look out toward the west and see the brilliant reds and oranges and purples as they changed momentarily. The snow had melted off lots of the dirt and gravel roads that criss-crossed Korea, and now dust rose thickly, producing flaming sunsets like those in the western deserts of the United States.

Then the jeep swung sharply to the northwest and headed for the line of foxholes and bunkers which constituted the segment of the United Nations front held by George Company of the Third Battalion, Fifth Marine Regiment, First Marine Division, Tenth Corps, Eighth Army Korea.

I was almost glad now that I could no longer see the sunset because I always got homesick when I saw it.

Now I looked out the back toward the east and could see cumulus clouds piled up thousands of feet, the higher ones still catching the rays of the dying sun, shining red like diluted blood, the lower ones white and fleecy like a pile of swabbing cotton. Even as I watched, the last of the sun's rays moved slowly up the massive cloud bank, transforming it before my eyes from a mountain covered with blood, to a white mountain topped with blood, and finally to an all-white glacier touching heaven.

The jeep hit a pothole, jolting me back into the present. Almost simultaneously a command, "Halt!" rang out. The jeep jerked to a stop. It was now nearly dark and the Marine issuing the challenge detached himself from the shadows and stepped into the road with his BAR at port arms, his right hand on the trigger housing.

"Ambulances from battalion aid coming through," Ned called out. He'd forgotten the password or hadn't been given it. In fact, the password for the day was seldom used. Sometimes we didn't even know it, although the S-2 section tried to disseminate it down to all units early in the day. But the word changed every day and usually you'd remember the word from the day before and couldn't think of the right one even if you'd heard it. So the usual reply to a challenge at a roadblock back of the lines was something similar to what Rohn had just said. Out in front of the lines, between the MLR and OPLR or in No-man's Land, security was much tighter.

I knew we'd just passed the George Company supply point, since it was there that you met the first sentry when headed for the lines on this road, except for the sentry on guard at the exit from the Battalion CP itself.

We were challenged once more at the junction with the road which led off to the H & S Company of the Second Battalion of the First Marine Regiment. A few minutes and a few hundred yards later we were on the backside of the MLR. Joe Tollander pulled in behind us and the corpsmen piled out and began unloading both jeeps. We left the jeeps in defilade, climbed up the ravine to the ridgeline, walked down to the trench and then alongside it toward the forward aid bunker.

I stood on the bunker for a moment and listened as the sounds of the two jeep ambulances faded away as Ned and Joe followed the tank road down the hillside toward

H & S. It was a bit unnerving to hear them go.

The first patrol of George Company—the second squad of the second platoon—was to leave the MLR and head for Gookland at 0500, one hour before daylight. This would give them about an hour to get well out on the nose of Hill 67, in position to strike.

I would be right behind them with my corpsmen. We would wait on the MLR until the patrol moved out, then follow in behind it, moving down the nose of Hill 67 until we were close enough to the fighting to be of some value, yet far enough away to be protected from the mortar and artillery fire that would be directed at the advancing line of men.

It promised to be a long night.

I spent it hunkered down in the forward aid bunker, talking sporadically with the corpsmen, dozing off periodically into fitful sleep. It was cold and I wasn't used to it like the men who lived in the bunkers. To them I was "rear-echelon," but a cut above the real pogues who weren't even assigned to front line outfits and never made it into the front line trenches at all.

It would be many weeks before I'd be able to look back with some perspective at that night, and at the next day and night. It would be even longer before I'd be able to piece together just what happened during the thirty-six hours it took the Third Battalion of the Fifth Marines to take Luke the Gook's Castle back from the Chinese Communists.

Book Three
The Taking of Hill 1052

Thirty-six

The men of the second platoon of George Company squatted Korean-style in their bunkers or lay awake, fully dressed, on their sleeping bags. No one could sleep. There was too much to think about.

Or rather, there was only one thing to think about.

In a few moments they would leave the relative safety of their bunkers and would set out against an entrenched and fanatical enemy. Whether they'd been in the lines for a year or had come over in the last replacement draft, they had one thing in common. They were all scared.

Yet they were all eager to go.

The boredom of the trenches produced this state of mind. Almost anything was better than sitting in a cold bunker waiting for something to happen.

Any minute now the word would come down the line and they'd be moving out.

They were ready to go.

They'd field-stripped and cleaned their weapons the night before. They'd filled magazines and bandoliers. They would carry all the ammunition they could and still be mobile. On the frozen floor, ready to be buckled on, lay their web belts with canvas ammo holders, canvas-sheathed bayonets, and grenades clipped by their handles. In the pockets of their field jackets each carried a small first aid kit, chocolate bars, and a packet of K-rations.

I knew almost all of these men by sight and many by name.

Orville Newman had come over with me on the *Willy Wiegel*, so we had a special relationship. He hated the name Orville and insisted I call him Buckshot, a nickname he'd picked up when he killed his first buck with a shotgun.

Buckshot was a colorful character. A real hill-billy from Arkansas. On the ship he sat by the hour strumming his git-tar, chain smoking, drinking beer, cussing a blue streak at the slightest provocation. He liked to brag about his "un-preacher-like encounters with the fair sex." His goal was to survive the war, go to OCS and become a chaplain. I liked him immensely. He was proud of his brother, who'd been killed at Inchon a year and a half earlier, and of his father, who'd been killed at Tarawa eight years earlier.

Ira Jensen was one of the guys I'd played volleyball and baseball with back in Camp Tripoli. He was a Dane from Alexandria, Minnesota, and was so big that everyone called him the Great Dane. He and I had fought many a battle at that volleyball net and I'd swallowed a lot of volleyballs off his fist.

The platoon corpsman was Jason Smith. I hoped he'd gotten more sleep than I had after our ordeal with the Chinaman with the hole in his head.

Those guys and all the rest had welcomed me into their bunkers when I was up on the line. Although few were in what we euphemistically called "our own socio-economic class," all were United States Marines and proud of it.

They'd accepted me and I was proud of that. Our friendship was based on mutual trust and respect. I trusted those grunts to keep the Chinese out of my aid station so I could work in relative safety. They trusted me to use my skills to keep them alive if they were wounded. As Al Chamberlin says in *Circle of Courage*, our friendship didn't depend on how we acted under normal conditions, but "how you performed when your guts were exposed."

Jim Jepson was with me in the bunker. I'd picked him to be with me down in our forward aid station. He'd crawled back into a corner where a candle was burning on a C-ration can lid stuck into the dirt wall. His pocket-sized New Testament lay open in his lap. He sat against the wall, head tipped back, helmet pulled down over his eyes, which I supposed were closed in prayer. I envied him his peace.

I didn't want to see any of those guys in my aid station today with a leg blown off or a lung perforated by a Chinese bullet or a belly full of shrapnel.

But I knew I would. And the strange thing was that I accepted it. How in *HELL* did I prepare my mind to accept what I was going to see in the next twenty-four hours or so?

It was now 0430. A penetrating cold had crept into the bunkers and most of the men had put on parkas over their field jackets.

Finally the word came down the line: "Second platoon and attached people, move out." "Second platoon and attached people, move out." I could hear it coming, getting louder each time it was repeated, finally coming to the aid bunker.

Jim Jepson shed his parka, crawled out through the flap, letting a blast of cold air in, and called to the next bunker, "Second platoon and attached people, move out."

Down the line I could hear the scuffling now as each man shucked off his parka, buckled on his ammo belt, slung a bandolier of ammo diagonally over his shoulder, picked up his M-l or BAR, and headed for the area back of Captain Fogarty's bunker where the patrol would form up.

I followed with my five corpsmen a few moments after the last Marine had rolled over the back edge of the trench. It was pitch dark, the moon not up yet. There was no wind. We stood with the Marines like a football team around our coach, Captain Fogarty: restless, attentive, cold with nervous sweat, scared, prayerful.

Second Lieutenant Stan Kowicki was the platoon leader. He was a seasoned campaigner. He was the one who'd been decorated with the Bronze Star shortly after we arrived back on the line in November. Now Fogarty ordered him to take an informal muster by fire teams. Actually, I think all he said was something like, "Is everybody here?" There was no rigid coming to attention, no crack of heels, no snapping salute, no "Second-squad-all-present-or-accounted-for-SIR!!"

Even in the dark these men knew each other so well that it would have been impossible for a fire-team member to be absent and not be missed. Try lining up a basketball team even in the dark, and imagine one of them absent and not missed.

Marne had decided—and had convinced McCallister that the strategy was appropriate—to send this platoon out intact. Ordinarily patrols were made up of men pulled from bunkers scattered along a wide sector in order to leave the main line essentially undiminished in defense capability. By sending out an intact platoon, Marne gained a cohesive fighting force in exchange for a huge gap in the George Company perimeter. He counted on the Chinese not knowing this or not being able to capitalize on it.

This was the platoon picked to form the base of fire and decoy raiding party. They would engage the enemy on the forward slope of The Rock and fake a slowdown if not actual retreat at first contact. Re-aligning then and under cover, they would furnish a base of fire from which to harass the enemy, keeping its attention focused in front of The Rock.

When the attack began from the rear by Micleson's helicopter-borne troops, this platoon would continue their pressure, denying the enemy the opportunity to concentrate wholly on Micleson's raiders.

Sean Fogarty gave them no pep talk now. In fact, I don't think I heard him say a word except to confirm the muster. The men knew their mission.

The four Marines forming the point started slowly down the trail, stepping as quietly as possible, avoiding bushes that would rasp against their clothes, lifting their boots with each step rather than scuffling through the snow, holding their weapons so that they wouldn't clink against any other gear but always careful to keep the muzzle pointed skyward or earthward.

They stayed close together, their eyes searching the inky blackness ahead for the faint glimmer of bare ground along which they must move. To step off the trail was extremely hazardous because of the danger of both enemy land mines and our own. The trail itself had been swept by men with mine detectors only hours before, so the trail was as safe as it could be.

Those mine-sweeping guys are another story. They liked to say to those of us who thought we were such brave, courageous, intrepid, hero-types, "Hey, guys, where you're going, we've been!"

Unfortunately, among the mines that the Chinese used was the "box" or "shoe" mine, which no metal detector could pick up. It was buried in a wooden box and it blew off a man's shoe—with his foot in it. In World War II the Germans had the same mine, called it a *schuh* mine. The theory was simple: a man with his foot or leg blown off was a living casualty, out of the battle as much as a dead man, but requiring one or two other men to get him back to his lines. A dead man could be left alone until it was convenient to move him.

So the men stayed close together in column, and on the path. There would be time later to break up the column and form a skirmish line. The usual maxim, "Spread out, men, one round—or one machine gun volley—will get us all," had to be dispensed with that night, for in the blackness they were forced to keep the man in front of them in sight or they might lose contact and straggle off.

This was always the nightmare of night missions. And it happened. Especially if a man was wounded: he'd be unable to move, yet afraid to make any noise by calling out for a corpsman. His patrol would get farther and farther away. But the abandonment usually wouldn't last very long because of the close-knit fire team association: his absence would soon be noted, sometimes within minutes.

My corpsmen and I brought up the rear, carrying boxes of dressings, serum albumin, basic surgical instruments, blankets, water in five gallon Jerry cans, and special triage sleeping bags that had half a dozen zippers in carefully selected places so we could work on any part of the body without exposing the entire patient to the cold.

One corpsman carried a huge bundle of half a dozen collapsed canvas stretchers on his back. In the dark he looked like Quasimodo. I was grimly amused, not because of the resemblance, but because even under those odd circumstances I was able to marvel once again at Hugo's genius in choosing the opening words of the Latin *introit* for his soft-hearted monster's name.

I felt like going around to each one of those guys to shake his hand and tell him that everything was going to be all right. That we really weren't going to be in danger. But that would've been a transparent lie. They'd all been in situations like this and they knew it was the luck of the draw if you came back okay.

As we fell into line and followed the second platoon of George Company down the nose of Hill 67, I wasn't really thinking of the situation in which I found myself, one which hardly anyone would envy. At the moment all I could feel was a release from the restlessness which had gripped me since I'd gotten the orders to back up this patrol.

It was a lot like the feeling I used to get back in school before a race. There was that feeling in my stomach which everyone said was like butterflies but which to me always felt more like a chunk of lead. I didn't feel hungry and yet I thought I ought to eat. I didn't feel sleepy, yet I had to sleep. And as the time for the race drew near, when I was actually out on the field all warmed up, my legs felt weaker and weaker and I knew I could never keep up the pace. Then I was in the crouch and there was the sound of the gun and I was straining for that pole before I came off the straightaway into the turn because I couldn't afford to lose an inch to anybody and all of a sudden my legs weren't weak any more and I felt hungry and I drove my legs with a one-two precision and breathed on the count like I'd been taught.

So now, as then, I could feel the strength coming back into my legs, the lead in my stomach melting away, and my breathing coming more easily. I was almost cheerful as I stared into the darkness ahead.

It really is a gift from God that we ordinary mortals can't see very far into the future.

Thirty-seven

While the Marines of the second platoon were fanning out into a skirmish line preparatory to launching their attack, my corpsmen and I found the abandoned bunker in the old trench system. It'd been built well originally, reinforced recently, and was actually in better shape than any of our three forward aid stations in George, How and Item Companies. It was also much bigger, about 10 x 20 feet and almost five feet high.

I'd been in it once before. It had smelled of garlic and unwashed bodies and I'd figured that North Korean troops had lived in it just recently. But then I found a beautiful little pottery bowl back in one corner. It was slate gray with a pattern of blue leaves and flowers. I stuck it in a box of dressings and later carried it back to rear aid where I asked Butch what it was used for.

His face turned red as he stammered, "Little boy-san pee." Apparently a civilian family had used the bunker and had forgotten the bowl when they moved out. That bowl survived the war better than I did and now sits on the floor of my living room beside a three-foot-high carving of an old papa-san.

Jim Jepson tied a new mantle onto the Coleman lantern, lit it, and placed it on an artillery shell box in the back.

We had to be extra careful here about maintaining blackout, so we covered it with a small canvas tarp each time someone went out or came in.

JJ grinned up at me as he tied on the mantle. He knew where it came from. Ingrid sent them out, three in every box of brownies or chocolate chip cookies. The corpsmen thought it was funny. It was, in a way. Millions and billions of dollars going down the drain in Korea, and we had light in our aid station bunker only if the doctor's wife remembered to send out mantles.

While I was setting up the aid bunker, Bob Marne was still back in his tent in Battalion CP, making last minute preparations for his part in the operation. He told me later that as he waited, he was struck by the difference between this operation and those earlier in the Korean War and also those in which he'd participated on Guam and Peleliu.

Somehow, he said, it didn't seem quite real to be sitting there alone in the half-light of the tent, waiting to embark on a mission for which he'd prepared for almost a month. Like acting in a play. First came the script, then learning the lines, now waiting for the curtain to go up.

A strange kind of war, he'd thought. No continuous battles anymore. No continuous movement of lines back and forth. Just kill and withdraw, kill and withdraw. Well, thank God he'd thought, this mission at least had an objective in mind—the control of the High Ground in front of the Third Battalion.

He'd tried to remember—and couldn't—what General Omar Bradley had written about such a situation. I've looked it up and it was apropos: "The rifleman fights without promise of either reward or relief. Behind every river there's another hill—and behind that hill, another river. After weeks or months in the line only a wound can offer him the comfort of safety, shelter, and a bed."

About 0430, while we were mustering with Captain Fogarty, Marne, still back in battalion headquarters, walked down to the 5-6 tent. Major Selkirk's nose was a bit out of joint. He'd wanted to go up with McCallister, but had been ordered to stay in H & S. "We can't both be up there," McCallister had said. "I need you back here to run things if they go wrong up front."

When McCallister was ready they headed for George Company's command bunker, taking the same route I'd taken the evening before, but with more precaution because of the darkness. They'd have to remain in contact with all elements of the operation and therefore would have to stay in or near Fogarty's command bunker which housed the radio equipment. This was the same bunker where I'd quoted Shakespeare to Everly and told him about the Golden Days. So it was back of us on the MLR, half a mile behind our new forward aid bunker where the base of fire would be established.

An hour later, Marne and McCallister sat in that bunker. McCallister looked at his watch. Oh-five-thirty.

"Half hour till dawn, Bob," he muttered.

"Just about, Colonel. Wish Stan Kowicki'd give us a report from the second platoon. He must be in position by now."

"He is and he will. He's a good man."

It was about then that I got on my walkie-talkie down in my forward aid station and reported in. Marne took the call.

"Jack Lord here," I said, skipping all the usual formal radio talk.

"Marne here, Doc, go ahead."

"Kimchi smells pretty good down here."

I heard a grunt, then, "Damn fool. You can't really smell it?"

"No, just whistling in the dark." Then I got serious. "We're all set, Major. In the bunker and waiting."

"Roger, Doc. Keep your head down."

"Don't worry, I will. You, too. Good luck. Out."

We were only a couple hundred yards apart but we were worlds away. He was on the MLR with a battalion of Marines around him. I was in No-man's Land with a platoon of Marines who would soon be moving forward, leaving us unprotected. If the Chinese counter-attacked—left their positions dug into and flanking The Rock—before our full force moved down the hill, we could be in trouble.

And, according to the game plan, that force wouldn't move until the helicopter-borne troops had landed behind The Rock and were pretty well into their assault. Marne knew this and knew that I knew it. But I settled down in my bunker and closed my eyes for a rest.

Back in George Company's command bunker, Marne took another radio call, this one from Kowicki. "In position, Major."

"Good," Marne answered. "Maintain strict fire control. We'll tell you when to go. Out." He released the butterfly.

McCallister made an impatient gesture. "That platoon's fire control is perfect, Major."

Marne answered softly, "Yeah, Colonel. Neale's platoon's fire control was perfect, too, over on Hill 812. Remember? Then the gooks started dancing around with lanterns on the end of long poles just to draw fire. And they drew it, too, and then they knew just exactly where to place the next few dozen rounds of 82s. It's lucky anybody got out of that alive. And what's more, by the time we could retaliate with our 81s they'd doused their lanterns and were gone..."

"Okay, okay, Major."

The minutes dragged by. Marne toyed with the idea of checking with Lt. Micleson back in the Battalion CP where the helicopter troops would be forming up. Just then the radioman said, "Platoon leader reporting from battalion, sir. They're standing by ready to go. Any message?"

"Negative."

Oh-five-forty-five. Fifteen minutes yet. I felt like I was in a state of suspended animation. Conversation was useless. I mean, what do you talk about?

Home? Family?

We didn't talk about home and families very much under ordinary circumstances. It was too painful and didn't get us out of Korea any faster.

The weather? This afternoon or tomorrow?

In a duck blind, waiting for dawn, you could drink some hot coffee, or snooze a bit, or talk about the weather or what you were going to do that afternoon or tomorrow. You could talk like that because you knew you were going to be around then.

We all just sat on the frozen ground, backs against the dirt walls.

I think it was the uncertainty that wore on us, that bore

down on us. I mean, if you're a *kamikaze* pilot you know you're going to die. I saw a picture once of a Japanese *kamikaze* unit waiting by its planes at dawn; they stood around laughing and talking. There was no uncertainty and they were at ease. They knew what was coming and they were happy.

We didn't know what was going to happen and we were not at ease. Jack Belden, a veteran of the war in Germany, wrote, "Uncertainty is in the very air which a battle breathes. It lies coiled at the heart of every combat. The unknown is the first-born son of combat and uncertainty is its other self."

But actually, we weren't in immediate danger like the guys just off the nose of Hill 67. They were the ones who were going to be shot at in just a few minutes. Just think about that. I did, often. Put yourself in such a place. In just a few minutes you're going to get up off your duff, go out there in a dark green uniform against a background of white snow, and trained Chinese riflemen are going to start shooting at you. Would you be brave?

I think you would. It comes down to this: you do what you have to do. Most people do, anyway. And I knew that those guys out there were all brave men, for they were all United States Marines. They gripped their steel with a courage that cannot be comprehended by a man who has never faced death on the battlefield.

So, what is courage?

Courage means lots of different things under many circumstances that have nothing to do with combat. In non-military situations, courage is personified by the person who can move figuratively into a battle and struggle to win even when he knows the risk of being "shot down."

But, in combat, courage is having the mind-set that

gives a man the ability to obey an order to move out of shelter into enemy fire. Simple as that. I pondered that for awhile and then asked myself, what, more specifically, is the look of courage?

I'd seen many courageous men in my time with the Corps. I knew I had because the deeds they did were brave deeds, and the situations they handled were difficult ones, and the medals they won said they were brave.

But what did their faces show while they were being brave?

I thought of the hard, lean, eye-squinting look of one professional Marine who was "just doing his job."

I thought of the wild, flushed, angry, frightened look of the hero of the last engagement who was repaying a debt for a fallen comrade.

I thought of the panting, sweating, beardless corpsman who'd just pulled two men to cover out of an open rice paddy.

I thought of the white-eyed, black-skinned, mountain of a man who I'd heard repeating, "Come Jesus, come Jesus, come Jesus, come Jesus," the whole time he was being brave.

They were all brave. They were all different, but they were all the same: later they all sat and trembled, and wished they were home.

Oh-five-fifty-five. Back in the Battalion CP the pilots sat in their copters, turning the blades slowly. Inside, Lt. Micleson and Sergeant Harold Rainey and Corporal Jerry Thorpe and the other men sat on their heels, waiting.

Thinking.

No, not really thinking.

Feeling.

Gripping their rifles.

A Marine's only friend—his rifle.

His only thought—keep your head down.

His only wish—tomorrow.

Oh-five-fifty-nine. I watched in my mind's eye the little group crouched in the draw in front of the nose of Hill 67. Muscles tense, waiting for the race to begin. The starter's gun was poised, and they knew it. But there were no gaping fans, no girls in jeans, no white tape to mark the end. No end, in fact. A convenient endless blur. If there was an end, they refused to think about it. But if there was an end, it would come soon.

The artillery and mortar fire had not slackened yet. The World War Two vintage, prop-driven Corsairs, however, had done their work, pitifully little, on The Rock, with their 500-pound bombs, .50 caliber machine guns and 20 millimeter cannons.

The Thunderjets had come, seemingly silent, ahead of their engines' roar, had dropped their sheets of napalm, and were gone. Areas around the base of The Rock still smoked and burned, but the napalm they'd dropped on The Rock itself had flamed and died, having no further fuel upon which to work. By now the Reds might begin to suspect something was up, but probably not, since early morning air-strikes were the rule, not the exception.

Oh-six-hundred. The entire world suddenly seemed a silent thing, without voice or breath or substance. Then as my ears began to realize their release from the almost constant noise of the bombardment, smaller sounds made their appearance. A bird-cry, a small animal skittering in the brush, the wind, the creak of leather on a corpsman's .45.

Then from the nose of Hill 67 came a shot, jarring the still air almost indecently. Soon the valley reverberated with the crack of rifles. I asked Jepson to cover the lantern with the tarp, pulled back the door flap, and looked out.

Thirty-eight

It was light now and I could see the steadily advancing line of Marines already a hundred yards down from my bunker. Although I couldn't see the other group, I knew a base of fire had been established all around me on the nose of Hill 67, protecting the advance of the decoy raiding patrol. It was from this base of fire most of the firing was coming.

The advancing line was moving faster now, almost running, realizing they were targets, knowing they had to be targets if the helicopter-borne troops were to come in as a surprise. Yet they still had to keep from getting killed. That wouldn't help anyone. Now the sharp staccato of a light machine gun interrupted the continuous crackling of rifles and occasionally a deeper thud gave warning that the Reds had gotten their mortar crews into the fight.

Suddenly a dense white cloud erupted near the line of advancing men, followed quickly by several more in succession down the line.

"Willy Peter," I muttered to myself. Willy Peter was what the men "affectionately" called the shells that splattered burning chunks of white phosphorus when they exploded. Every W. P. injury was a third degree burn, burning on contact through the entire thickness of skin into the fat or muscle below. The Chinese didn't use them much, so I figured they might have deduced that something big was in the offing.

The base-of-fire Marines who had stayed back on the nose of Hill 67 had now moved down the nose and had dug in just below our aid station. I could see several from my bunker. I could plainly hear Kowicki calling out orders to his thirteen-man squads. "First squad, your perimeter is 10 o'clock to 1 o'clock. Second squad, 12 o'clock to 3 o'clock. Third squad, 2 o'clock to 5 o'clock."

I knew this was a routine in case of a counter-attack from The Rock, and was not of much significance in this action. But the lieutenant was going according to the book. Better to over-estimate your enemy than to underestimate him.

One of the Marines, a private, crouched behind a splintered pine tree. He was no more than twenty yards from me and I could watch him as he shifted his gaze quickly from The Rock to the flanking lines of advancing Marines.

This was no battalion exercise in the treeless hills of Camp Pendleton where the "enemy" wore orange armbands and shot blanks and pointed a finger at you and said, "You're dead," or, "You're my prisoner." This was real.

The Marine I was watching was pretty well protected from small arms fire. By twisting his body a few degrees, he could keep his legs and hips behind the main trunk and still keep his chest and shoulders hidden by the splintered fragment. Only incoming shells could get to him, but they were dropping faster and faster as more enemy mortars were activated.

His job was to search the gook lines for signs of fire, then quickly shoot at that spot to keep the enemy deep in their holes while the raiding patrol moved up the hill.

He watched the line of advancing Marines even as I did. They ran, crouched, ducked, and hid, but always moved forward.

All except one.

I sucked in my breath with disappointment as one of the advancing Marines suddenly stood straight up, looked around him as if to see where he was, then collapsed in a heap.

He looked dead.

A corpsman soon appeared and dragged him back down the hill into the ravine. The corpsman was Jason Smith and from my bunker I could see him working on the Marine. He started a unit of serum albumin in an arm vein, but didn't strap on any combat dressings. I heaved a deep sigh of relief. He wasn't dead or Smitty wouldn't be starting an IV.

Jepson, crouched behind me and watching also, muttered, "Got him in the guts."

I nodded agreement and said, "Go get him."

Without answering me, Jepson turned and said to the bunker at large, "Nap time's over, boys. It's daylight in the swamp." And then I remembered that he was from northern Wisconsin where the giant white pines used to grow.

He and Rick Simpson scrambled down the hill with a stretcher and I soon lost sight of them in the brush. In just a few moments they reappeared in the ravine, startling Smitty into reaching for his .45. But just as quickly he grinned widely and helped load the Marine onto the stretcher, then dodged off through the trees to regain his platoon.

As I watched the action down in the ravine, the base of fire had been ordered forward to the next ridge line. The raiding patrol had already passed over to the other side of the ridge and had taken a tremendous volume of small arms and mortar fire. It was just as Marne had predicted on the day we viewed the area from the George Company bunker.

I could see a number of men lying wounded now on the ground along the back side of the ridge, waiting patiently for evacuation. There would be others that I couldn't see.

The base-of-fire squad, thinned out now by the increased length of line to be covered, settled in on top of the ridge and poured as heavy a volley as they could into The Rock, hoping to keep the enemy fire to a minimum of accuracy.

Our own artillery and mortar fire, which had stopped just prior to the six o'clock jump-off, had resumed again as the raiding patrol moved forward. Now it was also dropping a tremendous volume of fire on the Chinese MLR to keep them pinned down.

The decoy patrol was out of sight in the valley on the other side of the first ridge, but I could follow their progress by watching the exploding mortars and white phosphorus shells. It was six-twenty. Marne had guessed that it would take a full half hour or maybe longer to get the decoy raiding patrol up far enough on the hills surrounding The Rock that they would take the full attention of the Chinese.

Now the base of fire was moving up, trying to reach the ridge immediately behind the slowly-advancing line of attackers. It would take the base of fire another ten or fifteen minutes to establish themselves on the ridge and for the attacking patrol to move up far enough. Then Marne would be able to order in the helicopter troops, and the action would begin in earnest.

The raiding patrol was again easily seen in the bright morning sunlight climbing the slope directly beneath The Rock. Already they were using for protection boulders that had broken off from the rocky precipices above. The fire upon them was intense. It was obvious that the Chinese were now convinced that this was a major frontal attack on their fortress.

This was exactly what McCallister and Marne had hoped for. If the Chinese concentrated their men and weapons on our Marines out in front of their lines, there would be greater chance of surprising them with the 'copter troops. Then as they reversed their field to hold the rear of The Rock, the two-company assault on the front would be doubly effective.

Thirty-nine

Jepson and Simpson came dodging up the slope with the stretcher, unhappily ignoring for the moment the groans of the Marine, but unable to slow down for fear of making themselves an inviting target for fire from The Rock.

The Marine's face was covered with dirt and melting snow but I recognized him right away.

It was Orville "Buckshot" Newman, the guitar-playing Marine who wanted to be a chaplain.

"Hey, Buckshot," I said, "how we gonna take that hill without you?"

His face lit up with a wide grin. "Howdy, Doctor. Think I got a load a buckshot in my belly." He grimaced as a spasm of pain hit him, then said, "Always said huntin' coons at night with a trigger-happy bunch a hill-billies was dangerouser than Korea. Guess I was wrong."

He did have a belly wound as Jepson had predicted.

But not buckshot. Probably a .30 caliber rifle or machine gun bullet. I could picture the inside of his abdomen: multiple ragged holes in the bowel leaking semi-solid or liquid feces, mixing with blood and maybe bile or urine.

This would be a case for someone like Mike Lavierri and he'd fix this kid up and he'd be as good as new in a few weeks.

I gave Buckshot a quarter of morphine and the glazed look of unbearable pain slowly subsided. He'd need 'copter evac but I hesitated to call one in while the action was so heavy and so close. "Think you can get him back to the MLR?" I asked Jepson.

He didn't even hesitate. "Soon's as I catch my breath."

I radioed back to Everly in rear aid. "Get a Bell up to the 'copter strip back of George Company, will you, Ron?"

"Wilco, Jack. Thing's started up there?"

"With a vengeance. You can probably hear it."

"Oh, yeah. Y'want me up there?"

That caught me off guard and I practically stuttered as I said, "Not now. Not yet anyway." I resisted the temptation to say, "Hey there, Hahvahd Yahdian, you volunteering for action now?" But he didn't need that now and it was still better to have him back in battalion CP.

A few minutes later Jepson and Simpson took off up hill again with Orville "Buckshot" Newman. I've often wondered what happened to that guy, the first casualty of Operation Rock, which in turn was the first major helicopter assault in history.

It wasn't long before the second casualty was brought in. To my surprise it was Smitty who'd walked him back to us. Platoon corpsmen on patrol rarely left their units but this was different. One glance at the man he'd brought in told me instantly why Smitty had left the advance to bring this guy in. It was a man by the name of Ralph "Red" Dockerty, in his first action against the enemy. He was one of their buddies and he needed special attention.

"N. P.," Smitty said quietly and unnecessarily, and then scurried out.

N. P. Neuro-psychiatric casualty.

I moved over slowly toward "Red" Dockerty. He was just a boy, seventeen maybe. He gazed straight ahead, either not noticing my approach or not caring. His face was completely blank, no emotion registering.

No fear.

No anger.

No recognition.

Nothing.

His hands lay in his lap, palms up. He sat exactly as Smitty had placed him. His unloaded M-1 had been placed out of his reach against the mud wall of the cave-like bunker. His helmet was askew. His web belt, bayonet, and bandolier of extra ammo were missing.

He was, for all practical purposes, not of this world. His contact with reality was gone. His nose twitched. A faint glimmer of surprise appeared in his eyes then faded as quickly as it had come. He scratched his nose, then clenched his fist against his mouth.

In every war there are the wounded and the dead. But in addition to these there are the N. P. patients. In the first World War they called it shell-shock. In the Second World War they called it combat fatigue. In my war, the Korean War, we called it N. P. The name changed but the condition was the same.

Psychiatrists and psychologists in a combat zone listen to the same story over and over again. A man goes into combat after good training in the States. While on the move, taking an objective, for example, he does well, even distinguishes himself. The objective is obtained and the men begin to dig in.

There's no overhead cover, only open foxholes. The man sits in his hole while hundreds or even thousands of rounds of mortars and artillery fall on the hill. One by one the men of his platoon are hit and are carried away by corpsmen. The concussion waves spreading from shells exploding close by blur his vision and dampen his hearing, maybe even make him temporarily blind and deaf.

Every once in a while someone near him takes a direct hit and just disappears.

He himself is not hurt, but he begins to wonder how long he can escape. He begins to withdraw within himself. John Steinbeck once described how this progressive fear creeps up on the soldier: "Your skin feels thick and insensitive. There is a salty taste in your mouth. A hard, painful knot is in your stomach where the food is undigested. Your eyes do not pick up much detail and the sharp outlines of objects are slightly blurred. The whole world becomes unreal."

These are the preliminaries and they can be reversed by many things: a strong superior ordering the man to advance or retreat, a serious wound requiring evacuation, a resurgence of religious faith, the calming words of a buddy.

Or it can proceed along the downward track: the man's ego cracks, splinters, explodes, disappears like his buddy did. His eyes take on a glassy, starey look—the 2,000 yard stare. His face flushes. He stutters. He may be completely inarticulate. He is led back down to the battalion aid station and is evacuated to a forward hospital.

These, plus the dead, are the real casualties of war. In World War II they comprised 10% of the casualties. They, in their inarticulateness, speak louder than all the words of the generals at the Peace Table. These men know war. They are the unwounded wounded. As José Narosky once said, "In war, there are no unwounded soldiers."

I started talking. "Listen, Red, you just sit there now till you feel okay. No one's going to hurt you. We won't let them. Just sit there and try not to think. We'll have you out of here in no time."

Still no reaction.

I thought ahead to the future of this man. It was important that it be noted in writing by the first doctor to see him that this man was not deserting, not willfully disobeying an order. He had, rather, reached a state of being "incapable of differentiating right from wrong and adhering to the right." That's the way the division psychiatrist would put it.

I knew the psychiatrist, Dr. Jake Fenn, and could visualize the scene back at Able Med later that night. A corpsman leads Red Dockerty in, holding him and guiding him gently by the elbow.

Fenn, a big man with hooded brown eyes and cauliflower ears, sits on a wood-and-canvas folding chair behind a tiny table. A kerosene pressure lamp hanging from the center pole throws shadowed yellow light on Fenn's Slavic face. He sips black coffee from a canteen cup filled from a steaming container on the pot-belly stove. His eyes smolder and scintillas flick across the black pupils as he ponders whether my patient had willfully disobeyed an order or had been incapable of understanding it.

The difference was extremely important.

If this man was capable of differentiating right from wrong, and had willfully chosen the wrong, he was a deserter and would be given a general court-martial and receive a stiff punishment—ten to twenty-five years or more in prison. The maximum penalty, of course, was death, but this was seldom carried out nowadays.

But it was obvious to me that Ralph Dockerty was unable to differentiate right from wrong—he didn't know what he was doing. He needed treatment and probably a Section Eight discharge rather than the lock-up. I made this as clear as I could as I filled out the EMT and sent him up the hill with a corpsman. Jake Fenn should have little trouble with this decision. There would be no blood on his hands this time.

A more profound question, I think, is why more combat troops don't crack up. There isn't just one answer.

But one answer is simply that in the Marine Corps and all other well-trained outfits there's an incredible cohesion of personalities, a forging of friendship ties, an *esprit de corps*. The individual is supported by his fire team, squad, platoon, company, battalion, regiment, all the way up to his division. A wounded man will fight with the doctor to stay with his unit. He doesn't want "to let his buddies down." Which may translate in some cases to not wanting to appear chicken, but that's not a bad motivation in this case.

Another answer is that the man in combat has a cause to fight for. This motivation is the charge of the commanders and the better they do their job, the lower will be the N.P. rate. In Korea we knew we were fighting a Godless communism which had perpetrated a massive takeover of people who had already repudiated such a political life style.

Still another fundamental answer is summed up by Jack Belden: "It is just those men whose lives are most miserable, the very toughest soldiers, those whose job is to kill, maim and destroy, it is just those men who are the most gentle, considerate and moved by feelings of sympathy for others. War binds men more tightly together than almost any other branch of human activity. To undergo shame, fear, and death with scores of others of your age and mental coloring—who indeed would trade these comrades of the battlefield for friends made in times of peace?"

In the Marine Corps this binding together was sometimes demonstrated in a very concrete way. A Marine cut off from his unit by a serious wound knew that his guys would come after him, even at the risk of being killed themselves. I saw this time and again. Twice I saw Marines wade into enemy fire to recover the body of a buddy they knew was already dead. Marne had gone after the corpsman Chuck when he was quite certain he was dead.

Forty

Gunshot, mortar and Willy Peter wounds began to trickle into the bunker. As usual, about 70% of the wounds were shrapnel, the rest bullets. As each man was brought in, the corpsmen quickly filled out the Emergency Medical Tag, copying from the dog tag around the man's neck. Each small brown EMT was signed by the corpsman or myself, and the nature of the injury recorded. This facilitated triage back at the medical company and also made the man eligible for the Purple Heart.

I didn't have a Purple Heart. I didn't want one. I never got one.

Some of the wounds were relatively insignificant but bad enough to at least temporarily take the man out of action. We sent them walking back up the trail to Everly. They knew the way. They'd just come down that path in the dark.

Some of the wounds were mortal, at least where we

were. All we could give them was First Aid. With rare exceptions, the only thing I could do that a corpsman couldn't do was to call a 'copter. I probably shouldn't minimize the job of the battalion surgeon, but if anyone can, I can. I suppose the dregs of bitterness still lie in the bottom of my cup because I still wonder what the hell I was doing down there in No-man's Land on March 19th of 1952.

Well, anyway, we couldn't do much for some of those poor guys. We knew that. They knew that. So, in that time and place, they died. Some, in great agony, croaking or screaming for someone to do something. Some, quietly, fading quickly away from us to wherever combat Marines go when they die.

Old soldiers may never die, but believe me, General MacArthur, young Marines do.

We covered their faces with their helmets.

There's no mystery for me any more about why we close the eyes of the dead with pennies or cover their faces with a sheet or tip their helmets down over their faces. It's so that their dead uncovered eyes can't follow you around the room.

Forty-one

While we were up to our eyeballs in blood and gore in the valley out in front of the MLR, Marne in the George Company command bunker back on the MLR had been keeping close track of the position of his men as they stormed The Rock. Now, at 0720, he said to Colonel McCallister, "I think it's time to move."

McCallister grunted, nodded his head, and said to Sergeant Ruiz Gonzaga, his radioman, "Raise Lt. Micleson."

"Sir."

When Micleson came on, McCallister said sharply, in a pre-arranged code, "Shove off, coxswain, you're loaded."

"Aye, aye, sir!"

One at a time the eight Sikorskis lifted out of the H & S Company compound and formed into two tight formations of four. They maintained radio silence until all units were airborne and hovering in place over the Soyang-gang. Then Lt. Micleson, kneeling on the deck in the lead 'copter, shouted to his pilot, "When you're ready, Captain!"

The pilot raised his chin in acknowledgment, flipped on his radio and barked into it, "Opening kick-off! Go for six!"

Let the gooks try to break that code in time to do anything about it.

The eight big birds tipped forward as if tied to the same string. They roared down the river valley, which ran almost straight west for a quarter of a mile before swinging north over the Item Company MLR.

I was busy triaging—moving from man to man, determining which should be dressed and sent back to the lines, which should walk back to Everly at rear aid, which should be held temporarily until we could get them out by jeep ambulance or helicopter.

A roar in the sky drowned out all sound in the bunker. I thought with a start that a 'copter was coming in to take out the wounded. But I hadn't ordered one yet. I soon realized that the sound was considerably louder than one 'copter.

I crawled out into the trench line, followed by three or four corpsmen, and cautiously lifted my head above the edge of the ditch. We could see them coming as they skimmed the Item Company lines and swept over the ridge at Ku-dong, less than a quarter of a mile from us.

The element of surprise was now gone. The copters were obviously headed for the CCF lines. But would the Chinese have any idea that there were troops aboard? McCallister and Marne thought not. Both hoped that the Chinese would be stunned into inactivity, or at least would not do the right thing and order their own men onto the backside of The Rock.

Almost all the firing around us had stopped. I squatted on my heels, leaned back against the mud wall of the trench, and said, "Well, there go the boys to the back of that damn Rock."

"Ought to get a let-up here for a while, Doctor," Jepson said.

"Yeah, give us a chance to clear out the KIAs and the badly wounded. Maybe take a quick inventory of supplies."

We watched now as the two 'copter formations split off from each other and rose steadily up the flanks of Luke the Gook's Castle. One group went left, one went right, around The Rock. We lost sight of them then, but we could still hear them.

Forty-two

As the copters swung around The Rock, they broke formation and fanned out into a more or less regular semi-circular line half a mile long. This translated into one 'copter with five or six Marines every hundred yards. When the skirmish line was formed there would then be one Marine every 15-20 yards. "Not bad," Marne had said, "wouldn't want 'em any closer together. Not at first, anyway."

None of the pilots had ever seen the areas in which they were to land. But they'd pored over aerial photos and contour maps. They'd cursed the general for not allowing them to make runs in L-19s which would have given them a better idea of what the terrain looked like on the back side of The Rock.

Now each searched the ground below him for the landmarks in three dimensions that he'd picked out on the maps and aerial photos. Despite his past experience in correlating maps and photos with the actual terrain, almost every pilot had a moment of panic as he realized how different the terrain looked from the mental picture he'd developed.

But then as he got closer and started the descent, he picked out a hill here, a boulder there, a gully and a road over there. Somehow each 'copter headed for a different clearing. As in the practice runs, the air was vacuumed clean of all other sound by the flapping rotors.

Sergeant Rainey stood in the doorway of his 'copter, thinking grimly that this was not at all like jumping out of an LCP into the warm waters of a Pacific island beach. He slitted his eyes against the rush of icy wind, searching the ground for enemy troops. He braced himself with one hand on the hatch, knees slightly flexed, rifle gripped by the breech and trigger housing.

As the 'copter hit the ground, he jumped, nearly fell across a fallen tree, and started running. He heard five thumps behind him and knew his team had jumped.

The 'copter wasn't down for more than seven or eight seconds. In a maneuver he'd done literally thousands of times, the pilot lifted the 'copter a few feet, spun it through 180 degrees, tipped forward and took off. (We counted them as they came back across Ku-dong. When the eighth one appeared, a little cheer went up from where we were crouched in the trench outside our aid bunker.)

Now Rainey gripped his rifle with both hands in the port arms position, swinging his whole upper body in one taut unit. With each step his helmet strap cut into his neck (no chin-cups on our World War Two helmet straps!), his bayonet banged against his hip, his bandoliers of ammo slammed against his ribs. He didn't notice any of these things. Not because there wasn't pain, but because the adrenaline flowed and his concentration was so great. And massive loads of endorphins flood the bloodstream under these conditions, masking pain and producing a profound euphoria. Rainey only knew that he felt good.

The rest of the platoon had spewed out from copters all up and down the line. Rainey slowed a little, waiting for the line to form alongside him. Out of the corner of his eye he caught sight of a large boulder and had the fleeting desire to fling himself behind it.

No resistance yet.

Then came the command from Second Lieutenant Micleson, "Hit the deck."

And hit it he did, in one smooth and practiced motion, dropping to knees first to break his fall, then forearms and butt of rifle, and then belly. His canvas ammo case dug into his midriff. Snow sifted down the open sleeves of his field jacket and started to melt. Sweat formed on his forehead and dripped into his eyes and off his nose.

He started forward on his belly, crawling for the nearest cover. He could hear the grunts of his neighbors as they too crawled forward.

It wouldn't be long now, Rainey thought, before the stuff started coming in. First it would be bullets as the Chinese realized that they were in fact surrounded. They would come running out to the mouths of the tunnels in The Rock and start firing down the slope.

No sooner had that thought crossed his mind than a rifle cracked far off to his right, then another almost directly in front of him. Soon an almost continuous fire came from the back of The Rock. The line of advancing Marines was still two hundred yards from its objective.

Rainey assumed that the Chinese Command Post was behind him now, cut off from its own troops in The Rock, and likely to be ineffective. At least until the reserve troops could be brought up. What was it Major Marne had said? One battalion, three miles back, with five or six trucks to transport them? Something like that. That would take a while even if they were ready to go, which they probably were. The Chinese in The Rock and in the trenches around it were on their own except for radio contact.

Rainey raised up a bit, looking down the line for his squad leaders and for Lt. Micleson. Nobody hit yet that he could see. No machine gun fire yet either. Now, however, mortars started falling, coming from their rear, since the Marines had landed between the Red MLR and their supporting units.

Micleson stood up and started to run forward, making for a spot some thirty yards up the hill. As he ran he shouted orders which were relayed down both flanks until in a matter of seconds the entire line was moving forward, in short spurts of two or four or ten yards, always going from one cover or concealment to another. Very few rounds had been fired by the attacking patrol yet. There was too little time to search out the hillside for the backflash of rifle fire.

But many rounds had been fired by the enemy and the mortars were deadly, pinpointing with great accuracy the line of advancing Marines. Whenever a Marine stopped in one place for more than a minute or two, a saturation pattern of mortars dropped on him. They've got an FO up in that Rock somewhere, Rainey thought, and we gotta get him.

Several men were down now. Corpsmen pulled them behind boulders and trees, did what they could, then carried them or sent them forward with the advancing line. All evacuation would have to be forward and continuous. The wounded could not be left behind because no one knew how soon the CCF could get that battalion out of reserve and send them against the rear of the advancing Marines.

There was no respite from the counter-fire and still they couldn't do much in the way of returning the fire. Rainey thought to himself that here was where they needed a base of fire back of them to protect their advance. But there was none and they fought their way up the hill.

A machine gun opened fire. Rainey edged forward around a tree and tried to locate it. He found it directly in front of the fire team led by Jerry Thorpe, and off to the left of his own position. Another machine gun started chattering down the line but that one was going to be somebody else's business. Rainey called over to Thorpe, "Get that gun."

"Can't see it," Thorpe called back.

"Up behind that low outcropping of rocks—almost straight ahead of you. Wait'll it starts up again. There. There's big rocks and some sandbags piled up in front of it. See it?"

"Yeah, got 'er." Then to his fire team, "Schaeffer, you and Gingrich dig in. Try to keep 'em busy so they can't do much shootin'. Svenger 'n me'll start moving up on that gun."

Thorpe and Svenger began inching forward on their bellies. The gun was up the hill from them about a hundred yards, far out of grenade range and too well fortified to neutralize with small arms fire. They'd have to get up to within fifteen or twenty yards to be accurate with their grenades.

Our Marines loved their grenades. Rifles can jam with just a little sand or ice. Machine gun barrels can burn out. BARs can run out of ammo. Grenades always work.

Rainey watched Thorpe and Svenger and felt a fatherly

pride. He'd watched these two guys work together for three months in the George Company patrols and was greatly pleased when they'd both volunteered for this mission.

He smiled inwardly. They were sure a mismatched pair.

Jerry Thorpe was a city kid, hadn't even graduated from high school. His speech was from the streets. But he was intelligent and hard-working and maybe this hitch in the Marines would put him onto the right track.

Aage Svenger was a first generation American. His parents had come over from Denmark with a big family just before the war when Hitler was threatening all of Scandinavia. Aage was the caboose in a big family so his parents were now elderly. They'd wanted him to go to college but had no money to send him. He'd joined the Marines to fight for the country his parents had adopted. He'd get his college, Rainey thought, or at least part of it, through the GI Bill. That is, if he made it through these next few hours.

A simple prayer formed in Rainey's mind, "Take care a those kids, God, see 'em through this."

As Rainey watched, he began to consider just what must be done once that gun was silenced. That gun, and the others along the line. When they'd been taken or their operators forced to fall back, the Chinese resistance would be just yards short of The Rock itself.

Behind the machine gun the rock walls of Luke the Gook's Castle rose almost perpendicularly. Rainey knew that around the base of The Rock was the trench system which communicated with the main trench system running the entire length of the Red lines. Beyond the trenches at the base of The Rock, Rainey could now see excavations that extended right into The Rock itself. This they had suspected and now knew to be a fact. The Rock had been honeycombed with tunnels and caves.

It was from these that most of the small arms fire was coming. No wonder they couldn't find the riflemen. They were crouched in the semi-darkness of the tunnels and caves. Now that he'd found them, Rainey could pick out an occasional backflash. This was going to be tough. Those machine guns would actually be the easy part.

Thirty yards ahead of Rainey, a little off to his left, Thorpe and Svenger crouched behind trees twenty feet apart. Svenger was a little closer to their objective and Thorpe called to him.

"Can you get a grenade up there now?"

"No. Still too far."

"All right. Cover me. I'm gonna make a run for it."

He got cautiously to his hands and knees, peering at the terrain between him and the next good cover. It was nearly thirty yards across almost treeless ground, but with scattered bushes he could use for concealment. Within grenade throwing distance of the machine gun nest was a large ragged slab of grey-black granite that had fallen from The Rock eons ago.

That's where he had to go.

He'd have to run uphill on a grade of almost thirty degrees. As far as he could tell, there was no other way to do it. He'd been ordered to silence that gun. The thought never entered his mind to question Rainey's decision that this gun was important.

Besides, this was his big chance to show Rainey just what he could do. For another Marine the motivation might be to show his buddies, or to show the world, or to show Dad or Mom. For Jerry Thorpe, it was to show his hero, Harold Rainey.

He pulled his legs up under him until his feet were

planted firmly. Like a cross-country runner in a standing start, he dug the toes of his Mickey Mouse boots into the snow so he wouldn't fall on his face as he started his charge. He gripped his M-l in both hands, left on the barrel, right on the breech. He tightened the chin strap of his helmet.

He looked over at Svenger, who gave him the thumbs-up sign.

He nodded his head sharply in acknowledgment.

In a half-crouch he pushed off uphill, zig-zagging erratically, head down like a full-back, legs driving him upward. He changed pace, spurted forwards, threw his body one way and another.

The machine gun opened up and he heard the zinging of bullets like a swarm of bees all around him. One of them plowed into his left arm, grabbing it like a wrestler, yanking him backward and spinning him around. He fell heavily on his back. Pain ran down his arm from the elbow.

He rolled onto his belly, got up and started going again, more slowly this time because he couldn't get his left arm to pull with the rest of his body.

He tripped on an almost invisible wire at ankle level, heard the "phttt-whrrrr" in time, and threw himself flat on his face. Hot steel rained on his back from the Bouncing Betty that had exploded fifteen feet in the air. Cursing his stupidity, knowing he should've been watching for those, he sprang to his feet and lunged forward the remaining five yards.

He belly-flopped behind the boulder and took inventory of his wounds. His whole back felt numb. Sort of a dull ache there. No real pain. Blood ran down his back from half a dozen places. But, he thought with grim relief, at least it missed me on the way up, didn't rip off my balls like some guys I know.

His left arm hurt, though, a burning, throbbing pain in the muscles above the elbow. The thought "million-dollar wound" flicked through his mind and was gone. He was pretty sure his arm wasn't broken. Awful numb, though, below the part that was throbbing. Blood was beginning to flow in a steady stream from the bullet hole in his sleeve. His right calf ached. Must have a chunk of shrapnel there, too, he thought.

Carefully he propped his M-l against the boulder.

Detached two grenades from his web belt.

Pulled the cotter pin on one.

Let the handle fly off.

Heard the fuse pop.

Stood up and lobbed the grenade into the machine gun nest with an overhead motion like a cricket bowler's.

Pulled the cotter pin on the second grenade.

Let the handle fly off.

Heard the fuse pop.

Transferred it to his right hand.

Threw the grenade.

Two explosions, two seconds apart.

And silence.

He collapsed flat on his belly, exhausted and short of breath. His helmet strap cut into his chin so he popped it up and grabbed it with his teeth. It felt good to have something to grind his teeth on. Better'n a bullet to bite on, he thought. He tried to raise himself up but his strength was gone and he eased down into the snow.

Behind him he heard Svenger calling loudly for a corpsman, heard the crunch of snow under feet running toward him, listened for the machine gun to open up and, when it didn't, felt a glow of pride. Better'n a joint for givin' a guy a high, he thought.

He turned his head and saw Sol Epstein dropping to

his knees beside him. "Okay, Jerry," the corpsman said, "we got you now."

He made cuts in Thorpe's field jacket and fatigue jacket to expose the back wounds. Thick clotting blood covered Thorpe's back, soaked his underclothes and fatigue jacket. With each breath, pink frothy blood sprayed from a penetrating wound just below the right scapula. The coarse sucking noise of the wound seemed to originate in hell. Quickly the corpsman ripped open a large sterile battle dressing and tied it onto the wound. Then he fished a roll of tape out of his pocket and rapidly made an airtight seal over the dressings.

"Y'ain't gonna feel a whole lot better now, Jerry, but at least you won't get worse. Get ya out a here soon's I can get another guy to help."

Thorpe whispered, "Thanks, Sol, I owe ya one."

Epstein gripped Thorpe's shoulder and grinned. "I'll need about ten grand to get through med school."

"Ya got it!"

Sol moved on. There were men down all over who needed him and he couldn't do any more for Thorpe now.

Thorpe continued to gasp for breath. Epstein was right though. It wasn't getting any worse. Maybe even a little better. His whole back felt slimy as the blood started to clot and dry. His left arm ached like a toothache. His throat was dry from his rapid breathing. When he coughed, pains like knives jabbed the entire right side of his chest. His sputum was thick and bubbly and bright red.

Why, he asked himself, didn't he at least give me a shot of morphine? He started to call the doc back, then remembered one of my lectures the last time we were in reserve. No morphine for head and chest cases. He couldn't remember why. He wished he'd listened more carefully. Awfully cold though, it'd been, sitting in that unheated squad tent, their breath freezing as they listened, and no one asking any questions because that would've just prolonged their misery.

Forty-three

Harold Rainey continued his hazardous journey up the back of Hill 1052, Luke the Gook's Castle. He passed Thorpe lying on his stomach behind the boulder and knelt beside him. "Good job, Jerry."

Thorpe turned his head sideways and grinned, bloody saliva drooling into the snow. "Always wanted a Purple Heart."

"You'll get more'n that if I get my say." Rainey gripped Thorpe's hand and got to his feet, still in a crouch behind the boulder. "See ya, Mac."

"Yeah, see ya."

Rainey took off up the hill and cautiously approached the machine gun nest that Thorpe had grenaded. He peered over the rocks and sandbags that protected the nest. It was neutralized all right. There had been two men on the gun, a gunner and a loader. Both were sprawled beside the gun.

Rainey rolled over the sandbags and crouched beside the Chinese. One was almost buried under sand and dirt and snow. His left arm lay five feet from his body. His head was unrecognizable as human. The other one was still alive, his light brown quilted uniform and tennis shoes splattered with blood.

Rainey hesitated for a split second, then shot him in the head. "Ain't the time nor place to take prisoners," he said aloud, "and we sure as hell don't want him to come around and start raking our rear with that gun."

Rainey had seen a lot of dead Chinamen before, but these two were different somehow. These were the two that had shot Jerry Thorpe. And maybe Jerry wouldn't make it. He'd looked awful pale. Mouth foaming blood.

These two little dead men.

Rainey was glad they were dead.

He kicked the head of the one he'd just shot.

The head rolled limply to one side, and then rolled back where it had been. He kicked it again. The same thing happened.

In a frenzy, Rainey jumped up and down on the head.

"Rainey, what the hell you doing?" Lt. Micleson was shouting at him from behind a rock about ten yards to his left and behind him. "Cut it out! Damn you, cut it out! Can't you see he's dead?"

Rainey yelled back, "These are the two that got Jerry!"

"I know, I know! But they're dead now! They can't do any more. And you can't either. Get going now before I put you up for an N.P. evac."

As he stood quietly beside the dead Chinese, Micleson's order took a moment to sink in. Slowly he began to move forward, then realizing where he was, he lunged behind a tree. He lay still for a moment, catching his breath, then scrambled back on his hands and knees to the machine gun.

It was covered with dirt and snow but looked like it was still in working order, a couple dozen rounds still in the belt. The two Chinese, crouched over the gun, had taken most of the shrapnel.

Rainey reached for his canteen to wash it down, then thought better of using water he might need later. He stood up, stripped off his gloves, opened his fly, worked his fingers through the layers of clothes, and urinated on the gun. It worked.

The gun was locked in place on its tripod with vise-grips on both sides to prevent uncontrolled movement. Dials on the tripod and under the receiver permitted controlled vertical and horizontal movement a click at a time. Rainey released both vises, adjusted the headspace of barrel on barrel extension by tightening the barrel all the way and then unscrewing it a couple clicks. He gripped the handles, tipped the barrel toward the sky, squeezed the trigger, fired one round. He smiled grimly. Ain't many guys can do that, he thought.

He heaved at the legs of the tripod, one at a time, and freed them from sandbags and packed snow. Then he turned it around and pointed it up the hill at one of the caves he'd spotted earlier.

He readjusted the headspace so he could fire as many rounds as he wanted by just holding his finger on the trigger. He aimed the sights at the cave and locked the gun's traversing mechanism in place with the vise-grips.

Then he waited.

Finally, there it was. A backflash from the cave. He fired two quick bursts of three or four rounds into the cave entrance. He waited again. Nothing. He'd either gotten his man or had scared him back into his hole.

He looked down the Chinese line. There was one other cave he could get at without any of his own men in the line of fire. He rotated the dials and lined up the cave in his sights.

He watched for the tell-tale flash.

There.

Quickly he fired two bursts. This time he was answered by several rounds coming from somewhere outside the cave. He thought he saw a slight movement behind a low fir tree, and raked the tree with several long bursts. Then all was quiet in both places.

Micleson called to him, "Nice going, Hal. I think that's all you can do from there with that thing."

"Should I take it with me?"

"Hell, no! Destroy it!"

Rainey pulled the pin from a hand grenade, rolled it under the machine gun and darted behind a tree. As soon as the explosion came, Rainey started back up the hill. He'd fallen about twenty yards behind the line and made it up in three quick bursts of speed. They were now no more than fifty yards from the Red trenches. It was time to make the final rush that would carry them into those trenches. And then there were the caves.

Forty-four

"Cease fire," called Micleson. "Fix bayonets."

The counter-fire was now nearly a continuous roar. Mortars and artillery shells were coming in like rain despite the proximity of the two opposing lines. Nearly everyone had a wound of some kind. Nearly everyone would gladly have quit.

Everyone fixed their bayonets carefully to the muzzles of their M-1s. The BAR-men slung their twenty pound weapons over their shoulders and slammed bayonets onto their M-1s. Then they slung the M-1s back onto their shoulders and brought their BARs back to firing position. The flame throwers lay on their bellies under their steel tanks, patiently waiting. They would not use their rifles or bayonets except as a last resort.

The noise was intense. Those of us sitting on the nose of Hill 67 could hear it plainly and we looked at each other with the unspoken question: could anyone live through that?

I looked at my watch. 0945. I couldn't believe it. I thought at least four hours had gone by since the copters had roared by on their way to The Rock. But even so, the Chinese would've had time to get their reserve battalion down to the front, even without trucks, if they'd started them moving at the first sign of the copters.

Or had the Chinaman with the hole in his head known what he was talking about?

Back behind The Rock, corpsmen worked quietly on their wounded, determining whether their patients could make the remaining thirty yards under their own power or would have to be carried up. No one doubted that in a few moments he'd be able to nurse his wounds in the shelter of the caves, tunnels, and bunkers from which now came the enemy fire.

"Saddle up," shouted the lieutenant, the traditional "Get set" of the leathernecks, whether packs were to be lifted to tired, aching shoulders in the boondocks of Lejeune or Pendleton, or a final charge was to be made on the beaches of Iwo Jima or on the hills of Korea.

Fire team leaders called final instructions to what was left of their fire teams, making sure that each man knew which cave, bunker or section of trench system was his particular mission. Even as they spoke, men were hit, and re-assignments had to be made hurriedly. There was no time to think about decisions. They were made automatically in the few seconds between the order to fix bayonets and the warning to saddle up.

There were no drums or fifes or flying flags, no clash of cymbals or martial music to stir the blood. No need. Adrenaline pumped steadily and endorphins flowed.

And forget all the garbage you've seen on the screen or read in your books. Those guys weren't thinking about wives or sweethearts or mothers or fathers or love of country or heaven or hell—or anything.

Each man's mind waited only for his next order.

Before they got to this point, back in their bunkers, maybe even while crouched in the helicopters, they thought about some or all of those things. Some took pictures out of pockets and stared at them. Some read creased and greasy letters. Some read from pocket-size New Testaments. Some just sat and stared or closed their eyes and thought about girlfriends and God and hunting and apple pie.

But not now, as they waited for the next order.

And then it came.

"Let's go," screamed the lieutenant. The whole line was suddenly a crazy thing, a blur of motion, as the Marines stood up and started forward, a kaleidoscopic collage of men running, leaping, dodging, stumbling, firing, throwing grenades.

And falling in a heap or settling slowly to the ground with grunts or groans of pain.

Up to the trenches they went, screaming and cursing, firing point blank at the Chinese and throwing their grenades now like baseballs directly at the Chinese. Bodies and parts of bodies lay everywhere in the bottom of the trenches, some blown to bits by grenades, some lying crumpled where a rifle bullet had caught them.

Now men could be seen in hand-to-hand combat all along the line. Their magazines were empty and there was no time to reload. Their grenades were all thrown. So now the bayonet and the K-bar knife were the ultimate weapons of death. The Reds' burp guns were now silent, their machine guns unmanned, many of their caves flaming infernos.

The flame-throwers' special mission had been to attack the caves that had not been silenced by earlier fire, and into them they poured their burning mixture of oil and gasoline. The nozzles spewed brilliant reddish-yellow flames and immense clouds of the blackest of black smoke. Grotesque flaming figures ran out and rolled in the snow in front of their caves.

Some of the caves which the flame-throwers hadn't gotten to continued to return machine gun and rifle fire. BAR-men ran up to the entrances, threw grenades into them, waited for the explosion, then charged in, spraying the walls with bullets in a semi-circle at knee level.

And then, suddenly, it was all over.

Men stood back from their bloody tasks, rifle butts resting on the ground, gory K-bars gripped loosely in their left hands, eyes roaming up and down the trench system looking for more trouble.

But there was no one left to kill.

How did they feel now? What were their thoughts?

You wouldn't get them to admit it later when they sat drinking a beer in their suburban back yards. But the overwhelming majority felt a surge of power that made them omnipotent, gave them supremacy, even a sort of grandeur. This translated, for some, even for many, into *virility*, a sexual thrill that explodes into rape if captive women are present.

The endless stories from history of pillage and rape and sodomy following bloody victories are not extravagances from a cruder time. War brings out the beast as well as the best in man.

Men with bloodied swords or bloodied K-bars are men with swollen genitals.

Abram's men who stood against the Four Kings, Lief Erickson's Vikings who ravaged the English coast, Hitler's storm troopers who *blitzkrieged* the villages of France, Lt. Micleson's Marines on the backside of Hill 1052, all men who have bloodied themselves in war, share this memory.

This does not happen to the artillery man who shoots at his enemy from many miles away, nor to the bombardier who lets go his eggs from ten thousand feet up. It happens only to the man who kills a personal enemy with his bayonet or knife and sees the blood gush.

Forty-five

The Rock was ours by 1105. Precariously, to be sure, but nevertheless ours.

Rainey crouched in the mouth of a cave which moments before had sheltered the now dead Chinamen littering the floor. The Marine dead and wounded, including Jerry Thorpe, had been pulled up into the caves. They had taken no prisoners.

Rainey was talking by radio to Major Marne, thumbing the butterfly as he alternately spoke and listened. "Sir, Lieutenant Micleson says we gotta have reinforcements if we're gonna stay here much longer. Over."

"Negative. How and Item companies are pushing hard along both sides of The Rock. We'll have those flanks secured and can come to your aid directly. Let me talk to Lieutenant Micleson. Over."

"Lieutenant Micleson here, sir. Over."

"How long can you hold out? Over."

"An hour, no more, I'd guess, sir. Over."

"Your casualties? Over."

"Five dead, twenty seriously wounded. Almost everyone hit somewhere. Ten of the bad hit can still handle a weapon but couldn't move out of here under their own power. Even if there was a place to go, which right now there ain't. Over."

"Have the Chinks got their reserve battalion on the hill yet? Over."

"Crawling all over the place. Most of them still a couple hundred yards or more away, about where we landed, but working in closer all the time. Over."

"No further orders. Hang in there. Out."

It really was looking bad. Over half the men dead or seriously wounded. The hill below them alive with little quilted forms darting from tree to rock to bush. Incredibly fast. Hardly time to get off a shot.

The tables were turned, however. The enemy now must go into the open, must expose himself occasionally in order to move forward. And the shorter the distance he had to go, the less cover there was.

A bugle blared. The Chinese advance slowed and stopped. The soldiers disappeared behind trees, bushes and boulders. For almost ten minutes all was quiet. The waiting Marines tensed, assuming that the Chinese were preparing for a suicide charge up the hill.

Rainey thought that this was it, the end of everything. They could never hold out against all those men. He was going to die in the next few minutes. He closed his eyes. He breathed a good-bye to his wife Marion, then to his small boys, Paul and Clifford, and finally to his Dad and Mom. There were no tears, not for himself.

The bugle sounded again. One by one the Chinese began retreating as they had come, darting from cover to cover.

With audible sighs of relief the Marines in the caves began picking off as many of the retreating forms as they could.

Marne's timing had been so nearly perfect that the Chinese reserves attacking Micleson's men had been forced to retreat. The Marine assault group comprised of How and Item Companies had started moving shortly after the helicopters left the battalion CP. They trotted down the hill from their entrenched positions on the MLR, passed through the second platoon of George Company still forming the original base of fire just forward of our aid station. By the time the fighting was the heaviest behind The Rock they'd been able to move up almost to the Chinese positions.

The Chinese had been so taken by surprise by the helicopter invasion that their first move had been to pull troops out of the main line, directing them to the area around the back of The Rock. Too late they realized what was happening out in front of their positions.

Both How and Item Companies—240 riflemen, plus corpsmen, machine gunners, and flame throwers in each company—were on the line before the Chinese could reinforce it. The Chinese began to draw back from their entrenched positions, leaving unprotected the flanks of the reserve battalion counterattacking on the backside of The Rock.

This was when the first bugle sounded, halting the counter-attack.

Then, after hasty consultations with their division headquarters, they ordered the bugler to sound the retreat. Their officers preferred to withdraw their troops rather than risk having them surrounded and annihilated.

It was the break Micleson needed. Immediately he ordered every able-bodied man to start carrying the wounded around the west side of The Rock into the area south of The Rock secured earlier that morning by the raider platoon from George Company.

Forty-six

Chief Hoffman, handling the radio in our forward aid bunker, told me what was happening. I went outside and climbed up on the bunker and could see the first of the wounded being carried down the slope. I jumped down off the bunker and crawled into it. "Get Rohn down here, Chief," I said. He activated his walkie-talkie and called Rohn and his jeep ambulance down from the MLR.

Rohn came bouncing into the cleared area in front of our aid station, his eyes merry and a lopsided grin on his face. Somewhere in heaven he'd been programmed for this kind of work.

I hoped he'd live forever.

I sent him down the nose into the gully in front of The Rock. I stood on top of the aid bunker again and watched him dropping into the valley where Smitty had taken care of the very first casualty. He crossed the little rocky stream bed and then started working his way up higher so that he could begin moving the wounded out before the expected counter-attack.

He weaved his way between trees, stumps, and shell holes, his gears in double reduction and all four wheels driving. At last he could go no farther. He was still a hundred yards from The Rock, but that would have to do. He called up to a corpsman standing in the trench in front of The Rock.

"This is the last inch, Mac; far as we go. How many you got for me?"

"Ten walkers, eight riders. Four of the riders will probably be 'copter evacs when you get them back to forward aid. Better take them first."

The corpsman turned and I could see him giving orders to the wounded that could walk, and seeing to it that the stretcher cases were carried down the hill to the waiting jeep. Two were placed on the double decker racks. Rohn slammed up the jump seat and three men who couldn't walk but didn't need stretchers were helped into the back of the ambulance.

Jerry Thorpe was one of the stretcher cases. He was still very short of breath, and had begun to feel very weak. The ambulance bounced and jerked, causing severe pain in his arm. Some bleeding on his neck was continuing. He hadn't paid much attention to it before, and neither had the corpsmen, since his chest wound had been so much more important. Blood was now pooling on the stretcher from his neck. His skin was cold, clammy, and he felt a little dizzy. A unit of serum albumin was running into his right arm, the bottle hanging from the welded hook on the rack.

They pulled into the aid station area. Rohn and Jepson pulled Thorpe's stretcher out of the ambulance and I got to work on him. I put a compression dressing on the neck wound and started another unit of serum albumin in his other arm well below the bullet wound. He was in blood-loss shock but we had no blood.

I checked the dressing on his back, found it still airtight, but reinforced it with another combat dressing and tape. We put him into one of the multiple-zipper bags so he'd stay warm on the way back to Easy Med.

It was imperative to get a tube into his chest as soon as possible to get that collapsed lung re-expanded. I could have put in a tube but we had no way of maintaining an underwater seal.

Jerry's left arm was broken just above the elbow from the machine gun bullet. I didn't know at the time that he'd handled two live grenades with that left hand. When Rainey told me about it later, I couldn't believe it.

I asked Jerry to touch his little finger to his thumb and then spread his fingers. He could, indicating that his ulnar and median nerves were intact. The numbness he'd felt was from the shock waves radiating out from the bullet as it smashed the humerus.

When I'd done all I could, I squatted on my heels beside him for a moment. "Save some of those pheasants for me, Jerry," I said.

Between breaths he grinned and said, "Sure, Doc. You bet."

His grin faded. "Svenger come through here?"

"Who?"

"Aage Svenger."

I called out, "Anyone see Aage Svenger?"

No answer. "Guess not, Jerry. Friend of yours?"

"Same fire team."

"He's okay, Jerry, if he didn't come through here."

"What if he was dead?"

"He's okay, Jerry. We would've seen him."

He relaxed and some of the pain went out of his eyes.

I stood up and motioned to Chief Hoffman.

"I think he'll be all right now," I said, "but just keep him moving on over to the 'copter strip. I'll call a 'copter. And keep that serum albumin running full blast in both arms."

Ten minutes later the 'copter roared in to our "landing strip," simply a small patch of treeless ground flat enough so that the copter's rotors wouldn't hit the ground. Hardly had it landed than mortar fire also started landing, the whirring fins giving most of us a second or two warning. This was enough for us, but not for the pilot. He was in the act of stepping out of the cockpit when a mortar landed at his feet. We gaped with horror at what was left.

He wasn't quite dead yet but his whole left side was gone.

His face dripped blood.

Blood spurted from his side.

He died.

He slumped back into the 'copter.

I felt sick, felt like vomiting, and looked it. The corpsmen were watching me. I shouted, "Don't just stand there, get these men started back to battalion. Carry them on up to the road's end. I'll call for another jeep ambulance from battalion. That'll be faster than waiting for another 'copter."

Forty-seven

Back on The Rock and the flanking ridges, the Marines dug in to their new positions. Although the greatest resistance had been met at The Rock, both How and Item Companies had had to fight their way up to their new positions. We got those casualties, too, as well as a few men from 2/1 on the right and the KMC on the left.

As daylight waned, the noise of battle subsided. Occasionally a few rounds of mortars dropped almost desultorily out in what had been the back of The Rock and was now our new front line.

Ten-fifty-two was no longer Luke the Gook's Castle but a U. S. Marine stronghold. The entire front line in our sector had moved significantly.

In 3/5, How Company's sector now extended straight west from Hill 812 along the ridge that ran up to Hill 1052.

George Company, held in reserve except for the

second platoon which had started the entire action, now left the old MLR and moved up to The Rock to replace Rainey's raiders. Its sector therefore tied in with How Company east of 1052, ran west to 1052 which it encircled, then dropped south to tie in with Item Company.

Item Company moved forward of Hill 751 and the unnamed village on its north slope. Item's lines ran straight north and south.

On 3/5's right flank, the second battalion of the First Marine Regiment, not involved in the offensive, now extended west of its former position and held the ridge east of How Company, including Hill 812 itself.

On 3/5's left flank, the Korean Marine Corps had moved forward, maintaining its tie-in with Item Company on its right flank and a U. S. Army division on its left. The Army in turn swung one company northwest to reconstitute the line.

We medics joyfully escaped the confines of the bunkers and stood watching the first and third platoons of George Company stride down the path from the MLR, past our aid station, across the valley and up the slopes of 1052. One by one they tramped by, most with smiles and waves for me and my corpsmen.

There was a good bit of badinage between us because we'd been in the thick of it all day while these Marines had sat in their bunkers back on the MLR. But the exchanges were good-natured. Those grunts marching past had seen lots of combat, more than most of my corpsmen had, so it was time for the corpsmen to remind the Marines about the hard time they'd had.

McCallister pulled all of Rainey's raiders out of the line as soon as George Company moved up. Twenty had been hit seriously enough to evacuate, and five were dead. The 'copter pilot was dead. He'd been moved, but his disabled machine still sat in the clearing where it had landed, corpse-like itself, dead blades hanging limply from the main stem. The transparent bell covering the cockpit was shattered. One evac pod was gone, splintered into a thousand pieces by the same round that got the pilot. Fortunately, Jerry Thorpe had been in the other pod which was essentially undamaged.

By about 1600 the lines had been pretty well reconstituted. My forward aid station now lay comfortably behind the lines, almost as far back as our rear aid station had been behind the previous MLR.

I figured that H & S Company would probably stay where it was, at least temporarily, back where the Kanmu-gang joined the Soyang-gang. But I also suspected that Everly would be ordered to move rear aid forward once the lines really stabilized. He was now over a mile from George Company, and almost as far from How and Item. A good place would be at the unnamed village on the shelving north slope of 751 if there was a good bunker there, or on the south slope if no bunker was available. But that would be McCallister's decision. We were still getting the remainder of the wounded evacuated but we were no longer under fire. Most of the badly wounded were already gone, the others wrapped in blankets or triage bags and lying quietly in the snow outside.

Chief Hoffman stood in the center of the bunker, helmet off and head bent forward to clear the overhead logs, directing traffic. He didn't need any supervision, so I sat wearily on an empty ammo box, waiting for orders to move the station, or to stay put, or whatever, for the night. I cracked a carton of C-rations and ate a cold can of stew, a can of peaches, and a couple of stale graham crackers.

I smiled grimly as I looked around. The bunker was a

disaster. Everything was splattered with blood. Our clothes and faces and hands. Stretchers. Sleeping bags. Water cans.

Clothing cut off to get at wounds: boots and gloves and hats and pants and socks. Bloody combat dressings, pulled off to inspect wounds or to stop bleeding and thrown on the floor. Web belts. Bayonets. Helmets. Rifles stacked in one corner. Bandoliers.

Blood all over everything in sight.

Then there was the smell of cigarettes, blood, vomitus, feces, urine, cordite, unwashed bodies. I'd gotten used to the normal smell of the front line bunkers—oil smoke, cigarette smoke, body odor, gun-cleaning solvent and oil—but this was something else. For one thing, all these men packed into the small space had raised the room temperature and made the smells more noticeable.

I hoped with all my heart that we'd be ordered back to rear aid in the battalion CP, but that would depend on just how stable McCallister and Marne thought their new positions were. For once I was very happy to let the brass make the decisions.

Jim Jepson, his left thigh stiffening from a shrapnel fragment he'd taken on one of his runs, and which he obstinately refused to let me do anything about, knelt beside a Marine dying of a gun-shot wound of the head.

He looked up at me and said, "I know this guy. Jeff Hayes. Platoon sergeant over in 2/1 when he first came out. Got busted down to PFC for a little too much sheba-sheba-ing on company time. Hell of a nice guy. He'd do anything for you. "

"He just did," I said.

Jim nodded, looked down at Hayes, and said, "Yeah, I see what you mean. The greatest gift—to lay down your life for a friend."

He went back to work, a little embarrassed by his remark. But it wasn't out of character for him. He wasn't one of those foxhole Christians, nor a guy to pester you with that "Are you saved, brother?" crap. He was a real believer.

He finished doing what he could for Jeff Hayes, sat back on his haunches, and asked me, "Think they'll be back tonight, Doctor?"

"Who, the Chinese? No, I doubt it. They'll wait till tomorrow night."

"Moon's nearly full, Doctor. Just right for a night raid."

"Not tonight, I hope."

"I don't know, Doctor," Jim mused. "That's a pretty nice chunk of real estate they just got pushed off of. If I was a Chinaman, I might be tempted to try to get it right back. They never make daytime offensives so they won't wait till morning. They know we could be reinforced by tomorrow night, so they'll either come tonight or not at all."

"Sure hope you're wrong," I said.

Jepson jumped to his feet, wincing with pain.

I turned to see McCallister and Marne crawling through the doorway. They looked incongruously neat and clean compared to the aid station crew. They weren't, really, if you looked closer. Neither had shaved for a couple of days. Their eyes were tired, bloodshot, sooty. Their parkas were soiled with dirt and wet with snow. There was melting snow and ground-in dirt on the knees of their pants. But there was no blood.

"At ease, sailor," Marne said to Jepson and came over to me and shook my hand. "Jack, am I glad to see you're all right."

I laughed and punched him lightly in the belly. "I'd like to think you'd've heard if I wasn't!"

He grinned and laid a hand on my shoulder. "You look like you could use some sleep."

"We had a wild party here today." I waved my hand in the general direction of the mess on the floor. "As you can see." I smiled. "Someone suggested inviting you but I vetoed that."

McCallister just grunted and I suspected he figured I was a little too frivolous for the circumstances. But he said, "No need for you men to stay here tonight. Get on back to H & S." Then he lightened up a bit. "Ya still remember where it is?"

I laughed. "Back somewhere by Able Med?"

"Don't I wish."

But I knew he didn't. This was his life, right here. He held my eye for a moment and I think he read what I'd been thinking. Then he looked down at Jeff Hayes. "He gonna make it?"

I shook my head and said, "No, sir, I don't think so. Maybe they can fix him up back at Easy."

"Yeah, well, soon's you get these guys out of here you might as well get back to battalion and get some sleep. You might need it tomorrow."

"Aye, aye, sir," I said, but he was already crawling out of the bunker.

Marne said to the bunker at large, "You guys've done one hell of a job here today. We won't forget it."

Then he too was gone. I'd wanted to get a little more detailed information about possible new movements, whether or not they expected a counter-attack, and if so, when.

I sat down on the ammo box, glanced up at Jepson. "They must not expect a counter-attack tonight. Wouldn't send us back to battalion if they did. Guess your intuition was wrong."

"Guess so, Doctor. Glad to be wrong."

Forty-eight

But he wasn't wrong. He should've been a Marine officer because he was absolutely right and it was McCallister who'd guessed wrong. The Chinese did want their cozy bunkers back, and right now.

We'd cleared out all of the wounded by about 1900. With grunts and moans of disgust we'd picked up the worst of the mess on the floor, tossed it onto a couple of shelter halves, and dumped it all in the snow outside. I heard one of the corpsmen, Hn Lechner I think, griping to Chief Hoffman.

"Why can't we just leave this stuff in the bunker, Chief?"

I waited for the answer.

"'Cause we might be back, Mac," Hoffman said.

It was a prophetic answer.

We left the stretchers and boxes of serum albumin and most of the other heavy stuff and wearily slogged back up the hill in the dark to the backside of the old George Company lines. Joe Tollander was waiting for us there with the crackerbox to take us down to H & S.

The counter-attack began at about 2200, just after the moon came up. Marne and the colonel were still on line. I was snoring peacefully in my tent. Everly was down in sick bay, taking inventory, and counting noses.

The offensive had claimed two corpsmen from How, three from Item, and one from George's second platoon. These had to be replaced from the rear aid station.

The replacement system followed standard procedure. When a corpsman came out from the States he stayed in a rear area for five days to acclimate, mentally and physically, then went directly to a platoon on line and stayed for four to six months.

After his tour of line duty, he moved back to the battalion rear aid station, a considerably safer position, and stayed there for several more months. Finally, to finish up his tour in Korea he was sent back to a medical company, the aid station in regimental CP, or to some other rear-echelon outfit.

However, if a corpsman on line was incapacitated by wounds or illness, we had to send someone up, usually the last man to come down. In this way, the longer a corpsman was in Korea, the less likely he'd be sent back up to the front and therefore less likely to be killed or wounded.

Choosing the men to go back up was always a distasteful task for the battalion surgeon. But there was nothing else we could do and it was always accepted more or less gracefully by the corpsmen. Oh, they griped and mumbled and groaned. But they shouldered their packboards and with a rueful grin they went.

And sometimes they came back in a body bag.

Somebody always said, "It ain't fair." And in a way I guess it wasn't. The first time I saw a kid come back dead, who I'd sent back up after he was supposed to be off line, I felt a peculiar but real guilt. When someone said, "It ain't fair," I turned on him and said, "Tell me a better way." He was mature enough to recognize that I was under the gun and just answered, "Not your fault, Doctor. The system."

So Everly was looking through the list of twenty corpsmen to see who'd come off the line last. He started reading off the names to Chief Hoffman and the Chief wrote them down. The corpsmen stood around, knowing roughly who'd come when, but as each name and date of arrival was read, Hoffman checked it out with each man.

The phone rang. The Chief answered. It was Marne.

"Chief, get those corpsmen up here on the double. The gooks are back. Do you know where your men are to go—what platoons are short?"

"Yes, sir."

"Is Dr. Lord there?"

"No, sir, he's sleeping. Dr. Everly's here."

"Put him on."

"Everly speaking, sir."

"Doc, all hell has broken loose up here again. Will you or Jack get a forward aid station right back where it was before?"

"Yes, sir. Major, that 'copter strip may still be blocked by that shot-up 'copter."

"No, we've taken care of that. Now get going."

Everly's face burned from the tone of Marne's voice. It wasn't like him to be like that, he thought, must really feel we're in a jam.

He shoved the EE-8 back into its box and came over to our tent to wake me up. The simple little scene that followed is etched deeply in my memory: I'm lying in my mummy bag, half asleep. Everly sits on his cot five feet away, leaning forward a bit with his hands on his knees and elbows straight. He says, "Want me to go up this time?"

I lift up on one elbow. "No. I'm more familiar with the setup down there. I'll take Lechner and Jepson and the others who were with me before. Except this time you keep Chief Hoffman and Rick Simpson."

He nods and that's it. No argument this time. There'd be little difference in risk this time. Or so we thought.

It was like choosing up sides for a pickup baseball game.

All hell had indeed broken loose. The Chinese had counter-attacked with what seemed to be several battalions. They came in waves, shouting, screaming, bugles blaring, cymbals clanging, ten-penny whistles screeching. I could hear it all the way down in the valley as we moved back into the bunker we'd left just hours before. Not for the first time did I wonder if they were high on something.

So far, each successive wave had been repulsed with extremely high enemy casualties. The fighting was especially heavy on the right flank, where How Company tied in with the second battalion of the First Regiment. It was apparent even to a non-military mind like mine that the Chinese were hoping to break through there to create a corridor to the back of our George Company, thereby encircling The Rock again. An obvious plan, a test of strength, and it couldn't be stopped without reinforcements.

If the line gave way in How Company, even in an orderly retreat, McCallister's hand would be forced. If he held The Rock, for which we'd paid so dearly, George Company and part of Item might be surrounded as How Company fell back. But if he gave up The Rock, we'd be right back where we started and there'd be another fight to regain it some other day.

McCallister had two more cards to play in an attempt to hold The Rock. The first was to call out the Headquarters and Service Company—the "pots and pans brigade." In the battalion headquarters were the cooks, clerks, assistants to the officers, supply men, electricians, security detail, engineers, truckers, and others. About a hundred altogether. They'd all been trained as infantry Marines, but were mostly older men, men with special skills, less physically fit, and most had not been in actual combat since World War II and some not then.

The second card was to call out the regiment in reserve, which was again the Seventh Marines. They wouldn't think much of that. After coming out of Camp Tripoli in early January, they'd relieved the First Regiment. They'd taken a terrific shellacking but without losing any ground. Then they'd been relieved again just a week ago by the First. So they were still licking their wounds. But McCallister felt he had no choice and decided to play both cards.

"Marne, give Selkirk a call. Tell him to mobilize H & S. Get them into the line with How. Then ask Division to send up the Seventh."

"Aye, aye, sir!"

Forty-nine

So while we triaged and treated the flow of wounded through our aid station, replacements from H & S Company began filling in the gaps up on line caused by the evacuation of these wounded men. A grizzled 45-year-old supply sergeant fought alongside a 42-year-old cook. A 32-year-old electrician (a first lieutenant) joined the 20-year-old corporal who'd been the leader of a now non-existent fire team.

It was like this all up and down the line. This was a last-ditch maneuver—dig down deep into the barrel of man-power and hold that line. It wasn't a game, but it was like a game. The quarterback was out with a pulled hamstring. The wide receivers of Pro-bowl caliber were both out with wrenched knees. The giant right tackle was out with broken ribs. The second-stringers were in, showing the stuff they were made of.

Platoon leaders, many of them non-coms now, crawled

up and down the sector of the trench system for which they were responsible. It was imperative to re-establish a governable platoon by re-forming squads out of reconstituted fire teams.

And still the Chinese kept coming—and coming—and coming. The machine gunners traversed their weapons slowly from side to side, spitting lead constantly, occasionally holding in one position on a narrow corridor between trees or rocks where a steady stream of Chinese poured through like cattle through a corral gate.

The riflemen selected targets with more care and with more difficulty, peering down their iron sights in the dim light, often losing the bead on the muzzle in the darkness, waiting for a flash of light from explosions, sometimes merely pointing their weapons like a gun-fighter shooting from the hip.

Our mortar and artillery crews fired flares which drifted on tiny parachutes down over the line, lighting up the scene with an eerie whiter-than-white light. Sometimes the Chinese were back-lighted and sometimes front-lighted. I heard one Marine say that he couldn't shoot a silhouette; he had to see the face of the man he killed to make it real. He wanted personal revenge. I think I would've wanted it just the opposite: kill a shadow, not a man.

And still they came, tumbling and sagging and pitching and falling, piling up in the snow in front of the machine guns and rifles and grenades and BARs. Some lay dying in the moonlit snow, crying and groaning, in plain view of the Marines in the trenches. Others crawled on their bellies back down the hill. The Marines let them go. They were out of it, not worth the lead to kill.

A gentle breeze from the north wafted the smell of cordite and garlic and the acrid stench of burned-out flares into the nostrils of the Marines crouched in the trenches.

Onto the beaches of the How Company lines the human waves crashed and crashed, again and again, and then finally subsided, spent. The whistles screeched and the cymbals clanged no more. A far-off bugle sounded. The charging Chinese stopped, turned, retreated, dragging their wounded with them.

The counter-attack had failed.

Wispy streamers of fog out over the valley settled on the shattered pines where snow and blood now mingled. All was quiet for ten minutes, fifteen, twenty. The Marines relaxed, mumbling to each other, "Is it over?"

Yes and no.

The suicide charges were over, at least temporarily, but now mortars and artillery shells began falling and the Marines scrambled back into their bunkers.

We weren't getting any incoming where we were, down in the valley, but I knew what was happening now up on the line. Everybody sat in their bunkers listening to the stuff coming in, almost wishing that a new wave of Chinese would come up the hill because maybe the barrage would stop.

Marne and McCallister, sitting in their new command bunker on the right flank of 1052, were talking about that very thing. And then a strange thing happened, something that could only happen in an outfit where loyalty and selflessness and *esprit de corps* were at a maximum. McCallister told me all about it later.

"Pretty heavy barrage, Colonel," Marne had said.

"Yeah," McCallister had answered. "They're holding back their infantry now."

"Probably, but not for long." More than once Marne had seen CCF troops sent in under their own artillery fire with great loss of life. The first time he'd seen that done, he'd figured their signals had gotten crossed somehow.

They sat talking for awhile, each with his own thoughts. Then, "Major," McCallister said, "I don't think the Chinks know what a spot they've got us in. If they knew how close they were to a complete breakthrough in the How Company sector, they wouldn't have stopped their charge."

"Maybe, but we don't know what troops they've got available for a frontal assault. Maybe they've run out of men. They sure as hell lost a lot. They're stacked up in front of some of our bunkers like cordwood. No Army, not even the Reds, can keep feeding a machine gun that many men for very long and still throw in more replacements."

"You may be right, Major. Well, whatever the reason, they're giving us time to get the Seventh up here."

A voice sounded outside their bunker, "Meat packer, meat packer."

Marne recognized the password for the night and called out, "Get in here before you get your ass blown off!"

Sergeant Rainey came crawling in through the three-foot opening, pushing his M-1 ahead of him with a bandaged right hand. He waved a salute with his left hand and said with a big grin, "Howdy, Colonel. Major."

"What the hell are you doing up here, Rainey?" the colonel bellowed. "Your outfit's been relieved."

Rainey grinned again. "Yes, sir, I know. The pots and pans. Colonel, when I saw them guys leaving for the front, I couldn't feel safe back in battalion any longer."

He sat down and pushed his helmet back on his head. Then he reached down with both hands under his left knee and pulled up on his thigh. He saw Marne and McCallister watching him. "Yeah, got a leaf to stick on the Purple Heart I got on Guam."

"I asked you a question, Sergeant," McCallister said.

"Sorry, sir. What I come back for? Well, sir, most of what's left of my platoon come back, too. I been asked to tell you that we'd like to act as sort of a front line H & S Company long as you have to stay up here."

The colonel was visibly shaken. He wasn't fooled a moment by the "front line H & S Company" malarkey. Rainey was talking about a perimeter cordon, which would amount to a bodyguard for the colonel and his command post. This was a gesture he hadn't expected.

"Front line H & S?" he barked. "What the hell is that? Where'd'ya find that in the Table of Organization?"

"Well, sir..."

"No," McCallister interrupted. "I can't allow it. Take your men and get the hell off this hill."

Rainey wasn't surprised. He'd expected this.

"Look, Colonel," he said, "let's face it. You're in a vulnerable spot here. There's some as says y'oughta be back in battalion, but that's your decision..."

"Damn right," McCallister said.

Rainey went on unperturbed. "So is Doc Lord back there in Ku-dong. There's eighteen of us left out of Lt. Micleson's raiding patrol..."

"They're already talking about 'Rainey's Raiders,' Sergeant," McCallister said with a grin. "You're gonna go down in the history books as the first helicopter-borne attack patrol."

"Yeah," Marne said, also with a grin. "Rainey's Raiders. Got a ring to it."

I would've loved to see those grins. Here's these guys sitting in a front line bunker, under mortar and artillery attack, a breakthrough imminent in How Company that would surround their position with screaming Chinese. And joking about Sergeant Rainey making the history books!

Rainey screwed up his mouth, looked down at the ground, and shook his head back and forth. “That’s not right, sir. Lt. Micleson was the one who led the charge. He’s a very brave guy, Colonel.”

“I know he is, Rainey,” McCallister said, completely serious again. “I’m putting him up for a Bronze Star, Combat V, of course. I’m putting you up for one, too. Thorpe’ll get a Silver Star if what I’ve heard is correct.”

“Oh, you heard correct all right. I watched him. And there’s others…”

“We’ll sort that out later.”

“Yes, sir. Well, gettin’ back to why I come up here again, sir. We figgered maybe half of us could form a cordon around the aid station, half around your bunker here, just in case a real serious breakthrough occurs. Besides, like I said, we’d rather be up here with you and our buddies than back in battalion.”

McCallister knew this to be true. The majority of the men had such unit-spirit that to be separated from their units was the worst thing that could happen. He’d seen wounded men pleading not to be evacuated, pestering the doctors constantly to let them go back to their outfits. Their faces were black from the smoke of oil burned in empty cartridge cases. Their eyes were bloodshot from the smoke and from sleepless nights and the constant strain of incoming artillery and mortars exploding all around them.

They lived like animals in their caves, dirty, unshaven, hungry, enduring hours of unalleviated boredom alternating with moments of sheer terror. They were veterans, as Ernie Pyle put it, “in the cruel, fierce world of death.” Yet still they shouldered their pack boards and went back to the line the minute they could.

McCallister looked long at Rainey and thanked God for him and his ilk.

"All right, Sergeant," he said, "consider yourselves attached to this—what'd you call it?—this front line H & S Company, but you stay in here till this shelling lets up. Where are the rest of your men?"

"Scattered in bunkers down the..."

The high-pitched whistle of an incoming shell overhead stopped him. Then he grinned. "Our own. A sixteen incher from a battleship offshore."

"Probably the *Wisconsin*," Marne said.

"Five thousand bucks a shell," McCallister said. "You could buy a Cadillac."

"Kinda 'spensive launching platform, too, Colonel."

The enemy bombardment seemed to be easing a little. Rainey crawled out to organize his men. He knew that the letup meant that the Chinese were getting ready to attack again. Either that, or some of the Marines' fire was doing some good.

The enemy bombardment ceased. It was 2330. Working in my bunker on the casualties who'd been brought in despite the shelling, the only sounds I could hear now were our own artillery whistling high overhead. Some not so high. Some sounded as if you should get out with a broom and help them along. We were getting help now from the 11th Marines and from the *Wisconsin* out in the gulf.

Up in their bunker in How Company, Marne and McCallister waited. The colonel was busy talking by radio to each company commander in turn, issuing curt orders, asking pertinent questions about the number of casualties, the supply of ammunition, the morale. He learned from the acting CO of How Company (the CO, Captain Friberg, was dead) that from 2200 to 2330, a period of an hour and a half, over 1800 rounds of enemy mortar and artillery had landed on How Company alone.

One round every five seconds.

It was a wonder any one was alive. Not many were uninjured. One hundred and eighty men were evacuated from the How Company sector, roughly 90% of the company. Worse than the shelling that 2/1 had gotten back in September. And they would all come through my aid station.

No one could move during the bombardment. The whole line was paralyzed. As the shelling eased off and then stopped, corpsmen began crawling along the trenches, pulling the wounded out of their bunkers. They were helped by uninjured Marines, and by men with one arm in a sling, or with blood running down their faces, or limping grotesquely from leg wounds. They knew they must work fast, between the end of the shelling and the beginning of the CCF's next counter-attack.

As they came back down to us, we moved them on as fast as we could. I knew that Everly back in battalion would be on the EE-8 and walkie-talkie half the time, mobilizing trucks and jeeps and helicopters to get the stretcher cases out of the way before the lines crumbled and trapped them.

The walkers would have to take care of themselves, wending their way in the dark, back down the battalion road toward the regimental aid station.

I spent most of my time outside the bunker, moving from stretcher to stretcher, helping the corpsmen with splints and slings, making agonizing decisions about priorities for evacuation, joking with the wounded.

We did most of the work in the dark. It's amazing how well you can see when the moon is almost full and there's snow on the ground. We did have to take some men into the bunker where we had the Coleman lantern. There are some things you need light for. Starting an IV on a patient with no blood pressure. Catching an arterial bleeder that won't stop with pressure alone. Examining an eye wound to see if any steel can be removed on the spot. Things like that.

I didn't know these guys from How Company as well as I knew the George Company Marines, but they knew me. Part of my role as battalion surgeon was just to be there where the Marines could see me and know that a doctor was available if they got into serious trouble.

Not that these wounded Marines were fearful patients. Not at all. I rarely saw anxiety in their eyes. But I knew that deep down inside them there had to be concern. And part of their concern was that the corpsmen weren't trained to take care of the kind of an injury that they, the wounded, had suffered.

Fifty

The second attack began, worse than the first one, drawing every Marine out of the shelter of his bunker into the trenches or watch foxholes. Wave after wave of yelling, crazed Chinamen stormed up the hills. The Chinese knew that if they were repulsed this time, they'd have to wait until the following night, and by then the Marines would be reinforced. This was also their last-ditch maneuver.

Rainey and half a dozen of his troopers came down off the hill and Rainey told me what he was going to do.

"You guys are crazy," I told him.

He grinned. "Yeah, I guess so. But sitting back there in battalion was kinda like lying in bed at home on a October morning and you hear the wind howling and you know the ducks are gonna be skimming the marsh grass looking for a place to set down. And you just gotta get out there where the action is. Know what I mean, Doctor?"

Of course I did. And he knew I did. But I said, "No."

He laughed. "We'll be out there, Doctor." He waved his hand in a circle.

I no longer had to wonder how Fred Overman could keep working in the snow on a windy hillside when the Chinese were all around him. He—and now I—had a deep faith in the ability of those Marines out there.

To say that I was extremely busy would be an understatement. All available space in the aid bunker was filled with casualties. I moved some of the stable cases into the houses in Ku-dong, the little village cleaned out by the anti-guerrilla patrols. Marne sent two six-by-six trucks from a neighboring engineer battalion to help carry away the wounded, but they still kept coming faster than we could move them.

We ran out of triage sleeping bags, so I asked one of the truck drivers to load up with blankets from the store at battalion the next time he came back. We had plenty of combat dressings, serum albumin, and stretchers. What we really needed was more people but I knew that was a pipe dream.

Both of our jeep ambulances shuttled back and forth. Joe Tollander went grimly about his business, saying scarcely a word, gently handling the stretchers and driving as carefully as he could on the rough track.

Even Ned Rohn's nonchalance had faded. I hadn't seen his lop-sided grin for several hours. He had blood all over him. "None of it's mine," he told me with a parody of a grin.

We were all pretty bloody, mostly from wiping our hands on our jackets or pants, some of it from brushing against a bloody stretcher, some of it from arteries squirting on us while we clamped and tied and bandaged. We stopped to rinse our hands from the five-gallon Jerry cans only when the blood and other gurry interfered with our work.

I wondered how long we could hold out.

I got orders every hour or so to send up another corpsman to the line. By now there were only twenty corpsmen left in the whole battalion, less than half the optimum number. I'd sent word through Everly to the regimental surgeon, way back a million miles to the rear, where he sat, we knew, with a martini in his hand. He promised to pull men from other units in the regiment that weren't as hard hit. I'll believe that when I see it, I mumbled under my breath.

It was now 0200, four hours after the initial CCF counter-attack, and two hours since cessation of the bombardment signaled the second attack.

Bullets began to rip through the trees over our heads. I started. That means the Chinese are back on the MLR, I thought. In our sheltered position in the valley behind the ridge line, no bullets could reach us unless someone were on the ridge firing downward. Not directly at us of course—we were pretty well hidden by darkness and the trees—but at Marines on the line.

I started again. Not at what I heard, but at what I didn't hear. Our own artillery had stopped. At a time like this. Suddenly I knew why. A bugle blared—southeast of us. Somewhere on the ridge running east and west between 812 and 1052, How Company had been penetrated. We were cut off and the artillery spotters no longer knew where to direct their fire without hitting our own men.

Sweat broke out on my brow. The eyes of the corpsmen and the wounded Marines sought each other out and were not ashamed to show fear. Not the frantic, panic-button fear of the uninitiated, but the cold gripping fear of the battle-wise. Death was all around us, had doused the flames of life in too many of our comrades, had blown the light out of too many eyes. None of us wanted to lie down on that dark, cold, Korean mountain while our life's blood melted the snow.

None of us wanted our helmets pulled down over our dead eyes. None of us wanted to go home in a body bag.

For seconds no one moved. Not a word was spoken. But unheard orders emanated from some boot-camp source and each man went back to what he'd been doing.

There was nothing we could do but keep working and wait for orders to move out. But where? I could exercise my prerogative and move the aid station to the safest possible place. But I'd received no intelligence as to where that might be. I could only wait. And hope that communications to us were not cut off, too.

I suspected that sooner or later we'd have to join up with the front line outfits rather than fall back by ourselves. This could be done in one of two ways. If the line companies fell back to protect the flank that was exposed by the How Company breakthrough, they'd pick us up as they retreated.

But if McCallister elected to try to re-constitute the line, and thereby trap the Chinese who'd broken through, then it might be safer to move the aid station up closer to the lines.

I realized that the only sure way McCallister could reform the MLR on its present ridgeline—and save The Rock from recapture—was to use troops from the Seventh Regiment. And they weren't here yet as far as I knew.

I called to Jepson, "Better get everyone in the area ready to move out, JJ. I imagine we'll have to move up."

"Forward, Doctor?"

"Yeah, to get closer to our troops on line."

He eyed me for several seconds, the import of what I'd said sinking in. "Aye, aye, sir."

All the severely wounded men were moved into the underground bunkers in the old trench system. Everyone not too badly hurt was moved out of the bunkers and placed in rows between the trees. Those in the houses of Ku-dong were brought back to the main holding area. We covered everyone with wool blankets. It was warm enough for those of us moving around, but the guys lying in the snow would rapidly lose body heat.

The rattle of small arms fire was continuous, so constant that it seemed to be just background noise that I really didn't hear any more. What I heard were the voices of my corpsmen, Jepson and Lechner and all the rest.

"Hold your arm steady, Mac. Gotta get this needle in. Hey, come on now, you afraid of a little needle?"

"Just a flesh wound, Randy. Nothing too bad."

"Hey, JJ, gimme a hand here, will you? Hold a light on...yeah, like that."

"There y'go, bud. On your way. Yeah, back to your outfit! What're you smilin' for?"

"This guy's gone. Nothing I could do."

"Doctor Lord! Can you see this guy a minute?"

"Lech, get a coupla more blankets outta the bunker, will ya? This guy's shiverin' like it was cold out or somethin'."

"Hey, you asshole, what're you doin' here? Thought you'd gone back to Yong Dong Po with the rest of the bug-outs!"

"JJ, where'd that new case a serum albumin go?"

"Ned! Two more ready. Gimme a hand and we'll load 'em. Bring back a coupla shebas with you next time, hey?"

"Don't just stand there, Tollander, give us some guitar music, will ya?"

A runner came in from Colonel McCallister.

"Doctor, the colonel wants you to move into defilade about half a mile to the northwest."

"North*west*?"

"Yes, sir, that's what he said."

"Why'd he send a runner instead of radioing me?"

He grinned. "Nobody's answering the radio."

"The hell you say!"

"Skipper figures you're keeping busy!" He raised a hand in a half salute, said, "Gotta get back," and disappeared into the darkness.

"Northwest!" I mused to Rohn as I helped him load his ambulance with two more stretcher cases. "Why, that's off towards How Company's new lines."

"Yeah, Doctor, where the breakthrough occurred."

"What d'ya suppose happened?"

"I know what happened. The pots and pans plugged the How Company sector after the breakthrough. You know, when we first heard the bugles blowing south of us? Most of those Chinese were killed or captured. There weren't very many. Couple dozen."

"And now that part of the line is weakening again?"

"Must be, Doctor. Item has been taking a terrific shelling and I'd guess McCallister has had to reinforce them with some of the pots and pans from How."

"God, what a mess."

Rohn's information was correct. I heard the story from McCallister a month later—when I myself was recuperating on the Hospital Ship *Repose* and McCallister came through Inchon on his way home. "The H & S pots and pans," he said, "and the remnants of How Company closed the gap and stopped the advance."

But the tremendous bombardment the CCF had thrown onto the Item Company sector had weakened that sector to the point of an imminent breakthrough on the southwestern slopes of 1052. In desperation—and knowing what might happen in How Company—McCallister shifted the pots and pans down the valley and across to the Item Company sector.

"But then," McCallister said, "the How Company line, now minus the pots and pans, began to give way again."

There was no panic, no rout, no scrambling for safety. One by one a Marine would scurry out of the trench, run a few yards down the back of the ridge, fall behind a stump, rock, or clump of bushes, and continue firing at the oncoming Reds.

It was a bright moonlit night. The figures of the Chinese were outlined against the sky as they came across the ridge, and could be picked off then. But when one fell, another came, and then another, and eventually one would make it through the hail of bullets. When enough got through, the Marines were forced to fall back a little farther down the hillside.

"Within half an hour," McCallister said, "it became obvious that without the 7th Marines we couldn't hold 1052 any longer, that soon the entire line would have to fall back to more tenable positions."

It was difficult to maintain communications with other units in this situation. McCallister reluctantly ordered a slow, systematic withdrawal. "Gonzaga!" he barked.

"Sir!"

"Relay to CO How: pull back to position King Dog. To CO Item: pull back to position Zebra Sugar."

"Aye, aye, sir!"

When confirmation of orders received came back, McCallister, Marne, Washington, and Gonzaga slipped out of their bunker half a minute apart.

Gonzaga, carrying the fifty pound radio on his back, went first, then McCallister, then Washington, finally Marne. When Marne emerged from the bunker the radioman and the colonel were crouched down in the trench about twenty yards away.

The sergeant was twenty yards away in the other direction.

Five of Rainey's Raiders, all that were left of the eleven who'd stayed with McCallister and Marne, now stood along the trench system, facing north toward the enemy.

Flashes of fire from rifle and mortar lighted the trench system from time to time. A lone flare drifted five hundred feet up in the air and two hundred feet down the trench. McCallister watched Marne crawl down the trench a few yards to clear the bunker and look to him for a signal to move out.

All up and down the trenches McCallister could hear the scrunching of gear on the walls of the trench as the Marines of George Company crawled over the back wall and disappeared down the hill in the darkness. McCallister knew that on their flanks How and Item Companies would also be moving out.

"Marne was impatient," McCallister told me, "but I thought we had plenty of time. I'd already sent Rainey and half his men back to you. Now I let the rest of them go on ahead."

Finally McCallister swept his hand overhead to the rear. Marne relayed McCallister's signal, then lifted his right knee to place it on the back edge of the trench, preparatory to rolling out.

"I was still watching Marne," McCallister told me. "I saw him turn quick like he'd heard a new sound behind him." A Chinaman only yards away threw a grenade into the trench at his feet. "He didn't have time to think," McCallister said. Marne merely reacted. He pushed himself over the back wall of the trench and started to roll himself away.

He was too late.

A flash and a simultaneous explosion reverberated in the hollow of the bunker Marne had left. "Marne told me," McCallister said, "that a lightning-like pain shot down his left leg from buttocks to foot. His foot felt like it had exploded."

It had.

His leg gave way and he tumbled back into the trench.

McCallister, now less than twenty yards away, pulled his .45 and fired three or four times at the Chinaman. He saw him flinch but figured he'd missed because the Chinaman continued his charge the remaining few feet up the slope. He leaped into the trench and with fixed bayonet fell on Marne, its point burying itself in the right side of Marne's chest.

McCallister, Washington, and Gonzaga ran over now just as the Chinaman collapsed on top of Marne, his face dripping blood. He lay quite still, his breathing stopped.

He was dead.

McCallister hadn't missed. Washington steadied the rifle, which stood upright in Marne's chest and throbbed with the beat of Marne's heart. McCallister and Gonzaga cautiously pulled the Chinaman off Marne. "We had to pry that Chink's hands off his rifle," McCallister said, "and then tumble him to one side."

McCallister knelt beside Marne. "Got to pull that thing out, Bob."

Marne nodded, his eyes already glazing over.

McCallister stood up and grasped the rifle by stock and barrel. Washington released his hold and knelt by Marne's head. He placed his big hands on Marne's shoulders and said, "Steady there, Major." He looked up at McCallister and nodded curtly.

McCallister grunted with the effort and pulled upward on the rifle. The bayonet slipped out of Marne's chest with a slurping sound. Marne gasped in pain but had strength enough to clasp his hand over the wound. Air sucked in and out and blood bubbled between his fingers.

McCallister yelled, "Corpsman!" Again he called but the lines had already moved back too far and no corpsman responded. "Gonzaga, go get another guy!"

The radioman disappeared in the darkness and in moments was back with a rifleman, one of Rainey's men. Together they gently lifted Marne by his four extremities and stumbled down the trail off Luke the Gook's Castle until they found a stretcher.

But I didn't know any of those details as Rohn and I stood talking and then got to work moving the aid station. All I knew was that things weren't going right up front and we'd better get our butts in gear and go where the colonel had told us to go.

First I found Harold Rainey, told him where I wanted to go, and asked him to break a trail through to the new area.

"You know where I want to go?" I asked.

"Exactly, sir."

"Then come back and lead the first bunch over."

"Aye, aye, sir."

I watched him limp off in the dark at a half trot. God, what a man, I thought.

I figured we'd better take the wounded with us. In view of what happened, it was a smart move. But at the time I agonized a bit over the decision.

We had half a mile to go. Not very far. A fast man could run it in two minutes on a track. It took over two hours to move the aid station from Ku-dong on the nose of Hill 67 to the point the colonel had designated, in the valley behind the ridge that ran from 812 to 1052.

The stretcher cases went first. The walking wounded

helped. Men with bandaged heads and arms struggled with one pole of a stretcher, sometimes falling themselves, but getting up to struggle on. The corpsmen half ran, half walked with their stretchers, trying not to joggle their patients too much.

Finally all the wounded were moved to the new area.

The six-bys and jeep ambulances continued to carry casualties back to battalion while we made our move and then opened up a track to our new area and resumed evacuating the wounded.

The weary corpsmen and some of the wounded began trudging back and forth from the Ku-dong area with boxes of dressings, cases of serum albumin, stretchers, instruments, blankets, Jerry cans of water, and all the other equipment necessary for the maintenance of the aid station.

There were no goldbricks or malingerers in this outfit. Every one of those guys was a hero and should have gotten a Bronze Star or at least a Letter of Commendation, both with Combat V's. Almost none of them would because they were "just doing their jobs."

We were in an extremely vulnerable position and everyone knew it. The wounded Marines sat or lay with their rifles loaded and close at hand. Sergeant Rainey's men were scattered around the periphery of our work area again, moving slowly back and forth in the darkness, watching with dark-adapted eyes for signs of enemy infiltration.

I, like Colonel McCallister, thanked God for those…I almost said "heroes" again, because that's what they were, but we didn't talk or think like that. So I just thanked God for those guys out there trying to protect us with their rifles and BARs and grenades.

Three of Rainey's men had BARs and this made

everyone feel a little better. The BAR was an inaccurate weapon at long range, but for close-in fighting such as everyone expected it was nearly as good as the communists' burp guns, maybe better.

We all wondered where those Chinese were.

Wounded men continued to come back from the lines, faster than we could evacuate them. We could do very little for most of them except to tie on sterile bandages, splint fractures, stop hemorrhage, and treat shock. Many of them needed far more than that, far more than we could give them.

We did what we could.

But in our hearts we knew that we were losing The Rock.

Fifty-one

It was now four o'clock in the morning, still three hours till daylight. The sounds of rifles, burp guns, and BARs got closer and closer. At Ku-dong we'd been about a mile back of the new How Company lines stretching east of 1052 to 812. At this new position we were at first a good half mile back. Now the firefight sounded like it was only a couple of hundred yards away.

There was now no question about what was happening and what I had to do. The Rock was gone. How Company was moving south, George Company southeast, Item Company east. The newly established lines were imploding. My aid station was superfluous here. We'd become expendable in this place. We had to get out of here. Fast.

We were making good progress in evacuating our wounded.

The six-bys had helped a lot. They could carry four

stretchers or a dozen walking wounded. I flashed my light around the area in a quick circle and counted about fifteen casualties remaining. Only three or four needed stretchers. The rest had wounds that incapacitated them for further combat but didn't require stretcher evacuation.

A six-by roared in and loaded up all the walkers. At the same time Joe Tollander came back in his jeep ambulance to get two of the stretcher cases. It was time to move back.

I decided to send all the corpsmen back on the truck and jeep. I'd wait with the two remaining stretcher cases till Rohn came back with his jeep ambulance. It never crossed my mind to leave, too. I wasn't being a hero or playing the "captain goes down with the ship" routine. I was the battalion surgeon and the forward aid station was right where I was standing.

I gave the order. At first no one argued.

"What about the gear?" Lechner asked.

"Grab what you can carry easily and forget the rest."

Jepson started off and than came back. "I ain't goin'," he stated flatly.

"The hell you aren't. Get moving."

He didn't move. He smiled. "Ya can't make me."

I didn't try.

"Rest of you guys shove off."

Ten minutes later Rohn came back in his ambulance. He wasn't very happy with me. "Doctor," he said, "you better get outta here. No need for you to stay. We can clean up now."

He and JJ began loading the last two WIAs.

"You're probably right, Ned," I said, "Soon's we…"

There was a heavy tramping of feet in the brush to our northwest, the direction most of our last casualties had come from. We heard an agitated voice call out the password, then the sharp interrogation by one of Rainey's men. Soon four Marines carrying a stretcher scuffed rapidly through the snow into the aid station area.

I stared in amazement. One of the litter bearers was a Rainey Raider. A second was McCallister's radioman, Sergeant Ruiz Gonzaga. A third was Moses Washington, McCallister's gunny sergeant. The fourth was Colonel McCallister.

"Put him down," McCallister said. They lowered the stretcher to the ground. In the half light of moon and stars I looked down at the man on the stretcher. I shone a light in his face.

Bob Marne.

He was dead.

The whole front of his chest was covered with thick, clotting blood, purple in the glare of my flashlight. His left leg was a mangled mess of shredded muscle, fragmented bone, dirt, snow, and cloth. His foot wasn't even there.

McCallister's normally rocky face sagged at all four corners. Then I noticed that his left arm hung straight down at his side and a tightly drawn bandage ringed his upper arm. His face twisted slightly as he forced a smile. "We got out just a couple minutes too late."

That's all he said then. I got the rest of the story weeks later when McCallister visited me on the hospital ship and related the events to me that led up to this scene in what was left of our aid station just before we moved out.

What I didn't spell out was the horrible incongruity of my warm, soft bed, in that aseptic, white, hospital-ship room, and the unforgettable image of Marne lying there on a cold, dark, hillside in a frozen trench with a bayonet in his chest, the Chinaman breathing garlic in his face, Marne's hands gripping the cold steel barrel of the gun, wondering what he was going to do with it.

Russian roulette, or Chinese roulette. You spin the chambers enough times and eventually the bullet lines up with the firing pin and barrel.

Marne had played this game once too often.

Fifty-two

There wasn't room in the jeep for three stretchers so we lifted Marne off his and slid his limp body onto the floor between the jump seat and the lower stretcher rack.

The rifleman trotted off toward Ku-dong to rejoin Rainey. McCallister said to us, "You guys ride, I'll stay with Gunny and Gonzaga. Head for Ku-dong and we'll intercept you there with further orders."

They pushed off through the trees at a fast walk, cutting across country towards Ku-dong. We would have to follow the track but I figured we'd still beat them there.

Rohn slid into the driver's seat of the jeep ambulance. Jepson and I got in back and sat on the jump seat across from the stretchers. We had to put our feet on Marne's body. I heard myself mutter, "Sorry, Bob." I was glad the darkness hid Marne's face. There would be time to mourn later, but even now I brushed tears out of my eyes with the back of my glove.

I wondered how long it took for a soul to be reincarnated. I squeezed my eyes shut and could see an eagle soaring high in the cerulean blue sky above a white-capped mountain range. A gust of wind turned the eagle. Its head and tail feathers glowed pure white as the sun caught it.

Just before Rohn stepped on the starter, we could hear the rushing of many tennis-shoed feet to our rear, coming fast. Rohn mashed the starter, put the jeep into gear, and gunned the accelerator. The jeep slid sideways, straightened out, found the track, slewed again and crashed into a tree. Rohn threw the gears into reverse but we were stuck.

"Out!" I shouted. "Find cover."

We scattered and heard the sudden thunder of what seemed a hundred burp guns all around us. I ran about fifty yards and fell in under the low limbs of a spruce tree. The firing stopped. Then after about thirty seconds a single gun fired two short bursts with a clanging of metal. Oh God, I thought, they got the WIAs in the jeep.

I figured it was all over for me, too. What a way to go, I thought. Now I'd never see Ingrid and Lorrie again. I thought of trying to surrender but I knew that the Chinese would never let me live unless they needed prisoners for interrogation and that wasn't very likely at this stage of the game.

Ten minutes later I was still hunkered in under the lower limbs of the tree and the sounds of battle and the sussuration of feet running in the snow had bypassed me. I had no idea where Jepson and Rohn were. I didn't dare call out. I slid down a bit on my rear and found a more comfortable position. There was nothing to do but wait a while and see what happened.

I was exhausted. I'd been on the go for almost forty-eight hours with only a few hours sleep back in battalion earlier that night. I actually fell asleep, lying there under the thick branches of that spruce.

It wasn't a good sleep. It was as if I was awake while I was asleep, all the feelings of sadness and frustration and fear pestering my mind in fragmented phrases of voices I'd never hear again. The screen of my dreams flickered with scattered images just short of nightmares.

I jerked awake. It would be light in about two hours. Then where the hell would I go?

But I was alive.

Most of the sounds of the battle were half a mile away now, to the south, near Ku-dong. My God, I thought. Everything that'd been done, all the men who'd been killed and wounded, all the ammunition that'd been expended, all the time and trouble, all the heartbreak...all for nothing.

And Marne was dead.

Cautiously I crawled out from under the tree and walked slowly back towards the jeep. A few moments later I found it.

Rohn lay face down in the snow only yards from it.

Jepson was nowhere to be seen.

The two men on the stretchers were dead.

I stood looking down at Rohn's body for a long time. I tried not to be too maudlin but I couldn't help thinking about that big lop-sided grin and the jaunty way he wore his cap. He'd been a true friend. Only the difference in our rank had kept us from being buddies. Even that would have been no problem back in the States.

In sort of a daze I walked as quietly as I could in gradually increasing concentric circles, figuring Jepson would be close by whether he was dead or alive. Knowing it was stupid, but unable to stop myself, I called out, "Jim.

Jim. It's Jack Lord here, Jim. It's okay, JJ..."

I tripped and thought I'd stumbled over a tree root or a log in the snow. It was Jepson. He hadn't died right away, had had time to push into a snowbank and almost cover himself with snow. It had worked. The Chinese hadn't found him. But the Grim Reaper had.

The jeep was of no value to me now. I couldn't go back through both the Communist and Marine lines in it, even if I could somehow get it moving again. Slowly, ever so slowly, the hopelessness of my predicament sunk in. I was in CCF territory, much more dangerous even than No-man's Land. If I'd been alone out in No-man's Land, I could've moved back and made it to my own lines, even if I didn't know the password. I couldn't move back to my own lines now because the Chinese lines had to be crossed first. I knew it was impossible.

I sat on the back edge of the deck, sensing Marne and the other two Marines lying in there, out of it now, no longer caring what happened.

But I cared. I was still alive. A long, almost sobbing rush of air gushed from me. And, yes, tears filled my eyes. I was alive. No words can express that feeling and no one can truly comprehend the rapture that just seizes your whole being when the fact hits home: I'M ALIVE.

I was alive and I was going to get out of this somehow.

Fifty-three

I tried to pray and found it impossible. But it set my mind moving again. I remembered suddenly the Buddhist monastery only a few hundred yards away on the top of 1052. If I could get up there without being caught, there was just the slight chance that I could hide out there until the 7th Marines arrived and pushed the lines back where they'd been.

I heard a shuffling in the snow and scurried soundlessly away from the jeep. I stood absolutely still, knowing that in the half light I could not be detected unless the sentry shone a light around the area. A Chinese soldier appeared out of the shadows and walked slowly around the jeep. A vapor cloud puffed intermittently from his mouth.

He moved on.

I breathed again.

These guys would be all over the place. I'd never make it up to the monastery.

I went back to the jeep and pulled my parka and bunny hat out of the front seat. I put the parka on over everything else including my .45, snugged up and tied the drawstring around the bottom. I took my helmet off, put the alpaca-lined hat on, pulled the flaps down over my ears but left them untied so I could hear.

Then I stuck my helmet, minus the liner, on top of my hat. It felt funny, probably looked ludicrous, but I wasn't in any beauty contest. I didn't want to throw away either the hat or the helmet. The hat would keep me warm. The helmet—well, maybe it'd do me some good, at least make me feel better.

I looked briefly for my M-2 but it was gone. So was Rohn's .03 and Jepson's M-2. The Reds no doubt had taken them. I had my .45 with a full clip and some more rounds in the ammo holder on my web belt. It didn't make me feel much better. I didn't want to get into a shoot-out with a Chinaman spitting lead from a burp gun.

I also had my K-bar, honed to a razor's edge half a dozen times in the past few weeks. Rohn had made me do that. "Never know, Doctor," he'd say as we sat sipping the awful stuff we called coffee that we made from C-ration packets of powdered coffee, milk, and sugar.

Without really thinking about what I was doing, I zipped my parka open, unhooked the K-bar scabbard from my web belt and put it in the left pocket of my parka. I grunted a half-laugh as I thought, what the hell you doing, Jack? You gonna use that thing to kill a Chinaman?

Slowly I climbed the ridge, using the cant of the ground to guide me. It was tough going in the dark. I could see the dark trunks of the trees and could keep from running into them. But branches whipped my face and once caught the corner of my eye. I held my hands up in front of me to wedge through thickets. I stumbled over fallen logs and exposed roots and slipped on icy boulders. I fell flat on my face half a dozen times. Once I stepped in a deep shell hole and bent my knee backwards so far that I thought I'd sprained it. But I sat on the edge of the hole till the throbbing went away. Several times I had to squat in the snow to rest and get my bearings.

Fortunately I knew the terrain. I'd watched the second platoon of George Company taking that valley and climbing the slopes of 1052. I'd watched How to the north and Item to the southwest taking their ridges. Then I'd stood in the sunshine with my corpsmen shouting insults at the first and third platoons of George Company as they strode past us on their way to relieve Rainey's Raiders on The Rock itself.

I wanted to get to the top of the ridge that ran almost straight east and west between 812 and 1052. I figured if I angled slightly to the left of a straight up-hill line, I'd end up close to the base of 1052. When I found it I could work my way around to the back where there was supposed to be a path up to the monastery.

Twice I had to hunker down, waiting for the sound of sentries to move around me. I didn't have much time. There was already a faint line of light on the horizon in the east. But I couldn't move any faster, either, and risk stumbling onto a standing sentry or a bivouac.

I could feel the ground levelling off and knew I was almost to the top of the ridge. I started moving faster and tripped over a Chinese lying in the snow. I regained my balance, ready to run, but saw that the man was lying quietly on his side, half covered with a dark blanket.

I figured he must be dead but then he groaned and rolled over on his back. Half the side of his face was gone but his eyes were bright in the faint light of the coming dawn. His left arm lay at a grotesque angle and when he moved, it didn't move with him.

Without even thinking I pulled the scabbard of my K-bar from my pocket with my left hand and quickly pulled out the knife with my right. He closed his eyes as I flopped on my knees beside him. He knew what was coming. Perhaps he couldn't have called out. I'll never know because I didn't give him the chance.

It was over in a second.

I sat back on my heels with the bloody knife hanging from my hand. I started to shake, a gross trembling that racked my entire body. I knelt down again and pulled the blanket up over the man's face.

With the care my corpsmen would have used to clean a scalpel, I wiped the knife on the snow and then dried it on my pants. As I stood up I slipped it back into the scabbard, put the scabbard back in my pocket and zombie-like started back up the hill. The wet stuff running down my cheeks started to freeze and I wiped it away with the back of my mitten.

I had never killed a man before.

Fifty-four

I reached the ridgeline and now could see the outline of 1052 just to my left, that is, to the west. Cautiously I worked my way through the brush and almost accidentally stumbled onto the path to the monastery. It was wide and well-worn, curving indolently upward like a well-engineered ski run, ending another two hundred yards above me.

I climbed steadily now. Occasionally I stopped and lifted an ear flap to listen for sounds from the communist camps I knew must be below me somewhere in the darkness. I heard nothing. I saw nothing. Their sound-control and blackout were superb.

The resinous smell of pines filled the air. Above me the Milky Way shimmered. To the southwest Orion the hunter looked toward Diana the huntress but both were beginning to dim as the false dawn lighted the sky.

The Buddhist temple was unoccupied, as I'd hoped it

would be. We'd seen the monks leaving just a few weeks before, crossing the battle lines without contest from either side. I had thought it significant that they went south, not north. Their saffron robes had gleamed burnt orange in the late afternoon sun as they padded single file down the ridgeline I'd just climbed, their meager possessions in cloth bundles and battered wicker suitcases, chanting hymns of peace and solemn praise to Gautama, Lord Buddha.

I'm afraid I sensed none of the monks' peace as I approached the entrance to the temple. Above me towered the two-story wooden edifice, its twin-peaked pagodas outlined against the starry sky. An open porch projected twenty feet out from the main building. Colorfully decorated wooden panels enclosed the main structure but I could see very little of them in the dark.

Three deeply worn wooden steps led up to the veranda across the front. I brushed the snow off the top step and sat down. I shook my head slowly from side to side. Was this what I wanted? To try to hide here in hopes that 3/5 would come back with 2/7 and rescue me? Would the cavalry arrive in time to save the settlers from the Indians?

I climbed the railing and could then see through a rift in the trees bright pinpoints of light which could only be small-arms fire. Tracers flickered in long arcs northward from the Marine lines, which seemed to be almost back where we'd started from only two days ago. Bursting mortar and artillery shells occasionally lit up the scene but there really weren't very many. Neither side knew where to drop their charges.

I jumped down from the railing and instinctively scurried into the temple. My feet had made up my mind for me. My Mickey Mouse boots echoed eerily on the stone floor of the anteroom and then thumped on the hardwood floor of the large meditation room.

At the far end of the room, glinting in the gloom, a ten-foot-high Buddha sat in the classic lotus position: legs folded with feet turned soles-up upon knees, left hand in lap with palm turned up, right hand on right knee.

On each side of the idol was a paper door. I slid open the one on the right. The scent of incense lingered in the air like ozone long after the lightning has struck. I groped along the narrow corridor, in total darkness now, hands touching both walls with ease, and found a row of tiny rooms, the cells of the departed monks. Later I found a dozen more on the other side of the Buddha. I chose one at random, slid the lacquered paper door shut behind me and felt for a lock. There was none.

I felt a momentary panic, then grunted a half-laugh as I realized that if the temple were searched, no lock would keep me safe. I slumped to the floor with my back to a wall, wiped the sweat from my eyes, and sucked in my breath a few times to still the racing of my heart.

And waited.

Fifty-five

As light crept into the room I could see that the monks had built the temple well. Had built it without nails. Interlocking timbers of heavy cedar had been mortised so carefully that only loud noises penetrated to my cell. I could just barely hear the firefight and the occasional thuuuuump of an exploding shell in the valley below me as the Marines tried to stop the advancing Red troops.

It occurred to me that when the Marines counterattacked I would be a sitting duck for friendly fire.

Then there would be two ways to die: an enemy's bayonet or a friendly's mortar.

A third way didn't occur to me then. But it would.

Perhaps both sides would purposely leave the temple alone. Yeah, Marne had told me—I swallowed convulsively as I remembered that day only weeks before when Marne had been vibrantly alive and had told me—that our FOs had tried their damndest not to put rounds into that temple. They probably would try to avoid it again. There really wasn't much to be gained by shelling the top of The Rock unless there were troops up there. All of the fighting so far had been in the trenches around the base. The FOs might come back to their old positions in order to direct fire down onto the Marine lines, but McCallister would be unlikely to bother with them now.

I felt better after that little bit of unreasonable rationalization and began to relax. The human mind is a strange thing. For a long time it will constantly look on the bright side of whatever is happening.

Then I heard something that sent tremors up and down my spine. Tennis-shoed feet clumped into the meditation room. I cowered in the corner, armed only with my .45 and my K-bar, as vulnerable as a belly-up deer. Fifteen minutes later a bugle sounded fifty yards away. A high-pitched voice sang out an order and the soldiers left the temple.

I relaxed again but couldn't help thinking that now I was really in for it, unless there was one hell of a quick counter-attack. There were two lines to cross now without getting shot: theirs and ours. Suddenly I was very tired, and very hungry, and very sorry for myself.

I dozed fitfully in a half-sitting position, afraid to lie down and relax completely. Finally I did slide down onto the hard, cold floor, took off my helmet, pillowed my head on my doubled-up alpaca hat, and slept.

I awoke to the thud of wooden mallets driving tent stakes into the brittle ground. I could hear the camp being set up all around the temple. The lines must be way south, I thought, if they're putting up tents rather than digging in. Afraid to move for fear someone might be worshipping in the outer room, I lay back down and closed my eyes. I awoke again two hours later.

A gray light illuminated my cubicle from a tiny window high on the twelve-foot wall. The room was bare: no sleeping mat, no altar, no furniture. There had probably never been much in there, but whatever my unwitting host monk had owned he had taken away.

Staying flat on my back, I stretched my stiff, cold body, then with my hands under my hips I doubled up my knees and rode the bicycle a few times to get my blood stirring again. My nose was icy and my breath froze in white clouds.

I was thirsty, hungry, dirty, unshaven, still covered with blood which so far was not mine. I saw then Ned Rohn's laughing eyes and lop-sided smile as he told me that none of the blood splattered all over him was his. I heard Bob Marne's voice on the radio telling me to keep my head down. I heard Jim Jepson after Marne's Guam story saying he hoped Marne would be around if he ever caught it.

God…

I lay there in a daze, knowing that if I was honest with myself I'd admit that in time I'd have to give myself up to the Chinese, and would be sent to a POW camp somewhere in North Korea, or even China. The thought was overwhelming.

But perhaps the Marines would counter-attack before I died of thirst or hunger, or before I had to give myself up. Those splendid men of 3/5 knew I was out here somewhere. Knew that out here somewhere were Marne and Rohn and Jepson and the How Company WIAs. They'd be back! That idea comforted me and I relaxed and slept again.

I awoke later in the afternoon with bright sunlight streaming through the tiny window. My mouth and lips were dry and beginning to crack. I'd not had water for almost twenty-four hours. I didn't have my canteen on me. I'd taken it off the night before so the corpsmen could use it for the casualties. It was probably empty by now anyway.

In my thirst I almost forgot the nauseous feeling of hunger cramping my belly. How long could I live without water? Three days? More to the point: how long could I survive in the winter without food?

I wasn't worried about water. There was a whole forest full of snow out there. All I had to do was get to it. I licked my lips and scratched my crotch. That reminded me that my bladder was full, and I wondered for the first time if I could drink my own urine.

As the hours passed I thought of many things, of my aid station now working without me, of Bob Marne and of Ned Rohn and Jim Jepson. I shuddered and broke out in a sweat as I thought of the Chinaman I'd killed. Would he have had strength or will to call out? Would he have died anyway? Had his buddies left him to die? Were any close enough to hear him if he had called out?

Had I killed him unnecessarily?

I pushed those questions away and thought of home, so distant and unreal. For weeks now, at quiet times, I'd been thinking of what I'd do when I got home. The vision of Ingrid and little Lorrie filled the screen in my mind. Lorrie would be almost two now. I saw Ingrid sitting on the edge of the sandbox helping the baby wet down the sand to make a little house. There was a glass of lemonade on the ground by Ingrid's feet. She reached for it and held it for Lorrie. They grinned at each other.

Night came early in winter on the 38th parallel. I looked at my watch as the light faded and saw that it was 4:30. The front lines were ominously quiet, both sides licking their wounds. There'd be no counter-attack tonight. I wondered if McCallister would use copters when they moved out again. It had worked, hadn't it?

My hunger pains were not yet into the third stage where cramps cease and only a deep, aching craving takes over. So I thought about food. Back in the battalion H & S I'd be eating B-rations right now, dumped out of #10 cans into the big warming pots, heated through, then ladled onto my ice-cold messpan by a tired cook who'd held the line all night in How Company with the rest of the pots and pans. The cook would grin through chapped lips and say something like, "How ya' want your steak, Doctor?" And I'd return his grin and answer, "As usual, Mac—hot!"

But it would be food, and it would be hot, not like the cold C-rations I ate on line, and it would be better than the nothing I was going to eat tonight. Even K-rations sounded good to me. Why hadn't I filled my parka pockets with K-rations? All the real Marines did before setting out on a mission. My answer was in my question: real Marines.

My mind continued to torment me with visions of life back in H & S. Back there I could drink all the coffee I wanted, or maybe even powdered milk. And there was always water, towed in huge tanks from some purification depot farther back of the lines in rear-echelon-poguedom, back where men slept on cots in strong-backed tents and had two hot meals a day and got mail every day and…

I sighed deeply and pulled my daydreams back into my head with a jerk and whispered out loud that this was no way to start my vigil. If I was going to stick this out I had to begin to control my thoughts.

Fifty-six

Through the thick walls of my self-assigned prison, I could hear the life of the camp now clustered all around me. Men marched, orders were called, tire chains clanked and truck doors slammed. Once I even fancied that I heard a tank rumbling by but decided they wouldn't bring one up here. As if it made any difference.

It got dark and gradually the noises diminished in volume and frequency. Eventually all was quiet. I waited for what I considered to be another hour, then carefully flexed my muscles and worked my fingers in my mittens until they warmed up and responded to my commands.

I rose to a squatting position, bounced up and down several times, then stood up. I was stiff and cold from the long hours of idleness, but slowly my blood began to circulate and warmth surged into my toes as I ran softly in place.

Trusting the function of my body now, I carefully

opened the door to my cell and tiptoed down the hallway to the meditation room. Stealthily I slid open the paper door to the big room and listened for the sonorous sounds of sleeping soldiers, or snoring, or the rustle of sleeping bags. I sniffed the air for the odor of unwashed bodies and garlic.

With even more care I crossed the room, eased into the stone-floored anteroom, and opened the front door. Moonlight and starlight glittered on the snow just outside. It was all I could do to control the urge to run out and fall on my face in the snow.

Gently I lowered myself onto my belly and crawled soundlessly to the edge of the veranda. Off to the left I saw outlined against the moonlit sky a gnarled and twisted piñon pine. It looked like a Picasso painting of a headless torso with tortured arms raised as if in flight.

I shuddered.

The camp lay motionless, though I had no doubt that sentries stood alert and watchful around the perimeter. They would not be looking my way, I hoped. I slid off a mitten and scooped a mouthful of snow into my mouth. At first it burned like fire, then melted and trickled down my parched throat. For almost an hour I lay there, drinking snow by the handsful, savoring the sweet wetness. When one hand became numb, I put on my mitten and scooped with the other.

When my thirst was slaked, I inched backward until I felt the stones of the anteroom under my toes. I humped to hands and knees and peered out into the silent camp of the Chinese Communists.

A dark rage rose slowly, born in the realization of my helplessness, nurtured into a hate for the Chinese even now killing my buddies in the Third Battalion. I ground my teeth and saliva poured into my mouth. I swallowed convulsively half a dozen times, backed into the temple and with great deliberation closed the outside door.

I crouched there, still on hands and knees, head drooping. Tears streamed from my eyes and saliva from my lips, dripping unchecked onto the cold stone. In a hoarse whisper I couldn't control I cursed in a steady stream until the tears and saliva stopped flowing and my body stopped shaking. It was a release from the aching frustration of being trapped behind enemy lines, of the thirsty, frigid vigil in the Buddhist monk's cell.

But it was more.

It was the outpouring of emotions pent up for weeks on line, of the hours of anguish in the bunkers of the aid station treating the maimed men coming down off the hills.

It was knowing that no matter how long I lived, I'd never forget the blood and the broken bones and the mutilated boys and men I knew—had talked with, had eaten with, had played baseball and volleyball with, yes, and some I'd prayed with. I'd never forget all the others that I didn't know, coming to me on stretchers with their faces covered by a poncho or a blanket.

I knew that something had drained out of me this last few months and something else had taken its place: a gut-level hate for this war and every war, a hate for the men who perpetrated war and others who allowed them to continue. A hate for those who led each company, battalion, regiment, or division, into unnecessarily dangerous positions. A hate for those who reminded us that the casualty rate was low and that the mortality rate was the lowest of any war before now.

And once more I saw Jerry Thorpe, my pheasant-hunting friend, lying there with his steel-punctured lung and worried about his friend Aage Svenger…

…and Buckshot Newman, his belly muscles already board-like from the massive peritonitis…

…and Ned Rohn, Old 99's best friend and my friend, lying face down in the snow…

…and Jim Jepson, who had said, "Ya can't make me go, Doctor" and stayed when he could have gone…

…and Bob Marne…

Fifty-seven

I brushed the tears from my eyes and the saliva from my drooling lips and wondered for the first time if I could really make it. With the uncontrolled, jerky movements of the half-insane I rose to my feet and stumbled across the chamber toward the great Buddha. In impotent rage I struck out with my left foot at the bronze image. With a sickening thud I heard my toes crumple, and with a squawking rasp my rubber boot tear open.

Sobered now, grim-faced with self-pity, I limped into my cell and slumped to the floor. Gingerly I felt my boot and realized with terrible clarity that the vacuum seal was hopelessly damaged. My toes were already beginning to cool. I took off my boots, put both socks on the left foot, then put both boots back on.

Like a troop of Black Watch Fusiliers drumming out the dead march, the night wore on. I knew my foot was still alive because it ached. But each time I awoke after a restless doze, the foot was a little less painful and I knew I would inevitably lose the battle to the silent, creeping frost.

I fell asleep and dreamed that I was on a city street. I was the only one-legged man amongst the unshaven, rheumy-eyed derelicts stumbling fretfully along that sidewalk. An Arctic wind whistled through the steel and concrete canyons, lifting whole newspapers with devil-driven mini-tornadoes, spinning beer cans out of the gutter into the street where sleet-covered autos smashed them with an almost inaudible clink.

My crutches skidded on a mushy paper bag full of garbage and I tumbled grotesquely onto the stinking mess. Cursing the empty pantleg pinned carelessly to my left rear pocket, I pushed myself onto my right knee and brushed eggshells and grapefruit rinds from my worn leather jacket. Slowly, carefully, like a pregnant cow, I maneuvered my foot under my body and stood up, balancing unsteadily until I could cradle the crutches in my armpits. I brushed the soggy snow and filth from my gloves, settled stiff hands onto the crossbars of my crutches, and lumbered toward the Buckhorn Lounge a block away.

The blare of bugles tore me awake, and, as on the previous morning, I worked my arms and rode the bicycle and felt the warmth of my blood struggling through my aching body and limbs.

But I couldn't feel my left foot.

In the dim light of morning I took off my torn Mickey Mouse and peered anxiously at the foot and toes. I tried to move the dark toes and massage some color into the foot, but could not. Mechanically I pulled my boot back on and laced it.

I was thirsty again but my hunger had disappeared. I

hadn't urinated for almost thirty-six hours, but strangely had not felt the need. Then, as I thought of it, my bladder contracted in an overpowering urge and I rolled over on my side and emptied it on the floor. I knew I could never collect it and drink it.

The pattern of the first day repeated itself on the second and then on the third. I knew I was slowly driving myself into a corner from which I could never return. I found nothing in the deserted temple with which to wrap my foot. I stopped looking at it.

I crawled to the front veranda each night and filled my stomach with water, then stumped into one of the other cells and emptied my bladder on the floor. Once I had violent cramps from the ice water and emptied my bowels also. At first I worried about the odor and then knew there would be none in just a few minutes when the mess on the floor froze.

On the fourth night, through the haze of exhaustion and hunger, as I lay scooping snow into my parched mouth, I heard the sound of a firefight on the slopes of the mountain to the southeast. Closer and closer they came. I wanted to stand and cheer them on. But then they stopped, held steady for an hour, and finally retreated until I could hear them no more.

With one more desperate effort of the will, I forced myself back into the temple. I lay sobbing on the stones, knowing how close I'd come to rescue, knowing how close I was to standing up and running into the arms of the first Chinese I could find.

It was on the fifth night that the hallucinations began. My mother visited me and offered me food and wine, then snatched it away with a cackle. Chief Hoffman put his .45 to my head and pulled the trigger, only to find that the gun was empty. Wizened little brown men in scarlet shirts danced for me and held steaming bowls of rice to their lips and sucked in great mouthfuls of fishheads and cracked them with powerful teeth. The stench of garlic was everywhere.

In the morning I pulled myself to a sitting position, took off my torn boot, and looked at the shrunken black foot and toes. The frost had crept up the leg into the calf.

I could eat those toes, I thought. They're no longer a part of me, no longer members of my body. If thine eye offend thee, pluck it out and throw it away. Or eat it.

I vomited.

Fifty-eight

The fires in my tough young body were beginning to burn low. I knew what was happening. Stored carbohydrates had burned off during the first day or two. Stored fat was next and was gone from my lean body in less than a week. Heat and energy had to come from somewhere, so my muscles began to cannibalize themselves. The breakdown products of the muscle proteins released into my bloodstream acted as poisons in my brain. Ultimately I'd lose control completely.

Would lie down.

Would die.

For hours I lay in a daze, not awake yet not asleep. Uncontrollable shivering racked my body until I finally dragged myself to my feet and windmilled my arms and hobbled around the tiny room on one good foot and one wooden one.

I felt no pain, no hunger, no thirst.

Felt nothing.

Yet my left brain kept saying, move, move, move, move, or you'll die.

And my right brain kept answering, so what, so what, so what?

One mind said, keep going. The other asked, is being dead worse than dying?

The eleventh night was the worst. I didn't have the strength to crawl out to get water and when I rolled over to empty my bladder I caught what I could in my cupped hands and let the liquid run in a warm stream down my throat.

A tiny, sequestered area of my brain still knew I was alive. Periodically this part of my brain told me, stick it out, the 3/5 will be back, hang on, it's only a matter of time. But the rest of my brain was addled by the poison released by the degenerating muscles.

My living brain told me get food my dying brain asked where?

My living brain answered there isn't any my dying brain said your leg, you're going to lose it anyway.

My K-bar was in my hand, no conscious thought directing it, the blade shimmering eerily in the soft moonlight coming through the tiny window.

My living brain asked what the hell you doing?

My dying brain said I'm going to have dinner, it's about time, isn't it?

Dinner for one.

There was no pain as the razor-sharp edge gouged small chunks of black skin and purple muscle from the top of my foot and the back of my lower leg. I had no sensation of taste as I sucked at the frozen skin and chewed hungrily on the frozen muscle. Neither were there thoughts of ethics, morals, or religion. Nor of cannibalism, whether of one's friends, one's enemies, or one's self. There was just the dreadful, powerful instinct of self-preservation.

My body knew, even if my brain didn't, that the Aztecs were right: the best source of protein for human beings is human flesh.

And when I was done, I slept.

And dreamed of comic-opera ghouls pulling the wings off vampire bats and eating them, of movie-version cannibals singeing the life out of topeed missionaries…and then the dream was not a dream as the K-bar flashed once more and sliced hungrily at the frozen meat.

In the light of morning, my mind clearer than it had been for days, I looked at the mutilation. A faint shudder rippled across my shoulders and was gone. With an odd detachment I noted the slashed pantleg, the blackened foot and shriveled toes, and finally the white of bone showing through the purple meat of calf. I pulled off a glove and touched the bone, then tapped one taloned finger gently on it and cocked my head to the side and listened to the faint clicking sound. It reminded me of my mother playing the piano with too-long nails.

I ran my grimy fingers over what was left of the frozen muscle mass. Then with staring eyes and the infinite care of a surgeon operating under local anesthesia, I filetted a long thin slice of muscle and stuffed it into my mouth. Dreamily, eyes shut and brain out of gear, I chewed the icy meat until it softened and broke into little pieces and slid down my throat.

I hardly noticed the sudden flurry of activity outside as officers shouted orders. If I'd been able to get to the door I would have seen the trucks roar in and the Chinese hastily begin to strike their tents and load them. I would have seen them tie their bedrolls onto backpacks and stream off Hill 1052 in a panicky retreat.

The Seventh Regiment had arrived, I learned later, and had encountered elements of the CCF back near our artillery positions, nearly two miles behind the lines. They'd had to literally fight their way through the Chinese troops to salvage what was left of 3/5. Both Dog and Easy Companies of the Seventh had been ordered into the lines and were able to push those lines back to where they'd been when the breakthrough occurred. Fox Company of the Seventh had cleared the rear areas of the Chinese trapped there.

Then, two hours after the Chinese retreat from Hill 1052, the Second platoon of George Company strode up the path and fanned out on the barren summit of Luke the Gook's Castle.

Moses Washington eyed the pagoda and ordered a rifleteam to search it for stragglers.

THE SECRETARY OF THE NAVY
WASHINGTON

The President of the United States takes pleasure in presenting the BRONZE STAR MEDAL to

LIEUTENTANT JOHN QUINCY LORD
MEDICAL CORPS
UNITED STATES NAVAL RESERVE

for service as set forth in the following
CITATION

For excellent service in the line of his profession while serving with a Marine infantry battalion during operations against the enemy in KOREA on March 19th and 20th 1952. Serving as a surgeon, Lieutenant Lord displayed an outstanding degree of professional skill, personal bravery and fortitude in the performance of his duties. Working under adverse conditions, he employed his medical unit and evacuation facilities in such a manner that prompt attention to the wounded was constantly insured. During the two nights of the engagement, he established his aid station forward of the outpost line of resistance and, although extremely fatigued and under enemy small arms and mortar fire, treated wounded throughout the night and following morning. His actions contributed directly to saving the lives of many Marines. By his courage, resourcefulness, initiative and selfless devotion to duty, Lieutenant Lord upheld the highest traditions of the United States Naval Service.

Lieutenant Lord is authorized to wear the Combat "V"
For the President,
Secretary of the Navy

GLOSSARY

A-BAR Assistant to the BAR-man. Carries ammunition, assists in loading BAR.

BAR Browning Automatic Rifle. Light machine gun carried by one member of each fire team. Weighs almost twenty pounds. (See "Organization of the First Marine Division.")

BAR-man. The rifleman who carries the BAR.

Bouncing Betty Explosive device which flies into the air before exploding, usually triggered by a trip-wire rigged in thick brush close to the qround.

Carbine A short-barreled, lightweight, automatic or semiautomatic rifle, carried by troops that are not primarily riflemen. Weighs under ten pounds. See "M-2."

CCF Chinese Communist Forces.

CG Commanding General.

CIC Civilian Intelligence Corps.

CP Command Post.

Cumshaw Steal, usually from a neighboring rear-echelon Army unit. Originally a Shanghai Chinese word meaning bribe, such as one given to a police officer to close his eyes to illegal activities.

Debridement Surgical removal of dead or contaminated tissue, along with foreign bodies.

Defilade In a protected position from observation or fire from the ground, as behind a hill or in a ravine.

DI Drill instructor.

DMZ Demilitarized Zone. In Korea this was established at the end of the war, extended across the entire Korean peninsula, and was supposed to be clear of all military personnel and weapons.

EMT Emergency Medical Tag.

Enfield rifle A .30 caliber rifle first used in World War

I, developed in 1903 and called the Aught-Three. Supplanted first by a modification developed in 1906 and called the Aught-Six. Supplanted by the M-l Garand in World War II.

Enfilade In a position unprotected from observation or fire from the ground forces of the enemy.

Entrenching tool A small shovel with a folding blade, used primarily by infantry to dig foxholes and other shelters.

Fire step An elevated shelf of earth at the bottom of a deep foxhole, upon which the rifleman stands to watch the enemy lines and to fire from.

FMF Fleet Marine Force.

FO Forward observer, on MLR or OPLR, who watches where friendly mortar, artillery, or air fire lands in order to direct that fire more accurately.

FPO Fleet Post Office.

Friendly fire All forms of weapons firing from the side you are on.

G-l through G-6: Same duties as S-officers, at Division level. See S-l, etc.

Garand rifle See M-l.

"Gunny" sergeant Gunnery sergeant.

H & S Headquarters and Service, the command post of each battalion (See organization of the First Marine Division).

HA Hospital Apprentice. Designation on graduation from Corps School. Wears caduceus above two blue slashes on white uniform, white slashes on blue uniform.

Hill 1052 Height in meters, approximately three feet to a meter.

HM3, HM2, HMl, HMC Hospital Mate Third, Second, First, Chief. Progressive ranks above Hn. Wears caduceus between eagle above and chevron(s) below.

Hn Hospital man. First step up from HA. Wears

caduceus above three slashes.

Incoming Mortar and artillery fire landing on friendly outfits.

K-bar A twelve-inch knife with a seven-inch non-folding blade.

KIA Killed in action.

KMC Korean Marine Corps.

KSC Korean Service Corps.

LST Landing Ship, Tank. Large landing craft capable of carrying tanks, trucks, etc., or large numbers of troops, onto beaches where no port facilities exist.

M-l The Garand rifle, standard weapon for infantry Marines in Korea. Weighs about twelve pounds.

M-2 A carbine carried by officers, including doctors. See "carbine."

MASH Mobile Army Surgical Hospital.

MC Medical Corps.

MIA Missing in action.

Military alphabet Able—Baker—Charley—Dog—Easy—Fox—George—How—Item—Jig—King—Love—Mike—Nan—Oboe—Peter—Queen—Roger—Sugar—Tare—Uncle—Victor—Willy—Xray—Yoke—Zero.

Military script Paper money issued to the troops in Korea to be used in lieu of real money, e. g. in buying items from the PX (post exchange).

MLR Main Line of Resistance. The "front lines."

MS Morphine sulfate.

MSR Main Service Road.

Mummy bag A sleeping bag with a hood attachment, usually for cold weather and filled with goose down or other insulating material.

No-man's Land The territory between thle friendly and enemy MLRs.

Non-com Non-commissioned officer: corporal, sergeant, etc.

OD Olive drab. The gray-green color of most combat clothes, weapons, and other materiel.

OPLR Outpost Line of Resistance. Observation and communications posts forward of the MLR, usually on a high point.

S-l: Personnel Officer

S-2: Intelligence officer

S-3: Operations and Training Officer

S-4: Supply Officer

S-5: Executive Officer

S-6: Commanding Officer

TAD Temporary additional duty.

USNR United States Naval Reserve. Organization of men and officers not in the Regular Navy (USN).

WIA. Wounded in action.

U.S. Forces in Korea

The United States forces in Korea were all in the Eighth Army. The Eighth Army was comprised of three Corps: I, IX, X.

The units that fought in Korea were:

Eight U. S. Army divisions: First Cavalry. 2nd,
3rd, 7th, 24th, 25th, 45th Infantry

Korean Marine Corps

Republic of Korea Army

Commonwealth Division (Canada, Australia, Britain, etc.)

US FIRST MARINE DIVISION

THE ORGANIZATION OF THE FIRST MARINE DIVISION IN KOREA

The **Division**, commanded by a general, consisted of three infantry regiments, the First, Fifth, and Seventh, plus an artillery regiment, the Eleventh.

Each **regiment**, commanded by a colonel, had three battalions, the First, Second, and Third.

Each **battalion**, commanded by a lieutenant colonel, had three rifle companies. The First Battalion had Companies A, B, and C. The Second had D, E, and F. The Third had G, H, and I. Each battalion also had an H & S Company (Headquarters and Service Company) which contained all the "S" officers (see Glossary) and their staffs, medical personnel, cooks, truckers, security Marines, forward observers (FOs) for air and artillery, and all other support people. All told, there were about 1,000 men in each Marine battalion when it was committed to combat.

Each **rifle company**, which was led by a captain, was made up of three platoons. The company commander had a radio man, executive officer, first sergeant, gunnery sergeant, supply sergeant, and several runners. Attached to each rifle company in combat was a machine gun platoon of fifty-one men in three seventeen-man sections. Also attached was a nineteen-man mortar section. Counting all people in a combat rifle company, there were 235 men, of which seven were officers, and twenty-nine were sergeants.

Each **platoon**, which was led by a second lieutenant, was made up of three squads. Each platoon leader had a platoon sergeant, platoon guide, runner, radioman, and two Navy corpsmen, giving it forty-six men.

Each **squad**, which was led by a sergeant, was made up of three fire teams, giving it thirteen men.

Each **fire team**, the heart of the Marine rifle company, was led by a corporal, and had four men: a Browning Automatic Rifleman, an Assistant BAR-man, two riflemen with M-1s (Garand).

Lineage of the Fifth Marines

1917—Activated in Philadelphia as the Fifth Regiment of Marines.

1917-1918—Participated in World War I in the following campaigns:

AISNE
AISNE-MARNE
ST. MIHIEL
MEUSE-ARGONNE
TOULON-TRYON
CHATEAU-THIERRY
MARBACHE
LIMEY

1918-1919—Participated in the occupation of the German Rhineland.

1927-1930—Participated in operations against rebel forces in Nicaragua.

1942-1945—Participated in World War II as part of the Fleet Marine Force of the First Marine Division in the following campaigns:

GUADALCANAL
EASTERN NEW GUINEA
NEW BRITAIN
PELELIU
OKINAWA

1945-1947—Participated in the occupation of North China.

1950-1953—Participated in the Korean War as part of the First Marine Division in the following campaigns:

PUSAN PERIMETER
INCHON-SEOUL
CHOSIN RESERVOIR
EAST CENTRAL FRONT
WESTERN FRONT

1953-1955—Participated in defense of the Korean Demilitarized Zone.

1966-1971—Participated in the Vietnam War, operating from RUNG SAT, HUE, AN HOA, DA NANG, CHU LAI, PHU BAI, QUE SON, TAM KY